THE QUEEN'S LINE

Inheritance of Hunger - Book One

KATHRYN MOON

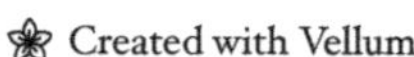
Created with Vellum

This is a Reverse Harem Paranormal Romance and is not suited for those under the age of 18.

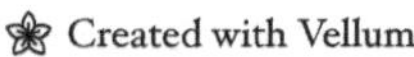 Created with Vellum

*For the fairy tale girls
wearing ballgowns, wielding blades*

CONTENTS

THE QUEEN'S LINE

INHERITANCE OF HUNGER
BOOK ONE

BY KATHRYN MOON

1.
BRYONY

"*Corinne, if I have to wait another moment to taste you...*" *Declan's rasp trailed off into an agonized sigh, his fingers gripping the Lady of Henwood Manor's waist like a vise.*

Corinne's body arched toward Declan, the refusal on her ripe lips wavering beneath his dark gaze.

"Your Highness, they are arriving."

My brow furrowed, my own fingers as tightly wrapped around the book as the disgraced knight Declan's hands were around his beloved. The air shimmered warmly around me, my heart racing with the passion provided from the page, my core hot and clenching. Out of the right corner of my eyes, my handmaid bounced anxiously on her toes, waiting for me to stir from my window seat in the library. And out of the left corner of my eyes...

I knew perfectly well the men were arriving. Every single, eligible man under fifty in Kimmery would be forcibly encouraged to attend a royal choosing ceremony. I could hear their voices shouting gaily to one another through the crack in the window, could see the dark trail of them just beyond the white jasmine-dressed gate as they gathered for entrance. The peace of my favorite place in the castle—the sight of the gardens out the window and the sea glittering in the horizon—was now marred by the rowdy sounds and bustling bodies of men. It was time for me to face my choosing, and not even my favorite book could delay this moment. All at once, the hint of desire I'd felt moments ago with my reading, vanished.

"The dowager queen is—"

"Yes, Una, I understand," I said with a sigh, and rose from my seat, turning my back on my formerly favorite view and sliding my beloved book into the deep pocket of my dress.

The dowager queen, my grandmother, would be growing impatient if not openly irate with the servants the longer I lingered. I'd already delayed the day of my first choosing for five years. Even my younger sister, Camellia, had taken her pick of men twice, and she'd only been of age for three years.

But how could I choose men when I failed to crave them when face to face? A man might be as perfectly formed as a work of art, but he didn't stir anything in me the way a hero from a book would. I was faulty. Broken in some way.

I followed Una out of the library and through the castle, down to the great hall where the choosing was about to take place. I could've managed the trip alone, certainly, but my grandmother was unlikely to leave me unchaperoned until I was pinned firmly beneath her hand, facing the sea of men I would have to draw lovers from.

I'd been a witness to both of Camellia's ceremonies, my grandmother of the incorrect opinion that watching my younger sister tackle a grown man to the floor and mount his barely erect cock would be some inducement to me to take my own Chosen. Instead, it had only made my own confusion more persistent.

Why could I feel heat and desire and the power of the queen's line—our legendary and potent Hunger—while reading a book, but never when faced with a man in real life? The Hunger was the dominant magic that sustained Kimmery's prosperity and power. Grandmother maintained her own small harem of Chosen but stepped down from sustaining her Hunger a few years ago. It was traditional for the queen's line to have at least two women keeping the Hunger rich and our people happy. If I joined my mother and Camellia, Kimmery might see an even greater golden age. I wanted to be a good queen for my country, wanted my people to be happy and healthy and wealthy.

All I had to do to ensure it was take a group of men to bed and slake my desires on them. Desires I had yet to feel for anyone in real life.

Una paused by the door, returning to her nervous bounce as my steps slowed in my own approach. The great hall was opened up and polished for the occasion, and I winced as I stepped into the room, sunlight catching on a dripping chandelier and casting a blinding ray into my eyes. Male murmurs sounded by the far end of the room, the procession trailing in at a single file, walking toward the platform where I would sit and observe them, making my choices.

My grandmother was there already, tall and imposing with a willowy figure and a stern gaze that moved from the men and fastened onto me. I resisted the urge to duck my chin as I would've as a child, and instead held my head high, ignoring the trail of men as I hurried to the platform to take my seat on my throne.

Grandmother's hand pinned me in place before I had finished bending. "You've been putting this off for years, Bryony."

"I know, Grandmother," I said softly.

The men were stripped down to their stockings and underwear. Some even less, as if I might be more tempted to choose them at the sight of their dangling flesh bouncing listlessly between their thighs. I had seen plenty of men and their cocks in my twenty-three years, and I wasn't convinced that buck naked was a man's best presentation. They took their place in organized lines so I could view ten of them at once, speeding up the process of the choosing, and their reflections bounced off the mirrors around the room and blurred over the ornate gilding until the great hall was an abstract of flesh.

"Your sister, Camellia, will have snatched up all the good ones by now," Grandmother said.

My face twitched as I wrestled down the urge to wrinkle my nose. I didn't like Camellia's men *at all*. But Camellia must have because ever since her second choosing ceremony, the only time I saw her was when she had one between her thighs. She was doing her part for the kingdom.

Now it was my turn. That was my only consolation—what I lacked in desire for the men trailing into the room, I at least had for seeing the betterment of my kingdom.

"Although, he's not bad, now is he?" Grandmother murmured, and this time I couldn't withhold my wince as her fingers dug into my shoulder at the sight of one of the men in the front line. "Millie, grab that one there. *No*, the one to the right of him!"

The man in question stepped out of the line and up to my grandmother's lady-in-waiting with a nod. He was terribly tall, much too tall for me, surely? And he did remind me a bit of the way men were described in the novels I loved so dearly. Ruggedly handsome with a dimpled chin and curling dark hair falling over his brow. He had thick, defined muscles and more dark hair curling over his chest and down his thighs. At least he was wearing underwear.

"Drop those, let us see it," Grandmother barked at him.

The man's eyes flicked to mine—a kind of cheerful, agree-ableness in his gaze—but he was as careful as I was to keep his face neutral in front of the dowager queen. His thumbs hooked into the laces of his underwear, and he shimmied the fabric down his hips, exposing his cock.

Can't fit, I thought, blinking at the over-generous appendage.

"Oh yes, that's very nice," Grandmother murmured. "Fluff it up for us a bit, won't you?"

I had seen sex. I had seen men waiting for their turn to worship my mother, and my sister seemed to revel in thrusting her sex life in my face. The women in my family were not shy in their appetites, nor were they expected to be. The queen's line *must* be virile, must have the Hunger. It was our duty and our gift to the kingdom. And yet I still shied away from the sight of the beautiful man reaching down to his own cock as he tried to stroke it to life for my grandmother's perusal.

"Very impressive, that's enough," Grandmother said. "Unless you'd like him now, Bryony?"

So here was the kind of man I was supposed to desire. Tall, big cock, quiet, aesthetically pleasing. I wanted to refuse. I knew nothing of him, he was only a man standing in front of me. What if he was rude, or his voice was too loud, or he was unkind? If I imagined him like Henry Fredericks, one of my favorite of all the romantic heroes I'd fallen in love with, then...

I blushed as a soft unfurling of warmth built in my center. *If* he was Henry Fredericks, then yes, I found him very pleasing.

But he *wasn't* the charming and humble duke to be. He was a stranger.

One my grandmother, my entire kingdom, was waiting to see if I desired. How could I explain to them that I lacked what everyone had always told me I was destined to rule with? There were some nights, alone in my bed, a book in hand and a vision of a looming hero in my thoughts, where I thought that I did possess the Hunger, the unquenchable craving to be *touched* and *satisfied*. But faced with the men of my mother's harem, my sister's, those alliance princes who came and went from the palace? I suspected I was missing a vital piece of myself. I wanted nothing of those men.

"Let him wait," I said, gesturing to the door leading to an antechamber that would take him to the lounge where the first round of my picks would be examined.

Camellia sampled three men over the course of her first choosing. I didn't think I could bring myself to sample one, but the least I could do was pick some of the men out of the line up as was expected of me. There would be some of the politically desirable matches—royals from nearby kingdoms, or ones especially advantageous for alliance—already waiting for me. But a woman from my line would be expected to find her own desires in our general populace. Grandmother said it made the people feel closer to our rulers. I suspected it was more likely that the Hunger demanded men who would *serve* and not see themselves as quite so equal in rank.

"Very good choice, Bryony. If he's quick to recover, he'll see you plenty satisfied," Grandmother said, watching the broad back of my first pick leaving the great hall as I waved my hand, happily dismissing the rest of the front line.

My grandmother was liberal with her advice and opinion, but as the endless sea of men moved through our hall, I devised my own system. There was a young man who looked like the sweetheart baker in a novel I'd loved growing up, and I gestured him into the antechamber, and then another who reminded me of the roguish and redeemed lead in *A Broken Promise*. It had been a terrible book with a worse main character, but Vlad Embario had always given me a bit of the swoons, and the man in front of me had a gaze that seemed equally as potent, watching me as fiercely as I'd studied him.

One by one, and with many rejected men between them, I made my choices. They were not based on Hunger, but on books I'd loved. If I possessed any secret Hunger, it wasn't making an appearance in this clinical parade of man-flesh and under my grandmother's opinionated eye.

"No, no, he's too old," Grandmother said, shaking her head as a tall, broad man stepped forward at my call, his movements rigid.

"He isn't," I said, eyeing the man and noting the surprised twitch of his head.

He had a wolfish look to him, and his features were classical and cool. There *was* silver in his hair, but I liked it and he reminded me of the noble Captain Beauregard, who'd rescued a young woman from pirates and had tenderly refused to deflower her until their wedding night.

"He may not be able to perform," Grandmother said.

And before she could demand he do so in front of us, I spoke up. "That will be known in the next round. Let him wait."

The older man's eyes fastened to mine and there was *ferocity* in his stare, but I wasn't sure it was of a passionate nature. Perhaps he was offended I would not let him prove himself? After a pause that left me nearly squirming in my seat, the man turned on his heel and strode to wait with the others.

"He looks willful," Grandmother said. "But that can be fun."

ॐ

GRANDMOTHER and I took our dinner together in her sitting room when I had finally dismissed the men for the day. Since I'd sampled none, I'd gotten through more than half of the single men of the kingdom in one sitting, although I'd started to lose any ability to differentiate them in my mind and asked for only one to wait in the entire last hour.

"They'll have their numbers soon, and then you may have your tastes of them," Grandmother said, dabbing at the corners of her mouth lightly with her napkin and pushing away her dinner tray. "You'll want to note any conflicts between the men. It's no good to you if they're too busy bickering with one another to fuck you properly, although a little tension can suit now and then. And of course, if any one of them says he's had enough for the day, you send him right out on his ass. No man should be less excited to spend himself in a woman than in his own hand, no matter how many times he's jerked off already."

I'd heard plenty of this when Camellia had decided to start choosing, but I nodded obediently now.

Grandmother, rather than appearing pleased, narrowed her eyes at me. "I have concerns, Bryony."

"You did not like my choices?"

"I do not like your complacency," Grandmother bit out, and I stiffened. "Your mother, your sister, and I were all but tearing down the doors to get to the men on the days of our choosing. You looked bored in the great hall, and now you look...well, certainly not inspired. Perhaps I was wrong to let you wait so long."

Perhaps she was. Perhaps I should've gotten this over with years ago like Camellia. I thought I would change, that I would grow into my Hunger, and instead it never came despite all my waiting.

I stood from my chair and brushed the crumbs from my skirt, striding to the door without waiting for my Grandmother.

"Perhaps you should give up playing chaperone if it disappoints you," I said. "I can manage the next part on my own. I *do* know what to look for in my lovers."

"Of course you do, I've trained you," Grandmother snapped back, but her smile was on at last. "Very well, go and manage the thing. We'll take your sheets in the morning."

I spun away and pushed the doors open, ignoring the sick swoop in my stomach at the reminder.

Choosing was only the first step, but that cold dinner was the last reprieve I'd get. I must cut down my list, meet the men remaining, and then...

And then soil my sheets with them, so that the palace may boast of the princess inherit's Hunger.

I stormed my way through the halls, my steps thunderous on

the marble, bouncing from pillar to pillar as if I were being chased. I could offer myself not one moment to think if I was going to see this through. I would take my grandmother's advice and choose the most virile of the men, in a wide variety, and then I would...

You'll fuck them. Just say it. Think it. Whatever you have to do. Prove you are worthy to take the throne.

The men were waiting, slightly more dressed than before while having a meal in the dining hall. My grandmother's favorite advisor was waiting for me by the door, a hawkish woman named Isolde, who I'd once caught sucking the cock of one of my mother's harem and who'd seemed mildly nervous around me ever since. As she should be. Touching a Chosen was forbidden to anyone but his mistress.

"Your Highness," Isolde said, dipping into a low curtsey at my arrival.

"Begin with the royals and nobles," I said in lieu of a greeting.

Isolde nodded, and her head remained ducked as she led me to the head of the table.

"Prince Dmitri of Quintaine," Isolde said as we stood by a very handsome young man with a stare that fastened to me and a lovely swoop of dark hair. "He ranks a five."

Ah, pity. Fives were the worst on the scale, small and not very girthy. Whoever had designed the rankings had decided it was better to place the worst in the middle and mix the rest up in a complicated code, so as to confuse the numbers and not to bruise the feelings of the men too much.

"Under two minutes, and remained uninspired," Isolde murmured.

So good looks weren't everything then. "Dismiss him," I answered softly.

Isolde crossed his name off her list. There were twenty nobles in total, and I realized they seemed to be a generally uninspired lot according to our statistics. Based on the criteria of penis size, stamina, and refractory period, only five so far met Grandmother's standards, and I'd happily dismissed the rest. We reached the last of the nobles, and I wondered if I could break my own promise to please Grandmother and simply keep him for aesthetics.

He was beautiful in an artful way. His shoulders were strikingly broad, and he remained bare-chested at the table, revealing an exquisite collection of tattoos on his tan body, done as carefully as paintings. His hair was sleek and black, and he was obviously from the Menarry Isles, with dark eyes and full lips.

"Prince Thao of the Menarry Isles, rank three." Three was good, nice and middle of the range. He might be long, or girthy, or average. Nothing too much or too little. An everyday cock by my grandmother's reporting. "His family line are all tiger shifters, but they took special note to say he prolonged for over twenty minutes, and was ready in under that."

The men were instructed not to acknowledge me as I learned their statistics, but Prince Thao glanced up and caught my eye. He didn't smirk, as many of the other nobles did. He looked... nervous. I wondered if it was because he didn't expect to be chosen, given his double nature. Shifters had a kind of magic that resisted our Hunger and was considered a poor choice for Chosen. If the prince were a commoner he wouldn't have been allowed to attend, but exceptions were made for royalty. He probably wasn't expecting to become my Chosen, but I found his nervousness called to me, in sympathy if nothing else.

"He will stay," I said, holding his gaze.

Isolde made her notes, and we moved to the next man.

"This is our ambassador to the Mennary Isles, Wendell Pope. He's a..." Isolde cleared her throat, cheeks flushing. "He's a nine, and he...prolonged for almost an hour."

I blinked at that. Would I even *want* to be made love to for an hour? Perhaps...if I had the Hunger. I was tempted to dismiss Wendell Pope simply to avoid such a possibility, except that he was so handsome, and Grandmother would probably disinherit me if she learned his statistics.

"We didn't have time to test him again," Isolde whispered.

Wendell Pope's cheeks flushed, and so did Prince Thao's. Was Thao jealous of Wendell's performance? Would that be some of the good tension or the bad tension?

"He will stay," I said.

I hadn't realized how many of my own people I had plucked from the lines, but it was more than double the number of nobles. I decided that if I kept five out of twenty nobles, I would keep twelve out of fifty commoners as if that might make it fairer. Having criteria at least made it a little easier to decide.

For the most part, the commoners favored much better by the statistics, and I let myself grow picky. That one was a two, which was quite good, but he was slurping. This one had a refractory period under ten minutes but only lasted five.

My rakish look-a-like from the great hall was named Cosmo Pianetta, and he ignored the rules in favor of looking back at me.

"A two at thirty minutes and refreshed in about that much," Isolde said, and then added to me, "But they noted that he watched the others as he did it."

I opened my mouth to ask—had the other men inspired him, or was he only prone to staring—and then snapped it shut again. "He will stay," I said, deciding that I could ask him later.

We moved on to a man who winked at me as he ate a chicken drumstick, red beard shining with grease.

"A twelve," Isolde informed me.

"Dismiss him," I said quickly. Anything above a ten was sure to injure me.

I kept a small few of the others, halfway through the group when we reached the older man I'd defied Grandmother to keep.

"Aric Martin, minor magician, an eight. He refused to perform," Isolde said, plenty loud enough for him to hear.

He ignored her and cut carefully at the meat on his plate, taking a bite and then reaching for his wine. Despite being instructed to ignore me, this man somehow made it feel like a defiance. The queen's line didn't usually take Chosen with magic, either mages or shifters, their magic supposedly clashing with the Hunger. Technically, a low magician wouldn't pose much threat, and would still be expected to arrive to the ceremony, but no one would expect me to choose one.

"He will stay," I said, finding his rudeness a strange relief in this situation.

"But, princess," Isolde hissed.

"I have asked for the facts on your list, not your opinion, Isolde. I might as well read it myself," I snapped back.

I was tired. I was anxious. I was a little bit frightened of what came after this. I didn't want to know which of the men Isolde thought would be good bed partners when I wasn't prepared to sleep with any of them yet.

I held my hand out for Isolde's list, my shoulders back and spine pin-straight as I stared up at her. She handed it over with a dark flush on her cheeks and then moved quickly to stand at the wall. When I glanced back, Aric Martin was staring at me, and this time his gaze was ice cold.

I pulled the list up, read the numbers in front of me, and called out my decisions for the table to hear, listing every name I'd marked to stay. Fuck decorum.

"The rest of you are dismissed," I said. "I will see my Chosen in the Rose Room."

From here on out, I would be alone with the men, permitted to do exactly as I pleased with no one to watch but the entire mess of them.

I strode out of the dining room, my hands clenched to fists, ignoring the dozens of eyes on my back.

2.
BRYONY

I'd stalled, just a little, to change into a new dress. If I'd been like Camellia or Grandmother, I probably would've removed all my clothes and waited in the Rose Room, ready to let the men race to impress me. The Rose Room was a sitting room attached to my own private rooms, although on the opposite side of my own personal sitting room. In the past, I had entertained the daughters of visiting diplomats over tea in that room. Now I was intended to host an orgy there.

Or at least, that would be the expectation.

I stood on the opposite side of the heavy door, listening to the low voices of the men waiting for me, some boisterous and taunting, others only murmurs. I stroked down the silken fabric of my gown, a looser and thinner dress than I was accustomed to wearing. I was grateful to be out of the corsets and ties and layers I'd been bound into as a princess, but it left me with an especially vulnerable feeling to know there was only my slip and this thin gown between me and the rest of the world. Suddenly, the boning of a corset sounded like a reasonable form of armor.

"She's a bit odd for her family, isn't she?" a voice called, a little too loud from the other side of the dense oak. "Almost shy."

The room of men grew muted, and I pressed my ear to the crease of the door to listen to the answering declaration.

"I'd be careful if I were you. She hears you, and you're likely to have your tongue cut off. Or something...smaller and even less likely to impress her."

My lips twitched. I wished I was watching in the room now. I would've liked to know who'd said that. I waited through the boisterous laughter and gathered my courage. I had to go in. I had to live up to the expectation of the queen's line. To our ruling Hunger. An appetite I appeared to be lacking.

The dying chuckles stuttered as I pushed the door open and stepped inside, forcing myself to raise my chin and meet the eyes of the men I'd called in.

"Princess," one purred, his fire-red hair catching the candle-light as he stepped forward and crowded me nearly right back out of the room. I held my feet still and stiffened as he moved into my chest, warm palms cupping my shoulders as he bent and kissed the corner of my jaw. He smelled of wine, and I'd already forgotten his name. "The anticipation of your presence has left me aching for you."

He rolled his hips insistently forward, and his name clicked in my brain with the slight nudge of a semi-aroused cock against my hip. Prince Everett of Fulledom. He was the fifth son in his line, and a position as one of my Chosen was sure to be a better a prospect than a general in one of his father's overly employed armies. I slipped free of his grip and worked my way around his side, dipping into a brief and shallow curtsey.

"Welcome back to Kimmery, Your Highness," I said, trying to back away from him. Except I only ended up stumbling into another body. I spun and pulled away before I could be grabbed up in another pair of over-eager arms.

This pair belonged to a tall and classical looking man with tan skin and shining brown hair. He had chosen to go shirtless, and his pectoral muscles bounced in invitation.

"Princess, I am ready to slake your desires, Lennon Barrett," he said with a little bow—one far too slight for my station. He rose up grinning, but it faltered at my blank expression. "I...I am a one, and I prolonged for forty-five minutes and was ready in five."

"Ah," I said, blinking and nodding, searching the room for some escape other than the way I'd come. "Noted. Please help yourself to the refreshments." I tossed a hand toward the table, where iced tea and small frosted cakes waited.

The eyes watching made my skin hot and itchy. I shouldn't have taken so many men, that was foolish of me, especially when

I knew I wanted nothing to do with any of them. Now I had seventeen men surrounding me, waiting for their turn to fuck.

The room was dimly lit by candlelight and a little warm due to the fire at the far end. Likely because it was expected that we'd all be naked soon enough. Men were quickly crowding closer, all the dignitaries and the more eager of the commoners.

Wendell Pope, the Mennary ambassador, reached my side next. He had the sense to bow low, one leg extended elegantly and spine straight.

"And would Your Highness appreciate any refreshment for herself?" he asked in a low and melodious tone. Behind him, Prince Thao bounced on the balls of his feet, eyes darting nervously between us.

It was on the tip of my tongue to refuse, but if I accepted, then Wendell Pope would be one less suitor breathing down the back of my neck, and perhaps he would take the beautiful Prince Thao with him on his errand.

"Water please, and some fruit," I said, straightening my shoulders before they collapsed under the weight of the room. I added to the others, "Excuse me, gentlemen."

It gave them enough pause, the words a clear dismissal, for me to escape to the far end of the room where a few men were seated by the fire, watching the scene without fighting for my attention personally. Disinterested Aric was there, silver hair glinting golden in the firelight, his chair turned to face the flames, with his back to me. With him was Cosmo, the man who had watched other men while pleasuring himself, and my first choice of the day, the big and handsome rough-looking man.

There was a space on the settee between Cosmo and the other one—he must've been one of the last handful I'd called for before storming out of the dining hall—and I rushed there with all of the finishing elegance of a well-trained princess. The bigger of the two men sat up straight at my approach, his legs shifting out of that masculine spread. Cosmo remained leaning against the arm of the settee, facing the room, his eyes smiling as I hurried and helped myself to the small space.

"Prin—"

"I feel as though I know all the wrong things about you," I

said, eyeing the three men quickly, careful not to glance at the rest of the room. "The choosing is a very strange ceremony. Please, tell me what is that you gentlemen do for a living."

By the fire, Aric had deep lines carving into his forehead and a dark storm in his eyes as they flicked to and away from me. Cosmo and the other man only grinned.

"I'm an artist, Your Highness. Sculpture mainly," Cosmo said.

"Any in our collection?" I asked, sitting up and brightening. I loved art. I could speak on art as long as he didn't try and turn the conversation into a seduction.

"No," Cosmo said, the corners of his dark eyes crinkling with humor. "I never apprenticed with one of the greats. But I've made sales to some of the better houses. Pope's father has one of my old works," he said, watching the other end of the room where Wendell and the others seemed to be bickering over my plate.

I glanced at Aric, but his eyes were still fixed on the fire so I turned to my first choice of the day. "And you? I called your name, but I missed knowing it was yours," I said, offering the man on my left a small, apologetic smile. He looked even more like a romantic hero from a story up close, the dimple on his chin growing deeper with his smile and a soft dark curl falling over his brow.

"Owen Dunne, Your Highness," he said, tone warm and soothing, head bowing respectfully. "I...I was a soldier in the army, and now I have a few jobs around Rumsbrooke in the north. I like working in the army stables best," he said.

I curled my legs up from the floor, tucking them under my skirt and nodded at big and gentle Owen Dunne. "Horses are lovely animals. And they have very good judgment, I think."

Owen's lips formed an exquisite smile, blue eyes clear and calming. "I absolutely agree. Aric, you said as much on the trip down here, didn't you?"

Aric grunted by the fire, and when I turned to look at him again, his head whipped toward the flames as if he'd been observing me while I wasn't looking.

"Aric owns a lively tavern in Rumsbrooke," Cosmo supplied slowly. "I used to sneak in there when I was a lad."

"No one sneaks around me, Pianetta," Aric growled, gray eyes cutting in a glare in our direction and then turning to the open room. "We let you in because the ladies liked you. Still do," he rasped with a skimming glance over me. "But it looks as though your competition will be more intent this time."

I stiffened as I saw what Aric meant. Someone must've wrestled my small plate of fruit from Wendell, and now all the neglected men of my Chosen were headed in our direction. Their gazes were more determined this time, and I didn't know if I was only being paranoid of or if there were hints of suspicion in their stares. I was already failing. I couldn't just sit here and play get-to-know-you with these men until dawn.

If I wanted to keep my position as princess inherit, then I had to perform.

I jumped up from the settee, grabbing up Owen and Cosmo's hands, finding Aric's narrow stare.

"I—please..." I swallowed hard, and Aric's head tipped as he watched me. "Would the three of you please retire to my bedroom with me?"

It shouldn't have been a question. It shouldn't even have been a statement. I should've stripped them bare and taken them on the couch like any other woman in the queen's line. But I didn't think I could stand to fake the Hunger in front of an audience so big.

Cosmo and Owen followed readily, but Aric's hands clenched around the arms of the chair he remained in and his head jerked in the briefest movement.

"Aric, you can't refuse," Cosmo whispered. "Especially not in front of the others."

The older man's jaw ticked, and he rose slowly from the chair, eyes fierce and full of anger on me. My own expression was tight as I tried to bury the panic in my own chest, and he blinked and made to follow. Owen cut our path smoothly through the sycophantic Chosen, and I hurried close at his back, grateful for the height and breadth of him giving me something to hide behind.

"Princess, please allow me—"

"You should have a prince with you to gentle their coarse habits—"

"Your water, Your Highness—"

"Your fruit, Your Grace—"

"I would drink from your apex like a dying man—"

I ignored them all, my eyes on the slight stain of Owen's coarse shirt. At the door, we found Prince Thao and Wendell Pope, who made identical and elegant bows to us.

"May we join you, Princess Bryony?" Thao asked in soft and accented Kimmerian.

The damn pair were blocking my escape. "Yes, fine. In, please," I bit out.

Wendell was quick with the door, and the voices followed close at our heels as we stepped into my dark bedchamber. There were candles lit on the mantle, but no fire and my balcony doors were open over the garden, the room fresh with the scent of orchids and gardenias and roses and peonies.

Owen turned and looked over my head. "A little faster, Aric, or you'll let the whole lot in," he said, smiling.

Behind me, a gentle pair of hands took my waist, drawing me back to a warm chest as the door clicked shut behind us. I nearly jumped out of my own skin as lips brushed over my shoulder, breath chuckling as Cosmo nuzzled my bare skin. He smelled nice, a little sweet and pleasantly fresh, and also a bit like plaster, but I couldn't force myself to relax. Instead, I reached for Owen's wrinkled shirt, pulling him to a bend. I made the mistake of stopping to look into his eyes, my own terrified and pained expression reflecting back at me, before I took his face in my hands, stubble scratching my palms, and brought his mouth to mine.

It was not my *first* kiss. One of Camellia's Chosen had tried to kiss me a year ago, his mouth bruising against mine before I'd wrestled him away. This was my first kiss I'd given freely, although I felt numb at the connection.

Was I doing it right, should I try to press my tongue in as Igor had with me? Owen's hands mirrored my own, gentle and scratching with callouses on my cheeks as he pulled at my lips softly with his, pressing and holding. It was tender and sweet, but my head refused to quiet. Cosmo's hands were petting softly around my waist and hips, a murmur of the others' voices over our shoulders. It didn't feel bad, or painful, but there was a knot of panic my throat couldn't swallow, and my stomach was queasy.

"You look pale, princess," Aric said. I pulled away from Owen's mouth, and he moved his kisses to my cheek and jaw. Aric was leaning against the bottom corner poster of my bed, arms crossed over his chest as he watched us. "Perhaps she is too warm, gentleman. Undress her."

"Should you really be the one making orders?" Prince Thao asked, raising a noble chin and glaring at Aric. The prince and Wendell were behind us, still near the door, and Wendell already had his hands raised to his throat, loosening the tie of his collar.

Aric shrugged, and his eyes never left mine. "If she doesn't like it, she can tell me what to do with my mouth."

Cosmo seemed happy enough to follow Aric's orders, his hands moving to my back to undo the laces of my gown. He pulled a few free, and I gasped as one of his hands reached down the collar of my gown to gently knead at my breast, a startling and vulnerable sensation.

Owen hummed into my cheek, stubble scratching as he nipped at my earlobe, his hands smoothing down my arms before reaching to gather up my skirts.

My heart trembled in my chest until I thought it might take flight. I stumbled out from between the two men with a moan, my hands wrestling myself free of them before moving to cradle my stomach as I hurried quickly to the other side of the room.

"You were too rough with her," Thao said.

I panted, pacing between my fainting couch and the door that would take me to my own sitting room, trying to ignore the shadows of the men by the bed.

"Your Highness?" Owen called.

I can't. I can't do it. I'm broken. I don't have the Hunger.

I will lose the crown and the kingdom. I will fail my family and my people.

"We'd better send for the others," Aric muttered.

"No!"

They stared at me as I spun to face them. It was there on their faces, the confusion, the obvious understanding that in *some* way, I was wrong. I was not what I ought to have been.

Only Aric's expression was clear. I marched back to him, my chin raised, and he remained still and relaxed at the tall pillar of my massive and unsoiled bed. He saw right through me, I realized. Any orders given were only tests to see if I could withstand them.

"Take control," I whispered to him, the warmth of his side radiating against me. Perhaps he could make something of this night when I could not.

Aric raised a pale eyebrow. "And force you?"

"Aric," Owen snapped as Wendell gasped.

I raised my hand to quiet them. "Yes," I said to Aric. And then I pretended we were alone and there was no one else to hear the words that followed in a whisper. "I can't do it myself."

Aric straightened. I only came to his chin, and he was broad right down to his hips—not as much as Owen, but there was something even more menacing about the man in front of me. He was not noble at all as I'd imagined him like a book character. There was steel in him, but it was more likely to cut me than protect me.

He reached to pinch my jaw between strong thick fingers, eyes flicking back and forth over mine as his head lowered. I braced myself. I didn't imagine he would be as gentle as Owen or Cosmo. I hoped he wouldn't because if he was tentative, I might find it possible to run away again. I hoped he was fast and efficient, and when he was done, I would be able to stomach the others too.

Aric's forehead rested against me and his lips skimmed mine, and I let out a shuddering sigh as I understood what he would say next.

"I will not." I whimpered and squeezed my eyes shut as he continued, "Neither will any of the others. And if you have it in mind to try your luck with the men outside, we'll bar the door."

Then I've failed, I thought, and the sobs came shattering out of my chest, cutting their way up my throat like shards of glass.

3.
OWEN

Aric bundled the little princess into his arms as she beat weak fists against his chest and cried with all the force of a new widow. What on earth had we all done wrong?

She was like a little confection, all her silk flounces and light brown curls like whips of cream around the sweet berry of flesh. I'd missed her younger sister's choosing while in the army, and I'd tried not to be too optimistic about my chances with Princess Bryony, but she'd called my name in her sharp and clear voice in the dining hall and here I was, exactly where I'd dreamed of landing one day. Being one of the Chosen wasn't just an honor, it was a life of destined luxury, something I'd imagined but never pictured clearly until arriving this morning in the capital.

Except now...

I had no idea *what* was happening.

"Shhhh," Aric soothed, gathering the young woman up and settling himself comfortably against the high pile of pillows in her massive throne of a bed. Princess Bryony only wept louder for all his soothing, but she clung to him, fingers fisted in his shirt as he stroked her back and her hair.

"I don't understand," the Mennary prince murmured, looking to his ambassador, who shook his equally perplexed head.

Cosmo, who I'd made easy conversation with in the waiting rooms, climbed onto the mattress as well, reaching his hand out to rest it over the top of her foot. She didn't pull away, although with the great heaping sobs and hiccups she was making against Aric's chest, she probably didn't have it in her to do much else.

"I'm...I'm *broken*," she cracked out, words muffled against Aric's shirt.

He rolled his eyes, but his hands made steady and soothing passes over the top of her head and down her back.

"You're nothing of the kind, princess," he said.

Princess Bryony pulled away from him then, eyes and cheeks shining with tears, a flush staining her skin. "I don't—I'm not—I don't..."

"You don't have the Hunger," Cosmo whispered.

She froze then, eyes as wide as a doe's, and her hands clenched in her lap, trembling until I thought she might slap him. Then she released a great sigh and her knees bundled up to her chest, hands covering her face.

"No, I don't."

The prince stumbled away from the bed, a hand covering his face, and I shot him and the pretty boy, Wendell Pope, a glare of warning before going to join the others on the bed.

"That doesn't make you broken," I said. I didn't really understand the Hunger. In my personal experience, if a girl liked a lad, she was plenty hungry for him, royalty or not. Usually, she got more than one look and a few numbers to decide if that was the case.

"It makes me unfit to rule," Bryony moaned, lifting her face from her hands to glance at me. She shifted, her dress making a pretty, liquid sound as she moved. She was, by far, the softest thing or person I'd ever touched in my entire life, and if it weren't for the clear memory of her own panic as she pulled away, I would've reached for her again.

"I've put this off for years, and my grandmother, she...she knows I'm not right. In the morning, they'll take my sheets and they'll see I've failed." Bryony wiped the tears off her cheeks with the back of her knuckle, sniffling until Cosmo drew out a paint marked handkerchief from his pocket.

She smiled at him, a wobbly and sweet little look, and brushed her thumb across one blue smudge, before raising it to her nose.

"If you knew you didn't have the Hunger, why on earth have the ceremony in the first place?" Thao asked, his voice rising.

"Keep your voice down," Wendell murmured to him,

catching him by the elbow and drawing him over to the bed. "Your Highness, we can fake the sheets easily enough."

Cosmo snorted and shrugged. "That's true. But sooner or later, the men in the next room will expect to be needed." We paused as the princess shuddered. Aric was watching her. He had been ever since she'd entered the dining hall this evening.

I'd heard of Aric Martin, owner of the Wing and Rook tavern and rumored magician and thief. I'd expected him to pay more attention to the riches that surrounded us than the princess herself, but he watched her like a hawk that had found its next prey. It wasn't sexual, like the other men, or even a sort of basic admiration, like the way Cosmo's eyes traveled over her. It was calculation.

"What happens when the queen discovers the first in line is lacking the Hunger?" Aric asked.

"The crown will go to my sister, Camellia," Bryony said softly, brow furrowing. "She has her Chosen already and can barely be sated by them as it is. She'll take more soon, no doubt, but Grandmother insisted I go first."

"What will happen to you?" I asked, my arm finding its way around her shoulders, sighing as she leaned willingly into my chest.

"I don't know. It isn't... I want to serve my people. Grandmother said that there being *two* daughters with the Hunger while my mother was still on the throne would bring Kimmery into a new golden age. Women of the queen's line have so few children, and for there to be *two* daughters was supposed to be a blessing to Kimmery. And now I've let them all down."

Aric scoffed and slid off the bed, boots hitting the floor and heading for one of the balconies. Good riddance. I didn't know enough about the man, and I'd thought he'd been prepared to force the nervous princess into sex earlier. He hadn't though, I reminded myself. I had to credit him that. He wasn't very kind to the young woman, but he wasn't a monster.

Aric paused in one of the open doorways and threw over his shoulder, "The last thing this kingdom needs is another woman on her back, princess."

And then he ducked out of sight. Princess Bryony stared after him, sitting upright and frowning.

"What does he mean?" she whispered, turning to look at the rest of us. "The Hunger is the force for prosperity in Kimmery."

Quiet answered the princess's declaration, and her gaze darted between us until Prince Thao cleared his throat.

"Certainly to be Chosen for your—the Hunger's use is a great honor," he said slowly and carefully. "But Kimmery's wealth is largely to do with your exports from the northern territory..."

The princess shifted away from me, kneeling to face us with her shoulders back and her chin high. I forced my eyes above the subtle curves of her breasts and then swallowed when I found her elegant throat equally fascinating.

"You believe the Hunger is...less responsible?" Bryony asked.

"Excuse me for the impertinence, Your Highness, but many find the Hunger to be a...a charming superstition," Wendell said, bowing lowly as if it might soften the words. "And a great honor to be Chosen, of course."

I looked to Cosmo, who was leaning back on his palms, watching the princess study us each in turn before gazing out after Aric on the balcony.

"Do you prefer women?" Cosmo asked. Bryony shook her head, and he pushed. "Are you certain?"

"I...I do have desires," she said, and my hands fisted against my thighs at the sight of her blush. "I enjoy reading and I...I daydream for the characters, the heroes. I fantasize," she said, with that perfectly proud tilt to her chin she used when she was embarrassed and refusing to admit as much. "It's just that you're all...strangers." Her nose wrinkled, and she shrugged. "Reasonably, I see that you are handsome, and I know that I should—"

"Should has nothing to do with it, princess," I murmured, and then found my own tongue useless as she turned green eyes to me. "Plenty of people wouldn't feel comfortable with a stranger."

Not that I'd minded the idea of bedding the princess on little more than a handful of words and an order from her. And it hadn't been any of the girls I'd met before I'd thought of when asked to perform earlier. It'd been her, pristine and polished and cold on her throne as she examined me in the great hall.

She's not cold at all though, I thought. Princess Bryony was warm to the touch and a little frightened, and she'd been stiff as I kissed her. It irritated me that Aric had seen how deep her discomfort went before I had.

"It's not right that a woman from the queen's line be like 'plenty of people,'" she said quietly. "But won't someone explain what you mean about the Hunger not being responsible for the kingdom's greatness?"

I dropped my eyes to my lap. Reassuring the princess that she wasn't broken was one thing. Explaining to her that Kimmery *was*...

That might be something like treason, and I wasn't a fool enough to speak. My eyes slid to Prince Thao. Perhaps someone of his rank might be able to get away with the words? Except he looked pale and preoccupied, pacing back and forth along the side of the bed.

"Kimmery does a great deal of trade, Your Highness," Cosmo said, sitting up. "Most of your labor comes from the north. Your citizens are paid very little and taxed very highly and that money is what ensures that the view outside your castle windows looks so...prosperous."

I bit my own lip as I watched Princess Bryony turn bright red, her eyes wide and her hands clenching the fabric of her skirt. There was shock and anger on her face, but also shame as she stared back at Cosmo, like she'd known such a thing might be possible but hadn't had to face the words before now.

"I don't—How can this be the case? Are you certain?" she asked, high and breathy. Her eyes glanced to Wendell, who nodded or bowed, or both at once.

"We come from the north, princess," Aric said, reappearing in the doorway. "Cosmo and I see every day what it costs Kimmerians to keep the capital shining and our queens coming on their Chosen's cocks."

"Aric," I snapped, and he raised an eyebrow at me.

"There are women and children working themselves into their graves, and you want me to apologize to the girl who lives in this?" he asked, swirling a hand through the air, eyes scanning over every ornate inch of the princess' bedroom.

He wasn't wrong; even I knew that. There was a reason why most men looked forward to the thought of being a Chosen, and it had less to do with bedding royalty than it did a lifetime away from labor. That was half my own hope in coming to the palace for the choosing.

"You know it isn't her fault," I said, glowering at Aric and ready to rise and toss him out and over the balcony until a light hand landed on my wrist.

"No, he's right. I had no idea," Bryony said with an open gaze directed to Aric. "But I should have, and that's my first failure to my people. It will be worse if I do nothing now that I've heard. I just...I have no proof that Kimmery is as well cared for as I've heard, but I have nothing but your word saying otherwise and..." Her brow furrowed, lips parted on a word that never found its voice.

She gathered her skirt in her hands, and Cosmo and I hurried to help lift her from the bed.

"You're going to...to do something now?" Thao asked, stepping forward. I didn't understand why the Mennary prince looked so nervous. I'd noticed it as soon as I'd entered the waiting room, after seeing the princess for the first time, and it had yet to abate.

"I'm going to go and...think. Make a decision," Bryony said softly, smoothing her silks. She couldn't meet our eyes, and I wished I was the kind of man who might insist on joining her, reassuring her more. But she probably didn't want a stablehand as a witness to her worries.

"We could make a show of it," Wendell offered, glancing at the rest of us. "You wouldn't even need to be in the room if you weren't comfortable. If they're going to look at your sheets—"

Bryony's nose was scrunched as she shook her head. "I don't want to lie, especially not if that's what the queen's line has been doing this whole time. You may—" Her voice wobbled and she pushed away from the bed, heading toward the private door on the far end of the room. "You may do as you please. I'll be back before the morning. Just don't let anyone else in, and try not to tell them anything until I've made a decision."

Her dress swished with every quick step away from us, candlelight rocking up the walls as she passed and all but ran through the doors, locking it shut behind her. Gone. The princess was gone, and my dream of being a Chosen was burst like a bubble. My eyes slit and turned to Aric Martin, his own gaze fixed on the locked doors that hid the princess.

"You could've been kinder to her," I said.

He blinked but didn't bother turning to me. "I could have. Maybe she needed to hear the truth."

"What does this mean for her? Pope, you'd know best," Cosmo said.

Wendell Pope, who was tall and handsome and practically glued to the prince's side as they whispered to each other in a rapid foreign tongue, whipped his head up and looked between the far doors and Cosmo.

"I wouldn't," he said, but when we all remained staring at him, he frowned. "She may...she may have to abdicate the throne. Or she may be able to convince the crown to give up the notion of the Hunger."

Aric scoffed at that suggestion. "The Hunger has reigned in this kingdom for hundreds of years, excusing the royals from any responsibility to their people."

"And now you have a princess who does not possess it," Thao spat back. "If it exists at all."

Aric and Cosmo frowned at one another, and I glared at them both. "What? What does that look mean?" I asked.

"We were both...present for Camellia's second choosing. She..." Cosmo trailed off, and Aric continued.

"She's a beast possessed, is what she is. Either by the Hunger or her own whims, who knows. But if the queen wants to keep the Hunger, she has the perfect daughter in the younger of the two. Pope is right. They'll toss that little flower right out onto the doorstep to greet her starving people," Aric finished, his eyes drifting back to the closed door, a line furrowing on his brow.

4.
BRYONY

You failed.

You failed at the Hunger, which might as well be made up.

Kimmery is failing its people.

Can I be as I am and do any better for the kingdom?

Around and around the thoughts turned. I was curled in the window seat of my personal study, staring down at the rose gardens in full bloom, the fountains bubbling under moonlight, until the moon was sliding behind my grandmother's turret and the sun was turning the water pink with dawn. And I had made no real decision, only worn my lip bruised with worrying. At the very edge of the horizon, the Coraletti Sea was a shimmering line. I'd never wondered why the castle seemed to face south, but now I understood, all our faults lay in the other direction. Who carried the cost of my favorite view? Were my people really suffering as they said, or was that only what my grandmother would call a commoner's right to unrest?

My eyes strayed to my bedroom door, and I wondered what the men I'd left there had done. Was it too late to ask them to fake some kind of debauchery? Could I just carry on pretending like I had for most of my life? Could I ask those men to give up their lives for that kind of charade?

Knock knock knock.

I startled on the bench at the alert and my tired eyes widened.

"Princess, it is—it is Thao," the soft voice whispered through the door. "May we speak?"

My legs were stiff as I unfolded them, stretching up from my nest of pillows and cool window panes, heading for the door. I ran my fingers across the pale velvet of my settee, a reassuring touch to ground myself before reaching the door and turning the key in the lock. I opened it, and my eyes trailed past Thao and into the room. Aric Martin was asleep on the chaise, hunched under his own coat with his back to me. In my bed, Owen and Cosmo lay sleeping, sprawled out in the sheets, mismatched curls over their faces.

Wendell Pope was awake and hovering by Thao's side, the pair of them looking as restless as I was.

"I haven't really made a decision," I admitted.

Wendell, who was a little taller than the prince, set his hand on Thao's shoulder. "Actually, we felt we owed you an explanation."

My heart hammered briefly. Another revelation was the *last* thing I wanted to deal with, especially so early in the morning. But I stepped back, and Thao and Wendell were quick to squeeze their way in through the parted door, Thao taking it from me and closing it behind himself, my eyebrows jumping at his forwardness.

"If you're about to try and seduce me—" I started. Wendell had been a little pushy the night before, at least compared to Owen or Cosmo. *Especially* compared to Aric, who'd barely bothered to hide his absolute loathing of me when he wasn't cradling me in his arms.

"Not at all, princess," Wendell said, stepping and bowing again. "In fact, I wanted to explain why I was so...*insistent* on being one of your Chosen."

I sighed and nodded, moving to my couch and gesturing for them to take the chairs. "Very well. It might be moot at this point. I'm not sure that a princess without the Hunger even needs Chosen."

Wendell and Thao both fidgeted their way into a set of armchairs that faced me, and it wasn't until their hands met in the space between that I had any notion of what was coming.

"Ambassador Pope is my lover," Thao said, straight backed and chin high, eyes locked to mine. "I knew the negotiations between our families would ensure my place here, and the only way to have Wen with me—"

"Was if he were Chosen," I finished for him, eyes widening

and heart gentling. I sighed and softened into my seat. "I understand. But what happens if I have no Chosen?"

Thao's eyes lowered to his lap, and Wendell's fingers squeezed around the prince's. "Thao's family had a marriage arranged for him in Jyndan as an alternative. I would remain Kimmery's ambassador to Mennary no doubt."

And the lovers would be separated. My lips parted as I looked between the two men, the weight of my unmade decision growing heavier.

"I don't...I don't know what to do," I admitted, exhaustion dredging up tears in my eyes once again.

Thao stood and crossed to me, helping himself to a seat next to mine and reaching for my cold fingers, wrapping them up in warmer hands. His black hair was loose around his face, strong chin dipping so he could meet my eyes.

"I was nervous for the choosing, whether Wendell found a place or not. The queen's line is notoriously possessive, and being chosen posed as many risks for my love as being separated did."

"I would never have tried to force the two of you apart," I said.

Thao's lips quirked. "Your sister, Camellia, likely would have if we'd arrived at her ceremony and not yours. I only want to say that...that if you wish to be a ruler to your kingdom, Hunger or not, Chosen or not, I will support you." He and Wendell exchanged a soft, appreciative smile between them, and my heart swelled. I might not feel a passion for the men individually, but I did have a wistful kind of longing for what they shared. And a desire to protect it.

"I don't know what will happen when I confess to my family, but I'll do my best to demand a place in my court for the both of you so you don't have to worry," I said.

Wendell's eyes winced, and he looked doubtful, but Thao beamed at me, dark eyes bright and clear, his hands squeezing around mine.

"I believe there is some record of members of the queen's line not taking part in the choosing, princess," Wendell said. "I don't know what became of those people, but if you can find anything written on them, it may offer you some guidance."

I groaned and pulled free of Thao's hold, rolling my shoulders and sitting up straight. "Then I'd better go searching now. The maids will be in soon with breakfast and to take the sheets. Try not to let Aric terrorize them."

I wasn't sure how I felt about the older man. He'd done his best to be harsh with me, to be cold or rude, but he'd been honest when others insisted on tiptoeing and I was grateful for the change. And he'd been so...tender when I'd fallen to pieces. I hadn't finished processing that feeling of being held, I only knew that I was curious about the dichotomy of the man.

"I'm sure he'll do his best," Wendell said, dark and dry as I headed for the doors that led to the hall.

◈

"I SHOULD'VE KNOWN I'd find you rutting up against a bookshelf rather than your Chosen."

I was sweating, climbing down the ladder in the library with an armful of royal history texts, when Camellia snapped and I nearly fell right to the marble tile.

My younger sister was in the center of the room, leaning up against a large, gleaming oak table, with one of her Chosen—I think his name was Sam—curled against her side, his hand in her hair and his mouth on her neck. Camellia's hips were twisted in his direction, her hand clamped on the back of his neck as her hooded eyes watched me, looking ready to fall shut. Any minute, and I was sure she'd be bent over the table, making as much noise as she liked as her Chosen served her from behind.

Camellia had taken great pleasure—*great* pleasure—in taunting me since she'd taken Chosen, fucking them in the garden below my windows while I was trying to read, nearly choking on her soup at dinner while one feasted on her below the table, taking up the public staircases with a pair of twins.

"Grandmother is looking for you," Camellia said, sighing as Sam ducked to suck along the collar of her dress.

I wanted to ask why she bothered dressing at all, except I was afraid it might just goad her into forgoing clothing.

I didn't find shame in public sex. My family had a history of performing it freely. But there was something in Camellia's habit of it that seemed cruelly focused on mocking me. If she'd been more absorbed in her Chosen than she was in making me a witness, I might not have minded so much.

"Mother is with her," Camellia added as I started to pass her. Her hair was up, or had been at some point, the color a lighter shade than mine and strands full of tangles. "Bry-bry, what have you done now?"

"Very little that should concern you," I said.

I stopped in my step and crossed my arms around the books I cradled, watching Sam ruck up Camellia's thin white skirt. It was a little stained, and his eyes slid away from Camellia's pale skin to find me. He looked tired...or bored, I wasn't sure, his lips chapped and his eyes too absent and unfocused to be lustful.

Camellia frowned and turned, blocking my view of her Chosen. "I don't understand you," she said to me, passing the words over her shoulder before pushing the man down to his knees.

I sighed and shook my head, heading for the doors. I didn't really understand me either. I thought I understood my family even less.

I tried to read on my way to my grandmother's suite, flipping through the pages of each book as I rotated them in the stack in my arms, searching for some mention of royals without the Hunger. The closest I found was a princess who died of a fever before reaching adulthood. Searching for the information provided a welcome distraction from my nerves as I made my way through the castle, my eyes down and avoiding any stray glance from the servants.

When I reached my grandmother's wing, I set the pile of books down on a side table before stepping up to the door, smoothing back my hair. I hadn't bothered dressing for the day, partly to avoid the giggles of the maidservants, and partly to avoid Aric and the others in my bedroom. But it wasn't so uncommon for the queen's line to look disheveled, although I was lacking the usual excuse.

The servant posted outside of the door stepped in to announce me, waving me through after a sharp "Send her in" from my Grandmother. I stalled in the doorway however, when I saw my mother. It had been several weeks since I'd seen her last. She preferred to remain shut up with her Chosen in her wing, leaving Grandmother as the mouthpiece to the queen's line.

My mother was small, like me, with rounded hips and small breasts. Camellia took after Grandmother, tall and thin, although all four of us had the same sharp chin and high brow. Mother, Queen Peony of Kimmery, was reclined on Grandmother's chaise, her feet in the lap of one of her Chosen, who smiled warmly at me before going back to massaging Mother's feet.

"Darling," my mother said, hands reaching for me, although she made no other move in my direction.

"Your Majesty," I said, dipping into the lowest curtsey I could give and then turning my bowed head to my grandmother. "Your Majesty."

"Bryony, come here and kiss my cheek," Mother said.

I was keenly aware of my grandmother's stare scorching into my cheek as I stepped further into her chambers and headed for my mother. Technically, my mother held the real command in our hierarchy, but it wasn't in her nature to wrestle the control away from Grandmother, and I was sure at any moment I was about to be chastised.

My mother's eyes were glassy, her cheeks flushed, and her curls were braided softly over her shoulder. She went without a corset generally when I saw her, and at the moment she was wearing only a silk robe over a night dress. I bent, and she turned her head side to side for me to kiss her soft skin.

"Do you know...I think she might be Michael's," my mother said, and it took me a moment to realize she was speaking to her Chosen and not to me. "He has those eyes too."

The man answered her with a docile hum as my mother stared absently up at me.

"Bryony," Grandmother said, patience at an end. I turned and curtseyed to her again before she snapped. "What are these?"

White sheets were fisted in her hand, piled high on the floor.

I opened my mouth to give her the simplest answer and then shut again. Saying 'sheets' would only earn me ire.

"I did not make use of my Chosen last night," I said.

Grandmother glared at me, and I wondered if it might've been better to play stupid instead. "I know you did not make use of them, girl, because the sheets are practically untouched, although they smell of—of *horse*."

I almost wanted to smile. That would be Owen, who seemed unrefined but sweet and patient. Horses would like that, and I had been grateful for it the night before too.

"Oh, Bryony, you took Chosen?" my mother asked, her voice high and bright at my back.

"Oh she named them, but she did not *take* them," Grandmother answered for me. "I should have known when you refused to even sample. You exhibited a complete lack of interest, but I'd assumed we'd given you enough time—"

"I don't have the Hunger," I blurted out.

Mother gasped, and I heard her rustling softly on the chaise. Grandmother only gave me a look of triumph, and I bit down around the question in my mouth.

But you knew that didn't you?

"Oh, Bryony," my mother sighed, and I was surprised to find her hand on my shoulder. I saw my mother rarely as it was, and I saw her moving of her own accord even less. She reached for my cheek next and turned me to face her, blue eyes sorrowful and studying. "What do you mean, darling?"

I had cried in front of the men last night, but I refused to do so in front of my grandmother. She was too sharp, and I knew she'd turn my tears into knives to use against me. Instead, I bound the exhaustion and turmoil tight in my chest and met my mother's stare.

"I do possess lust, but it—it isn't the same. I can't feel desire for a stranger."

My mother frowned, puzzled, and glanced to my grandmother and then back to me. "And...women?"

"No, not to my knowledge. Men are *attractive*—"

"Of course they are," mother said, brightening.

"But admiration does not come with craving," I said. "I have *tried*."

"The sheets say otherwise," Grandmother bit out, and I flinched, but our queen only rolled her eyes. "It will have to be Camellia, Peony. I've been telling you this from the start."

"Oh, give it a little time," Mother said.

"Time? You heard the girl, she has no Hunger! Are you asking me to condemn Kimmery on behalf of this...this mutation in the queen's line?"

I gasped, the word striking me in the heart. A *mutation*. A confirmation of my worst feelings for myself. I spun to my grandmother and opened my mouth to spew back at her—everything I'd learned from the men the night before, the taxation and the labor and the cruelty of our kingdom upon its own people. But these were things I wasn't even sure of yet.

My mother's hand squeezed my shoulder, and the words died in my throat.

"Bryony's Hunger may grow," my mother said, and the sweetness of her voice had hardened to a queen's command. "Camellia is full of appetite, but she does not have Bryony's love of our people. Bryony will be given time. None of the queen's line ever keeps *all* of their first Chosen. Perhaps she simply needs to rearrange their numbers."

Thao and Wendell immediately came to mind, sparking a whole new idea in my thoughts, my indecision washing away under a plan. "There are a few I like," I said quickly, turning to my mother's warm smile to avoid the chill on the other end of the room. "And I...I was thinking that it might be nice to get to know them better away from the...busyness in the capital."

"Away? Away *where*?" Grandmother squawked.

"Oh, how lovely! Like a common little honeymoon," my mother cooed.

"We could go north," I said. I would find the truth and the answers for myself.

5.
Bryony

I hadn't *forgotten* about the men I'd left in my bedroom, but I wasn't expecting them to still be there when I returned.

"Oh." I paused in the doorway and looked over the small collection of them.

Aric's shadow was hovering on the balcony, although he'd left his heavy dark coat behind on my chaise. Cosmo was there too, lounging on the floor in the sun like a cat, with my writing desk on his lap and what looked like art sketches scribbled over my best stationary. Wendell and Thao were sitting up in the bed, apparently having taken a turn sleeping there after the sheets were changed. And sweet Owen was sitting carefully on the bench at the end of my bed, a tray full of last night's confectionary collections and this morning's ample breakfast balanced on his lap.

"How did it go? Are you all right?" he asked immediately, rattling the trays when he shifted as if to rise.

"I...I hardly know," I said, my hand coming up to rest over my forehead. And then I caught sight of myself in a mirror to my right and realized I looked like one of those fainting damsels while Aric was glaring at me, and I dropped my hand immediately and began to pace the room.

What would I be permitted to take with me? Trunks of clothes, of course, but could I keep my books in the north? I'd give up all my gowns in exchange for my books.

My Chosen—if I could even call them that, when I had declared them so by necessity rather than desire—remained quiet as I moved to a dresser, fiddling with my jewelry there. I startled as a knock thundered on the far door.

"We heard voices. Is she back yet?" a man called through.

"The other men have been knocking all morning," Cosmo whispered to me. "We'll answer no?"

I started to nod, my hands wringing in front of me, before I pressed them down at my sides and marched to the door.

"Your Highness, we're more than happy to stall for you," Wendell murmured, rising from the bed.

"I have been stalling for five years," I muttered, straightening my shoulders and grabbing for the door. I swung it open, and the man on the other side—one of the commoners—straightened and puffed up his bare chest.

I blinked at the dozen men in the other room, all stripped down to their underwear to catch my attention. In my pause, the one in front of me reached for my waist, and I dodged neatly out of the way at the last possible second.

"Princess, we have been longing—"

"You are dismissed," I snapped, pressing my lips hard together as shock made a few of them stumble backwards. "All of you. I apologize for the inconvenience of your time—"

"Inconvenience? Princess Bryony, I have come all the way from Noren." Ah yes, Prince Holden. Tall and icy fair, and fully indignant at my announcement.

"Then I suggest you put your clothes on again and travel back there," I said, raising my chin. "Your summers are not so forgiving as ours."

The men broke out into a cacophony of complaints, and Wendell was quick to jump between us, helping me press the door shut to their pounding fists and managing the lock for me. I spun and ran for the bed, leaping across the end of it, burying my face in the mattress and releasing a muffled and strangled scream of frustration into the soft fabric of my sheets. The bed rustled as Thao shifted away from me, and my body ached with restrained tension as the fire of confusion and anger seemed to bleed out of me and into the silk.

Someone, probably Owen, smoothed a hand down my back, circling gently at the base until I softened and rolled over to face the room again.

The first I saw were Cosmo and Aric, standing in the

doorway of the balcony, Cosmo's smile upside down and Aric's frown tilted the wrong way.

"I am to go north, to the Winter Palace," I said.

"North?" Aric growled.

"And are we dismissed like the others?" Cosmo asked instead.

I let out an un-princessly grunt as I squirmed myself into sitting upright, Owen leaning onto the bed at my side, Wendell standing at the corner with Thao leaning into his chest.

"That will be up to you," I said, sharing a look with Thao and Wendell. "I may not ever amount to what I—to what the queen's line would *wish* me to be. However, for the time being, I've been given a little time with my Chosen. Her Majesty hopes I might grow into my Hunger, and I hope I might see for myself what goes on in my own kingdom."

Aric scoffed. "You're taking court to the north?"

"I'm taking myself. And...those of you who would join me, even if it's only for the appearance of having Chosen," I said, looking them each in the eye. "Arrangements are already being made to hire staff from the villages surrounding the northern estate, but it will be...less lavish by comparison to living here."

There, that was enough of a warning, wasn't it? I had a momentary flash of regret that I'd tossed the rest of the Chosen out. How was I to know who I might warm to when I felt so little at the start? Except...I did share something with these men, even if it wasn't passion. Cosmo and Owen weren't pushy and had listened to me. Thao and Wendell were honest with me about their own needs. And Aric...

I tried to avoid turning to him, but there was an itchy craving in my chest to know what he thought of my plan. Instead of approval, his narrow-eyed gaze was only full of study and suspicion, as if he was already searching for my next failing and would be only too happy to point it out to me when he'd found it.

"We—*I* am your Chosen," Thao said immediately, his eyes pulling away from Wendell to meet mine. His head dipped, and I answered it in kind, aware of the gratitude in his gaze. I didn't know what I would've done if the couple hadn't spoken to me in the morning, but they certainly helped spark my stalling tactic in front of my mother and grandmother.

"I will remain your Chosen as long as it pleases you," Wendell said, a galant echo of his lover's sentiment. His smile was more sincere than it had been the night before, a softer and more humored version of the ambassador's insistent charm.

"I will rely on you both not just for the sake of the illusion, but to help guide me through some of the misinformation I have been fed," I said quietly. "My understanding of my own kingdom has been vastly twisted by an education designed for a girl with the Hunger. And you all as well," I said turning to the others, trying to catch Aric's eye. "You are my people and my best judgement of the disservice the crown has done the kingdom."

Owen blushed a little, and Cosmo offered me a warm smile. "I'm less in tune with politics than you might assume, but I would happily take a place as your Chosen, and as an artist in residency in the Winter Palace."

I grinned, and the prickling weight in my chest of the day—no, month, ever since I'd known I couldn't stall any longer—lightened. "The palace would be honored."

A rough hand found mine on the bed, Owen's eyes dropping shyly. I wondered how he was with other women. Still so shy and sweet? It tugged at me strangely, a not unfamiliar feeling, but an unexpected one I would examine later.

"You may make use of me in any way you see fit, Your Highness," Owen said, low and soft, blue eyes flicking up to mine. "As your Chosen or a stablehand, I am at your service."

It grew stronger, the warmth in my veins and the gentle pull in Owen's direction. Was this desire? This softer version of the swelling feeling I'd felt while reading passionate romantic scenes in stories? Whatever it was, Aric cut through it with a low rumble of annoyance.

"I want no place in your palace or the pretense of being your Chosen," he announced, and I tried not to grimace at the shame that swelled at his declaration. "But these four will only flatter your naïvety. Rumsbrooke is my territory, and I will tell you the truth of your foundling efforts at ruling your people, princess. If you ever deign to visit the city, that is."

"I'll make a point of it," I snapped back at the older man. There was no reason to take offense at his not wanting to be one of my Chosen, except that seemed to be his exact aim in telling me so.

Cosmo sat up and pulled Aric onto the balcony, voice hissing and too quiet for me to hear, and I glared at their backs.

"When do we leave, Your Highness?" Wendell asked.

I sighed and raised my hands to cover the heat in my cheeks and settle my thoughts. "The sooner the better. I'd hate to have Camellia come crowing victory to me, and she may decide to try and claim some of you if we're not quick enough." I peeked through my fingers at Owen. "Unless you might prefer to be claimed?"

Owen frowned at the others before realizing the question was directed at himself. He shook his head quickly. "Not by anyone other than you."

My stomach flipped, and I returned to hiding behind my hands. Something was definitely shifting. Not an urge to pin Owen down and ride him like my sister would've done but...*something*. It was every bit as sweet and shy as the massive man in front of me, but it was welcome to continue.

⚜

IF I HAD NEEDED any proof of Aric's claim that my kingdom was suffering, I saw it all on the carriage ride north the next day. It was as if I was watching a flower decay with every mile we traveled. Kimmery's capital was exquisite, glittering, and smooth. The villages that surrounded it were sweet, like scenes from quaint paintings, and the people who strolled the streets in the south seemed happy enough, if comparatively shabby to what I'd grown up surrounded by.

By evening of the first day, everything had changed.

I winced as the wheel of the carriage hit a deep pock in the road, jostling me between Thao and Cosmo. Wendell sat across from Thao, and Owen took up the rest of the bench, his head leaning against the top of the carriage by the window, mouth hanging open and letting out soft little sighs of sleep. Outside of

Thao's window, farmland stretched, men in the fields with their backs bowed low, shirts hanging loose on their bodies. With farmland so rich, the men who worked the fields should've looked hale and healthy, but instead, the faces that turned to watch our traveling were gaunt and hollow-eyed.

"Does all the food go to the capital?" I asked softly, turning to Cosmo.

His own gaze was watchful out the window, eyes equal parts sympathetic and observant, like he couldn't decide between empathy for the men, or the desire to paint them. Perhaps both.

"Most of the farmland is owned by merchants rather than townspeople," Cosmo said. "The food goes south and is shipped away. The farmers are paid a small stipend of the food and a little money."

"It was a law passed at least one hundred years ago that farm-land must be owned by no less than two hundred acres for mass and uniform crops. Most farmers couldn't afford to and were reluctant to try and buy each other out. They ended up selling to merchants."

I twisted my own fingers in my lap and tried to force my jaw to unclench. "It should be abolished."

Cosmo hummed, and Owen snuffled in his sleep, softening some of the tension.

A set of horse hooves clapped closer to our carriage, until Aric appeared on a grand red stallion, bending forward to peer inside at us. "There's an inn a few miles ahead where we could eat a rough meal and get back on the road after watering and changing the horses, or we might travel a little east and stay with some local lord."

I frowned and heard the test in Aric's voice. "I think a local inn would suit fine."

"The ride won't get more comfortable through the night, princess," Aric said.

"Well if you think it will be too much for you, you may come and sit inside and I will take the horse," I tossed back.

Cosmo chuckled, and Wendell gave me a glowing smile from his corner of the carriage as Aric sat up straight and clucked to his horse, driving it forward. Only Thao was quiet, if we ignored Owen's snoring.

"I'm sorry, I should've asked the rest of you where you might've liked to stay," I said, realizing that Prince Thao would probably have preferred a night in a proper bed at an overly hospitable lord's home. It was only that I wasn't feeling especially fond of the aristocracy at the moment, and I'd known that Aric had expected me to prefer pampering to seeing what common men and women of my kingdom were living with daily.

And I just desperately wanted Aric to be wrong about me, so much so that I was confusing myself about what I really preferred.

"I don't like him. I don't *trust* him," Thao said, glaring out the window. "Whatever your own faults, you *are* a princess and—"

Wendell's foot shifted and struck Thao's, cutting off the prince. "Oh, apologies," Wendell said, while glaring at his lover.

"Aric has a good heart, if a prejudiced one," Cosmo murmured to me. "I don't condone his rudeness, of course. I only..."

"I will have to earn his trust before he gives me any reason to build my own for him," I said, raising an eyebrow.

Cosmo flashed a smile at me, his eyes flicking down to my mouth, and then the low collar of my gown before his head quickly lifted. "Just so, Your Highness. If it's any consolation, I've told him he's an idiot."

"We all have," Owen grunted, frowning and twisting awake, his head knocking against the roof of the carriage as he tried to sit up. "I may take a horse for some of the night myself. I feel wadded up in this little box."

My lips twitched as I watched Owen try to work out the kinks of sleeping without elbowing Wendell in the gut or kneeing Cosmo in the groin. I was tempted to offer to switch places with Wendell, but that little blooming feeling I'd discovered for Owen just a day ago had yet to abate and I wasn't sure what would happen if I were pressed up against him.

The carriage slowed as we reached the edge of a village, the sunset turning the mildewy browns and greens of the dilapidated buildings into a silky and jewel toned range of darkness. The inn we were waiting outside of was a low building with a peaked roof that sank in on one side. The windows of the inn were parted, letting the sounds and smells drift out to the street. Our carriage door opened, Owen jumping out, all too eager to stretch his long legs...and his broad back, and his muscular arms, and rolling his head on his dense shoulders. I swallowed and shook myself out of my staring, only to choke lightly on a whiff of the inn's stench. Sausage and stale ale and... My nose wrinkled. Was that the smell of piss?

The men emptied the carriage, and it was Aric who stepped up to the door, holding out a hand to help me out. No, not to help me, to stop me.

"I've charmed the carriage to avoid attracting attention, but I think we'd better do the same to you, if you don't object, princess," Aric said, quiet and low. He had a cloth bag in his hand and a few beads of sweat on his brow that hadn't been there when he'd spoken to us before.

My eyes widened, and I nodded before I'd even thought it through. Aric's hands raised to cup my face, the bag dangling from his wrist, and it was the first time he'd touched me since the night of my choosing. I held my breath at the prick of his magic dancing over my skin. For a brief moment, it was suffocating, like someone had pressed a pillow over my face, and then it gentled and sank in—a tight feeling, and a little itchy, but manageable. His fingers trailed down my throat to the collar of my dress, and my lips parted as his touch skimmed over my breast bone.

In books, a hero was always described with 'heat in his gaze,' but I couldn't tell if that was what was in Aric's eyes. It was certainly...focused, and it brought goosebumps out all over me and made my breasts feel both heavy and tight. And then my gown whispered and shifted from golden silk to a slightly rough texture and an earthy green.

"That should do," Aric said, words scratching against my ear, his breath short and rapid.

And then he was gone, leaving me gaping in my seat, and with no escort down from the carriage until Wendell appeared a moment later, gallant and golden. His eyebrows bounced as he took me in.

"He's made a joke of me, hasn't he?" I asked.

Wendell shook his head and then frowned. "You're just...well, you won't attract too much attention at least. I just didn't realize he had so much talent. Allow me," he said, and I took his hand as he helped me down.

Aric had tweaked Thao's own ornate outfit as well, although not as much as my own, and the prince had tied back his silky black hair. Cosmo and Owen were missing altogether.

"We'll sit in two different groups," Aric said, and he still sounded a little breathless. I wondered if his magic cost him to use. He was registered as a minor magician, but when I checked myself in the reflection of the carriage window, I jumped at the sight of a completely different woman. This wasn't *minor* magic at all.

I'd never given a great deal of consideration to my own looks, but one thing was painfully clear—Aric had made me *plain*. My hair was missing all its shine, my ears were larger, my eyes smaller. He was pale when I spun around again, but smirking.

"How did you do that?" I asked, eyes wide.

"I'm a mage," he said, brow arching. Then he jiggled the bag. It sounded like stones or shells shaking together. "There's power in the charm. I got it before we left the south."

"You're very talented," I said primly, just to watch the smirk falter.

"Stay within reach of one of us, prin—" Aric shook his head and turned his back to me. "I did what I could, but you're still a maid and some men will grab whatever bit of flesh they can."

Wendell tucked me securely between himself and Thao, and together we followed Aric into the inn.

The scent of ale and sausage was stronger inside, and the piss smell blessedly faint—although not altogether lost. The mood of the bar was not exactly energetic, but there was an air of determination about the men drinking and talking loudly throughout the dim space. Lanterns flickered from wooden beams, casting shadows and offering a faint view of the slop on the plates and the weak foam in glasses. I drank in every detail I could, relieved to note that Aric's glamour was doing the trick. Men eyed me, but it was surveying and cursory, and their gazes immediately moved to Thao.

Even with his shine dulled and his hair pulled back, Thao moved and stood and kept his gaze over the heads of the room like a prince. I didn't know if it was because he was uncomfortable or simply naturally haughty, but when I squeezed my fingers around his, he answered back in kind.

Owen and Cosmo were by the front windows with a group of men, and it took me a moment to realize they were our royal guard, their uniforms softened to common clothing by Aric's magic. He led the four of us to a corner table on the opposite end of the room and pulled me out from Thao's grasp, guiding me down into a chair at his side without a glance in my direction.

"So I can keep an eye on the glamour," he said under his breath, brow furrowing and eyes watching the room.

"It isn't *small* magic that you work," I murmured back, eyeing the the carved top of the table Aric had placed us at. There were stains and half-finished notes dug out of the wood grain, and a moment later there was a sloshing mug of ale landing in front of me, courtesy of a harried barmaid.

Aric grunted in answer to my questioning tone and I faced him, waiting for him to glance at me. Wendell sat across from us, and Aric had pushed Thao to my other side, keeping his back to the room that was too curious about the prince's foreign looks.

"I know you didn't want to be Chosen," I whispered. Aric blinked at me, and his shoulder jerked in a brief shrug. "If you'd said what kind of magic you could really work, they probably wouldn't even have let you through the front door."

I didn't understand it, but Grandmother said the magical kinds were no good to the Hunger. It was part of why I was glad to take Thao with his tiger shifting, just to spite my grandmother a little. But being honest might've meant Aric didn't even have to go through with my farcical choosing ceremony.

"I'm unregistered," Aric said, his voice dark and gravelly. "I report a little so I can get away with it when I need to, but no more."

I frowned up at him. "What do you mean registered?"

He frowned back and then looked across the table to Wendell. "Your—um, Bryony," Wendell started carefully, dropping my title. Which was nice, actually. I wanted to ask them all to leave it and simply call me by my name instead. "Every Kimmerian citizen skilled in magical arts must be registered."

"I don't—"

"The good magicians go to the army's frontlines in a battle. The great ones go to court," Aric said, cutting off my question. "Shifters have it worse."

When he didn't elaborate with my stare, I turned back to Wendell.

"Those who can shift into animals are generally assigned a position in the army or some kind of labor. Mining or sea faring..." Wendell said, nodding, careful not to look in Thao's direction.

"Assigned?" I asked.

"It means they're not given a choice," Aric bit out. "Their bodies fare better than single-natured humans. They can take more abuse."

I reached for the sticky mug of ale as worry over this round of ugly news hit me, and resisted the urge to spit the liquid right back out of my mouth as the tart and bitter flavor hit my tongue. Aric seemed to shake, but if he was laughing he did me the rare courtesy of not being obvious about it.

"I wonder who is really running this kingdom when the future ruler knows so little about what's going on," Aric muttered, wincing through his own gulp of ale.

He might not have meant that comment as a slight against me. Not like he usually did. But it stung in my chest long after our plates arrived—a strange mess of food that seemed just nearly uniform in texture and color. He was right though. I could imagine my grandmother holding to some of these laws I was learning, but was my mother aware? If the Hunger of the queen's line was not a source of power for Kimmery, then it was clearly a source of distraction for its rulers and I was becoming glad not to possess it.

6.
BRYONY

I woke with a groan, stretching in my seat of the carriage at dawn, my feet tangling with the others on the floor. I felt gritty and sweaty from being cooped up in the carriage for so long, and as I sat up I realized at least one of the men had escaped.

Wendell was still pressed to one corner, Owen at his side, but it was only Cosmo on the other bench with me, rustling and turning away as I shifted in my seat.

"Look," whispered Wendell, and he pointed out the window to my right.

There, on the rocky terrain just next to us, an orange striped tiger moved fluidly along our path.

"Thao," I said, my eyes widening, and Wendell hummed the affirmative.

He was enormous, easily twice the size of his human form or even giant Owen, and I watched with rapt fascination as he moved over boulders and down to the road and then back up, body fluid and muscular. His head turned and he glanced at us, amber eyes blinking at me, before going back to staring ahead. He yawned, and I gasped as I realized that in his tiger form, Thao could easily bite my head off in one snap.

"He doesn't spook the horses?" I whispered, turning and finding Wendell's stare on his lover, something pained and wistful in his blue eyes.

"No, single natured animals seem to be able to tell the differ-ence." Wendell's blue eyes tracked every movement of Thao as a tiger, but I didn't think it was simply admiration in his gaze.

"Do you worry for him? He looks...indestructible to me."

"Worry?" Wendell asked, straightening. He blinked and then

shook his head, a gentle smile growing. "No, Your Highness. I think I'm only a little jealous."

Ah! Well, that made sense. It would be nice to be able to shift into an enormous, free beast, rather than kept cooped up and held to expectations I couldn't meet.

It would be nice until they forced you into an army or some kind of strenuous labor, I reminded myself, thinking of what I'd learned the night before.

Just the thought made my heart pinch uncomfortably in my chest, the confines of the carriage suddenly unbearable.

"Are there extra horses behind us?" I asked.

Wendell frowned and shrugged. "I believe so."

I nodded and reached for the door handle. "I'm going to ride for a few hours."

"Oh, I'll tell them to stop the—"

"Don't bother," I answered Wendell, opening the door and jumping down with a great gasp of relief, my feet jogging lightly to keep myself from tripping.

Thao leapt down from the rocks, and I found myself fighting the impulse to scoot away from the massive, lanky form of him padding closer, his paws twice the size of my own feet. But he brushed up against my side and followed me as I moved back to the horses that kept pace with the carriage from behind. Thao paused, sitting on his haunches like a house cat as the horse handler passed me the reins of a powdery white and grey gelding.

"We don't have a saddle for you," he said, but I was already pulling myself up onto the horse's back.

Here was the amount of my education. Taking my Chosen once I was of age—which I'd failed at—horseback riding, and fencing. Or so it felt when at every turn I learned something new and horrid about my own kingdom. If I'd had any doubts about the wealth and health of my own people, yesterday had squashed those. I believed the men and what they'd told me, or at least, more than I believed my own family.

"It's not necessary," I called to the handler over my shoulder.

I arranged my plentiful skirts around my legs and squeezed gently, coaxing the gelding into a trot. Thao joined us, loping along before rising back up into the mountainside. Wendell's smile was tilted up as I passed the carriage and driver, taking in deep lungfuls of fresh air. I'd seen paintings of the northern terrain of Kimmery around the castle, including depictions of the Winter Palace, but my mother had never wanted to leave the south. I wondered now if that neglect on visiting the north was intentional.

The rocky hills rising up around us were lush with greenery, still ripe with Kimmery's long summers. I'd known rich, mani-cured gardens my entire life, and a little of forests when Mother wanted a royal hunt or picnic, but I'd never been anywhere so wild or with such a sense of the unknown. In the south, I could see for miles out my window, into the sea on one side over the castle, or over the villages and into the woods from the other. Here the hills hid what was over the next bend, like tempting secrets to tease me.

"I never realized what a long journey it was," I said, urging my horse up to ride alongside Aric.

He startled in his seat, and I smothered my laugh as I real-ized I'd caught him sleeping in his saddle.

"How long did you think three hundred miles would take?" Aric grunted.

My teeth clenched, and I fixed my eyes to the curling road ahead of us, two royal guards at the lead.

"I think we both know by now that my education has lacked a great deal of value," I said.

Aric groaned and stretched in the saddle, back cracking as he twisted. My own bottom was already sore from the carriage ride, and I couldn't imagine how his felt from riding for over a day. If I wasn't perfectly aware of how it would slow us down, I might've asked to walk on my own for a few miles, but I didn't want to be more of an inconvenience to the small collection of guards and staff or my Chosen than I already was.

"You have the ambition to learn, at least," Aric said, grudg-ingly and quiet. "And you appear to see things for what they are."

"Be careful, you're getting complimentary," I said, delighted to see his lips twitch.

"Princess, I promise to never compliment you where you

don't deserve it," Aric said with a mocking kind of regality. "And to always tell you when I think you're doing a piss poor job."

We rode alongside one another, and it was the most companionable time I'd spent with Aric since he'd held me while I'd broken down on the night of my choosing.

He'd smelled like pipe smoke and plums that night, and no one had ever held me in such a way before. Not since I was a little girl at least. There was a complicated push and pull between us. I desperately wanted to prove myself to him, which I found equally and deeply irritating. And at the same time, I craved that brief softness he'd shown me. How could I show him my own strength when I wanted just as badly to have him scoop me up against his chest again?

"If you lack the Hunger, you may be the best ruler this country could see," Aric said. "You'd actually be focused on your people instead of your—" And then he stopped himself abruptly and cleared his throat.

I glanced at him, eyeing the flush spreading over his cheeks that he steadfastly ignored. A sharp pang struck me low in the belly, and I nearly swayed on my horse before whipping my stare away.

I *did* lack the Hunger...didn't I?

◈

WE REACHED the edges of the northern city Rumsbrooke at nightfall. I'd napped in the carriage while the others rode the horses during the afternoon, and then returned to my gray gelding as the sun set.

If I'd hoped to see Rumsbrooke as an improvement on the crumbling towns between here and the sea, I was disappointed. The city was large and contained in an old stone wall that was giving away beneath dense vines. Even from outside, the scent of decay was on the air.

"I leave you here. You're only an hour's ride from the Winter Palace," Aric said, turning his horse away from our caravan. "If you make it into Rumsbrooke, you might find me at the Wing and Rook."

"I'll make a point of it," I said, my hands tight around the reins as Aric's head tipped to me and he nudged his horse to the city gates. "Aric!"

Thao was back in his tiger form, tongue licking his chops, and he padded up to my side as Aric paused and looked over his shoulder. I suspected Thao'd hunted his own dinner for the night, rather than dining on the scraps the rest of us had shared.

"You've promised to give me your honest opinion. I hope you'll come to the Winter Palace to see me. I'd hate to get spoiled without your tempering influence."

Thao huffed and twisted sinuously away, no doubt annoyed with my declaration. My heart pounded in my chest as I stared across the road at Aric. His face was in profile, one steel gray eye visible and holding my gaze. I wasn't sure who was in battle, only that I felt the struggle in my veins as he nodded once more and trotted to the gate.

"You should stay in the carriage for the rest of the ride, princess," Aric called. "The woods between here and the palace can be dangerous."

I wanted to leap down from my seat and drag him back, make him promise to see me at the palace, and I didn't even entirely understand why. Everything was jumbling together in my head, leaving a slow, pounding ache behind. Aric was not the noble gentleman, but he wasn't the coarse blade either. And it hardly seemed to matter because he was riding away from me.

Perhaps you are simply spoiled and don't like something being taken away from you, I thought. It seemed like something he might say.

Fabric rustled behind me, and I glanced over my shoulder to find Thao standing by the waiting carriage.

"Come, Bryony. For once, the rogue is right."

My lips twitched, and I had an odd understanding that *this* was the kind of tension between men that might be amusing. Or at least I found it so. I slid off the back of my horse and Thao took the reins, passing it back to the handler before following me into the carriage.

I moved to sit with Owen, fairly certain that his and Thao's shoulders would exceed the width of the carriage. Owen hummed as I settled in at his side, and Thao rapped on the roof, shutting the door as it jerked forward.

"I hope whatever staff was hired for the palace has prepared the rooms and baths before we arrive," Thao grumbled.

"I don't care what we arrive to. I'd sleep in the stable with the horses," Owen offered, his arm sliding over my shoulders and carelessly pulling me into his warm side. It was more comfortable than I expected, and I sank against him.

"How different would that be to your usual accommodations?" Thao asked, eyes narrowing, but he didn't seem to be vicious with the question, although Wendell shot him a warning look.

"Not very," Owen answered with an easy laugh.

"You are Chosen now," I said, reaching up to touch the hand Owen rested over my shoulder and finding myself happily tangling my fingers with his. "You should be able to sleep wherever you please, stables or suites."

I shared an apple with Owen, watching the woods pass outside the carriage window for the hour. I saw at least three herds of deer as we traveled, and heard a whole cacophony of other animals calling to one another.

"I didn't expect to see the woods so well stocked," I said, watching three rabbits race out from under brush near the edge of the woods. "Does no one hunt here?"

"No one is allowed to hunt in the queen's woods," Wendell said.

"Why? It's not as though court has come up north in ages!"

"It's an old law, but one that's never been lifted," Cosmo said with a shrug.

Wendell's lips twisted into a frown and with a nudge from Thao, he added, "Some of the local lords prefer it that way. Easier hunting when they come up for a party."

I hummed and turned back to the window, eyeing a brave doe through the trees. It was beautiful to see the woods so full of life, but I wondered if it might be manageable to give some of this abundance back to the people.

"I need a diary to make a list of all the things I want to fix," I murmured. "I'm afraid I'll forget something, and there's so much to do."

"Wendell's very organized, he could be your secretary," Thao said, smirking slightly.

Wendell tried to smooth away the irritation on his face, but I only smiled at him. "Wendell already has a position in my court."

The blond brightened at that and rolled his eyes at his lover before turning back to me. "I would be happy to assist you in any way."

"I think we have our first view," Cosmo murmured, ducking in his seat and pointing out the window.

I stiffened and leaned, blocking the view from the others as I searched through the lines of trees for the Winter Palace.

The castle by the sea that I'd grown up in was ivory and gold, the roof almost pink with clay tiles, and rose trellis vines climbing the stone partway up. It smelled of the gardens, of the bakeries in the city, and occasionally the sea.

The building growing before me was none of those things. By moonlight, it was cold and imposing and... I squinted at the dark splotches of the stone. It appeared dilapidated. The paintings I'd seen before had been...austere, not so bright with color as things were in the south, but certainly clean and polished.

As we rode closer, we reached a massive iron gate, torches in posts and guards waiting in bronze armor and blue uniforms. The gate was draped in dark ivy, and a few of the twisting lines of iron were bent in one direction or another.

"It has been a...a long time since anyone has lived here," I murmured.

Owen's arms slid from my waist and found my hands, large rough fingers taking mine, and I squeezed them gratefully. "We'll make do, Your Highness."

I held onto Owen as my anchor as we circled up the long road that led to the palace until there was no denying the reality of it. The Winter Palace was overgrown, stone cracking in spots. There were weeds growing up the front steps, and the only sign of light and life were the flickering candles in cracked windows.

Thao cursed in Mennarian, and I refrained from mentioning that I was fluent, because the palace *was* a shit hole.

On the top of the tall staircase leading up to a door that hung crookedly on its hinges stood two figures. One was another guard, tall and broad with skin that matched the armor he wore, and his eyes focused straight ahead. The other was a shorter man, and much rounder, dressed in formal garb and draped in furs. It was cooler here in the north, but as I stepped out of the carriage, I didn't feel the need for fur. Cool, but in a way, more pleasant than the muggy humidity of the south.

"Your Royal Highness," the shorter man moaned and bent in a low bow. "At last you've arrived. We were so concerned. Although we might've used several more days to prepare for your party. As you can see, the Winter Palace is not in its...finest shape."

"I can see, yes," I said, eyeing the steps up carefully, Owen's hand in mine helping guide me in the dark over the broken stone.

The stout man frowned as if he'd expected me to contradict him. "We were given very little notice of your coming."

"Does the palace have no steward?" I asked.

The guard's wide mouth twitched with the briefest smile as the other man puffed. "I *am* the steward, Your Highness. Sir Hubert of Rumsbrooke," he added with another quick bow.

"Then I *am* surprised by the condition, regardless of how soon our arrival was," I said.

My Chosen were at my back, and I felt their presence as a strength against this pompous man. It had never been my place to deal with stewards or guards before now, but my grandmother was—thankfully—absent, and I felt a small thrill at staring down my nose at this man as he gave a panicked look to the palace behind him.

"My instructions until now were to *leave* it," he muttered.

My triumph faltered. "I see. Well, you will have new instructions in the morning. Tonight, however, I hope there was enough time to prepare rooms for myself and my—"

"R-rooms?" Sir Hubert stuttered, his eyes trailing over my Chosen. Because he expected me to take them in mine. *Of course,* I hissed to myself mentally.

The Chosen had their own place in the castle, a collection of suites connected to their mistress's, and I assumed as much would be available here.

"If I gave up my own quarters next to yours, we might have two," Sir Hubert said, grimacing.

"Good. Two rooms will do," I said, resisting the urge to balk at the notion that he might have taken a room next to mine. Winter Palace or Kimmerian Castle, a steward had no place that close to his princess. I turned my chin to the guard at Sir Hubert's side, ignoring the older man's ruffled feathers. "And you are?"

"Cresswell Stark, Your Highness," he said, all velvet and low in tone as he bowed. "Captain of the Guard here in the North."

"And how long have you had your position?"

"Since to-today, Your Highness," he said, paling slightly.

I only nodded. "I'd like to speak with you soon, but not tonight. Perhaps you would join us for breakfast tomorrow. There will be breakfast tomorrow, yes, Sir Hubert?"

"Ye-yes, Your Highness," Sir Hubert choked out as Cresswell bowed to me.

"Good, then you may show us our rooms."

As the two men turned their back to me, I sighed and sagged slightly, looking over my shoulder at Thao. He grinned back at me and dipped his head lightly in approval. I didn't want a man like Sir Hubert deciding he could take a hand to me—to guide me politically or otherwise. It required me playing the part of high-handed princess more than I'd ever bothered doing in my life until now, but there was satisfaction in getting my way in something. And I didn't like to see a man like Sir Hubert dressed in furs and dripping in gold chains when I knew his people—*my* people—were starving, overtaxed, and dressed in rags.

Inside, at least, the palace showed a little less of its wear, especially as we traveled deeper in. Some of the chandeliers were lopsided, many of the candelabras were cold, and a few discolored gaps on the walls showed where a painting had gone missing. Overall though, the halls were clean if a little drafty. That could likely be repaired by winter.

Hubert led us to a hall at the back of the palace, pausing

outside of a set of tall doors. "There is a meal waiting inside for you all, as well as a bath, and if you'll give me an hour—"

"Less than that," I said.

"Yes, Your Highness," he puffed. "A little time, I will arrange the second suite for..."

He trailed off, waiting for me to reveal who would be where.

"Thank you, that will be all," I said instead, ignoring his grimace.

7.
BRYONY

I resisted the urge to release a heavy sigh. I'd already indulged myself in many. Instead, I scooped a last cup full of fresh water over my shoulders, rinsing away the oils and suds from my bath, and rose up from the tub. There was a screen blocking the view from the bedroom, and I grabbed the towel draped over the top of it, patting myself dry before pulling on my night slip. And then remembering that I'd be sharing my bed tonight, I grabbed my silk robe as well.

Thao and Wendell had left for the second suite after eating with the rest of us, and I'd turned down the offer of help from the young maid who'd been barely brave enough to stick her head in the doorway. I could manage a bath for myself, and after two full days packed into the carriage with men, I was grateful to be alone in the tub for longer than the bath really required.

Now I slipped out from behind the screened washroom to find Owen and Cosmo reclining over the slightly moth-eaten covers of the *enormous* bed in my suite.

"Want me to start the water for you?" I asked Cosmo as he shuffled off the bed.

He smiled at me and shook his head, fingers already traveling to the buttons of his shirt as he walked past me. "I'm more than happy to manage my own bath. Are you sure you wouldn't prefer Owen or I to take a couch in the next room?"

"No, it seems silly with the size of that bed," I said, eyeing the almost miraculously large piece of furniture. It could've fit the three of us, and Thao and Wendell, and Aric too, and maybe even a few of the Chosen I'd dismissed days ago. "Anyway, the servants will be sneaking in and out of there with our luggage and I..."

Cosmo nodded and stepped behind the screen. "We're keeping up pretenses. I understand."

Owen peeked out from behind the pages of a book as I neared the bed, and I was so charmed by the sight of him, massive fingers holding its ornate binding, that it took me a moment to realize it was a favorite of mine.

"*The Lovers of Invernette*!" I scrambled for the bed, tangling my legs in my robe and skirt as I wormed my way to the head-board in the middle, peeking over Owen's shoulder to see where he was.

"It's making me blush," he said. "If this was the kind of reading I'd done in school, I would've been a more enthusiastic student."

"It's utter trash," I said, grinning. "I adore it. Will you read to me?"

If Owen hadn't been blushing before, he certainly was now, cheeks rosy and hair rumpled, his shirt half undone to reveal those appealing dark curls on his chest. "I'm not a very good reader."

"You have a nice voice. And I'm so tired, I think my eyes would cross if I tried to read so much as a sentence. Just until I fall asleep? It won't take long, I promise," I said, and I leaned into Owen's side, cuddling to his shoulder and resting my chin there to gaze up at him with a coaxing smile.

His throat cleared as his eyes scanned my face, that lovely color growing even deeper by the candlelight. "All right, Your Highness."

I pinched his side and caught his eye before it turned to the page. "Bryony. Please."

"Bryony," he said with a nod, and I almost shivered with the sound of my name on his tongue.

Very few people had the right to call me by my name, and mostly I'd heard it from my Grandmother. It sounded much sweeter on Owen's tongue, all low and a little gravelly and clumsy with his shyness.

"*His hand on her waist was feather light, no more than a graze. But Amelia felt the touch as if it were a brand against her skin*," Owen read, his words slow but very careful. He didn't read with a great deal of *feeling*, but he took care with the words and there was a kind of melody to his rhythm that was soothing as he continued.

It was one of my favorite scenes in the book, full of the kind of romantic tension that made my chest ache and my sex throb. Even with Owen's almost clumsy delivery, the words raised heat under my skin. I untied my robe, distracting Owen from the page momentarily as I slid out of the silk and then under the sheets on the bed, nestling into the pillows at my back and smiling at him. He was *very* pretty, coarse stubble on his jaw and full lips, a brow that furrowed as he troubled over a word. His Adam's apple bobbed in his throat, and my hand raised of its own accord as if I'd been about to reach out and touch the spot. I curled onto my side and rested my hand on his chest, closing my eyes to enjoy the vibration of his voice in his chest, pretending I didn't feel the echo of it between my thighs.

This was just...this was *normal* desire, wasn't it? A young woman's crush, and not the Hunger? I wished briefly that it'd made itself known the night of my choosing, instead of waiting until I was hundreds of miles away from home.

"Her lips tingled with the imagined kiss, and the back of her hand burned where his lips had rested."

My own lips were tingling, and I tried to imagine kissing Owen. It came easily. I knew how he kissed, except instead of the anxiety I'd felt at that moment, I now had an aching throb in my core. If I'd been alone, I would've reached down between my legs to dull the ache. But I'd brought these men with me under the assumption that they *wouldn't* be playing a real role as my Chosen. And anyway, I wasn't even sure things had changed so much. Maybe this was only a reaction to Owen reading to me, some mix of my feelings for the hero in the book and the availability of the man at my side.

The pulsing heat grew steady and lulling, my hands fisting in the fabric of Owen's shirt and breaths puffing a little more intensely than normal, as his sweet and droning voice coaxed me into a hazy kind of drowse. At some point, when I was too deep at the edge of sleep, Cosmo returned and the men traded places, Owen untangling my fingers from his shirt and passing the book to Cosmo.

The artist was a better reader, and after his bath he smelled salty and clean. I blinked once, my eyelids as heavy and dry as bricks, but it was enough to see his bare chest in the bed next to me. I rolled in his direction, and he tucked me against his side, continuing to read until I was fast asleep.

⊱❦⊰

I woke up on rougher sheets than home, feeling hotter and more stifled than usual. But it only took a moment. One soft puff of breath against the back of my neck and a nudge of a stiff length against the bottom of my ass, and I remembered where I was and who I was with.

Cosmo was absent from the bed, and it was undeniably Owen's massive arm that was wrapped around my waist, holding me against his chest as he ground himself against my bottom. He groaned into my hair and began to work himself a little faster, breaths panting on the back of my neck. All at once, his arm tightened, his pants halted with a gasp, and his grinding froze.

"Fuck," he muttered, hips slowly pulling away from mine.

I tried to contain the giggle building in my chest as Owen wiggled away from me, carefully loosening his arm from around my waist, but with a ticklish brush of his fingers against my side, the sound broke free and I rolled to face him.

"I'm sorry," we both said in a rush.

"I don't mean to laugh at you," I said quickly.

Owen was rumpled and his face was flushed, throat bobbing and chest still heaving. I tried very very hard not to look down— or at least I told myself I tried—and then bit my lip at the bulge of his arousal tenting the sheet.

"I didn't mean to..." He cleared his throat and leaned toward the bed, trying to hide the outline of his cock. "I'm sorry. I—"

"You were asleep, Owen. It's all right," I said.

He was shirtless now too, like Cosmo had been when he'd come to bed. For never sharing my bed with anyone before, I'd found it no trouble at all to sleep through the night. The curtains to the room were still pulled shut, but I could see bright sunlight trying to make its way through little tears in the old velvet.

Owen was rumpled and warm, and he was studying me with the same interest I had while gazing back at him.

"I should—" He made to move out of the bed, and an impulse struck me.

My hand reached his chest before he could escape, his heartbeat just barely detectable against my palm through the thick planes of muscle. I stretched up from the pillows, Owen held in place by just the pressure of my palm pausing him. I craned my neck, watching his eyes as my mouth lifted to brush against his. Owen had nibbled at my lips when he'd kissed me on my orders, and I did the same to him now, sucking softly on his bottom lip.

There was a taste to him, not sweet but not unpleasant either, just the unfamiliar flavor of another person, and I hummed as he pressed back, both our eyes falling shut. My fingers curled into Owen's chest hair as he leaned into me, and then further, pushing me back into the pillows. The kiss was slow and exploratory and cautious, Owen taking frequent pauses to wait and see if I would come back for more. When our tongues flicked together and a lick of heat flashed against my sex, I gasped and he pulled away, waiting and watching me.

I swallowed hard, staring up at the shadow of Owen and wondering what I wanted next. More kisses? Yes. More *than* kisses?

Not...not quite yet.

"I was just curious," I said, my cheeks echoing Owen's growing smile.

He grinned, and I held my breath as he pressed down, but it was only to drop a kiss against my forehead, my nose, my chin, and then once more, briefly, on my lips.

"Feel free to be curious any time, Your—Bryony," he said. And then he cleared his throat and leaned back, glancing towards his lap. "I think I'd better...umm..."

He moved to rise from the bed at the same time that knuckles rapped on the door. Owen shuffled to sit in front of me, blocking me from view, but it was only Cosmo coming in. Dark eyes looked over Owen and I briefly, Cosmo's roguish smile flickering.

"'Morning, you two. I think there's something you'd better come see in Thao and Wendell's room," Cosmo said.

I followed Owen out of the bed but shooed him to the washroom. "Go on and meet us there," I said, trying not to blush with the knowledge of what he might need to do before joining us. I scooped my robe up from the end of the bed and my cheeks went pinker as Owen ducked, smacking a firm kiss against my cheek before jogging away, his hand held in front of his crotch as if to preserve his modesty.

"I wouldn't have interrupted if I'd known," Cosmo murmured when I reached him.

I shook my head. "You didn't really. It was just..." I didn't know how to explain it. Just a day ago, I'd told these men that their position as my Chosen was for show. And it might still be, I wasn't entirely certain what was happening, only that this morning's kiss with Owen hadn't been full of stress or worry like the night of my choosing. This time, there was only interest and playfulness between us.

"Owen wanted to be Chosen, you know," Cosmo said, catching my hand and squeezing it as he led me into the suite's sitting room.

"Did you?" I asked, frowning. It hadn't occurred to me before now to wonder how the men felt about attending the choosing. I'd been too stressed with my own part to play. Aric had made it abundantly clear he was opposed to my claiming him, and Thao and Wendell were... Well, they'd found their place comfortably, although it had nothing to do with desiring *me*. Cosmo I was less sure about.

He hummed and pulled the hand he held into the crook of his arm, drawing me closer with a soft twitch of his lips. "Not until you sat down on the couch with us in your panic and rushed to ask us about ourselves. And then I was very happy to be picked in the ceremony," Cosmo said, and before I could answer him, he stopped by the buffet table near the door and pulled a napkin off a plate, revealing a collection of my favorites —melon, salty thinly sliced ham, and a chocolate tart. "I saved these for you. There's plenty of food left for Owen too, but you and Wendell have similar tastes, and I wanted to make sure you didn't miss out."

I squeezed his arm before taking the plate, eating a piece of melon and ham together in one bite and humming at the syrupy sweetness of the fruit contrasting against the salt of the meat. "Thank you. What am I going to see?"

Cosmo sobered, and his hand moved to my back to guide me out to the hall. "Right. Well, breakfast was the good news. Thao and Wendell found the bad, I'm afraid."

Ominous as that sounded, it wasn't enough to stop me from savoring the bites of food. The chocolate tart was especially good, the pastry even butterier than the ones at home.

Our cook is good, even if the castle is drafty and the stairs are broken and the roads are weedy, I thought, and then immediately felt guilty because I was enjoying melon and ham and chocolate for breakfast and the people of Rumsbrooke were...well, certainly not experiencing the same.

"I was thinking we ought to do something about the woods," I said as Cosmo led me to the other suite of rooms. "It might be rash to open them to general hunting, but we could appoint someone from the city as...as royal hunter? Someone who would hunt responsibly."

"Are you...especially carnivorous?" Cosmo asked, frowning. "Even with the staff we have here—"

"Not for us! For the people. If food is scarce then...it may be a silly idea."

Cosmo's steps slowed, and his smile grew. He leaned into me and then wavered back again. "No, not silly at all. You want the food to go to the people?" I nodded, and his hand passed up and down my back again, spreading warmth. "It can be made practical and fair, I think."

"I'll call the magistrate...or maybe I'd better make the visit myself?" I mused.

Cosmo opened the door into the second suite, one that mirrored my own, and I paused to take it in. The colors were darker, more cherry wood and less marble and gold, but all in all, it was equally well kept. I narrowed my eyes at the curtains, which seemed whole and uneaten. It might've been a little better.

"Princess Bryony, there you are," Thao called from the right side door.

I could see a glimpse of the vast bed over his shoulder. It was tucked beneath a small balcony like nook—a chair set up, and a little table, and Wendell standing there with his hands against the railing, overlooking the room.

"Oh, I wish I had one of those! How sweet."

Wendell grimaced and looked behind him. "Less sweet than it appears, Your Highness. Come and see for yourself."

I followed Cosmo to the narrow and steep set of stairs that led up to the small landing. There was enough room there for three people at most, and Wendell moved to the corner to leave me room before pointing to a device in the wall I hadn't initially seen. It was the end of a spy scope, sticking out of the wall, the chair close and convenient. I bent to the eyepiece and closed my other eye to peer through. Adjusting the lens, I frowned as a mess of rumpled sheets appeared and then gasped as Owen dropped onto the bed, naked and shimmying into a pair of trousers, his cheeks flushed.

I yanked back, blinking away the memory of his bouncing length as he tucked it away, muscular knots of his stomach flexing as he moved. I glanced at Wendell, and for a moment, I was only embarrassed by what I'd seen. Finally, it clicked.

"Oh! That slimy little—" I cut myself off, and Thao finished the thought for me in his own tongue. "He wanted to spy on me!"

"Your bed specifically, unless there are more things like that around the castle," Wendell said with a nod.

I shuddered and clenched my fists at the thought of Sir Hubert watching me in *any* fashion. Nothing had really taken place in the bed until this morning, but I was still relieved that I'd insisted on taking this bedroom for my Chosen.

"Invading royal privacy is one of the highest offenses in my court," Thao said, shoulders squared as he stared up at me.

I wrinkled my nose. I wasn't so sure what kind of privacy was normal in my mother's court, but Thao wasn't about to give me lessons on my own preferences.

"If the state of the palace, of his *city*, weren't enough of an offense, this is," I said with a nod. "He has to go."

Thao *hmph'ed* in agreement, and Wendell hid a small chuckle behind his hand.

8.
CRESSWELL

I was nearly done pulling on my armor when a knock sounded on my door from the guard's bunk room.

"Come in," I called.

The door opened, and I strained to remember the name of the face I was staring back at.

"She's asking for you," the younger guard said. Stanley! That was his name. He'd been in the army before being let off duty for an injury, and then almost immediately being turned around and given a position as a royal guard. We were meant to be the best of the best, and instead, I was getting the impression we were the leftovers.

And then, finally, his words sunk in as he stared expectantly back at me.

"Oh! Yes, all right," I said nodding and fumbling my last buckle in my haste.

"She's in the garden study," Stanley offered as I made to pass him.

"Who's with her?" *If you aren't*, I left off at the end.

"Yorley's outside cracking jokes," Stanley said with a roll of his eyes before blinking quickly. "But I don't think she can hear him."

I stifled my growl in front of the others and headed for the door.

"He looks like he thinks he's on his way to be Chosen," one man said under his breath.

"The queen's line don't take mutts like him," another hissed back.

I paused, back stiff, wondering if they meant my skin color or my status as a shifter, either of which might make me unlikely to be picked as a Chosen, although only my second nature prevented me from going to the choosing ceremony.

Just go, she's waiting on you, my human brain sighed.

Tear into them, the animal snarled.

I kept moving, rushing as much as my armor allowed, up to the decrepit palace. This was no place for a princess, and I couldn't understand why she'd come at all.

Yorley was leaned against the doorframe when I arrived, pretty clearly listening in, but he shrugged at me as if it were part of his job description.

"Not fucking, far as I can tell," he whispered.

"That's not for you to know," I answered.

He rolled his eyes, and I knocked on the door. "Guard Stark, Your Highness."

"Come in, please."

I stepped in, already bending to a bow, aware of the shadows of the figures in front of me.

"At ease, Guard Stark." The voice was feminine, almost laughing too, and I tried to fight the urge to stare as I stood up.

Whatever I'd expected of the princess, the young woman in front of me was not it. I'd heard mixed rumors as men returned north from the choosing ceremony. That she'd cut the ceremony short, she hadn't sampled a single man, she dismissed three-quarters of her first selection without a second glance. After Camellia's choosing ceremonies, men always spoke of the younger princess like a lion—conquering men, dragging them to the floor to be devoured. I'd imagined Princess Bryony as some cross between Camellia and the dowager queen—tall, fearsome, and maybe cold.

Instead, the woman in front of me looked...edible. Kissable. A temptation to devour, rather than the predator who conquered men. Her hair was down and draped in curls over one shoulder, a golden version of brown that I thought would look especially nice mussed over a pillow.

"What do you know of Sir Hubert?" she asked me, and I blinked away the fantasy.

Her Chosen surrounded her in the sparsely furnished sitting room that overlooked the gnarled orchard on the western end of the palace. It was gray out, and the lace of the curtains blocked what little light did try and make its way into the room, but the princess seemed to shine in amber silk, her hands folded on her lap. For all the sweetness in her face and the wide look in her eyes, she did have steel in her spine. I'd seen it the night before when she'd cut the steward down to size, and I liked the sharpness in her tone in contrast to the softness of her appearance.

"Very little, Your Highness," I said, with a dip of my waist. "I met him only yesterday."

The princess pursed her lips, and her eyes narrowed slightly. If she were any other girl in the world, I would've teased her for her severity and tried to catch a kiss. That was a pout that deserved to be flirted with.

"But is he known generally here in the north?"

My eyebrows raised. "His...reputation is known. I'm sure the other lords and the like know him, but he's not one to mix with..." *With the rest of us*, I thought but didn't say. She didn't need to know where I came from, and she certainly didn't appear interested.

"He's not liked then," she said. I gaped at her, and she only nodded. "If his neglect of the castle is any indication of that of his people, I'm not surprised. I would like you to find him and bring him to speak to me here. When I'm done, I'll need you to escort him from the palace and ensure he doesn't find his way back here without an explicit invitation from myself. Is that..." She frowned at herself, and the big one—the one I'd known vaguely from the army stables—squeezed her hand as the Mennarian prince rested his hand on her opposite shoulder. "Will you be able to manage that?"

I bowed. "Easily, Your Highness." Hubert would probably spit in my eye for it, but as Head of the Royal Guard, my orders were the ones that came from the princess's lips. And it would be a genuine pleasure to toss Hubert out. He was known for not only his general neglect of duty and miserly hoarding of money, but also the misery he put young female staff through.

I left the room, trying to catch the murmur that rose up at my back, but the princess and her Chosen were careful to keep their conversation private. I could guess roughly where I'd find the older man and headed for the kitchens, my steps soft on the tile, even in my heavy boots. I didn't mind the royal guard uniform, although the armor was heavier and less necessary in my opinion than that of the army's. I would be a better guard to the princess without any armor at all, but I kept that personal fact to myself. The army general who'd given me my new assignment had made it very clear I was *not* chosen for my second nature. I was trained and capable, and that was all she needed if any threat *did* arise.

Passing the larder, I heard the telltale scuffle and whimper, and I dove into the room to find Hubert holding a young girl to the wall—the princess's new maid. He barely had a grip on her, and he startled as I entered, the girl slipping free with a gasp and a sob.

"Go and find Granny Umber in the kitchens," I said to her. Bertha Umber, the new head cook of the Winter Palace, was a motherly legend in Rumsbrooke. She'd nearly reared me herself, and she'd manage the girl's frightened trembles and bruised wrists with ease. I would manage Hubert.

"What are you doing in here?" Hubert blustered, quick to try and right his trousers. "You should be at the gate."

"The princess wants to see you. I have orders to take you to her," I said, stepping forward and blocking Hubert's sight of the girl running out the door.

Hubert stiffened and stood taller, a smug smile painting over his lips. "Does she? Well, of course. I am at Her Highness's disposal."

I resisted the urge to grin at his choice of language. Disposal, indeed. As if a princess like the one I'd left in the other room would want a man as slimy and foul-hearted as Hubert.

"Don't stand so proud, you idiot," Hubert spat at me as he tucked his shirt away and smoothed back his thinning strands. "You interfere with my business again, and I'll be sure to see the princess tosses you out of this promotion as quick as it was handed down to you."

Keep talking, you old pervert. I'll enjoy walking you out to the gates every bit more in a few minutes.

When Hubert was as presentable as a man who thought that

fur was fashionable in the dead of summer *could* be, I stood back and allowed him to pretend to lead the way.

"The garden study," I said when he veered toward the stairs that would take us up to the bedrooms.

He chuckled. "Ah, christening every room, are they?"

I would've rolled my eyes, but there were too many mirrors, even in the dark hall. When we made it back to the study, the princess's Chosen had provided her more space and I noted the way it gave her a more imposing position, guarded at her back with her chin high and the gentleness in her expression wiped away.

"Your Royal Highness," Hubert simpered, rushing forward and reaching for the Princess's hand.

"That's close enough," she bit out, and then blinked at me as I caught Hubert by the back of his coat before he could throw himself at her.

"Unhand me, you mixed-blooded wretch!" Hubert growled.

The slur was one I'd heard plenty of in Kimmery. No one knew quite where I'd come from, whether it was my mother or my father who was the supposed blot on my family line. Only that I'd appeared on the docks as a child, darker than a Kimmerian child, but with the right shade of green in my eyes. Someone's bastard, no doubt.

"Sir Hubert, compose yourself," Princess Bryony said, and Hubert stilled and stood, trying to draw himself up higher. "It goes without saying that I am unimpressed with your management of this estate. The condition of the palace, the grounds, is deplorable. And yet it was the discovery of the device in your bedroom, intended to spy on myself and my Chosen—"

"Your Highness, I would *never*! That was there of course, but I would certainly never presume..." Hubert spluttered, and even I couldn't keep my eyebrows from rising.

I'd thought it strange that a steward would try and insist on taking the suite next to the princess and her Chosen, but to do so for the sake of *spying*...

No, not spying. Watching them have sex, I realized. He'd been trying to peep in on the princess. It was less surprising than it was *brave* for him to still be here after having his plan ruined.

"I don't believe you," Princess Bryony said in the face of his panic. Behind her, the men of her Chosen seemed to swell with protective energy, even the shorter and less severe looking of the group glaring down at Sir Hubert. "Whatever you have or have not been doing with this palace ends now. You are dismissed from your duties and the premises."

I made to reach for him, but he wasn't done.

"Your Highness, with all due respect, it was the *council* who hired me," Hubert said, chest puffing.

The princess stood, and I realized she wasn't *so* small. She was a little taller than Hubert, although still dainty by comparison to his girth. But she stood with the kind of pride one expected in a royal, that must've been reared in them from their first steps.

"And does the council have more authority in my palace than I do?" she asked. The question was dark and sharp, and I wondered if I imagined the softest thread of doubt in her tone.

Hubert wavered and then sagged. "No, Your Highness."

"Then you are dismissed," Princess Bryony repeated. "Guard Stark, you are to accompany Sir Hubert to retrieve his *personal* belongings and then see him off the grounds. This should take no more than a half hour, I should think."

"Less than that, I'd imagine, Your Highness," I said, smiling and bowing for her as Hubert snarled at me.

I grabbed his arm and dragged him from the room as he began to try and plead for leniency.

I already loved my new position, even if I was a leftover.

9.
BRYONY

I might've been imagining it simply due to my own relief, but I thought the palace felt a little lighter with Sir Hubert's absence. I was curled on the couch, leaning against Owen's side as if he were my own personal furniture—he didn't seem to mind and had his arm securely around my waist—as I took notes in an old journal Wendell had found for me.

"Begging your pardon, Your Majest—I mean highness, *Your* Highness."

I looked up with a smile already on my face as a young woman, maybe a few years younger than Camellia, came into the study we occupied, repeating an unsteady curtsey as she carried a tray that Cosmo hurried to rescue from her.

"We in the kitchen just thought you might like some cake," she said. Her head was ducked shyly, red curls peeking out from under her cap. I thought her eyes looked a little swollen, as if she'd been crying, but she could barely restrain the grin on her lips. "No one below minds to hear that Sir Hubert is leaving, and we just—that is to say, we just had some cake about. Begging your pardon." She added two more curtsies and then scurried from the room.

"You're winning favor with the people already," Wendell said, flashing me a bright smile as Cosmo set the tray down on the table in front of us.

There were far too many cakes—or I thought so, until Owen picked up two at once and popped them both in his mouth—but they were frosted with a soft pink and topped with a candied duplication of my namesake flower, white and green and delicate.

"I doubt it'll be always so easy and satisfying, but I'll take this win," I said, sighing and stealing the next cake out of Owen's fingers. He grinned at me, and I forgot all about pastry as I watched his tongue flick out over his lips.

My reverie was interrupted by the return of Guard Stark, who looked just about as pleased with his duty of the morning as the maid had been to deliver us cake.

"He's gone now, Your Highness. I watched him down the road myself. Think I managed to keep him from stealing a fair number of trinkets as well," Cresswell Stark announced, pride shining into those sharp green eyes of his.

"Good," I said, at the same time that Thao scoffed and said, "It looks as though he's taken plenty others during his time here."

Cresswell started to bow again, and I interrupted him. "Would you like a cake?"

Thao frowned at me and the message was clear. Princesses don't offer their guards cake. Well, this one was going to, and that wasn't the only reason I wanted to delay Cresswell.

"Would I—no, no thank you, Your Highness. I appreciate it," he said, color warming his face.

"Are you from Rumsbrooke, Guard Stark? Do you know the local magistrate?" I added when he frowned.

"Oh! Well, I did. But he died a few years ago. His wife has taken over his duties as the council hasn't bothered to appoint a new one. Rebecca Sanders, she lives in Rumsbrooke and runs his old printing business as well."

"If she's taken over his duties, why hasn't *she* been appointed?" I asked, and when the guard gaped I waved my hand in the air. "Never mind. If she's doing the work, then she's the person I want to speak to."

"I can...have her sent for," Cresswell said with a nod.

I nearly agreed, when it occurred to me that Rebecca Sanders might not be the only person I wanted to speak to in Rumsbrooke.

He won't be glad to see you, I thought, and then decided I didn't care. The offer had been made, and we could all live with the consequences.

"Actually, I think I'd like to go and see the city for myself and speak to her there," I said.

"I know where the Sanders house is," Cosmo offered. "Rebecca took pity on me and bought one of my first pieces."

Wendell leaned forward and added softly, "We should at least send word. A royal visit would catch anyone off guard, especially since it's still so...new to have you here."

I looked back to Cresswell, aware that he'd watched every detail of our interactions with keen interest. I was probably not what he'd imagined when he'd heard a princess was coming with her Chosen. And no doubt dismissing Sir Hubert and taking a trip to speak to the local magistrate—honorary title or otherwise —would fracture any attempt to appear as if we were all playing along with my Hunger. But after our travels, I didn't want to waste any more time playing pretend.

"I'll have word sent down to the city, and if you don't object, I think it's best if I and some of the guard attend you on your trip, Your Highness," Cresswell said with a respectful bow.

How eccentric would I appear if I asked my royal guard to dismiss with my title and bowing as well as my Chosen? Probably a little too much so.

"I defer to your judgment in this," I said, and Cresswell bowed again before leaving.

"I don't think a local magistrate is worthy of house calls from the crown princess of Kimmery," Thao said, taking a cake for himself and raising an eyebrow at me.

"The crown princess thinks she is," I volleyed back, and Thao's smile fractured and he dipped his head. "Cosmo, will you come and help ease the introduction? Wendell, I think you might be best prepared of all of us to help me navigate subjects like a new steward and lowering taxes and hunting licenses."

Wendell's eyebrows shot up, and he looked to Thao in a reflex before realizing that it wasn't up to his lover to decide. "I... I will do my best, Your—"

"Bryony," I said before he could finish.

"I will do my best to help, Bryony," he said, nodding and ignoring Prince Thao's stare.

"Prince Thao and I will explore the palace while you're gone," Owen said, turning a grin in the prince's direction.

Thao made an uncomfortable face, but nodded in agreement.

RUMSBROOKE DIDN'T IMPROVE from inside the gate. The buildings were close and almost universally in disrepair, at least at the edges of the city. I was glad that Cresswell had insisted on not only the guards, but also a more modest black carriage, and I felt guilty that I was relieved to be tucked away from my own people.

Wendell looked equally grave at my side as he stared out the window. "You may have to decide between forgoing their taxes and repairing the palace, Your Highness."

"Forgoing the taxes, obviously," I said, and Wendell's head turned to me, his gaze softening.

"If you can spare taxes and some of the upcoming harvest, you'll do better for these people than they've seen in years," Cosmo said from across the carriage.

As reassuring as it was probably meant to be, his words only left me queasy. No wonder Aric hated me and the palace and the choosing. No wonder men submitted themselves to the humiliation of the process if it offered relief from a life of scraping by on nothing. Kimmery was broken, and I didn't know if I had the power to fix it. Not fully, not with my position of inheriting the crown at risk.

"It...it *will* be temporary unless we can do something about the legislations in place that prevent economic growth for the masses," Wendell said, shifting nervously in place.

"You don't need to be ashamed to tell me the truth," I said, catching Wendell's pale gaze. "You know more on this subject than I do, and I hope I've made it clear that I'd like to learn."

I liked Wendell's smile. It—like the rest of him—was gentle, but full and warm and focused when he granted it. "I wanted a seat on the council, I wanted to make changes like these for Kimmery," Wendell said softly.

"Why didn't you take one?" I asked.

"The council votes on new members, and I had no connections within its circle. When they offered me the position of ambassador, it was too good to refuse, but I knew it was to keep me from campaigning for one of their seats. And then..."

And then in Mennary, he met the love of his life. Wendell smiled and shrugged, and I reached over to squeeze his hand.

"As much as I wish you were on my council, I'm glad for the way things worked out," I said.

"We're here," Cosmo said at the same time the carriage rolled to a slow stop.

We were near the heart of Rumsbrooke, dark buildings tall and narrow and made of large stone. It had the look of a once wealthy and now dilapidated neighborhood, but it was an improvement on the lean-tos we'd passed on our way. I stepped out after Wendell, and he was quick to catch me by my waist, lifting me over a little running mess of refuse and water that ran at the edge of the sidewalk. My breath caught in my chest, caught off guard by the gesture and the absolute ease with which he managed it. Wendell was very tall, probably as much as Owen, and while he wasn't *slim* by any sense of the word, he appeared so in comparison to Owen and Thao's muscular bodies. But he was strong, and he set me down on my toes as gently as if I weighed nothing before offering me his arm to hold.

Cosmo's hand touched my back as he leapt over the gutter, and I returned to my senses, staring up the narrow, crooked stairs of the building we were in front of, my eyes landing on the woman waiting for us. For a second, I had the strange impulse to curtsey to her, but she beat me to it, bending low. She reminded me a little of my grandmother, tall and thin, with a firm and examining expression. Her features were softer, however, and there was still some brown in her hair. Her dark grey dress was frayed at the hem and discolored at the cuffs, but it was tidy and the lines were pressed smooth, and when she pushed herself up by her dark polished cane, she stood straight with pride.

"Thank you for seeing me on such short notice, Mistress Sanders," I said, taking Wendell's hand and following him up the stairs, watching the older woman's eyes widen briefly with surprise.

"The honor is mine, Your Majesty," she said.

I squeezed Wendell's fingers before he could correct her use of the title. "Princess Bryony, please."

"Please, come inside. I—I haven't prepared a tea, but—"

"I really came for business, you don't need to exert yourself for our sake," I said quickly.

The house was clean and bright inside, although there was a funny feeling as I stepped through the doorway as if everything might've been leaning slightly to the left. Rebecca Sanders led us slowly down a hall and then into a well-organized office on the left. Behind me, Cosmo followed close with Cresswell Stark, who left another two guards at the front door.

Two mismatched chairs faced a long desk, and Rebecca's lips pursed as she glanced between us and them. Wendell managed the ceremony, pulling out the chair with the cushion for me and then gesturing Rebecca to sit before taking the empty seat, as Cosmo leaned in at my back casually.

"It's good to see you again, Pianetta," Rebecca said swiftly, her eyes bouncing over the four of us from behind her desk.

"It's good to be home again. I hope the city is behaving itself for you," Cosmo said.

Rebecca huffed and didn't answer, instead meeting my gaze with her own soft brown eyes. "I take it you've chosen a replacement for my late husband Frederick?"

"I—" *Don't stutter. Don't look nervous.* "I would like *you* to take the position, unless you object. If it's been a burden for you, I'm sure we can find—"

"You want *me* to be magistrate?" Rebecca asked, jaw dropping slightly. All at once, the firm and steady woman of the front steps seemed to falter, and I recognized the expression in front of me. Not my grandmother's, but my own.

"Guard Stark and Cosmo have said you already are serving as magistrate, and if you aren't unhappy with the work, then I'm glad to make it official," I said.

She restored herself, lips pressing firmly and eyes traveling over the surface of her desk.

"I do have...changes I would like to implement, with your help," I said.

Her shoulders slumped and she didn't look up. "You'll want to raise the taxes now that you're living in the north, I take it."

"I'd like to lower them, actually. Well, I'd like to forgo them for the time being," I said.

It was as if I'd struck her with the announcement. Rebecca Sanders dropped back in her chair, twice as shocked as when I'd said I wanted her to keep the position.

"Forgo the taxes?" she breathed.

"I've dismissed Sir Hubert as steward of the Winter Palace, and I...suppose I will be in need of another. But I'm not entirely sure what kind of state the coffers are in or what I'll need the steward to be handling while I'm in residence. Also, there is the matter of the ban on hunting in the woods. I'd like it to be lifted, but I am concerned that might lead to a rush that's not sustainable. I was thinking of appointing a royal hunter who might... donate the meat to the citizens in some way."

Cosmo's hand passed gently over my shoulder, and I looked up to see the laughter in his eyes and the gentle smile. "Mistress Sanders looks as though she might faint."

She did look pale, and I wondered if she'd heard everything I said or if she was still stuck on the bit about the taxes. "A...royal hunter who gives his catch to the citizens?" she murmured.

Oh good, she had caught that part. "Yes, I know. I haven't sorted out how it would be most widely beneficial yet, but I'm open to input."

"I...I accept the position of Northern Magistrate, Your— Princess Bryony. And I will happily make the announcement of taxes being waived. I do... I am aware," Rebecca began cautiously, pulling a bound book out of a drawer of the desk, "that Sir Hubert borrowed against the Winter Palace's coffers. There was also a great deal transferred south last year. The current total is...not impressive," she said, turning the book to face me.

Wendell hummed, and I realized as I stared at the numbers that I had little to no idea what any of it meant. I could do that math, but in terms of what it would cost to maintain the castle versus what was available? I was lost. I turned to Wendell, and he frowned at me.

"It's...it's enough for good wages to the current staff and good meals, I would guess to last us through winter. Not much else," he said.

"Then that's where it will have to go," I said, nodding.

Wendell smiled, and Rebecca's eyes volleyed between us as I turned to her again. "Waive taxes until the harvest and we'll revisit the subject then. As for the steward...I'd rather not leave it to the council to decide. I'm not a great fan of their first choice."

"Let me think of a few people, and I'll send them up to the palace for an interview?" Rebecca suggested. "There is—if you're considering lifting the ban on hunting, I wonder if you'd be willing to consider waiving some of the upcoming poaching convictions. In particular, there is a young boy, under sixteen, who is the sole provider for his younger siblings and—"

"Oh! Pardon him, please," I said, sitting forward.

Rebecca sighed and nodded. "I hoped you might say that. Yes, gladly."

I smiled at her, and she answered in kind, the first smile on her lips since our arrival on her doorstep. I wondered if Rebecca Sanders' late husband would've been as agreeable to work with as she was, but either way, I was glad to have her as a resource now.

❃

WE STAYED with Mistress Sanders for almost another hour, and it was Wendell and Cosmo who managed to lead the conversation after my initial planning outburst. Rebecca confirmed that as crown princess, I had the power to lift bans and rearrange my court as I pleased, it was just that I wouldn't be currying favor with the council for every change I made.

"I think I need to meet the council for myself," I said, frowning as we got into the carriage again. "But not just yet. I want to have a better handle on what's going on and what needs changed."

"You're doing good work already, Bryony," Wendell said, following me in.

"He's right. And Rebecca Sanders is closer to the collective ear of Rumsbrooke than any council member," Cosmo added.

Cresswell, who'd remained mostly silent and watchful during the meeting, was closing the door behind Wendell when I remembered there was one more stop I wanted to make while we were in the city.

"Guard Stark, will you take us to the Wing and Rook?"

"The—the *tavern*, Your Highness?" Cresswell's brow furrowed beneath the gleaming brass helmet he wore.

"And inn, yes," I said nodding.

"It's in a very unsavory neighborhood, even for Rumsbrooke," Cresswell said, standing at the open door.

"That's all right. You and the guards may remain with the carriage while my Chosen and I go in to speak with an acquaintance."

"An acquaintance...at the Wing and Rook," Cresswell said slowly, suspicion or something along those lines in his eyes.

I sat up straighter and reached for the door handle. "Yes, now please, so we may get back before dark." And then I pulled the door shut on my own. I leaned back to find Wendell and Cosmo smirking at me. "What?"

"I don't think Aric Martin was really expecting you to take him up on that offer," Wendell said with a shrug, his smile growing. I liked Wendell on his own. He was reserved around Thao in a way he wasn't when it was us together. I would have to keep my eye on that and be sure it wasn't a problem. Thao obviously felt himself above my other Chosen—he *was* a prince—but I wouldn't allow it to make anyone uncomfortable.

"If Aric is there, I can guarantee he won't expect you to walk in. It's barely been a day," Cosmo added.

I sat back in my seat in the carriage and hid my fiddling hands in the fabric of my skirt. "I said if I was in Rumsbrooke that I would go. I am here, and I will."

"Of course, princess," Cosmo said, that glitter of laughter in his dark eyes again. It wasn't cruel—in fact, there was a fondness to it that made me want to squirm in my seat.

The ride to the Wing and Rook didn't take long, but Cresswell was correct that the neighborhood did change a great deal. The road grew narrow and crowded with stalls. There were plenty of people out, and they eyed the carriage with calculating stares, a few even spitting in our direction. Definitely Aric's people then.

"Are you sure we shouldn't take in a guard?" Wendell murmured, meeting the harsh stares above hollow cheeks through the glass of the carriage window.

"I don't want to attract too much attention," I said.

Wendell choked, and Cosmo grinned. "Bryony, you would do that anywhere. But I think you're right. The guards will rile up Aric's patrons. You... Well, Aric won't let anything happen to any of us if we go in, and I know a few of his crowd myself."

"You're well connected here in the north," I said, grinning back at Cosmo.

His brows jumped and his head tipped side to side. "*Well* connected? I don't know about that. But I grew up in the poor end of the city and made friends with the patrons. I know plenty of people here, that's true."

The carriage stopped, and this time, it was Cosmo who lifted me down. Perhaps I misjudged men's strength in general because he was the slimmest of my Chosen and he still handled me with ease. I hadn't had many occasions to be carried about in my life, but I was beginning to think it was something I would enjoy growing used to.

"You stay close to my side or at my back in there. And move quickly and keep your eyes off strangers, yes?" Cosmo murmured to me, his hands coming up to hold my chin briefly. His touch was rougher than I expected, and I remembered that his medium was primarily sculpture.

I reached for his hand as I nodded, and Cosmo's fingers linked with mine as Wendell slid his arm loosely around my waist.

"In and out if Aric's not in," Cosmo said, and then drew us forward.

With two steps into the narrow hall leading in the tavern, I was blind. It wasn't an especially bright day and Rumsbrooke didn't leave room for a great deal of sunlight to shine down on its residents, but in comparison to the inside of the Wing and Rook, it'd been positively sunny on the street.

Cosmo at least seemed confident in his steps, even as Wendell stumbled against my side. Slowly, my eyes adjusted, just in time for Cosmo to guide me gently down a set of narrow stairs into a stone cellar. A few candles were lit, only just enough for you to see the general layout of the room, and I barely remembered to keep my eyes up and off the hooded patrons at their tables. Wendell's fingers squeezed urgently against my waist.

"That you, Pianetta? Wasn't expecting to see—" A short man with a dark patch over one eye and a tangled mess of indistinguishably colored hair stood behind a counter, enormous barrels of ale propped against the wall behind him. He gaped at our approach.

"Is His Majesty in?" Cosmo asked, voice bright and calm.

"Aye, he's in the back. Let me tell him...he has visitors," the bartender said slowly, without turning away from us. He was staring at me, and I wasn't sure if he was someone I was meant to avoid looking at or not, but it was impossible to resist the urge to glance directly back at the one eye fixed to me. He grinned, and it was gap-toothed but not unfriendly, then he chuckled and turned away to a crank that rolled one of the barrels out of the row and revealed a tunnel.

"Oi! You got someone here to see you."

"Who?"

The word was barely audible but I knew the irritable tone, and I bit my lip at the sudden flare of goosebumps and excitement. *Oh, you idiot*, I thought. *How is he any more attainable than a book character?*

"Hello, love, ain't you pretty," rasped a voice at my back, the fabric of my skirt rustling.

"Royalty," the bartender called down the tunnel.

I twisted between my Chosen and nearly startled at the figure behind me. They were...not put together as I thought they ought to have been, shoulders at different angles and a smile hanging in the opposite direction.

"Oh dear," Wendell murmured, and I pressed my foot to the top of his to stop him from saying anything else.

"Hello," I said, smiling. "I like your vest."

It was patched together, in a not completely dissimilar way to the man I was looking at, but it was colorful and the stitches were even and minuscule, perfectly crafted. The crooked smile spread over the unusual face, and there was no mistaking the keen intelligence in this man's gaze. He straightened slightly, a brief reveal that some of his deformity was in fact an act, and he winked at me.

"Need another fella?"

"I think I'm a bit over-stocked at the moment, but I'll keep you in mind," I said, and the man looked delighted with me.

"Scrapper! Leave the girl alone!"

I startled at Aric's bark but Scrapper, my new friend, just leaned cooly to the left, staring across the bar to see Aric where he stood at the mouth of the tunnel.

"Was just being cordial," he said, and made to leave.

"Give it back first," Aric growled, and I volleyed my gaze between them.

"Don't know what you—"

"Scrapper, I'm not joking around. Turn it over. All of it."

Scrapper sighed, and gnarled hands dipped into patches of his vest which were in fact pockets, pulling out a pretty pin and chain set that had been at the back of my dress, as well as my handkerchief, and something that looked like it might've been a trinket of Wendell's.

"Oh," I said, as he pushed my ornaments into my palm. "Here, keep this. As a memento."

I tried to push the pin back, and Scrapper only shook his head. "I'd rather have the handkerchief, Your Loveliness."

Aric huffed as I gave Scrapper my handkerchief after pressing a stained kiss to the corner. Scrapper waved it like a flag in the direction of Aric's scowl before ducking and disappearing into one of the bar's shadows. Aric waited behind the counter for us, frowning and glaring around the room.

"Vic, give the gentlemen a pint while they wait and make sure no one works them for coin," Aric muttered. "Pri—Bryony, in here."

"Would you rather we—?" Wendell started, but I only shook my head at him.

"I'm fine. Have a drink." I stepped into the tunnel, and a second later Aric was at my back, hand splayed on my spine and pushing me forward.

"What on earth do you think you're doing here?" Aric hissed.

"You invited me."

"I—You—" He scoffed and sighed as we moved out of the density of darkness in the tunnel and into a room lit from thick glass skylights and a collection of lanterns. It was cool and clearly underground, but made comfortable with dense rugs and good, well-worn furniture. "I should've known you'd actually take me up on it."

"Of course you should have," I said, and marveled at the tremble that ran through me at Aric's resulting growl. "Aric, this isn't really a normal tavern, is it? And they call you Your Majesty. I probably shouldn't have come with the royal guard, should I?"

"You *what?*" Aric gasped, spinning me to face him in front of a desk. It was bigger than Rebecca's and infinitely less organized, covered in unusual instruments and maps and scraps of paper. In fact, the entire room was filled with little interesting bits of machinery and dried plants and odd collections.

"You're not really just a tavern owner, are you?" I asked, looking up at Aric's stoned expression.

He gaped at me, slowly gathering control of his face, righting it back to his usual cool and irritated calm. "Will the royal guard be joining us here?" he asked.

"No, I told them to wait outside. I thought it might attract less attention."

Aric's eyes scanned me head to toe, and my skin seemed to respond by growing extra sensitive to my own clothing. "I'm not certain of that, but I'm glad for your instinct. Your Highness, I... I *am* a tavern owner, and a mage. I'm also the King of Thieves."

I blinked at him, laughter my first impulse, but it died immediately when I thought of Scrapper and even Cosmo's advice about caution in the bar. "Oh. *Oh*, I see. Next time I visit, I won't bring the guard with me," I said.

"Next time," Aric responded flatly.

"What does it mean to be the King of Thieves? Who do you steal from?" I asked frowning. "How is being a thief any better than—than—" Than being a princess who doesn't look after her people?

"I'm not stealing from starving people! None of my court is. We're trying to give *back*," Aric hissed.

"Then *who*, Aric?"

"Do you want me to confess to *you*? Not a chance, princess. With the royal guard standing outside?" Aric scoffed and shook his head, eyes turning toward the tunnel. He looked like he wanted to drag me back out again. "We steal from those who can afford it, who are making it worse for everyone else. Does that satisfy you?"

"Do you steal from men like Sir Hubert?" I asked, relaxing again. Maybe it was absurd, he'd admitted to being a criminal, but I believed Aric. He'd steal from me, but he wouldn't steal from the people in the street we passed. I wanted to trust him, I needed to because I didn't have very many other people I *could* trust.

Aric's brow twitched. "Hubert?"

"The steward of the north. Do you know him? I had to fire him. He tried to take the suite next to mine in the palace so he could watch the princess with her Chosen in bed," I said, and Aric stiffened and his head whipped back to face me. "Also, I think he must've been generally hated anyway because the cook made me cakes when he left. And I've made Rebecca Sanders the Northern Magistrate, officially." Aric's hands were still holding me by my shoulders, and his fingers tightened slightly as I went on. "We're going to waive taxes for the time being, and I'll think of a way to help with the harvest too. And do you know anyone who might make a good royal hunter? Or how I could fairly feed the people with what might be hunted in the woods? I still haven't sorted that out yet."

Aric's eyes widened, and I could've sworn he was *just* about to smile. "Princess," he purred, and I would've melted at that sound if not for his hands holding me up. He guided me down into a deep armchair before finally releasing me, stepping back and dragging another chair closer. He leaned forward in his seat, elbows on his knees, and I sat primly at the edge of my own.

"You've been very busy," he said, and I realized that he was at the edge of laughter.

"A great deal needs to get done," I said, smoothing my skirt over my knees and letting the texture of the fabric distract me from the force of Aric's stare.

He had a strange kind of effect on me. One moment, I found him magnetic and I wanted to curl up against him. The next, I wanted to shy away. And then a second later, I wanted to stomp on his foot and remind him that *I* was his princess and he was...

A King of Thieves.

"How do you become a King of Thieves?" I asked.

Aric's eyes narrowed and his smile finally broke free, sly and simple. "I think if I tell you, you might try and take it from me. We'd better just focus on what you've wrought already. Sir Hubert will take this to the council."

"I have the higher authority," I said.

Aric nodded, and a lock of silver hair fell over his forehead. I wondered if it was soft or thick and coarse. "You do, but the crown doesn't usually step between the council and their authority over the people. You're ruffling feathers. Sanders is a good magistrate, better even than her husband, and I have no doubt you've already won her loyalty. She hates taking taxes."

Aric and Rebecca Sanders knew one another then, well enough for him to know this about her? Were they...did they have feelings for one another? Perhaps that was why Aric was so determined not to be one of my Chosen. The widow of the magistrate and a King of Thieves was a romantic sort of pairing, the kind of thing I would've loved to read about.

I like it less when it is Aric, I realized, frowning at my own possessive impulse.

"As for hunting...the woods are often occupied by...unregistered shifters," Aric said slowly, watching my face.

"Oh! Then I'd better not. Or should I just make it public knowledge?" I asked.

"If it were a shifter doing the hunting, they would be able to communicate with the rest of the community and have a better sense while in the woods. And they'd have appropriate respect for the animals being hunted," Aric said, words slow and eyes drifting around the room with thought.

"You have someone in mind," I said.

His lips twitched again. "I might."

"Aric, I trust your judgment. I feel as though I've made that clear," I said, straightening in my seat.

His expression sobered, and his eyes narrowed in a suspicion I hadn't expected. "Princess, you are sitting across from the King of Thieves. Trust isn't something I'd recommend we share between us."

I held myself still, resisting the urge to flinch. "Why did you want your crown, Aric? For wealth?" I glanced around the room where everything inside looked used and worn. "I doubt it. You can hate the crown I'm after, but I think you know my motivations are the same as yours. I want to help Kimmery. I don't want you to have to try and fix the balance on your own at the risk of being arrested. I'm sorry I didn't realize before this week what being queen would really mean, everything that needs changed, but we're on the same side now."

I stood, and Aric's eyes remained lowered. "You'll find me a hunter?" I asked.

He was quiet for a long time, and I wondered if I'd pushed him a little too far with my speech until he dipped his head once in a nod and finally met my eyes again. "I'll bring them to the palace to meet you."

"Thank you." I turned and headed for the exit, deciding I'd had enough of our brand of conflict for today.

"Bryony."

Perhaps he will apologize and we can be friends again. Were we ever friends?

I spun, knowing my smile had brightened at his call and feeling it falter at his stern stare.

"Don't come back here unless I call for you," he said.

I bit down on my tongue and stormed back down the tunnel and into the dismal bar.

10.
BRYONY

Cosmo combed his fingers through my hair as I sat on the bed with my back to him, Owen stretched out at our side.

"So your day was fruitful, and ours was as well," Owen said as Cosmo began to make a braid.

We'd arrived back to the palace after dark, and I could feel the evidence of so many days riding in the carriage wearing on me, my head starting to pound as I sipped our wine over a hasty dinner. Thao and Wendell had already left us for the suite next door and I had my remaining two Chosen in bed, for all that I would really do with them.

You might do a little *more with Owen if you liked*, a wicked voice in my thoughts offered.

"How does Thao seem to be adjusting?" I asked, wondering what a prince from the southern islands might think of the northern end of Kimmery.

"Mm, he's a bit high, isn't he?" Owen asked, and Cosmo stifled a laugh at the understatement. "But I think I might've won him over a touch by the end of the day. Or worn him down."

I smiled and stretched my hand back until Owen's fingers caught mine and squeezed gently.

"We found a number of bedrooms. They were a little dusty, but the maid said she'd have them ready by tonight if you'd rather sleep alone," Owen said, words softening as he went. "Oh, and I made friends with a family of raccoons and introduced them to some better hiding spots outside, but they'll probably try and return."

Cosmos fingers stilled in my hair briefly and then tied off the end of my braid with a ribbon. I mulled over Owen's offer, fingers twisting in my lap.

"Is it...is it difficult for you to lie next to me? Be honest," I rushed to add. "I know a little of these things, and I..."

I'm aware you were both more than willing to have sex with me days ago, if I'd been prepared.

Cosmo touched my shoulder, guiding me to twist to meet his gaze. He leaned forward and paused, and then leaned in again until our noses were only an inch apart, his eyes flicking back and forth over mine, waiting. I lifted my chin and Cosmo smiled, dipping his head and pressing a soft, brief kiss against my lips. He pulled away quickly and I waited a moment, considering myself.

There wasn't the same hammering anticipation and craving I'd had this morning with Owen, but my lips tingled and my cheeks grew warm. I liked the kiss, even if I wasn't waiting for another.

"I'm happy to sleep in your bed if you like the company. I'm happy to sleep in my own too," Cosmo said. Which didn't mean he didn't find it uncomfortable, I noticed. "If you ever desired more than friendship and a kiss between us, you'd have it," he added grinning.

"I prefer your bed," Owen said, his own smile bright.

I laughed and shook off the buzzing tension in my veins, Cosmo sliding out of my way so I could fall back into the pillows.

"It may not be Hunger, but there's something growing here," I said as Cosmo and Owen settled me between them. I stared up at the cracks in the high ceiling of the room as Cosmo leaned into my side, his fingers tangling with mine over my ribs. I turned my head and craned my neck to find Owen's face. "You wanted to be Chosen?"

"I did."

"Why?"

Owen pursed his lips, shoulders shrugging but careful not to jostle me. "I wanted to be wanted. I'm the oldest boy of... Think it's eleven of us, altogether," he said, grinning sheepishly. "Lost count when my parents had to put me into an early apprenticeship with the army groomsman. And then he had kids and couldn't afford to feed me on top of them, so I went into the army. And now there's peace again and... I'm useful, I can work and I can manage for myself, but I wanted a place that was more than temporary, that needed me. I didn't really think I had much of a chance at being Chosen if I'm honest, but it was going to be better than what I already had. It is a great deal better." I felt a touch at the top of my head, a kiss maybe, or just Owen leaning into me.

"Even if we aren't..." *Even if I wasn't what I was supposed to be, who he'd thought he'd have a place with?*

Owen shuffled down in the bed until we were nose to nose, his smile beaming. He didn't seem to mind Cosmo on the other side of me, even granted the man a grin before looking back to me. "It's been the best week of my life yet, Bryony. Like Cosmo said, whatever you need of me is yours."

This time, I *did* need. I pressed into Owen, holding tight to Cosmo's hand, and sucked at Owen's bottom lip, my eyes falling shut at his pleased hum. He kissed me back, gentle nibbles and licking at my lips. Both he and Cosmo pressed closer until I was pinned between their bodies and heat, a sudden stab of longing striking me in my core. Cosmo's lips touched my shoulder, just a graze, and Owen's cock stirred against my thigh as he sucked on my tongue.

I didn't realize that I'd been holding my breath until Owen released me and I gasped for air, making both men chuckle and retreat. Owen kissed my nose and my cheek, and then settled into the pillows as Cosmo leaned back, giving me a little room. He pulled his hand from mine, but just as I started to frown at the loss, Cosmo's fingers dipped into my hair under my braid, digging into the tense muscle at the base of my skull.

I hummed, and Owen skimmed his own hand over my side to cup my hip.

"Sleep, Bryony. We'll have new adventures in the morning," Owen said.

"Read to her a little," Cosmo said.

But I didn't need so much coaxing. I fell asleep to Cosmo's touches and the rhythm of Owen's heartbeat under my palm.

IT WAS JUST me and Owen again when I woke in the morning. My head was still beating like an unwelcome drum, and much of my body was stiff. I'd done almost no traveling growing up, and I'd forgotten that it would leave me feeling so jumbled and sore.

I rolled in the bed, biting off my own groan, and came nose to chest with Owen, pressing my face to his warmth and wiggling in to feel the soft stab of his cock against my stomach.

"Don't mind that," Owen said, and I smiled into his skin. "It's to do with you, but also just the morning."

"I don't mind, really."

"What needs doing today?" Owen asked, his arms finding their way around me and gathering me closer to his chest. His cock pressed between my thighs, and I resisted the impulse to wiggle against it just to see what sounds he made.

"I wanted to make a list of what needs to be repaired around the palace, at least until we have a new steward to help, but Wendell says the finances might not allow for much work," I said. "I suppose today I only have to wait for news."

Owen's arms shifted, one sliding lower to cup around my hips. "Are you feeling better?"

"A little worse, I think. It will pass."

"No one would think ill of you if you wanted to spend the day in bed," Owen said.

"Mm, I might. What would I do in bed all day, anyway?"

He shrugged, his chest shifting against my cheek. "Read... sleep, ignore some of the worries you've been nursing since the choosing."

"Since before," I corrected gently. My eyes drifted shut, and for a moment, I soaked up the warmth of the embrace. Somehow, even though he'd bathed twice in the palace already, Owen still smelled a little like hay and horses, but in the sweetest way. He made it easy to relax, to spend time so close with him as if he weren't someone I'd only known for a handful of days.

Owen leaned back, and I opened my eyes again to look up at him, finding him staring and studying me in the way that Cosmo or Aric sometimes did.

"Come here," I said, even though we were already so close.

Owen seemed to understand, hunching and dipping his face to mine. I was feeling curious again, and we smiled before our lips connected, soft sips from one another that grew deeper with every pass. I cupped his rough jaw in my hands, holding him in place for my tasting, and then gasped as his own gripped my ass through my thin nightgown. His tongue flicked between my lips, brushing over mine and then stroking and pulling away.

"How curious are you feeling this morning?" he breathed, voice rough.

"A little more," I answered immediately, craning my neck for more and ignoring the ache that twinged through my muscles.

Owen rolled us, hands sliding down the backs of my thighs to guide them open. We both groaned as his hips settled between mine, heat and rigid length nestling against the bunched fabric pressed to my sex. He held himself over me, moving one hand to brace by my shoulder, and he stared down to watch my reaction.

"Is this how it would be?" I asked, glancing down between us.

"Not at first," Owen said, catching my eye again.

I raised an eyebrow. "No? I thought this was the general premise."

He grinned and rocked, and my breath caught in my lungs at the soft pressure. "It is, but I think first I'd like to..." He paused and then his grin grew. He shifted, and I swallowed as his hips pulled away from mine and he shimmed down my body, pausing briefly with his face above my chest to dip and kiss my breast bone. He settled, making room for his own broad shoulders between my thighs, creating a stretch in my muscles that was shockingly delicious.

"If you were feeling patient, I think I'd like to kiss every sweet inch of you. But if you were very curious, and you really needed me, I'd start here," Owen said, holding my gaze as his face lowered, breaths brushing my nightgown, heat bleeding through and radiating against my flesh. He moved slowly but he didn't pause, just held my gaze until his mouth pressed over my core, the kiss pressing into me through the thin layer of fabric, fire following under my skin. He rose up with an equally patient pace, and I realized I was panting, my eyes wide and fixed on his lips.

I sat up and Owen pulled me up onto his lap, holding me by my bottom. "I am getting very curious," I said, biting my lip.

Owen nodded and dipped his head, plucking my lip free with his own teeth. "You'll know when you're ready."

I looped my arms around his neck, and Owen lowered me back to the bed as I kissed his rough chin and long throat. He settled on top of me again, both of us rocking into one another, the friction of fabric rougher than skin but also stimulating. I'd tried touching myself in the past, bringing myself to the same climax the characters in stories found, but it seemed as if I always stalled on the brink. My hands grew unreliable, fidgeting wildly without my permission, right when I thought I might've reached the precipice, and then the feeling would fade away again.

Owen was careful with his own weight and seemed to avoid the steady thump of us together that I was starting to wish for. His kisses were gentler too, testing and tasting. He wanted me to take control before we went further and I...

I was still a little nervous, still stuck in my own head and wondering where to put my hands.

He's not rushing you, so you don't have to either, I realized. I sighed, and Owen kissed my jaw and then lifted one of his legs, bracing his knee outside my hip before slowly rolling back to my side. I turned with him, stealing another kiss from his mouth before we parted at the same time. Owen's fingers pushed some of my hair back over my shoulder, blue eyes glittering with a hidden grin.

"You smell like a meadow," Owen said, flashing that bright smile of his.

"I'm glad you came to the choosing," I answered, leaning in to press my lips to the dimple on his chin. "I'm going to dress and explore the palace."

"I'll join you...in a minute," he added with pink cheeks.

I decided it was wholly unfair that Owen could resolve the simmering desire left from our kisses, but also that I didn't mind carrying that heady sensation for a little while longer.

11.
THAO

"This is a good room for light," Cosmo mused, standing at the center of one of the court rooms of the palace.

"Will it make a good studio for you?" Princess Bryony asked, pausing in the slow dancing turns she'd been making over the tile. I'd been watching her delicate movements and the almost childlike enjoyment she got as her skirt flared around her with each spin. The princess was graceful, and I was fascinated by the way she could seem delicate and shy one moment, and then demonstrate a ferocious strength and authority in the next.

I was raised with strength and force and authority, taught to never reveal weakness. Bryony's own occasional fragility worked well to disarm her opponent, hiding the steely determination beneath her perfumes and silks.

"It seems too grand," Cosmo answered, and then tipped his head in thought, taking in the room once more. "It would allow me to make larger works, I suppose."

"There might be a room equally suitable that isn't designed for hosting affairs on matters of state. Perhaps on the second floor," I said. "This is a palace, after all. Not an artist's commune."

Wendell shot me an impatient glance, but I waited for Bryony's whip turn and glare flashing in my direction. Was I a glutton for the woman's punishment? *Perhaps.*

"I'm not a great lover of meetings, and it seems to me there's more than enough of those rooms already," Bryony said. "And anyway, I imagine it's rather difficult to be hauling materials all the way up to the second floor. See, here Cosmo can just open the doors onto the veranda and carts might be brought around there. We could make a path."

"You're sounding like a patroness," Cosmo said, grinning and taking Bryony's hand, pulling her into another graceful spin.

The room was huge, on the northeastern corner of the palace, with an open overlook of the dense and tangled orchard and plenty of sunlight dressing the bright diamond patterned marble floor. It had probably been a ballroom or some room for the royals to conference with advisors, but it seemed as though most of the palace furniture had migrated to the northern wing, where the drafts were less severe. Several of the southern rooms needed windows replaced, and Owen had again discovered animal residents—a family of cats behind a desk. I wondered if he was so talented with wild animals from being so close to one himself. Although Bryony was fairly delighted to know we now had kittens and had the maid move them into the kitchens for scraps of fish and a warmer hiding place.

"You should sculpt our princess," I suggested, hoping to make up for my previous slight against the artist.

Bryony's head ducked, her cheeks flushing, and Cosmo kept his hold on her hand, his eyes drinking her up like a man who'd just discovered an oasis in the desert.

"She'd make an excellent muse," Cosmo agreed, tugging on her hand and raising it up to his lips to press a kiss to her palm.

My eyes slid to Wendell, and I was surprised to find him watching them as avidly as I had, a soft smile on his lips. For whom? The princess or the artist? Visually, I liked them both. I searched the room and found Owen fiddling with a broken lamp in the corner. He glanced up, and his own lips curled as he took in Cosmo's flirting.

If Bryony had a favorite of us, I suspected it was Owen thus far, but he didn't appear jealous. And I was...surprised to find that I wasn't bothered by Wendell's attention turned away from me either. That was good. If he and I were going to have any longevity here as Bryony's Chosen—because I had no doubt she *would* be making use of us, sooner or later—our own romance was going to have to be open to new members, or at least guests.

I wasn't sure about Cosmo yet, but I certainly didn't mind the idea of sharing Wendell with Bryony. Or vice versa.

"I can't think of a use for a statue of myself, but I'll help in any way I can," Bryony said, charmingly pink down to her throat now.

"Done with this," Owen called, righting the lamp against the wall and moving to join us.

"Owen, you don't have to make the repairs yourself, you know," Bryony murmured, reaching for him and enfolding herself between the two men.

He shrugged. "Seems like a waste to wait for someone else to do it when I know how. I don't mind. Come on, there's another room I want you to see," he said.

Wendell waited for me as they passed him and headed back to the dark hall.

"I can't tell if you're goading her intentionally," Wendell whispered in his slightly clunky Mennarian. He often mixed up the words from formal tongue and common when we were only speaking with one another.

"Neither can I," I answered.

I usually settled on the common tongue; the grammar was closer to Kimmerian for Wendell. Before, when I was only a Mennarian prince and Wendell was only the ambassador, we should've spoken exclusively in formal tongue, regardless of our intimacy. If one of us had been a woman, using the common tongue would've been a demonstration of our intentions to one another, but there was no allowance for relationships between men. It was a relief to finally be in an environment where none of that mattered.

"Treat the others with respect," Wendell said, even more quietly. "It's one thing to tease her, but she rises to their defense quickly and she might mistake your intent."

My back tightened at the caution, and I reined myself in before I snapped at Wendell. He wasn't wrong—I couldn't remember a time Wendell had ever been wrong—I was just notoriously irritable when corrected, the inflexibility of my own upbringing was finding its way into uncomfortable places in my personal relationships.

I nodded to Wendell, and it was worth ignoring my own discomfort for the tilt of his lips and the brush of his hand against my back. Ahead of us, Bryony leaned into Owen's side, her right hand tangled with Cosmo's left. They were so at ease with each other, and they'd only known one another for a handful of days. Wendell and I had been lovers for years, but we were so used to hiding the fact that we barely knew how to express it outside of our sex life. I reached for his hand and felt his steps falter before he squeezed tight around my fingers and granted me a shining smile. A simple offering with a powerful return. I sighed, and my tension unwound.

Owen led us through the dim halls to the back corner of the palace and into the gymnasium he and I had found the day before. It still had a stale smell to it, equipment left out to gather dust, and I was surprised by the gleeful note from Bryony.

"Oh, look! Everything's been left," she said, freeing herself from between her Chosen and running across the room to examine the swords resting in the notches on the wall. My eyebrows lifted as she rose to her toes, drawing up a long sabre and pulling it from its thin sleeve.

"Kimmery loves its fencing," Wendell reminded me. "And our queen's line has a reputation for being the fiercest swordswomen." He bowed lightly in Bryony's direction and she rolled her eyes a little.

I could see it though, with the way she held the blade to rest against her knuckles as she examined its length. A sabre for sport was a needle by comparison to the inukat—the long, flat, Mennarian blade with a slight curve to its length—I'd trained to fight with for battle, but a needle could still cut an important artery in well trained hands. She bounced the blade lightly and then took the hilt, cutting through the air with a resulting whistle.

"It's still good," she said. "Do you duel, Wendell?"

"I could easily lose to you," Wendell said, laughing at Bryony's frown. "I'm terrible, not modest. Thao would be a better sparring partner for you."

It might've seemed like an innocent suggestion, if it weren't for Wendell's glance at me out of the corner of his eye.

"It's not my weapon, but I might serve with a little tutelage," I agreed, moving to join Bryony at the wall.

If I were sword-fighting for sport in Mennary, I would never choose an opponent as diminutive as the princess, let alone a woman. But watching her rotate her wrist and arm, learning the weight of the weapon she held comfortably in one hand, I had no doubt that it would be a mistake to underestimate Bryony with a blade of any kind.

"I'll gladly teach you sabre fencing if you will teach me the art of inukat," Bryony said, glancing up at me from beneath her lashes.

"If I do not faint at the sight of you holding a sword as tall as you are, I will happily teach you to wield it," I said, grinning.

Bryony's smile was my own reward, sly and delighted, bouncing slightly on the balls of her feet as if she were ready to lunge and gut me already. I would have to be on my guard with this woman.

⚜

"Mmm, I feel...I feel spoiled," Wendell said, still trying to catch his breath as I wiped our stomachs clean with a towel.

"By my lovemaking?" I asked, grinning.

"Ha! Well, yes, but more...isn't it better this way?" Wendell asked, and then blinked up at me, a sleepy satisfied smile painted over his lips. He was exquisite, my hazy sunlight of a man, all pale and golden with eyes to match a good day's sky. "Maybe you didn't worry about it the way I did," Wendell mumbled, eyelids growing heavy.

I tossed the towel in the direction of our laundry before collapsing against Wendell's side, pressing a long kiss to his warm shoulder, catching a drop of salt on his skin and searching for another.

"Worry how?" I mumbled into him.

"That we'd be discovered. That a servant would walk in at any moment and not keep what they see to themselves. Your mother and father would've sent me packing to Kimmery if they'd discovered our relationship."

I decided not to mention to Wendell that my father *had* been aware, and the promises I'd made so that Wendell's place as ambassador wouldn't be interrupted. One of those promises, to submit myself to the Kimmerian choosing ceremony, had brought us to this moment where it didn't matter now.

"I just feel spoiled to know that I can share this bed with you every night and to touch you openly," Wendell said.

"You don't...miss what you've sacrificed?" I asked, brow furrowing.

Wendell blinked slowly and sighed. "I do, but I think that's something that might be overcome."

He looked as though he were ready to fall asleep, and I suspected it was his way of hiding from my possible response. To reassure him, I reached for his cheek, turning his face to mine and pressing my lips firmly to his.

"I love you," I said in my own language, and then I repeated the simple words in his until Wendell's smile was wide.

"I love you too," he said.

I settled on my side, propping my head in one hand and letting the other play up and down over Wen's chest. "You don't worry that she'll dismiss us?"

His eyes opened wider, and he blinked up at me. "Not...not really. Provided we don't make things difficult for her...or the others," he said, echoing his warning to me earlier. "Even then, she strikes me as someone who *still* might try to help us. She is... she is sweet, isn't she?"

I hummed in agreement, idly playing with Wendell's nipple until he huffed and batted me away, laughing at my wicked smile.

"What would we have done if she'd been like the rest of the queen's line?" I asked.

Wendell swallowed and frowned. "It's strange to think of it now. At the time, I sort of dreaded being Chosen as much as I was determined. I didn't think the Hunger would allow for you and I to be this...comfortable. And now..."

It had to be said. *One* of us had to say it before the other would admit it, and I just hoped I wasn't wrong about Wendell's interest.

"Now I wish she'd call us to her bed," I said, and then stiffened for the three seconds it took Wendell to answer.

"Ugh, me too. She's so... I want to nibble on her. And every time she narrows her eyes at you, my cock seems to take it as an invitation to rise to a call she hasn't even made," Wen released in a rush of words so fast, it took me a moment to sort through them.

I laughed and pushed my long hair out of my face. "Yes. I can't decide if I want to turn her over my knee or put myself over hers."

Wen's eyebrows waggled. "Take turns and let me watch."

There. Of course we're on the same page. We always have been.

I sank down, and Wen moved his arm to pull me into his side, turning and meeting me for a long kiss.

"You can be charming, I know it," Wendell mumbled against my lips.

I pulled back and glared at him. "You're saying *I'm* the obstacle?"

Wendell only laughed and wrestled me back into the pillows, whispering suggestions of how we could woo the princess, and then seduce, and then *possess* her.

12.
BRYONY

"At the ready," I said, still sucking in deep breaths and moving back to position.

Thao wrestled with the face guard he was wearing and huffed. "Couldn't we do this with less...wrappings?"

I huffed back and then shook my head. "Fine, yes, go ahead. I'm leaving mine on, but I know I won't scratch you."

He paused, and then his ungloved hand whipped the helmet off, black hair flying wildly about his face. It wasn't regulation, his hair was too long and it covered useable space for me to attack, but his frustration seemed to be infectious and I didn't want to fight with him on the topic.

Whatever I'd expected from dueling with Thao, it wasn't this temper tantrum behavior over wearing the appropriate safety gear. It probably also wasn't for him to be quite so quick to learn the art of sabre fencing. It appeared some of his ego *wasn't* unwarranted. I was ahead by three points, but he had four of his own and it was galling. I was supposed to be *teaching* him, not being trounced by him.

"When I teach you in inukat, there's no helmets and binding clothing to prevent your movement," Thao said. He was flushed and sweaty, but I could absolutely guarantee that I looked worse beneath my own face shield. "Although, I suppose I will have to grant you the right to wear a shirt," he added, grinning like a cat.

I rolled my eyes and realized there was a disadvantage to letting Thao unmask himself. I had to combat the distraction of his flirting.

"At the ready," I repeated.

Thao groaned and rolled his shoulders before relaxing into

the correct stance, right foot ahead of the left and knees bent, sabre raised loosely in front of him.

"Begin," I said, and we jumped into movement.

I loved sabre fencing. It was quick, efficient, and comparatively brutal in offensive attacks. I practiced in foil and epee to keep myself versatile, but sabre was my favorite. I wanted *action*.

Thao answered three strikes, and I forced myself to focus on him below the neck, although it was impossible to miss the intensity of his focus or the snarl of effort on his lips as I beat him back and caught the tip of my blade against his left side. He jumped away with a growl, whipping the blade down and back and forth as he shook himself loose again.

"You are too fast," he said.

"I am winning, so I think I must be the right kind of fast," I said, and then lost my own train of thought as he spun around with a grin on his face.

Thao had suggested to Cosmo that I might make a good subject of a sculpture. Thao would've been even better. It was a shame he was so rude to the others, because he had a look I admired and it might've been nice to feel for him the way I did for Owen. At the very least, I would've liked to examine his tattoos again, but the fencing gear didn't allow for that either. We were both strapped in from toe to throat.

"I'm exhausted," Thao said. "How long do you usually do this?"

"I think I just wanted to beat you once more," I admitted, reaching up and pulling my own mask off, turning away to hide myself as I tried to wipe away my sweat and smooth my mess of hair.

When I turned back, Thao was significantly closer than I remembered.

"If you are feeling unsatisfied, I could think of better remedies, Bryony," Thao said, words silky and teeth glinting at me in his smile.

I gaped back at him and then settled my confusion. Did he really think that would work with me?

It'd been three mornings of waking up in bed next to Owen and feeling...curious. This morning, he hadn't even waited for my command, just scooped me up and kissed me until I was whimpering and trying to sort my thoughts through the haze of warmth and touch. Owen said I would know when I was ready, but instead, I only found myself constantly *wondering* if I was ready. So yes, I was unsatisfied, and maybe I had been trying to distract myself or burn away some of the simmer still left in my veins with a bit of sport. That didn't mean I wanted to be so transparent about it, or that the simmer was for *this* man.

Thao stepped closer, enough that I caught the spicy whiff of him, and then his eyes drifted over my shoulder and his grin grew wider.

"I wondered where you two were."

I spun to see Wendell leaning in the tall doorway of the room, head tipped and smile soft. "Who won?" he asked.

"Bryony, a number of times," Thao said, the pass of his hand over my back muffled through his glove and my dense jacket.

He moved to Wendell then, and it didn't occur to me to look away until Thao had his lover pressed to the door frame, their lips connected in a fierce kiss. And even when it did occur, I still watched. Wendell groaned into the kiss, pulling away and stretching his throat for Thao to nip and lick down its length. Bright blue eyes met mine and I flushed, caught in my curiosity as Wendell smiled softly at me.

"Join us, Bryony," Wendell said, and my eyes widened until he added, "For lunch."

"I...I think I will go for a ride first," I said, tearing my eyes away from the lovers and ripping the glove from my hand, pulling open the collar of the jacket.

"A ride? We can join you," Thao said, panting a little and leaning into Wendell, who circled the other man's waist with his arms.

They were a pretty pair, all wrapped in one another, but they misunderstood my attention. I'd never seen men together in all the sexual displays I'd grown up around. While I wanted to be touched, I didn't really know Wendell yet and half the time I didn't even like Thao. Thao was courteous to me, but not to Owen or Cosmo, and Wendell seemed to have a little too much of the diplomat in him for me to really break through to the man underneath.

I shook my head, unlacing the jacket with clumsy fingers. "No, just my own company for this, I think."

Thao frowned and Wendell took his cheek in hand, drawing him in for another, softer kiss as I passed them in the door and headed for my room. Cosmo was working on arranging his new studio to his liking, and Owen had mentioned over breakfast that he wanted to explore the grounds. With Wendell and Thao behind me, and the palace staff still a small number, I was able to travel the halls unobserved aside from a few stationed guards. I shook out my hair from its pins and freed myself from the tight fencing jacket by the time I made it back to my room. I had on a light blouse over my corset, and I wrestled myself out of the pants, moving quickly to find a skirt to wear while riding.

I wanted to fly, to take off into the sky and get the wind and sunlight on my skin and to finally catch my breath. But I was missing wings, so a saddle and a fast horse would have to do.

I managed to skirt around the guards, who seemed mostly to ignore me anyway, and took a garden door out of the palace. The gardens were horribly neglected and overgrown, grasses thigh high, but there were still flowers blooming in the midst of all the chaos—roses overtaking trellises and magic lilies peeking shyly around sapling trees. I found a route, feathered grasses clinging to my skirt and leaving seeds behind as I followed stepping stones over to a break in the hedge. The stables were on the other side, down a gravel path and on a plateau below the outcrop the palace was perched on.

I moved as quietly and quickly as I could, half expecting Guard Stark to appear unexpectedly. I'd never lived much of my life outside of observation. There were always servants on hand in the capital, always someone watching under the guise of being helpful. I'd learned how to slip around corners at a young age, to lose the tail of a watchful guard, but my freedom usually only lasted for a handful of minutes, maybe an hour if I was lucky.

As I approached the stables, it seemed I'd have even less than that. There was a low masculine murmur from inside, likely a groomsmen I hadn't come across. I tiptoed up to the wide open doors and then paused, a slow smile stretching across my lips. Former groomsmen, as it turned out.

"Yes, you are sweet, aren't you?" Owen murmured, brushing down the length of my gray gelding's back inside of its stall. "Just like your princess. She's as lucky to have a horse like you as we are to have a princess like her."

The horse snickered and danced in place, and Owen laughed, cheeks full with his smile.

"I think you do her justice just fine," Owen said with a dip of his head, as if the two were carrying on a conversation. "I'll have to take some notes, won't I? Don't want to disappoint someone as perfect as her."

It was like being struck in the stomach, nearly bowling me over in one great burst of heat and...and a *clench* of need. My feet were moving before I knew what was in my head, and Owen looked up from the gelding at my rapid approach.

"Just thought they could use a little company," Owen said, his smile even brighter for me than it had been for the horse. My blood flashed in my veins, a spark to fuel.

The stall door was open and I reached inside, grabbing Owen's free hand and yanking him towards me. The brush in his hand clattered to the floor, and my gelding huffed as Owen came stumbling over, our chests crashing together. I was high on my toes, arms around his neck, when he caught on. He lifted me from the dusty floor and up into his hold as our lips slanted over one another.

I was starving, desperate, *aching*. I needed *Owen*. Not touch or kisses or sex in general, but *this* man specifically. His flavor on my tongue, his brittle moan caught in our kiss, his dense arms squeezing me tighter. He stumbled, and my back hit the gate of an empty stall, our hips pressing closer together. I dug my fingers through his unruly dark hair, clutching the strands in my fist as I licked my way into his mouth and rolled my hips into his.

"Bryony," he gasped, drawing away with wide eyes.

"I'm *very* curious. I need you badly," I answered, leaning in again and scratching my teeth over his jaw as I used his own words from days ago. His skin was smooth now, although I knew by nightfall it'd be scratchy and coarse again, and he tasted like salt on his neck and cloves on his lips.

Owen groaned and shuddered, his nose pressing into the corner of my jaw, breath panting and warming my throat. "Are you—"

"Owen, please," I said, and even though I was begging, I was also pushing on his shoulders, trying to drive him to his knees.

So this was what *knowing* felt like. I didn't care where my hands went, or if anyone else was nearby, I just had to have Owen against me, the weight and strength of him, his sweetness as he gazed at me.

Owen's left arm tightened around me and he pulled the gate open, falling into the stall with me, pushing me into the far corner where no one would see us if they walked into the stable. He was hunched, mouthing down my throat as I scratched and tugged at his loose shirt, pulling the collar back so I could slide my hands beneath to touch his skin.

"Quick then?" Owen asked, voice ragged.

"Like you promised." I'd been thinking about Owen's mouth on my sex since he'd pulled away three mornings ago, and what had seemed awkward and too personal to me at the time was now intensely fascinating to me. I had to know how it would feel.

He had to bend to kiss my collarbone, and he plucked at the buttons of my blouse, opening the collar and pushing it down over my shoulders, the callouses of his hands scratching at my skin. I moaned, my arms slightly trapped against my sides, as he sucked along the top of my corset.

"Can I...?" He tugged at the top of the corset, and I arched for him, pressing my breasts up to the edge.

My breaths were getting high and quick, little whimpering sighs snagging in my throat. Owen's thumb slipped under fabric, pulling one breast free and up to his mouth for him to suck at the tip. My knees shook, and his arm slid down to my hips to hold me in place. The corset was a tight pressure on the under-side of my breast, but also stimulating, the ache soothed by the silky swipes of his tongue on my skin and the suction of his lips.

"Owen," I whined, holding his face to me. He drifted to the

other side, repeating the gesture and exposing my wet breast to cool air until my nipple pebbled. "No more, I need..."

He pulled away with a pop and lowered himself to his knees in a mess of old hay. "You need my mouth on your perfect cunt like I promised?" he asked, blinking those big dark eyes of his up at me, curls mussed over his forehead.

I swallowed hard and every inch of me was over sensitive, thrumming with a need to be touched everywhere and all at once. My pulse was pounding in my veins, in my nipples, in my *cunt* as he'd called it. I nodded and sighed as Owen leaned forward, nuzzling into my skirt. He bit into the fabric, catching my mound with a dull and playful pressure, and my legs nearly crumpled beneath me.

"Do you want to lift your skirt so you can watch, or for me to slip under it?" Owen asked, grinning up at me, rolling his chin against my sex. Just that little gesture made me pang and ache and want to cry for more.

I pulled my skirt up in great wads and then frowned when I realized I wouldn't be able to touch Owen. But I would rather be able to see him, to watch as he sat down on his heels and dipped his head to kiss my knees, ignoring my exposed sex as he worked back and forth up my legs.

"You said quick," I breathed, pulling my skirt a little higher so I could touch my own breasts now that they were out.

Owen laughed, and strands of his hair skimmed over my mound as he continued his path of soft kisses up the tops of my thighs. His hand reached up and petted between my legs, his brow furrowing as he touched my lips and found them damp. I moaned and my head fell back, thumping against the walls of the stable, my hips jerking into his touch as he trailed them back and forth, up and down, coating every inch of me in my own arousal.

"Please, Owen. Please. Please. Please, you said—" I broke off with a cry as his hand gripped my right thigh and threw it over his shoulder, his mouth immediately replacing his fingers.

My eyes flashed wide at the first soft lap of his tongue. It was so light but almost *feverish* against me, and Owen pressed in deeper, humming at my taste and quickly returning for more. The pang and clench of need that had struck me when I'd watched him brushing my gelding didn't abate as he kissed and sucked and feasted on my sex—it only grew stronger, winding me up tight and making me beg for more.

Owen groaned, and his free shoulder pressed to the inside of my thigh, forcing me to wiggle my balancing foot and give him more room. His tongue became urgent against me, thrusting as he suckled, probing lightly at my entrance and making me gasp and squeeze my hands on my breasts.

The pulse in my veins grew louder, deeper, galloping with every nudge of Owen's lips and tongue. I was losing control of myself, my hips riding over his mouth, but Owen only moaned and encouraged me, his hands squeezing tight on the back of my thighs. A tickling, racing, powerful sensation ran up and down my spine, my voice high and aching and crying out to Owen.

Here was the familiar edge I'd met before, the grip on my own flesh and the fabric failing as my hands began to spasm. Owen laughed as my skirt fell around him like a curtain, but it didn't deter him. He moved his lips to the top of the crease of my sex, parting the flesh and sucking over a lightning sensitive nerve.

"Owen, yes!"

My hands slid over the wall behind me, too weak and clumsy to find purchase. I crashed as Owen dipped a thick finger inside of me, teasing me in two places as thunder roared through me, swallowing me under. Energy rushed through me, needle pricks coating my skin before flying away from me like sparks off a log. I shook through the wave, pleading, and Owen sucked once more before reappearing from beneath my skirt, slowly guiding me down to his lap.

His chin was shining with slick release. Actually, the whole room was shining, the stable taking on a hazy golden glow. His finger was still inside me, pumping through the soft flutters.

"Better?" he asked.

I opened my mouth to say 'yes' and then realized that my whole body was tense. I wanted to push Owen down into the hay and tear away his clothes and *ride* him into another immediate release. The hollow clench seized inside of me, taking my muscles in a tight grip and making me cry out.

Owen leaned in, kissing my throat. "What is it? What's wrong."

"I need...I need your cock," I gasped, grinding down onto his hand, searching for more. "Please, Owen."

My big, lovely, sweet Chosen pulled back, brow folding. "Bryony...I'm not sure we should—"

The heaviness under my skin, the drumming pulse, the painful clench all compounded together, and the demand slipped out of my lips as I dug my fingers into Owen's shoulders.

"Fuck me, Owen Dunne."

The stables weren't golden at all now, but a deep and shimmering red, and Owen's brow smoothed, his gaze going blank. He rolled, tipping me into the prickly bed of hay beneath us and rising up to his knees, pulling at the buckle of his belt.

My skirt had flipped up with the movement, and Owen was quick to yank down his pants, but it was his eyes I was fixated on. That blank stare. I knew that stare. It was the look of Camellia's Chosen, and sometimes even my mother's.

Owen grunted, pulling on his stiff cock and then started to bend down.

"Wait!" I pressed my hands to his shoulders, and Owen paused obediently, unblinking. I shuddered and closed my eyes, trying to push away the power racing through me.

The Hunger. This wasn't desire, this was *magic*.

I possessed the Hunger, or rather in this case it had possessed me.

Owen groaned above me, and I pulled my hands off him as if he'd caught fire, pushing them down into the hay. His cock was out and weeping profusely. He shivered as I released him, his stare still distant.

"Oh, I'm sorry," I whispered, trying to wrestle back the Hunger. I leaned forward and rested my forehead against Owen's shoulder. "Owen, I'm sorry, I'm sorry."

In their stalls, horses whinnied, and the stable seemed to groan and shiver before going silent. The pressure that'd been riding me vanished, and all I was left with was weak and trembly nerves and the soft pound of pleasure burning slowly away from my cunt.

"I'm so sorry."

Owen puffed and shook himself, and then his arms circled me. I stiffened as his lips pressed to the top of my head.

"Bryony, what's wrong?" Owen murmured. "What—What's happened? Are you alright?"

I gasped and wrestled myself upright, throwing myself against his chest, ignoring the tangle of my skirts and the disassembled drop of his pants in favor of wrapping myself around the man.

"I...I have the Hunger. I used it on you, I didn't mean to! I'm sorry!" I shook, and Owen squeezed me tight.

"Shhh, it's all right, Mistress. It's all right."

13.
BRYONY

Neither Owen or I mentioned what had taken place to any of the others. We took a lunch together out on the deck, staying mostly quiet. Owen kept me close, leaving kisses on my shoulders and running his fingers over my curls.

The Hunger didn't return.

When nightfall came and a slightly stilted dinner was over with, Owen exchanged brief words with Cosmo, and then escorted me up to the bedroom we'd been sharing. I wasn't sure what he'd said, but it left us alone together for the night.

There was a tap on the screen of the washroom, and I stiffened in the tub and then forced myself to relax. "Yes?"

"Can I come join you?"

I brushed my soapy hands over the surface of the bubbly water as I considered Owen's offer. The tub was big enough for two, although it'd be a squeeze. That didn't sound unpleasant, just intimate, and I was full of jagged nerves. But Owen...

"Yes, join me."

Owen moved quickly into the small space, lit only by a set of candles in the windowsill. He flashed me a quick and careful smile before pulling his shirt off over his head and stripping out of his pants and underwear in two quick steps. I'd seen him more or less naked before, the morning of my choosing, but it was so different now. He wasn't just beautiful to look at. I wanted to touch him, to learn the ways we fit together, to be entirely surrounded by him.

I pushed myself to one side of the tub and Owen slid in on the other, his knees breaking through the bubbles and his feets resting against my bottom as he faced me.

"Did what happened in the stable happen too soon?" Owen asked, leaning forward. He ignored washing himself, and my hands itched with the impulse to do the work for him.

"I—no! No, it wasn't too soon," I said, blushing and swishing water in his direction to lap at his chest. "It's just that I didn't realize the Hunger would *force* you to..." I swallowed and shook my head when words failed me.

Owen hummed and his arms stretched, hands circling my wrists. "What happened? That part is foggy. I just remember having you on my tongue and listening to you shout my name," he said, grinning.

He tugged on one of my wrists and I laughed, ducking my head and letting him pull me through the water to cuddle against his chest.

"It was like...it was as if it wasn't enough," I said. "Which it *was*. It was wonderful! I've never..." I looked up and Owen's smile was warm, his eyes a little hooded with interest. "And I told you I wanted to..."

"My cock," he said, eyebrows jumping. His grin grew even prouder in that moment. "I just remembered. You said you needed my cock."

"And you said no, and then I *told* you to and you just sort of... you disappeared. It was like you were unconscious but just obeying orders."

Owen hummed and settled us deeper in the water, pulling me closer and pressing a kiss to my forehead. "It's a bit fuzzy, but I remember just feeling a...like I was about to burst with wanting to be inside you. Which, I mean, I am generally," he said, laughing. "I definitely was while I was tasting you. I only said no because I'm...I'm kind of big, and I'm a little bit worried about hurting you. Not sure I'm the best choice for your first...you know."

I blinked, and then my eyes widened. My first cock. Owen *was* the biggest of my Chosen.

"You think it might hurt?" I asked, resting a hand over his steady heartbeat.

"It might, if we don't take enough time to ready you. But

there's lots we can do first, and it'll all feel good for both of us," Owen said. He leaned back to grin at me, and then his brow furrowed, a wet hand reaching up out of the water and his fingertip running down the length of my nose. "What's wrong?"

"What if the Hunger comes back and I force you to do something?"

Owen's nose and mouth scrunched up. "Not sure there's much you could tell me to do I wouldn't want to anyway."

I huffed and fought my smile. "Owen! I don't want to have sex with someone who's being forced by my magic. I want to have sex with *you*. I want to see this smile while it's happening," I said, tracing said smile with my own touch, giggling as Owen nipped at my fingers. "I want to control the Hunger, not have it control you."

"Fair enough, I'd want the same for you," Owen murmured.

And as much as I feared a repeat of what had happened in the stables, I couldn't resist the impulse to stretch, my chest pressing to Owen's as I arched up for a kiss. I moaned and shivered in the warm water as he kissed my mouth the same way he had my sex, with licks and nibbles and the vibration of his own groan. When I tried to pull away, Owen held me in place with one hand splayed on my bare back, his nose nuzzling mine.

"What if—"

"You can't learn to control the Hunger if you don't test it a little bit, right?" Owen whispered, nipping at my lips. "Like I said, there's lots we can do with our hands and mouths that will feel just as good. When you want to touch, try and think of it as practice."

I *had* been able to push the Hunger away when I'd realized what had happened. As quick as the power came on, I'd managed to clear my head and stop it from completely taking over.

I turned and pressed myself to the side of the tub, lips quirking as I scooped up handfuls of water and then poured them over Owen's chest. "And if I want to practice touching now?" He reached for me and I grinned, pushing his hands back. "I said touching. Not being touched."

Owen's eyebrows jumped. "I'm not sure a Chosen's priority is being touched."

"I think it's up to his mistress to decide that," I said, lifting my chin.

Owen grinned and sighed, his arms rising to the edges of the tub, water beading and rolling off the muscular limbs. He leaned back and closed his eyes. "Then I am at your disposal, Mistress."

I grinned and squirmed, drinking him in, gazing down at the distorted length of him under the water. Perhaps if I focused on Owen's pleasure, I wouldn't lose control to my own. Either way, it would be fun to explore the terrain of a man. I pushed his legs to either side of the tub and knelt in the water between them, reaching for the soap and oil and cloth I'd used to wash myself, my hands and eyes already greedy at the beautiful display of Owen in front of me.

I would take my time, even if the water grew cool before I was done.

❦

THE BED DIPPED and I opened my eyes to see Cosmo, fully dressed and leaning toward me on the mattress.

"Hello, beautiful," he said, smiling, but his eyes remained tight. "I don't mean to barge in—"

"Don't worry about that," I said, wiggling out from under Owen's heavy arm and sitting up.

I'd had my fun in the tub, then a little more once Owen was dried on the bed, and I learned how to handle his cock until it had suddenly spurt and made me jump and laugh at the suddenness. I'd never seen a man come outside of a woman before, but aside from the mess, it'd been beautiful to watch him fall apart. Owen and I had both dressed before finally resting, and I hadn't let him take his own turn with me, still a little nervous about the Hunger coming back and taking over.

Cosmo sat up and his eyes moved leisurely over me, expression relaxing. "You didn't mind me missing last night?"

"Mmm, no, although...I might need your advice later," I said, picking at the embroidery on my nightgown and wondering what Cosmo would think of the predicament of my powers.

He laughed and shrugged. "That's sure to be an interesting conversation, but I'm happy to help. For now, I came because Guard Stark is detaining Aric at the gate."

"What?!"

Owen grunted as I nearly kicked him in my scramble to get out of bed. Cosmo scooped me up, lifting me off the mattress and setting me on my feet before I raced away, grabbing my robe and tying it around myself.

"You don't want to dress?" Cosmo asked as I hurried for the door.

"No, this will do. Why is he detaining Aric?" I asked.

"Because Aric is a thief," Cosmo answered, following me and taking my hand to help me balance as I tried to jump into my boots. "Stark's probably familiar with his reputation. Aric's not alone. There's a woman with him I didn't recognize from this far. Not Rebecca Sanders through."

"Why—never mind, I should've warned Stark about Aric, I suppose," I huffed.

"Aric probably thought he was clever enough to get in the palace without bothering with the guards. Don't worry, Stark probably won't behead him before we get down there."

"Cosmo!"

Cosmo laughed as I rushed into the hall, trying to comb through my tangles with one hand and braid my hair with the other.

"I was only joking, Bryony," Cosmo called to my back. I made it to the grand staircase, my hand taking the wide railing as I flew down the twisting steps.

"If Aric speaks to the royal guard the way he speaks to me, you might be right though," I answered in a shout.

Cosmo grunted in response, his own steps quick behind mine. I headed straight when I reached the bottom of the stairs, racing for the long entrance hall that led to the front stairs. When I was nearly to the door, I saw the gleam of armor on the drive outside, and the dark, hooded figures behind hauled between guards.

I threw myself at the front doors, groaning with the effort to push them open and then paused on the top step, realizing my hair was half braided and half tangled and that I was in a delicate nightgown and a billowing silk robe. So be it.

"Guard Stark, release them," I shouted down to the drive.

I couldn't pick my head guard out of the group at first, too caught by the lift of Aric's face and his stare finding me at the top of the steps, eyes widening a little. It was a woman with him, and she was beautiful, even in the ragged cloak. She had vivid red hair and she was as tall as Aric, dressed in simple pants and several layers of tops fastened by a belt. Stark was at her back, holding her arms behind her and marching her forward.

"Princess, this man is a rogue and this woman—"

"Guard Stark that man is a member of my Chosen," I said, giving up my shout as they neared. Cosmo finally reached me, and he took my hand as we moved down the uneven steps.

"A—he's *what?*" Stark called, his grip on the woman slipping. She pulled her arms free and stepped out of his reach but didn't move further away.

"Aric Martin is one of my Chosen," I said, and I didn't miss the surprise on the woman's face, or the struggle on her face as she fought against her own laughter. I also didn't miss the simmering irritation on Aric's. "And being Chosen, any arrest, punishment, or imprisonment would be at *my* discretion."

If looks could've killed, I might've been twice dead in that moment, both Aric and Cresswell Stark's stares glowering up at me.

"He was trespassing in the woods," Stark said, hanging by threads onto his argument.

"He has an open invitation here," I answered. "The woods included. My apologies, Miss..."

The redheaded woman's lips pursed, and her eyes were narrow with amusement. "Griffin, no Miss."

"Griffin," I said, dipping my head. She wobbled and then settled on a bow instead of a curtsey. I turned to Aric, who was now smirking at Cresswell Stark. "Aric. Please, both of you come in. We'll speak over breakfast."

Aric took the stairs two at a time, and Griffin's steps were just as quick. I met Cosmo's eyes as I turned away from the disappointed guards.

"Don't laugh or I'll laugh," I whispered, and Cosmo's grin flashed before he leaned in, catching my lips in a quick kiss.

"Your hair is rioting," Cosmo murmured against me and then jumped away before I could pinch him.

I SPARED myself just enough time for our breakfast to be rerouted to the greenhouse, and for me to comb my hair and put on a proper dress. Griffin was at the iron table, drinking rich coffee from a tea cup and picking at a slice of bacon. Aric was moving around the greenhouse, examining the remains of the plants and the ones who had survived the many years of neglect.

"This would've been a good collection for a magician's stores," Aric said, crouching with his back to me.

Cosmo had gone back to speak to Guard Stark, to remind the man that his studio supplies would be arriving and to please not detain the cart. I'd told Owen to occupy Wendell and Thao if they left their room. Thao liked to antagonize Aric and vice versa, and I wasn't in the mood to referee.

"I'm hoping I might be able to rescue some of what's here," I said, and Aric startled and stood, Griffin slurping her coffee, her eyes bouncing between us. "I apologize for the manner of your arrival. I should've thought to give the guards better instructions for visitors."

Aric didn't respond, and it was Griffin who cleared her throat and sat up in her chair. "No harm done, Your Highness."

Neither man or woman bowed to me at my entrance. In Aric's case it was clear defiance, but with Griffin, it seemed more like a test. I moved to the table, picking up the coffee pot and refilling her cup before choosing one for myself.

"You must be Aric's recommendation for a royal hunter," I said, taking a seat and eyeing the woman out the corner of my eye.

She was older than me, maybe in her thirties instead of twenties, and she appeared equal parts athletic and feminine, the belt tight around a small waist and her pants hugging around full hips. There was a whisper of gray braided back into her red hair, but her face was smooth and ageless.

"I am a hunter. And I'd gladly hunt in the royal woods knowing that my catch went to the citizens," Griffin said slowly, watching me with equal interest.

I nodded. "I suppose civil hunter might be a better term."

Griffin straightened and looked at Aric lurking in the overgrown bushes and wilted remains of the background. "Yes, I...I like that. As for how to get the meat to the people..."

Aric cleared his throat and stepped forward. "I've spoken with some of the taverns in and around Rumsbrooke. If Griffin will bring us the meat, we'll stretch it enough to make free meals to serve."

"I wanted to call them princess dinners, but Aric growled at me," Griffin said, grinning and snapping on her slice of bacon as he demonstrated the sound. "Yes. Just like that."

"I think I'd rather avoid that name as well," I said, taking a drink of my coffee to hide the warmth in my cheeks. "But I like the premise. Call it whatever suits. What will you want for your commission? Until I'm able to take back Sir Hubert's debts to the palace, we are being careful with the funds that remain, but I think we should be able to—"

"Your Highness, you've waived taxes and you're asking me to assist you in feeding your people in a way that requires no cost to them. I volunteer to do the work," Griffin said quickly.

"You should be paid for your time," I said.

Griffin's smile was faint. "I think any other royal would say the position was an honor."

I sat up straight just as Aric muttered something under his breath. "I'm not any other royal," I said. "If you won't take coin as payment, at least take a small commission of the meat."

"Don't argue with her, Griff, you won't win," Aric said.

I whipped to glare at him. "I hope this is a lesson you plan on learning for yourself."

Griffin's laugh was bright and cheerful, and she rose quickly from the table, finishing her coffee and grabbing a small quiche in her palm. "If no one minds, I'd like to walk the woods a little to get a better understanding of what's available and where I might start."

"Of course," I said, and Aric grunted. He had a pie of his own in hand, and I hadn't even seen him come close enough to the table to take it.

Griffin left the greenhouse, and Aric turned to me. "She'll do?"

"Yes, I like her," I said.

"She liked you too," Aric said, and then he nodded once and turned for the door.

"Aric. I'm...I'm sorry for claiming you in front of the guard. It was the first thing I thought of," I said.

Aric rolled back on his heels, raising the hand holding the pie up to his lips to catch a crumb on his tongue. Sunlight was falling through the moldy windows of the greenhouse, landing on his blade sharp cheekbones.

"It's true that I can't be imprisoned unless you say so?" Aric asked, smirking a little.

"Yes, but it doesn't mean I won't give the order if I think you deserve it," I said, narrowing my eyes.

Aric laughed, and then he moved to take Griffin's seat, pouring himself a new cup of coffee. "I don't doubt that, princess."

"What is... Do you know what kind of shifter she is?" I asked, scooting forward in my seat.

"Mm, red hawk, I think. Haven't seen for myself. Kimmery's shifters aren't so bold as your Prince Thao," Aric said. "But his transformation is a secret process the Mennarian royals keep for themselves."

I'd heard that the tiger gene in Mennary was exclusive to the royals, not that it was a process, but I trusted Aric to know his magic. "And Kimmery's shifters?"

"Northern blood," Aric said, shrugging. "I've always assumed it might be a mineral that gets into the water and affects babes pre-birth. It's more common away from the wealthier homes so..."

"So less likely to occur in families drinking wine and water that's been cleaned and treated," I said, and Aric nodded. "And the Hunger is..."

"The Hunger is exclusive to the women of your family," Aric said, frowning. "Perhaps it's growing weaker since you don't seem to share it with your sister."

Oh. I hadn't... Well, of course I hadn't *told* Aric about the Hunger finally rearing its head. I wasn't likely to be telling Aric about what I was doing with Owen in the stable regardless. And now I found I didn't want to. Aric might know more about magic than anyone else I could speak to, but whatever trust he had in me was due to the fact that we'd believed I was *missing* the Hunger. Now that I knew what the power was really capable of, I was less apt to trust myself too. I'd felt the stirrings of Hunger while toying with Owen the night before, but it was less distinguishable from everyday desire.

"How long do you plan on continuing the charade of Hunger and Chosen and the like?" Aric asked, watching me too closely for my comfort in the moment.

"Until I've secured the crown and I know that my grandmother won't talk my mother into passing it to Camellia," I said, squaring my shoulders. That'd been true before it had shown up, at least.

Aric leaned into the arm of the chair, and my eyes snagged on the elegant perch of his fingers as his head tilted into his hand. "Have you heard from the council?"

"Not yet. I'll have to reach out perhaps," I said.

"See how much they let you get away with first," Aric said, smiling lightly. "If you ignore them, you can act without the pretense of wanting their approval. Save diplomacy for when it's called on."

Footsteps approached, and we both looked up as Cosmo entered. "Hello, Aric."

"Pianetta," Aric said with a dip of his head. He sighed and pushed up from his seat. "I should get back to the city before the vultures circle my crown."

"Is King of Thieves a much sought after title?" I asked, wanting to delay Aric a little longer.

He shrugged. "I have my rivals, same as you. At least mine aren't blood."

I chewed over that unpleasant truth as Aric saw himself out and Cosmo joined me for quiche and coffee.

14.
COSMO

I wasn't usually jealous with my lovers, and to be fair, Bryony wasn't rightly my lover, but I watched her fiddling with Owen's hands idly with a bitter kind of fondness. They stood together by the window of my studio, picturesque and sweet. She was easy with me, but she and Owen kept near constant physical contact with one another for the past couple days. If I was more keen on painting, I would've asked them to pose for me.

"So...you do have the Hunger?" I asked.

Bryony nodded shyly, and Owen flipped his hand and squeezed hers reassuringly.

"And it's like a force of desire?"

"It forces desire," Bryony muttered.

"No, the desire was there," Owen said softly, ducking his head and bumping it to hers before looking up at me. "But I don't really remember what happened when it hit, and Bryony said it was like she was controlling me."

"Which I don't want," Bryony said.

Owen grinned and shrugged. "And I'd really rather remember everything that happens between us."

I laughed and nodded, swallowing hard around the envious stab in my throat. I would've felt the same if there'd been anything happening with Bryony other than the occasional kiss, always initiated by me.

"If this is all the Hunger is, I would've rather continued not having it," Bryony said with a sigh. She slid off the bench by the window, leaving Owen behind as she came to watch me. "What are you making?"

"I hadn't really decided," I admitted, wrinkling my nose at the block of clay waiting for me at the center of my workspace.

"How do you decide?" Bryony asked, the distraction from our conversation on her powers leaving her mood brighter.

"I usually only buy supplies when I'm inspired. I thought I might try it the other way around for once, but maybe that was a mistake."

"You're not inspired?"

I turned to look at her, the swell of her breasts at the collar of her dress, the tiny pinch of her waist from her corset. I could imagine the curve of her full hips under the sway of her skirt, painfully familiar with their shape as they nestled against me at night.

"My muse is shy of being admired," I said as Bryony began to turn pink beneath my stare.

She feigned pushing her hair away from her face, pressed the back of her hand against her warm cheek, and fought her smile. "Not of being admired, but maybe of being put on display," she said softly.

My heart thumped, and I nodded. I could relate to that, I preferred being the observer rather than the other way around. Bryony was a strong princess, determined to rule, and it was obviously not for the glory of recognition. The thump of my heart turned into a pang, and when I reached for her, she came willingly, pressing into my chest and wrapping her arms around my waist as I stretched mine around her shoulders.

"Private sketches sometime," I whispered, trying to stamp down my desire to *push* when she gasped against my throat and her breath cascaded damply down my neck.

"All right," she breathed. "For now...how is Owen for inspiration?"

I blinked and stared over to where Owen was stretched out over the bench Bryony had vacated, ready to nap. I'd noticed how beautiful he was, a fact almost disguised by his easy going and simple nature. Almost, but not quite. If Owen had been a model in my studio, I definitely would've attempted a seduction. He seemed wholly Bryony's now, but if she was willing to share...

"Owen, how would you feel about posing for me?" I called. "Just sketches to start."

"Happy to," he said.

"Naked," Bryony called, and I laughed at her wicked grin.

Owen opened one eye and tilted his head to stare at us, cheeks swelling with a smile. "Fine," he said with a shrug.

"Go and find something to read to us while we work," I whispered to Bryony, holding her tight to add, "Nothing too inspiring. There's a fine line between art and pornography."

Bryony laughed and ran away, skirt flying behind her as she left the room, both of us watching her back as she went.

Owen stood from the bench and crossed to me, pulling the hem of his shirt out from the waistband of his pants. I moved to find my sheets of parchment, pinning it to a board on my easel.

"How big are you?" Owen asked.

I hissed as I struck my own thumb with a pin, distracted by Owen's question. "Wha—Big? What do you mean?"

Owen waggled his eyebrows and looked down at his own crotch. "You know."

"Oh! Um..." My brow furrowed, and my face heated. What did he want me to do? Show him?

"I'm afraid of hurting Bryony. I don't think I should be her first," Owen said. "Otherwise, I'd be trying a little harder to help her get over this Hunger thing."

"Shouldn't it be Bryony who decides that though?" I asked, trying to focus on my work instead of the wild questions running through my head.

"Well, yes. But she already likes you. Don't worry about giving us so much privacy."

I hummed. I'd slept on the couch in the studio last night for their sake. If Owen was comfortable with it, I'd be more than happy to return to Bryony's bed.

"What about children? Does she want to get pregnant?" I asked, frowning. I wasn't sure I was ready to be a father now that I thought of it.

Owen shrugged. "She says her family's fertility is supposed to do with the kingdom, not children. Lots of sex, very few pregnancies."

"I don't think that should be relied on," I murmured, although it made sense. It was rare for there to be two princesses of the queen's line. I'd just assumed that had to do with some kind of contraception. "I'll talk to her about it. Bertha Umber makes a tea for some women that helps prevent, just in case."

Owen finished undressing, kicking his clothes to the side and stretching with a total lack of self-consciousness that made me smile. "What should I do?"

"Hmm, just move around a bit for now. I'll sketch a few poses before I make up my mind."

Bryony came rushing back a moment later, three books cradled in her arms and color high in her cheeks. She grinned at the sight of Owen stretched and naked in the center of the room, but came directly to my side.

"Will I be in your way if I watch you work?"

I shook my head. "Between Owen's form and your voice in my ear, I will be perfectly inspired," I said.

Bryony beamed at me and slid the books onto a safe spot on my table before reaching out and tugging me closer by a button-hole on my open vest. I stumbled against her and Bryony rose to her toes, pressing her lips to my chin, my mouth, and my nose in quick succession. When she made to return for a second kiss, I didn't hesitate.

My hands snatched at her waist and I tilted my head, licking at the seam of her mouth, sucking on her bottom lip when she parted them for me. She hummed, leaning into me, and victory was like lightning running through me. This kiss was hers to grant and twice as sweet for it. Bryony's arms slid over my shoulders as I held her against me, my hands moving down to cup her ass and pin her hips against mine. She was perfect, an exact fit against me, her head tilted back and body surrendering in my arms.

When her hands clutched at my shoulder blades, magic struck, dizzying me. Bryony froze and I held still, my teeth gripping her lip.

"There," I whispered, pulling away slightly so I could see her eyes. They were wide with shock and worry. "It's all right. I'm still here. The Hunger?"

"Yes," Bryony said, barely forcing the word out as if she was too afraid to move.

"Can you let it go?"

Her brow furrowed, and she breathed slowly out, sinking down from her toes to stand fully. She nodded and I ducked, nipping at her jaw and then over her throat. Bryony moaned, and her hands cupped my shoulders, debating on whether to pull me in or push me away.

"Back?" I asked. Owen was moving closer out of the corner of my eye, watching us. Bryony nodded as I licked over her pulse, tasting violets on her skin. "Push it away again."

She sighed and sagged in my arms.

"See? You control it." I kissed her jaw again and then stood straight, smiling down at her. "Owen is right. We just need to practice."

Bryony's smile was tenuous, but Owen and I looked at one another, equally smug. Our princess hungered for us. That was an enviable position to be in.

15.
BRYONY

"**Y**our Highness, I have made a discovery," Cresswell Stark announced, pausing in the doorway of Cosmo's studio, his eyes growing wide at the sight in front of him.

Owen was holding a complicated pose, his hips thrust forward as he lunged, chest back and hand pressed gallantly over his heart. Cosmo said he was meant to look as though he was swooning for me, or professing his love. Except I'd been in the middle of reading an intense and sensual scene in a book so Owen's cock was slightly hard, bobbing in the air in front of him.

My court *was* starting to look a little like the capital, I realized. I hoped someone reported it to my grandmother.

"A discovery," I repeated.

"Uhh err, yes. A... We've found boats for the ponds behind the palace. Only one is water safe, but one of my men used to be a shipwright so he says he can have the others ready. I just thought you might be..." He trailed off, staring at Owen for a moment before frowning and shaking his head. "Bored, or—"

"I could do with a break from this position," Owen said, his eyes turning to us. "And I wouldn't mind getting back to the stables to check on the horses."

It was our third day in the studio. Cosmo had made a beautiful, small model of Owen in a relaxed stance the day before, but he was less impressed with his own work than I was. I thought it might be a good time to get him away from the project before he got frustrated with himself.

Cosmo set down his pencil and nodded before spinning to me. "What do you say to a picnic on the water with me?"

I grinned and slid down from my perch, nodding. "That

sounds lovely. I've been wanting to see the grounds behind the palace."

Cosmo rolled up his sleeves, now dusted with dark marks from his drawings, and Owen groaned as he stood straight.

"Thank you, Guard Stark. That was thoughtful of you to bring us the news," I said, offering the man a smile.

He was out of his armor, dressed in a well-tailored uniform, and his spine straightened, eyes flicking back and forth between the three of us. "I could...I could accompany you, if you like, Your Highness."

I waved the offer away. "No, that won't be necessary. Cosmo and I will manage fine, and I'm sure no unexpected guests will appear from the pond."

Cosmo tucked his chuckle behind his hand, and Cresswell Stark delivered a stiff bow. "I'll tell the kitchens to pack a basket."

He left, and I frowned at where he'd stood in the doorway, wondering why I felt as though I'd disappointed him in some way.

"He seems very helpful," I mused. Owen and Cosmo both chuckled, and I turned to them. "What? What is it?"

"Bryony, I think he'd like it if you made him one of your Chosen," Cosmo said.

"Or at least if you let him rock your boat," Owen added, grinning and jumping into his trousers.

I scoffed and shook my head, even though I knew they might be right. A place as Chosen was considered to be coveted...if you weren't already in love with someone...or if you weren't Aric. *Aric might already be in love with someone. Like Griffin. Or Rebecca Sanders.*

"Come on," Cosmo murmured, taking my hand. "We can have as smooth or as rocky a ride as we please together."

I'd seen some of the lower grounds from the windows—heavy willows hanging over the water, brushing against lily pads, over-grown rose bushes, and iris blooming amongst the weeds. Some-one, I'd missed who, had already begun to cut away the tall grasses that'd been left to run rampant in the palace's abandonment, and there was a wide path available that ran down to the shore.

The little maid who sometimes helped lace me into my corsets and dresses came jogging out from the low kitchen doors, bringing an over-full basket of fruit and sandwiches and cheeses.

"Just be careful of any geese. They can be rude when they get a whiff of food," she warned us.

The guards were quick, or Cosmo was right and Cresswell had been hoping to accompany me on the boat ride, because it was there on the edge of the water, floating with its oars waiting inside and two cushions likely stolen from within the palace.

"You don't mind me coming and not Owen?" Cosmo asked softly.

I clutched at his arm, waiting for him to look up and meet my eyes. "Why would you expect that to be the case?"

Cosmo's smile was wry. "You are...partial to him." He set his foot down on the edge of the boat, holding it steady for me to step inside, before passing me the basket.

I settled into the seat at the prow, mulling over his words. "I like you both, very much. Owen is a little more forward than you."

Cosmo's eyebrows rose, and he climbed into the belly of the boat. "Noted," he said, taking an oar and using it to push us away from shore.

"Not that I need you to be more like Owen," I rushed to say. "Just that maybe he's given me more opportunities to grow my feelings for him." I grimaced and shook my head, wishing I could erase the whole comparison between one man and the other.

"That's true," Cosmo said, without seeming offended. "Owen knew he wanted to be Chosen, that he would share your attention with others."

"Does it bother you?" I asked, watching him as he settled the oars into their holders and began to row us out from under the cover of a willow and into the sunshine.

"No, I think I was just waiting for you to come to me," Cosmo said with a shrug. "Especially after you tore away the first night. I didn't want you to feel uncomfortable again."

I hummed and leaned carefully forward, watching Cosmo's smile stretch as he mirrored me, our mouths grazing briefly.

"My patience bears good fruit," Cosmo murmured, nose nudging against mine before he leaned back and rowed.

I turned my own attention to the basket of food, gradually trading places with it so I could sit on the cushion at Cosmo's knees. "Are you hungry?" I asked, unwrapping a sandwich from paper.

"Muse, if you're asking if you can feed me, I am starving," Cosmo said, his voice dropping.

I bit my smile and raised the food up for him to lean down and take a bite, his teeth nipping at my fingers and dark eyes shining.

"Mm, now, where are we traveling?" Cosmo asked as I took my own bite.

I sat up and stared around the lake and its slight arch. Behind us sat the palace, and ahead of us looked like briars on the shore of another wood. There were willows all to the right, but on the left there was a stone archway and a narrow tunnel leading to more water.

"Can we explore?" I asked, pointing in the tunnel's direction.

"Of course!"

I fed Cosmo as he rowed, trying not to shy away from his stare as he licked the ends of my fingers, cleaning away crumbs or dripping juice. He paused his rowing once to catch my hand, lifting it to his mouth and licking a rivulet of strawberry juice from my palm to the tip of my thumb, sucking the digit and swirling his tongue around the tip. My breath caught as Hunger surged inside of me, biting and begging for more touch.

"Your pupils get very wide when it hits," Cosmo murmured, releasing my hand and returning to his work of rowing.

I grinned. "Are you experimenting?"

"Observing. How did it happen with Owen first? You were in the stables...kissing?"

"No, I'd only just arrived and Owen was talking to my horse," I said. Cosmo laughed, and I smiled at the memory. "He was just being...Owen. You know, sweet and funny, saying nice things to a horse because Owen is the kind of person who would think to do so. He's so...*good*. And then it hit, although I didn't know what it was at first. I just *needed* him."

Cosmo's smile was wide, shining, although I was a little bit distracted by the strain of his arms working in smooth rotations.

"What are you thinking?" I asked.

"That your Hunger isn't born out of lust. It comes from affection," Cosmo said. "Or at least in part."

We were moving into the tunnel now, my eyes adjusting slowly to the dark. "I suppose that's true. Does it matter?"

"I don't know. I just think it's sweet," Cosmo admitted. The water swished as the oars cut through. "It makes sense that you're attracted to Owen's goodness, you have so much yourself."

"I—"

"Don't object. Think of the position that you're in, the privilege that you were born with. Not even your own people expect you to do anything for them, they're so used to the way things have been. You have the Hunger. You could turn back to the capital now and return to the way things were."

"No, I couldn't," I said, twisting to watch as we emerged onto a larger pond. The tunnel had been for a bridge, probably to the woods surrounded by briars. We were on the western side of the palace now, closer to the stables.

"You wouldn't," Cosmo corrected, and when I turned back to him, I finally saw the softness of his expression. "Owen has easier burdens than you, but I suppose that hasn't stopped others in his place from being bitter or cruel."

"I might be a little bitter," I said.

"I won't tell anyone," Cosmo said. He crossed the oars for a rest, and I stretched up as he bent down, lifting my face to his for his kiss. It was gentle, lingering and tempting, and Cosmo hovered there in place for a long moment. "Don't be hard on yourself, Bryony. You're making changes."

"In a boat, on a lake, behind my palace?" I asked, grinning wryly.

Cosmo chuckled and sat up straight. "When does Griffin start hunting?"

"Today."

"Then, yes. In a boat, on a lake, behind your palace. What

have I done today with my sketches?" Cosmo shrugged and picked up the oars.

"Art has value. It can educate, or bring joy, or illuminate a new audience to experiences or cultures they never imagined," I said.

Cosmo grinned, steering us over into a large pool of lily pads missing their blooms. "Great art can. And my art can be beautiful, which might bring someone joy. I'm not sure I've succeeded more than that yet."

"But you weren't born with a pencil and chisel attached to your hands, so you must continue to pick them up because you love the work," I teased.

"I do love it. That must be why. For the last year or so, I've wondered if I was only continuing because it's all I know. Not that I'm uninspired. Only that my work seems to be solely for aesthetics."

"I like aesthetics," I said, taking a berry for myself and eyeing the pond. There was an old crippled oak tree on the bank and a flock of the geese we'd been warned about farther down. "Do you really only want to sculpt if the product is important?"

Cosmo hummed and shook his head. "No. No, I...I love sculpting because it's as if I'm getting to know someone with my hands. Almost like creating them, except it feels as though they already existed in the clay before I ever arrived. I sketched Owen today, but when I plan the piece, it won't be him who appears. There will be someone new, and I learn them as I build them. Learn the strains in their muscles and imagine where they might've come from. Their age as it shows on their face or in their stance. Their moods and behaviors from their expression."

Cosmo was somewhere else now, not with me in the boat, and I wanted to reach out and drag him back to me, to fall into that same place in his head where he went when he was working. My body tightened, and I huffed out an irritated breath as I lurched up to my knees, the boat rocking a little at my movement.

Cosmo's gaze fell back to me, eyes widening and lips parting, but I didn't wait for him to ask. My arms circled his shoulders, and I pulled him to me, claiming his mouth with a kiss.

He was right. The Hunger was more than physical lust, that was just how it manifested. It was Cosmo who'd triggered it, simply by being himself.

"Bryony," he gasped, and then groaned and returned to my kiss, slipping gently down from the bench he'd been sitting on, pushing the oars to the back of the boat. We were floating toward the oak on the bank, the boat rocking slightly as we rushed to press closer.

We'd probably be fine. I didn't really care either way.

All I wanted in the moment was Cosmo, and I dragged him down on top of me, my back pushing the basket to the tip of the prow and out of my way. Cosmo laughed as the boat moved with every little jostle of our bodies as we tried to fit together in the small space. We were on our sides by the end, hands groping over clothes to try and hold each other closer, mouths meeting messily, nibbling at any flesh they could find.

"Please," I begged, my body trying to work itself against Cosmo.

"It's all right. I have you."

He did, but not enough. I nearly tipped us over trying to climb on top of him, and the Hunger didn't care if Cosmo was laughing wildly, if I was giggling too. It still wanted *more*. I settled my knees on either side of his hips and tried to grind down on his lap, my hands braced on either side of Cosmo's beaming smile, but there was too much fabric between us for real friction.

"Is this you?" Cosmo murmured, a little fold appearing between his dark brows. "Are you as much possessed by the magic as you could make me be?"

I paused to catch my breath, sitting up over his lap and staring down at him. Cosmo Pianetta was handsome, although it was in an earthier way than the others. His lips were full and strong, and his nose had a distinctive line down the tip. His curls were black and thick, and I indulged in the impulse to reach out and dig my fingers in, watching in fascination as Cosmo's eyes fell shut and his head tilted back under my grip, throat bobbing with his swallow.

"It's me," I said, realizing it was true. The Hunger was on my back, panting and salivating like a wolf waiting to leap on its prey, but it was willing to be patient if I demanded it. "I want you."

Cosmo grinned, eyes opening and finding mine. "Then I'm yours, muse."

Which is, of course, when the goose arrived on the boat.

16.
BRYONY

I screamed, and Cosmo broke into immediate rowdy laughter. The goose spread its wings and honked, leaning forward, snapping at me and bouncing closer, perching on the wobbling oars like a gargoyle. A second bird appeared by Cosmo's head, and his laughter died abruptly as we both sat up and the geese began their attack, claiming our picnic basket and cornering us against the side.

We were up, clutching each other, trying to shoo the geese away, when the balance tipped and the water rushed in and I went spilling out. Sky and the tall green branches of trees spinning over my head as Cosmo fell out with me, something like a scream and a laugh rising out of my throat. The water was a cool caress against my back, until it started to swallow me and Cosmo at my side, his arm still wrapped around my waist.

"Ugh, pleh! Hang on!" Cosmo said, coughing water out. I could just barely feel the resistance of a mossy stone under my toes, with water up to my ears, but Cosmo was tall enough to slip and walk and pull me forward to the bank.

"Geese are monsters," he gasped.

I coughed and spat, but the lake water was reasonably clear. "We were warned," I croaked, reaching under the water and wrestling with too much fabric around my legs.

Cosmo snorted, lifting me up with both arms, my dress sopping and heavy, pouring water back to the surface as he grunted and hauled us to shore. My giggles broke free next, and he grinned at me, black hair hanging around his ears in sodden curls.

"I hope you weren't very hungry," I said, grinning and looking back over Cosmo's shoulder to see the geese rescuing what was left of our picnic as it bobbed up from beneath the boat.

"I'll be fine. What of your hunger?" he asked, the double meaning hovering in the question. Cosmo sank to his knees at the very edge of the water and set me down in a soft nest of grass and sand. He hovered next to me, undoing the buttons of his soaked vest and peeling it off his shoulders. The white fabric of his shirt was now transparent, and I admired the familiar path of dark hair over his chest and down his stomach.

I swallowed and struggled to my own knees, pulling wet fabric away from my legs. "I am...in need of assistance in getting out of this dress," I said.

I liked Cosmo's smile; there was something secretive about it, as if the expression was entirely for my own eyes whether we were alone or not. He reached out, hooking his index finger in the collar of my dress, his touch sliding down between my breasts and yanking me forward. My balance failed, and I fell into Cosmo's chest, my face turned up to his as his mouth slanted over mine, tongue licking in immediately. I moaned into the kiss, my hands grabbing onto Cosmo's shoulders. There was a slightly bitter flavor between us, the taste of the lake, but it melted away the longer we kissed until there was only Cosmo and berries and honey.

His finger had retreated, and I wanted it and *more* back on my skin, until a moment later there was a tug on the back of my dress. I gasped as Cosmo pulled away, and then stiffened at the *ripping* down my spine and the sticky cling of fabric loosened. Cosmo grinned at me and then revealed a penknife in his hand.

"I'll find you new ribbons to lace with," he said, and then he flipped the knife closed and began to pull the dress off of me.

No one had ever gotten that close to me with a knife in my life, and there was no *logical* reason for my heart to beat faster and my blood to run hotter, but I moaned as Cosmo peeled me out of the gown.

"Are you going to ruin my corset too?" I asked, wondering if I sounded as hopeful as I felt.

"I don't know why you bother with them, you're perfectly

made as it is," Cosmo said, staring down at the swell of my small breasts against the binding of my corset.

I wiggled my hips out of the skirt, falling back into the grass as Cosmo pulled his shirt off over his head. Sunlight wove its way through the gnarled branches of the dead oak above us, freckling over his tanned skin and catching on the droplets of water that clung to him like kisses. I gaped at him, and he laughed as he caught me at it.

"Do you really want me to cut it?" he asked, nodding down at my corset before scooping up my dress and tossing it away from us.

I raised my knees, planting my heels on either side of Cosmo, watching the instantaneous flick of his eyes move down to my center. "I do," I said.

Cosmo's lips curled, and his eyes traveled back up to mine. "Is my muse a little attracted to danger?"

"Maybe. Or I am simply impatient to have your mouth on my breasts," I said, flush flooding my cheeks.

I had been more than ready to fuck Owen in the stables, but I'd also been ridden heavily by the Hunger. It was here now between Cosmo and I, but it wasn't the painful clench and demand, more of a sinuous cloud of desire floating between us.

Cosmo was broad shouldered and lean. He bent over me, arms bracing himself to hover above me, the tips of grasses reaching out to tickle his cheek. The damp fabric of my shift stretched and then rose higher up my thighs as Cosmo sank against me. His hips rocked, and my eyes fell shut, lips parted on a silent cry as the warm pressure against my sex flared, a match catching its flame. His lips pressed to my pulse.

"Now? Here?" he whispered, but there was something missing in the question.

I nodded and kissed his lips. "With you, yes."

He wasn't a convenient body. He was Cosmo, my observant artist, and I wanted him intensely and immediately.

"And your tea?"

"Every morning," I answered, speaking of the contraceptive tea Cosmo had convinced me to ask Cook Umber for. I wasn't like the rest of my family, even if I did have the hunger and

Cosmo was probably right to caution me on this front too. I wanted to claim a kingdom before creating an heir.

Cosmo sighed, and I wrapped my arms around his back, tapping my fingers over knots of muscle and sun-warmed skin. He settled on top of me and the weight of him, pressing my thighs open to make room for his body against mine, was exquisite pressure. He rocked softly over me, and every nudge of our hips connecting made my breath catch.

"I want to draw one hundred sketches of you like this, just to memorize the moment," he whispered.

I ignored my own blush and nipped his chin. "That would take a lot of time. I'd rather memorize the feel of you inside me with one hundred thrusts," I said.

Cosmo's belly laugh always hit him suddenly, and I grinned at the low and loud happy sound as it poured out of him. "Bryony!" His eyebrows raised, and his tone softened. "You've never had sex before."

I narrowed my eyes. "I've never had *this* kind of sex before. A cock inside me. Will it make a difference for you?"

"Ha! I...I am more concerned for your sake."

I sighed and lifted my hips, smiling and letting my eyes fall shut as I ground myself against Cosmo and listened to his guttural groan. "I...I had Owen's mouth on me. That seems more...obscene or intimate in some way. His eyes were awfully close to a part of me I've seen very little of. This simply seems equitable by comparison."

I opened my eyes just in time to see Cosmo's eyes fixed to my straining breasts. His tongue licked his lip and he grinned at me.

"Well...that's a valid argument."

"Are you worried about hurting me like Owen is?" I asked.

Cosmo hummed and passed his lips over mine. "No. It will be intense, but I can make sure I don't hurt you."

And with that, the discussion ended. Cosmo rolled to the side, one of his hands diving into my hair to clutch at my roots and hold me in place for a plunging, rough kiss. The other hand traveled to the top of my corset, pulling at the laces there. No knife then. Maybe I could convince him another time? Instead, he kissed me, on and on, until I struggled for air. There was no purchase for me to find in the kiss, it was entirely under Cosmo's control, licks and nibbles, his tongue thrusting against mine. Without him between my legs, I could only press them together to try and relieve the pressure the kiss created. It was a poor replacement, and my hands grappled over the planes of his back, trying to drag him back on top of me, but he refused to budge.

Slowly, the simmering Hunger began to boil, my skin too tight, my lips clumsy as I tried to find a measure of control. I needed to be filled, needed the pressure of Cosmo's body to pin me back on the ground. I barely noticed as the corset loosened, falling away from my sides like petals. I wouldn't have felt it at all, except without the occupation of my laces, Cosmo's hand found a new task.

Fingertips grazed against my core, and I whimpered at the touch. And then Cosmo pulled away from the kiss with the first slow plunge of a finger inside of me.

"Oh! Cosmo!" My eyes opened wide and he was there above me, grinning and looking over every inch of me as his finger pumped inside of me, the others grazing around my clit but never touching directly.

"That's it, muse. Fuck yourself, just like that," Cosmo murmured, sitting up and watching me riding his finger. "Too much?"

"Nooo, I need more," I whined, and then I swallowed my squeal as he responded by pressing another finger in immediately.

I moaned and my head tossed, my hair pulling in his grip. He took over the pace, soft and slow as I adjusted. Owen had teased me a little with a finger in our "practicing" but almost shyly. There was nothing shy about Cosmo, and in that moment I felt molded by him, as if we were both learning my limits and my desires while he worked on me like a sculpture.

"You're very wet," he said, and I was relieved he sounded a little breathless. "That's good. I think I can make you even more so."

His touch curled inside of me, and my back arched, cool air running over my chest and making my nipples pebble under the wet fabric of my shift as Cosmo fucked me with his fingers. My hands trembled and fell from his shoulders, and I pressed them down into the sand and grass as my feet slipped at the edge of the pond.

"I'm going to—" I whimpered at a shivery threat of pleasure licking over me. I bit my lips to bury the demand that he *fuck* me properly, the chasm of Hunger growing vast in my chest and core. Cosmo leaned down, kissing me and conquering my mouth with his tongue at the same pace of his fingers in my cunt.

"Come, little muse," Cosmo whispered, and then he wedged in a third finger, twisting them inside of me.

I broke and warmth threaded through me as I cried out, driven through the cascading ecstasy by Cosmo's urging touch. My fingers dug into the earth, and my eyes opened wide as I reached the peak of the crest. For a moment, everything was blurred, sunlight swimming through branches, and then the world seemed to vibrate and the sunlight landing on us dimmed. I blinked, and the great oak shuddered above me, unfurling a sudden rush of green leaves, blooming them like flowers in a rushing pace.

Cosmo's attention was equally caught, his fingers stilling inside of me as he gazed up, and then back down to me.

"Bryony?"

"The oak..." I blinked and shook my head. Did orgasms cause hallucinations?

Cosmo laughed softly and then sat up on his knees, grinning down at me, reminding the Hunger of exactly what I wanted to focus on. I reached for him, our hands meeting on his waistband at the same moment, fumbling together until it was open. I pushed Cosmo's pants down his hips, and his hand cupped my face, stealing gentler kisses.

"You know what happened, don't you?" Cosmo murmured.

I huffed, trying to drag him down on top of me, biting down on my lip at the sight of his dark, thick cock and its leaking head. "I don't really care. I just want you *in* me."

Cosmo tilted my chin up and caught my eyes. "You do, or the Hunger does?"

I took a slow breath and then leaned in, pressing my breasts against him. "Both. I'm here."

He shuffled out of his pants, throwing them toward my dress, and then stopped my hands before I could pull my shift over my head. "So the grass doesn't scratch you. Leave it. I'll enjoy you stripped bare in bed later."

The Hunger approved of this argument, and I fell back into the grass. Cosmo settled on top of me, his cock pressed to my wet sex, sliding through my release. I moaned at the contact and wiggled beneath him, trying to fit him inside of me. He grinned and shook his head, continuing the roll of his hips as his head lowered to my breasts, sucking on them through the fabric.

"Bryony, do you know what the Hunger does?" he asked.

I squeezed his sides, grinding up against him, the front half of my shift wadded up against my stomach and squelching wetly with our motions. "It—it forced Owen."

"They say it brings prosperity," Cosmo said.

"Cosmo, we both know that's not true. Enough lessons, *please*. I want you."

He laughed and then pressed his mouth to mine, hips pulling away and making me whine until I felt the graze of his knuckles against me as he lined himself up at my entrance.

You're going to have sex, I thought suddenly, stilling beneath him.

Finally, the Hunger seemed to answer.

I was still lax with surprise as Cosmo started to press inside me with short thrusts, my lips parting on a sigh.

"Bryony," Cosmo breathed against my lips. "Have I—ungh— have I mentioned how glad I am to be Chosen?"

I smiled and my breath caught at the next thrust. It *was* intense. It was as if he were filling more than just my cunt, as if he was there in my chest too, my throat, in my head. Not painful, but foreign and unfamiliar, growing heavier by the second.

Cosmo's thumb stroked my cheek, drawing my eyes to his. "Too much?" Before I could answer, his free hand fit between us, rolling over my clit and turning pressure into craving.

I moaned and shook my head, lifting my hips, both of us crying out as he slid deeper. The more he played his finger over that spot, the more it was impossible for me to stay still. I squeezed him inside of me, rocked beneath him, held him tight in my arms and whined, pleading his name for more. There was pinching and strain, but there was also simmering heat and flashing pleasure, reminding where this all led. Cosmo fell into me, hips finally striking against mine, pinning my legs open as he began to thrust in earnest.

"Bryony."

"Don't stop," I answered quickly, voice strangled, as if by taking Cosmo into me I'd lost room for myself. I didn't care, I wanted more of him.

Cosmo hunched, making more room for his hand to work me into a new frenzy and allowing his mouth to travel up and down my neck, sucking and marking me, and then even to my breasts, pulling my nipple between his lips and biting down.

The Hunger surged, and I pulled my hands off his skin, pressing them back into the earth above my head. Cosmo knew my body better than I did, shifting his hips to reach that place inside of me he'd found earlier with his fingers. I cried out at the stab of crushing pleasure that shook me with every nudge of him over that place. Someone would hear me like this, might even come and witness us.

I hope it's Owen, I thought, wondering what it would be like to have Owen's hands and mouth on me as Cosmo fucked me.

And with that image passing through me, I came again, light flaring behind my eyes. Water from the pond licked at my toes until Cosmo pulled my legs up around his waist, his slow and steady thrust growing rough and slapping.

"Yes!" I gasped, my eyes flying wide to stare between us. "Am I—are you—"

"I'm here, I have you," Cosmo said, brow furrowed and grin tense, his focus on his own movements. "You're going to come again, little muse. I want to feel you squeezing around me once more before I finish."

He could make me come a thousand times for all I cared. I bit my lip and tried an experimental clench around his length, and Cosmo groaned and laughed.

"That's not fair," he gasped, his rutting against me pushing me through the grass, his own hips following eagerly. "Focus on the Hunger, Bryony."

"But—"

"Push it to the water next," he said. And then his arms circled my hips and he held me so tight, I thought I might burst as he fucked me with wild enthusiasm.

I couldn't think about the Hunger, I was *made* of it, writhing in Cosmo's arms as it surged through me. I squeezed my eyes shut as I cried out, our bodies seeming to tie together as we connected. Whatever came next, orgasm or Hunger or something new, seemed to go on and on. Cosmo's breath was panting on my neck, his own voice clear and aching in my ear. I lost our edges, unaware of where I started and ran into him, there was just a drowning sensation that I welcomed, vaguely aware of his instructions before it started.

The pond. I groaned and tensed, pushing the feeling toward the water, and Cosmo shuddered, heat blooming sweetly inside of me. Kisses pressed to my jaw, and my body jostled as Cosmo rolled us.

Clarity came back slowly, my face pressed to Cosmo's throat, breaths hiccuping. Our skin was sticky with sweat, and I grimaced, irritated by the presence of my wet shift still clinging to me. Cosmo chuckled, sitting up with me over his lap, and helped me out of the fabric, the pair of us catching our breaths. I leaned in as he cupped my cheek, ready for his kiss, wanting the sweeter, softer connection to help me come down from the intensity of the moment before. His nose nudged against mine, and he grinned as I nudged back.

"Mmm, I think I did better than I expected," he teased.

I laughed and tucked my face back into his shoulder. "I agree." I circled my arms around his shoulders, and Cosmo petted my back.

"You liked it?"

I laughed and lifted my head, surprised to find the little hints of worry on his face. "Cosmo! I...I don't have words, I..."

He grinned and relaxed. "I agree. Feel free to stroke my ego if you find them though. For instance, I have never found such sweet satisfaction in my life. Your thighs were made to hold me."

I blushed and pinched his skin. Cosmo was deadly with flattery. He'd have made a good courtier if it suited him. "I thought you made the earth move," I said.

His eyebrows raised. "Ah. About that. I think that might've been you, little muse. Look," he said, nodding behind me.

I twisted to glance at the pond and froze in Cosmo's arms. There lay the green lily pads we'd passed earlier, and now they were dressed in full blooms, creams and pinks and yellow water lilies bright and open, teacups on saucers.

"But..."

"Also, the meadow," Cosmo murmured, nuzzling my throat.

He leaned back as I turned and stared at the sudden burst of color through the grasses, yellow daisies and red poppies and purple coneflowers.

"Whatever happened with Owen, that's not *all* the Hunger does," Cosmo said, waiting patiently for me to stare my fill through the meadow and back up to the oak on my left, the previously dead and undressed one that was now rich with new growth.

"It works," I whispered. "It works. My family has just been using it wrong?"

Cosmo hummed and kissed my lips. "You can bring the north back to life, Bryony."

17.
BRYONY

"Nothing like that happened in the stables though, so we can't—" I started, glancing at the others around the low table filled with books.

"Actually, I meant to tell you," Owen said, interrupting me with a kiss on my cheek. "I didn't notice it at the time, but when I went in the morning, it looked as though someone had gone over the place with a fresh coat of paint. Everything was tidy and fresh, right down to the hay in the loft."

I gaped at Owen. What was he saying? I had worked some kind change over the *stables* too?

We were gathered together, my Chosen and I, in the Winter Palace library, a place that smelled of mildew and which I'd outright refused to enter until Owen had run through, laughing as he cleared away genuinely monstrous cobwebs. I was still feeling itchy, waiting for whatever beastly spider had fashioned those cobwebs to come out of its hiding spot.

"Here's a record of royal stays in the Winter Palace," Wendell murmured, sitting up in his armchair, raising the book he held. "It marks it by the final harvest, a festival, and then through the winter until the 'Ground Blessing.' But it appears to have stopped...over one hundred fifty years ago. I wonder why."

"I've never, in all my life, heard any mention of my grandmother or my mother having actual...*contact* with the land we were supposed to be gifting with prosperity. I feel so stupid not to have thought of it," I muttered, flipping blindly through the pages in front of me before taking a deep breath and sinking back into the chair.

My body was still *thrumming* with the rush of sex with Cosmo, and when he reached over and soothed his hand down my arm, the Hunger panged softly inside of me, tugging me in his direction.

"Traditions get watered down all the time. The meaning may have gotten lost," Cosmo offered.

"Perhaps there was an especially lazy queen in your ancestry," Thao offered with a shrug. "Not all royalty chooses to do their duty. My great-great grandfather was a resounding disappointment to Mennary."

My lips twitched, and Thao smiled back at me, sitting next to Wendell but not bothering to look at the book in front of him. Owen was on my other side, his legs spread and his knee resting against my thigh. Cosmo and I had snuck back to the palace in our wet clothes, washing the sand and grass away quickly and redressing before going to find the others.

"Are you sure the oak was dead?" Wendell asked, eyes tracing the words on the page in front of him.

"Positive," Cosmo said, his fingers trailing back and forth on the inside of my wrist. "Hollow branches and not a leaf in sight until..."

Until I'd come on his fingers. I looked up and met Cosmo's eyes on mine, my lungs freezing for a moment in response to the warmth of his stare. The corner of his eyes crinkled with laughter, and I wondered if he was intentionally stirring me up to see what would happen.

You could be like Camellia and plant yourself on his lap right now, just hike your skirts up and he could slide right—

"Ah, wait a moment. The year the queen stopped attending the harvest festival, the council replaced her and attended themselves," Wendell said, looking up.

"What do we know about the council?" I asked, more to myself than the others.

"They're intended to lighten the load for the queen. They're universally nobles, and they manage local magistrates. They appoint ambassadors, set taxes, and coordinate kingdom spending," Wendell said, looking up from the page.

"All which seems to go to the capital," Cosmo added.

"Or their own pockets," I said, and then I laughed. "We sound like Aric."

"We could call him here," Cosmo offered, and I flashed him a glare.

"I think I'd rather he wasn't...aware of this new development," I murmured. "He thinks the queen's line and the Hunger are the cause of the inequity of wealth in the kingdom. And in some way, he might be right. I'd rather he wasn't suspicious of me while I'm trying to help."

"At this point, I wouldn't recommend attracting any unnecessary attention to your newly revealed magic at all," Wendell said. "Most people are assuming you have it, but I don't know of anyone who would expect the Hunger to manifest so..."

"Lushly," Cosmo said, tongue wrapping decadently around the word.

I rolled my eyes at him, and he laughed as my hand seemed to rise unconsciously to toy around my collar. I was growing too warm.

"There should be texts in here somewhere on the council's duties and the formation of their number, wouldn't you think?" I asked, wiggling away from Cosmo and Owen's stray touches.

My skin was itchy and tight, Hunger nipping at me and trying to drag my eyes back to the men at the table. I moved around my chair and bounced on my toes, trying to ignore my cravings to focus on the actual conversation.

"Are you tired?" Cosmo asked, and I shook my head. "Owen, why don't you go with her to find more useful material on the council."

"Here's a candle," Thao said, lighting one and placing it in a holder before passing it across the table.

I didn't argue with them, although I wasn't sure having Owen at my side would make me feel *calmer* at the moment. Mostly, I was left thinking about the rich pressure and *full* feeling Cosmo had given me and now what that might feel like with Owen.

The candlelight cast my shadow up the dark and warped shelves as we moved down the aisles. Owen's palm was warm at the base of my back, seeping through my dress and directly to my skin. I'd taken Cosmo's advice and left my uncomfortable corset behind in my bedroom with my shift, and the kiss of silk directly against my skin was liberating and tantalizing.

"Are you excited at all?" Owen asked.

"I...I am a little," I said, and then I blushed and looked back at Owen, grinning. "I think I am more excited about sex than I am about the magic. Perhaps that's the flaw in the queen's line anyway. I just don't know how I'm supposed to help the entire kingdom. Am I meant to go have a fuck in every field?"

Owen nearly dropped the candle laughing, and I grinned up at him. "If it comes down to it, I'll do my best to help," he said. "Cosmo and I both would."

"Well it's an option at least," I said with a sigh.

"You're trying to heal an entire kingdom overnight," Owen said softly, voice lowering and gentling. "It can't be done, Bryony, even *with* magic. I'm just glad Kimmery has you at all. But don't wear yourself out trying to take an axe to make a road through a mountain."

I paused, and Owen passed me, turning to face me as I stared up at him. "Thank you, Owen," I said, reaching and catching the front of his shirt, pulling him in as I rose to my toes to kiss him softly.

"I'm your Chosen," Owen said, beaming at me. "I'm here for you for any reason."

I kissed him again for that, trying to ignore the growing, gnawing need that gaped inside of me in exchange for simple affection with my sweetest Chosen. Except it was his gentleness and sweetness that seemed to stir up my desire. Cosmo was right, the more affection I held for them, the more I craved them.

Owen chuckled and nudged my nose with his as my kisses grew more urgent, my hands fisting tighter in his shirt. "It's back?" he rasped.

"I don't think it ever really left," I breathed, trying to hold myself away from him.

"And you enjoyed it?" Owen raised an eyebrow and spoke softly. "Being fucked in the grass?"

"Mm, not the grass specifically," I said, laughing. "The sex? Yes, I enjoyed it."

"And your first cock?" Owen asked, words growing gritty and his eyes hooding.

I swallowed and nodded, and watched as Owen stretched his arm up, easily placing the candle on the top of a bookshelf, the glow softening over our heads. His hands cupped my hips then, guiding me with slow steps backwards until we were hidden away between two shelves. My back bumped against a shelf, and my breath hitched as I nodded.

"I—very much. Is that... Does it make you jealous?" I asked.

"Does it make me jealous that you...?" His brow furrowed.

"That you weren't first when we'd already had—"

"Bryony, *no*." Owen ducked and took my mouth in a firm, sucking kiss. "No. I told you."

I blushed as I recalled the reason for his reluctance to be my first. "You did. I just wasn't sure if it would feel different."

"All I want is your pleasure," Owen murmured. "However you arrive at it, and with anyone you like."

"What about yours?" I wrinkled my nose. "Aren't I allowed to want the same for you?"

Owen smiled and stepped forward, lifting me off my toes and making me gasp and clutch at the glossy wood behind me. My feet slipped on air for a moment before finding a grip on a low shelf, and Owen pressed in closer, taking my left leg and raising it up by another step, stretching me open so he could rest his hips against mine.

"Are you sore?" he asked.

"Not at all. I only feel the Hunger," I said, my eyes dropping to where Owen started to push my skirt up to my waist. "Owen—"

"We said we would practice," Owen murmured, leaning in and dropping feather light kisses against my mouth over and over again. "What do you think your Hunger will do in the library? More flowers?"

My eyes widened and I glanced up. My hands were on the shelves, Owen had me pinned in place and positioned perfectly for his control. We hadn't really tested much of the direction or control of the magic, but I knew that when I'd been touching Owen was when I'd forced him to respond to me. If I could concentrate like I had at the pond, and resist the urge to grab onto Owen and bully him into satisfying me, then it would be *interesting* to see what the magic did in the room.

Which is exactly why you're panting like a dog in the sun at the prospect. It's all in the name of experimentation. Specifically, experimenting with how Owen's cock will feel.

"The others," I murmured at the sound of their voices at the other end of the long room.

"Stay quiet," Owen murmured, and then his fingertips were on my skin, grazing against the inside of my thighs.

I whimpered and then forced out a long breath as my eyes shut and my nails dug into the wood shelf. "If you see a spider, you'd better pull me down from here," I hissed, and then I bit my lip as Owen pressed one long, thick finger inside of me.

"How long have you been so wet?" Owen asked.

"Since you and Cosmo sat down on either side of me," I breathed in a whisper as Owen's finger slid out, spreading my arousal over my sex, and then pressed back in again.

Owen huffed and I opened my eyes, my lips parting in an 'o' as he pumped his finger inside of me. He was careful not to touch anywhere else, but he leaned in and sucked along my throat and down to my shoulder, leaving my skin wet from long licks of his tongue. My pulse pounded in my ear and my breath sounded twenty times louder than usual, even as I tried to keep it quiet and shallow. Owen added a second finger as soon as the first was completely slippery, and I failed to stifle my groan.

"Please," I whispered, nuzzling against Owen's ear as he bit gently on the muscle of my shoulder.

"I should let you come," he said.

"Yes!"

"But I'd rather you do it on my cock."

I swallowed my whine and let my head fall back onto the shelf, staring up at the glow of the candlelight barely illuminating a darkened discolored painting over the ceiling.

"It doesn't hurt?" Owen asked.

I shook my head quickly. "Add another."

I was growing used to the feeling of being filled, or rather, growing addicted to it, and I arched in place as Owen pressed a third finger into me. His hands were bigger than Cosmo's, and this was a new and beautiful stretch. I wanted to ride his hand like I had with Cosmo, but I was already at the very edge of keeping my balance. His fingers twisted inside of me, and my head fell back to the shelf with a *thunk,* hair bumping into dusty books as my mouth parted on a silent cry. Owen's fingers could barely move inside of me. The stretching sensation was a heavier version of Cosmo's initial intrusion, but with a little wiggle, my silence broke with a ragged moan.

The fingers dragged out of me with perfect, agonizing slowness, my body trembling with every tiny retreat, my chest heaving as I attempted to catch my breath. I lifted my head and Owen was there, his tongue thrusting into my open mouth, licking and battling against my own as his hands rustled between us, occasionally nudging me lightly. I was ready to jump down from my forced position on the shelf when I finally felt the fat, blunt head of his cock pressing against me, sliding in my wetness.

"I want you to watch, Mistress," Owen breathed, and my head dropped forward, my skirts bunched just high enough to reveal my naked sex and his massive cock poised to take me. "But you must be quiet," he added, one arm wrapping around my waist.

His other hand, the one with the fingers that had been inside me, raised to my mouth. I thought he meant to cover my lips to stifle my cries at first, until he forced the fingers I'd taken in my sex between my lips, filling my mouth with my own tart flavor. My eyes widened, and I moaned around his fingers, sucking on them roughly and making Owen grin. He might be the one to call me Mistress, but he excelled at mastering me.

I didn't bother trying to stay quiet, and I don't think Owen really meant for me to, because his smile grew wider as he began to thrust his way into me, my sex resisting the thick intrusion for a moment before giving him passage. I was loud and eager, fascinated by the overwhelming sensation of being stuffed by him. It was at the threshold of pain, but Owen was gentle and patient.

"Watch," he reminded me, and my eyes dropped.

My sex was red, and some of the wetness was glinting from the high candlelight as I watched him push and retreat, growing shining and slick with every short thrust. The deeper he went, the closer he moved until his chest blocked my view. His fingers pressed down on my tongue and his hips rolled, demanding every nerve inside of me to *feel* him, and my eyes fell shut. Tightness turned into a pulsing, pounding feeling, even as Owen remained still, slowly sinking upwards into me.

"You can only take so much of me like this," Owen said, and I groaned at the thought that there might be more, both wary and craving to learn it. "Do you like it?"

I nodded rapidly, sucking and licking on the fingers in my mouth, and Owen rewarded me by starting to fuck. The first real thrust, and I was breathless. The second, and I cried out, stunned by the places he reached inside of me. Cosmo had made sure to stimulate my clit, but Owen ignored it entirely, and the pleasure was heavier and less sharp, but also more uncertain. I didn't know if I would come, but I enjoyed the overwhelming drive and stretch of him inside me all the same.

My hands and feet slipped on the wood as I started to sweat. I wanted to move. To drag Owen down on the floor and learn all of him, ride him like a saddle made perfectly for my pleasure and release. Instead, I let him control the slow and steady pace, my body still learning how to accommodate him, every buck of his body growing sweeter. This was like drinking a bottle of wine by myself, a sort of dragging, dizzy, giggling feeling.

Owen panted, his eyes taking in a view I couldn't see for myself, watching my body swallow him up, sucking on his length as he pulled away. His thrusts grew more urgent, faster and a little deeper, and I moaned loudly and bit on his fingers to show my approval. Owen grunted and our skin began to slap, a little wetness smacking at the inside of my thighs.

I begged, but the words were muffled, and then I praised and crooned nonsensically in thanks as I realized I *would* come, and it would be strong. Owen gasped as I started to clutch.

"That's it, little Mistress. Gush and squeeze around me. I'm going to carry you to the table and give you all of me next, whether the others are still there or not. Would you like that?"

Apparently, I would, because I came with a surprised little scream, my hands slipping. Owen's hand pulled from my mouth, and he pinned me in place, hands on my waist, as he fucked me roughly through my orgasm. The magic was there on my fingertips, and I wanted badly to cling to Owen, to drag him under its force with me, but my fingers flashed wide.

Candlelight flared, not just from above, but all around us, and the library groaned, wooden shelves straightening. There was a sound of glass sprinkling and mending with a squeak, the opposite of a shattering.

And all through it, I trembled and clutched gratefully around Owen's cock. He pressed in deep, arms circling my waist and his mouth sucking on my throat as I shuddered and began to settle, his hips still nudging.

"Good work, Mistress," Owen chuckled. "Do you want more?"

I panted and my arms looped around Owen's broad shoulders, but I was careful not to touch him. Owen was still hard inside of me, and the Hunger was still there, gnawing and growling and waiting for more.

"You promised," I said, and then giggled as Owen's hands cupped my ass through my skirt, holding me to him.

"Tighter," Owen breathed, voice a little strained. I squeezed him tighter, everywhere, and Owen grunted and nearly started bucking again, before lifting me off the shelf and carrying me out into the aisle.

With one glance back over my shoulder, I sighed. The others had left the table and probably the library altogether. I couldn't decide if I was relieved or disappointed. It might've been fun to have Cosmo waiting for us, and there was something intriguingly dangerous about the idea of Thao and Wendell watching.

Maybe they might entertain themselves?

"You knew they were gone," I said to Owen, who smiled, although he looked a little strained and desperate.

"With your first moans," he said, grinning. And then he set me down at the edge of the table, lifting my hips up to meet his and letting me fall backward onto the books. "Hold on, Bryony," he gasped.

I reached for the edges of the table, but not before Owen began to rut wildly into me, my voice spilling out on a thrilled yell. He *was* deeper, and one of his hands turned immediately to my clit, stirring me into a kicking frenzy as I bucked to meet his thrusts. There was an occasional sting of too much, but Owen was careful to distract me with pleasure, warmth growing where we were joined.

"Give me your breasts," he grunted, and I wrestled into my own bodice to pull them up to the edges of my collar, Owen falling forward to feast on them with licks and bites and ferocious sucks, pulling a direct line between my cunt and his mouth.

"Yes! Yes, Owen!" I whimpered and then gave into the urge to hold him to me. The table squawked in protest beneath us, and one of the books on the other end of the table clattered over the edge.

"If I come before you, you should use your magic to make me hard again," Owen growled, and then he nipped at my breast.

I laughed and gasped, shaking my head, and Owen's thumb strummed over my clit faster. I didn't care who came first, as long as we both would this time.

In the end, it was me, shouting his name with a chorus of pleas, and then Owen, groaning out mine in one long song before collapsing onto me. All the dust and grime of the room evaporated with our sighs, and left us in a shining, bright, majestic library we had just enthusiastically defiled.

On the ceiling above us, the painting was revealed to be a decadent orgy of flesh, every member of the party smiling beatifically down on Owen and I as if in congratulation.

18.
ARIC

I rested my head against the back of my hands, the tangy smell of coin in front of my face making me grimace. I'd had lofty dreams when I defeated my father-in-law and took the crown of King of Thieves—of stealing from the queen and righting the inequality in Kimmery. Of snatching priceless jewels off the throats of fine ladies and delivering them into my darling Charlotte's rough hands.

In reality, I was the underpaid equivalent of an accountant, constantly counting coin before passing it back into the rightful hands.

You could leave it all behind and take up in the palace as a useless Chosen. I scoffed at the stray thought, brushing away the brief glimmer in my head of green eyes and pink cheeks just as a knock echoed down the chamber. I looked up at the scraping of the turning keg, my eyes narrowing at the approaching figure.

"I should look a great deal more cheerful than you if I were surrounded by coin in that way."

I groaned and pushed myself away from my desk, back into the cushion of my armchair as Griffin pushed back the hood of her cloak just in time for a little candlelight to catch on her crimson hair.

"Not if you knew you'd never keep it," I said, and the woman hummed and shrugged her shoulder, unfastening her cloak and letting it fall from her shoulders as she took the chair across from me. I narrowed my eyes and watched her carefully.

Griffin wasn't a favorite in my court. She went to the law when it suited her, and stole from thieves when she felt they didn't deserve what they'd caught. But she paid her dues, and while I upheld the rules of my community, I appreciated Griffin's personal application of her morals. She didn't tolerate assholes or brutes, whether they were wealthy and respectable, or part of the thriving underbelly she moved through. Charlotte had adored the younger woman.

"How do you like your new position?" I asked. "Have you started?"

"I've just finished dropping off my catches," she said with a nod, her eyes traveling the room, while I kept my own in the direction of her hands. She couldn't steal from me with her eyes, and I wouldn't let her distract me while I was in the middle of preparing the thief's exchange. Our earnings mostly went to the families in most pressing need, but we took our own cuts, and I wouldn't put it past Griffin to skim from those.

"It's easy pickings in the royal woods," Griffin mused, her brow furrowing and turning back to me. "And I've never seen anything like the late-season mating of yesterday. All at once, the whole woods seemed to go mad with it."

I frowned back at her, head shaking slightly. "I know very little of that."

Griffin hummed, lips smirking. "Of course not. City boy. You should let yourself out of your cage more often. Get some fresh air. Go up and visit *your princess*," she said, eyes laughing and words sweetening strangely.

"She plucked me out of the line up. Nothing more," I growled, my teeth grinding.

"She declared you Chosen," Griffin parried, an eyebrow arching. "To the royal guard."

I cleared my throat and resisted the urge to scrub my hand over my eyes. The woman in front of me was far too opportunistic to be trusted that far. "Yes. That was convenient. But she knows perfectly well I am not her Chosen." *Not that she has need of them*, I thought, although I didn't want to say it out loud. I didn't know if it was important to Bryony that the kingdom generally still believed her to possess the Hunger, but I wasn't in the habit of giving away other people's secrets. "I may be technically eligible for the ceremony, but we both know I am not fit."

Griffin blinked, and her head turned with an avian tip, eyes landing immediately on the portrait of Charlotte in the corner.

Black hair, ice blue eyes, skin a little too dark for this far North. The most beautiful and dangerous woman I'd known in all my life. My wife.

"I think Charlotte would have a good laugh to see you set up in a palace."

"I think Charlotte would spit in my eye for bedding a girl so young."

"She's not *so* young. She's the elder of the two," Griffin said with a shrug.

I narrowed my eyes at her, trying to decide if she was goading me to embarrass me. "I love my wife, Griffin. And I love my court."

Griffin's teasing expression faltered, and I winced away from the look in her eyes. "I loved Charlotte too, Aric. But she is gone now. And your court will falter soon unless you point in the direction of an heir."

Loved.

I understood what Griffin meant. Charlotte was dead, we spoke of her in past tense now. But Charlotte's absence—from my court, my bed, my house—didn't alter my love for her.

"I will manage the succession when it's time," I said instead.

"See that you do, or the vultures will circle and I'd hate to see them cut you down," Griffin murmured, pushing back in her chair and pocketing a few stray coins as she rose, as if I didn't notice.

"You would make a good king," I said. It wasn't the first time I'd thought as much. Griffin had the hardness and the strength in her to rule a pack of thieves disinclined to taking orders and accepting punishment.

"I would make a dead king," Griffin corrected. "Most of the court hates me. Find someone more likable."

"They tell me Emory is likeable," I said, thinking of the young man who'd been gathering his own court of thieves on the other end of the city. They played nicely with us, but by setting themselves apart there was always cause for concern.

"Is he?" Griffin asked, eyes narrowing at me. "I'm not so sure of that."

My eyebrows bounced. "No? Do you have proof?"

"Not yet," Griffin said, swinging her cloak back onto her shoulders. "I'll let you know when I do."

When, not if. Griffin had suspicions about the young man who charmed our community. I trusted her judgement a little better than my own.

"In the meantime," she continued, coy and slow as she retreated down the passage. "You should consider an alliance with that princess. She *is* soft for you, Aric."

I sucked in a deep breath and swallowed down the flurry of denial and insult that rose to my tongue. It would only prove Griffin right. *The red hawk has suspicions about you too*, I thought. And she wasn't wrong. Bryony did have some kind of girlish favor for me, I'd been aware of it since the journey north. Or at least since her visit to the Wing and Rook.

And she is *soft*, a wicked voice reminded me, conjuring a buried memory of a crumpled young woman weeping against my chest. *She won't be tremulous and terrified of sex forever, and if her passion for her kingdom is any indication of her fire...*

I scowled and turned back to organizing the collection of coins in front of me, irritated with Griffin for picking at the subject and myself for bearing it as a weak spot in the first place. A new set of steps echoed in the passage and I shook my head.

"Whatever it is, I'm not in the mood."

"Not even if it's very curious?"

I looked up, my frown quirking up in one corner as I watched Scrapper slouch his way into my office, fingers deftly turning a fold of paper over one digit and then another, like a street magician's coin.

"If this conversation ends with you pocketing anything at all, I'll drag you out of here by your collar," I said.

Scrapper's grin was practically sideways, his head tilted strangely on his neck as he moved closer, bracing himself against the chair Griffin had just abandoned.

"What did that two-face want?" Scrapper asked.

"That's not a very curious question, and it's none of your business. What do you want, Scrapper?"

"Stole this off of Sir Hubert's man on his way out of Rumsbrooke," Scrapper said, holding up the note. No, a letter, folded and sealed. "It's to Lord Roderick."

I shrugged. "That's not so surprising. I'm sure he's complaining about losing his position at the Winter Palace."

"Nah. I go through all Hubey's outgoing mail. His complaint went out the day he came back to the city with his raggedy furs hanging between his legs. Couldn't get my hands on the reply, but I thought this one was interesting."

I frowned up at Scrapper. Who had told him to go through Sir Hubert's mail, and if no one, why hadn't I thought to earlier? I reached a hand out, and Scrapper raised an eyebrow at me.

"Are you going to let me read it?" I asked.

"Are you going to tell me to leave once you have?" Scrapper asked.

"Oh, for fuck's sake, Scrap!"

He tossed the letter to the table, and I ignored the chink of metal sliding into Scrapper's pocket as I ripped the seal off.

"Oi! Be more careful. I always send them on their way once I've read 'em," Scrapper snapped.

I certainly accept the pause on my position, Lord Roderick. I absolutely understand the necessity of patience. However, if we know that the remaining queen's line is willing to cooperate, why do we entertain the girl? Surely something could be done about her sooner rather than later. I myself could find the necessary means to manage the problem if the royal guard or the crown itself shies from its duty. Ever your humble servant,

Sir Hubert of Scathe

"Bold, isn't it?" Scrapper asked.

My blood was iron in my veins. Bryony was Kimmery's *one* hope at a decent monarch, at a queen willing to listen to her people, willing to *see* them. And the council, or at the very least, Sir Hubert, wanted her out of the picture.

"Treasonous," I said, reading the words again.

The necessary means to manage the problem. The royal guard *or* the crown itself. That left Bryony with enemies at every side of her.

"Wasn't sure who ought to see it," Scrapper murmured. "Not with the way it talks."

I hummed my agreement, but the sound was low and feral.

"Better no one for the moment," I said, reading it again. And then again. I looked up from the page at last and Scrapper was there, thoughtful and patient, and probably a good few coins richer for my distraction. He could take it from my cut. This was worth it. "What can you discover about the royal guard stationed at the Winter Palace?"

"Plenty," Scrapper said, wobbling with his crooked shrug. "I'll see who favors the council and who the crown and who is left."

"Good."

"We like her then?" Scrapper asked.

Why, all of the sudden, did it feel as though I was choking on my own tongue? "The princess?" I managed to squeeze out. Scrapper nodded. "We...we prefer her."

Scrapper's lips pursed oddly, his eyes widening too much. "I don't mind that. She seemed good folk. There was talk in court when she dropped by."

I nodded. "There was bound to be."

"And that talk spread through the city some."

"I take it there were objections to my meeting with the princess?" I asked.

"Some. I squashed most. Then they stirred up again," Scrapper said slowly.

I did not have a right-hand man. I had been my predecessor's until I deposed him, and it seemed to be tempting fate to take one of my own. But if I had, it would've been Scrapper. He didn't look powerful, and he could trick anyone—even me—into under-estimating him. But even without the title or the respect he might've earned as my second, Scrapper was loyal. Surprisingly so, for a thief.

"Did you notice where it seemed to be coming from?" I asked.

"Far as I could tell, the news landed in Emory's lap and he seemed keen to let it swirl again anytime it could," Scrapper said.

"That's the second time someone's said his name to me today in warning," I said.

Scrapper grinned. "Three and it'll be bad luck."

"How many ears do you have?" I asked, grinning back at Scrapper.

He eyed the gold and waggled his eyebrows. "Might be enough to listen to the guards and our neighboring court. Might not be."

I scoffed and picked a short stack of gold coins, pinching them between my fingers and letting Scrapper count.

"Well," he said with a great and labored sigh. "It'll be thin and exhausting work, but I'll manage."

I laughed at last and shook my head. "Go and help yourself to whatever cook's done with Griffin's catch, and I'll hear no more about it."

Scrapper took his new gold and turned away from me with the tip of an imaginary hat. "Will she stay good, you think? Or go rotten like the others?" It was an aimless question and he was already on his way out, but the answer was on the tip of my tongue, pinched between my teeth.

She may save us, if we can rescue her crown for her. She'll stay good.

But that seemed an awfully optimistic idea, and I shook it out of my head before it could take root.

19.
BRYONY

The Hunger took hold of me for the next few days, and the excuse of curiosity and experimentation with the magic made it too tempting to resist.

"Shhh..." Cosmo stilled at my back, and my fingers scratched against the glass of the window he had me pressed to. "Shh, someone's coming."

"I was coming," I whispered back, and Cosmo shook against my back with a soft laugh.

We were in the entrance of the palace, tucked in an alcove behind a curtain, and I could hear the soft boots of a passing guard treading slowly by as Cosmo and I held our breath. He was practically throbbing inside me, and when I closed my eyes and relaxed into the feeling, my lips fell open at the slow and steady sensation. Cosmo didn't wait for the steps to move fully out of hearing, but his next nudges were short, deep thrusts that made me squeak and press my mouth shut again.

"Focus on the chandelier next," Cosmo whispered.

The chandelier in the hall behind us was dull, chipped, and missing some of its dripping crystals. I wasn't sure what the Hunger was really capable of, but that was the whole point of learning, wasn't it?

I swallowed a strangled moan as Cosmo picked up his pace, his hands under my skirt pushing me into a deeper arch until every thrust dragged against my front walls.

Perhaps magic wasn't the *only* thing we were experimenting with for the day.

My sweaty palms squeaked against the glass, nails trying to dig and grab on to the smooth surface.

"I'm going to—Oh, god, Cosmo there's a guard on the stairs,"

I gasped, my eyes widening as I watched the guard who had passed us stepping slowly down the grand and broken front steps of the palace. If he turned around, he'd be sure to see me pressed up against the window like this, even if he couldn't make out any explicit details.

"Quickly then," Cosmo said, laughing. "And quietly."

He reached around, toying with my clit, and I keened, watching the guard's head turn just enough for me to make out that it was Cresswell Stark. Then I came, forgetting to be quiet at all as heat and magic rushed through me. The glass of the window rattled and I slammed my eyes shut, not caring who might see or hear us as I let out a soft cry and tried to focus on the hall behind us rather than the glass in front of me, when all I really wanted to think of was the thrust and strike of Cosmo inside me.

Never stop. Never stop.

Cosmo groaned, sagging forward, and I whimpered as he came in a wet rush that leaked out between us as he pinned me to the window. Glass chinked behind the curtain, and Cosmo dragged me away from the window. Our feet stumbled together as he leaned back against the alcove wall and propped me up against his chest, flicking back the curtain for us to look up.

I gasped, eyes widening. It was not the chandelier of minutes ago, carefully carved crystal bars and delicate drops. Now it was a flurry of petal thin blossoms, swirling in a whirlwind, catching candle flames in the hearts of their blooms.

"I didn't mean to do that," I breathed.

Cosmo hummed and tipped my head to the side, sucking on my pulse until I squirmed. "Owen will have lunch for us in the greenhouse. We can see what kind of work you can do there if you'd like."

⁂

MY THIGHS BURNED and my head was tossed back, knees aching against the cracked tile floor of the greenhouse as I rode Owen's cock with an anxious fervor.

"Oh please, please, I'm so close," I whined.

Cosmo had wrestled my dress off my shoulders and down below my breasts, and he was also straddling Owen's thighs, sitting behind me with his hands on my breasts and his mouth on my throat. Owen groaned as I clutched his length, his thumb urgent on my swollen clit.

I wasn't even coming and the room was blooming, massive red flowers with bright yellow stamens coming to life, old stems and herbs and trees growing lush with life again as the Hunger swam through my veins, thrilled to be sated, to be fed.

"Please," I breathed, and then shouted as Cosmo pinched the tips of my breasts and Owen bucked roughly in his own finish.

I came with a long series of shudders, and the colors of fresh flowers went wild around the room, iron groaning above us as the greenhouse repaired itself, stained glass shining tinted light to the floor, iron wrapping into swirling patterns with a great exclamation of relief. One that I echoed with a whimper as I fell forward onto Owen's heaving chest.

⚜

I TREMBLED, skin sweaty and covered in goosebumps since Owen had thrown the windows of my bedroom open. Cosmo kissed the inside of my thigh, gently pulling his fingers free, an embarrassing flood of fluids trailing after his touch. Owen turned his head against my breast, nibbling lightly on my nipple and laughing as I swatted him away.

"No-no more. I...can't," I said weakly. That was the thing though—I *could*. The Hunger was there, even after the day of indulging the urge it remained, mingling with the aftershocks and exhaustion, nipping along my sensitive skin and everywhere that Cosmo and Owen touched me.

"Sore?" Cosmo rasped, pushing himself up on wobbling arms and rolling slowly away from me. Cool air filled his place, and it was every bit as sensual a touch as his, slightly humid from an approaching rainstorm.

We'd indulged the Hunger for three days, but it was as if feeding it only made it that much stronger, every morning it would wake twice as voracious. Today the three of us had barely rested, *I* had barely taken a breath, since I'd woken with Owen hard against my ass. An entire day of hiding away from anyone else, moving through the castle and experimenting with the Hunger. With each other, really.

Cosmo leaned down on the bed, close to my side without touching, and reached out to brush sweaty strands of hair away from my forehead.

I shook my head and furrowed my brow. "No. Awareness, yes, but not sore. I can't think of ever hearing my mother or any of the queen's line complain of soreness," I said. Cosmo and Owen had taken their turns with me until their cocks tired after a brief dinner, and then they had sated the Hunger with their fingers and mouths until the air around us was hot and heavy with magic.

"Mm, perhaps it's part of the gift of your family," Cosmo said.

"The Hunger has passed now?" Owen asked, settling in at my back, although he had none of Cosmo's qualms for touching me.

I bit my lip, and Cosmo's lips twitched as he watched me. "I... No, it hasn't. Having the two of you close doesn't really...calm it."

"We don't have to stop," Owen rumbled, kissing my shoulder and draping a heavy arm around my waist to reach up and palm my breast, making my breath catch.

"I...I'm not sure..." My eyes fell shut as Owen mouthed along my throat. My skin was tender from all the attention I'd already received, but there was a burn and itch for more beneath that.

"I'm not sure Bryony's lust and the Hunger's exactly overlap," Cosmo said gently, making Owen pause, his rough cheek tickling against the lobe of my ear.

"Oh! Is that...?" Owen started to pull away, and my hand slapped over his arm, moving his hand down to my ribs but keeping him close as I rolled and pushed myself up against the pillows so I could see them both.

"I don't know," I admitted, my eyes trailing over their languid forms around me on the bed. Perhaps seeing them wasn't the wisest idea. Owen and Cosmo were exquisite, similar and contrasting all at once. They both had *spectacular* asses, ones I thrilled in clutching as they thrust into me over and over while I—

I bit my lip as my core clenched on nothing at the memory.

Cosmo laughed, startling me out of my reverie as he reached a hand up and covered my eyes with his palm. "Clear your head, Bryony. Owen, get her a robe and find us something to cover up in. I think we ought to speak a little more before we continue to indulge."

I sighed and let my eyes fall shut again as Owen slid away and the cool air from the open windows reached me, clearing away some of the fog of sex and sweat with the fresh night's empty fragrance. Silk followed, kissing over my shoulders, and Cosmo's hands joined mine in dressing me. The bed rustled around me as I took deep, clean breaths until my men went still and Owen's fingers brushed my knee.

It wasn't really better to open my eyes again. Cosmo and Owen were still bare chested, and my fingers itched to comb through the dark hair on their broad chests, to warm my lips on their skin and find traces of our flavors mingling there. I turned my head to the window instead, admiring the faint moonlight gilding the leaves of the trees outside the palace, instead of the candlelight playing on skin I still longed to taste and touch again.

"I am...afraid I will become like the rest of the women in the queen's line. Indulging in the power and neglecting my duties to the kingdom," I said after a pause of quiet, finding it easier to speak to the night rather than the men across from me. "I still don't know everything I can and can't do with this power, it seems to act on its own instruction."

"You know you can direct it," Cosmo reminded me gently. "How much focus did it take you to repair the chandelier?"

"A little, not a great deal. But did I repair it or make an entirely new one?" I asked, glancing at him with a frown. "Just because I can send magic in a direction, doesn't make me reliable if I don't know what will happen as a result. All evening with you both, I've made no effort to control it aside from being careful not to force either of you."

"Well, the curtains and bedding are mended and the drafts are likely gone too," Owen said, and I could see his easy shrug out of the corner of my eyes. "And I think you should practice your control over us. If we're comfortable with it, it would be better for you to know exactly how it works."

"Bryony," Cosmo said softly, leaning forward and reaching for my chin, turning my face to his. Dark eyes snagged against mine. "You have a good heart. A better heart than most monarchs. Your enjoyment of sex won't change that. You have already proven that *you* control your Hunger to a degree. It's only been three days, and nothing bad has happened as a result."

As if it felt the need to prove him wrong, Hunger surged. Or perhaps it was only affection. Either way, it launched me forward, Cosmo catching me easily around the waist as I pressed my mouth to his, my hands holding him in place for my tasting. He had me on his lips, tart and musky, and I sucked on the flavor, more interested in remembering how it had gotten there than the actual taste.

Then I slowed the kiss, holding the Hunger back as I eased away to smile up at him. "Thank you."

He kissed the end of my nose. "Of course. I see your magic as a creative force. We know a little of how it works with natural things, bringing plants back to life. You wanted a list of tasks to focus on for the kingdom. Perhaps you need to make another list of your magic."

Cosmo released me and I shuffled on my knees to Owen, who lifted me up and arranged me on his lap. I tried not to recall what it was like to ride him in that position, and instead, kissed his cheeks and swollen lips briefly.

"You are right. I should learn all the aspects of this power, even the ones that worry me," I said to Owen, looping my arms around his neck.

"If you are afraid of forgetting your kingdom, we can always come up with an arrangement," he said, grinning down at me. "Very good deeds for your people in exchange for very wicked acts with your Chosen."

Owen squeezed me tighter, falling back into the bed with Cosmo quick to follow as I laughed.

"Rewards for good princessly behavior!" Cosmo said, waggling his eyebrows.

"Grandmother would say good princessly behavior *was* the wicked deed, but for myself, I think I prefer something concrete that others will appreciate," I said. "I'll have to think of what to do next. I'm afraid it may involve finally confronting the council."

"Not tonight it won't," Cosmo said, pressing a kiss to my forehead. He and Owen seemed comfortable in each other's space, although I knew Cosmo appreciated watching Owen as much as I did, and the same didn't appear to be true in reverse.

"Do you want to bathe and we can read to you?" Owen asked.

My eyes widened and I twisted my lips in thought. It *was* an appealing offer, but perhaps a little too much so. "I think I'd better just bathe alone and come back to bed."

"And then rest," Cosmo said, more to Owen than to me. "You've had a busy day."

I blushed and nodded, sliding out from between them, Owen raising a hand to help me balance as I tiptoed over the enormous bed and let myself down. My eyes widened as I felt the slippery release leaking out and cooling against my thighs. I'd been debauched! I glanced back to the bed and caught Owen and Cosmo on their sides facing one another and whispering, and my cheeks warmed and swelled with an enormous smile as I ran for the bath. The water was probably cold by now, but I would be back between them soon.

I paused at the tub, staring down at the hazy water, filled with my favorite oils. It was cool to the touch, and my hand skimmed just on the very surface as an idea occurred to me. Cosmo was right. I knew that I could push my magic in a direction, but I was always too preoccupied by enjoying the sex I was having to worry about what the power wrought. I studied my own body for the moment, searching for the Hunger, finding it easily even without my men in front of me. Was there still a little power in me?

I bit my lip and imagined the release of an orgasm, but this time I focused on the water, thinking of the heat that rushed through me as I came. The smooth opaque surface of the bath rippled, thin strands of steam rising, and my hand clutched, fingers skimming through warm water.

My robe fell from my shoulders, and I climbed into the tub with a sense of triumph, sighing at the warm caress of the water. Maybe I was a *little* sore. Not pained, but certainly stretched. My eyes fell shut, and I let myself doze for a moment. I would wash and return to the bed, but it was nice to have a few moments alone, even if the day had been blissful in its company.

The screen rustled, and I smiled as a warm hand brushed over my shoulders, my eyes opening to find Owen sitting on the floor by the massive tub.

"I haven't come to distract or tempt you. I just wanted to say that the Hunger and its magic isn't the most important part of what happens between us," Owen said softly. His hand on the back of my neck worked gently into muscle, melting me further into the warm water, my eyelids drooping.

"I know," I said, nodding lightly. "I just want to be sure—"

Owen leaned forward and nipped at my lips. "Does it feel good? Are you happy?"

I sighed and grinned. "Yes and yes."

Owen's smile echoed mine. "Me too. Today was fun."

My cheeks swelled and I nodded. It had been fun, more than fun. It had been hazy and decadent and delicious and—

I swallowed hard and glanced down to the water before I gave the Hunger too much fuel and it demanded another performance. Owen made to stand and I stopped him with a touch on his arm, looking up from the water to meet his blue eyes.

"I'm very lucky I chose you, Owen," I said. "You and Cosmo. I didn't know how to pick men out of a crowd like that, but I'm so happy that I did and it was you."

Owen leaned forward, his fingers cupping around the back of my neck, pulling my mouth up to his for a slow, sipping kiss. He leaned back and nodded, a firm kind of certainty making his face uncommonly stern. "I won't ever be your grandest Chosen, but I will be good to you. I promise you that."

My chest throbbed and my arms lifted from the tub, water cascading off so I could hold Owen closer to me, kiss him deeply until my lungs begged for breath. "Stay," I gasped, clinging to him, tugging him to the edge of the tub.

He shook his head and grinned. "Wash up. Come to bed and rest. Or more. Whatever you need."

I whined as he pulled away, and Owen laughed and ducked around the screen as I sank under the water, trying to clear the happy fog from my brain.

20.
CRESSWELL

Something strange was going on in the palace.

I paused in my slow pace of the princess's hall as the floor creaked and the walls shuddered. Candlelight flared in the sconces on the wall, and my eyes widened at the way the hall seemed to brighten and gleam. A door threw open, two male voices hissing to one another, and I turned my eyes down to the floor as two of the Chosen stepped out into the hall.

Even without looking, I knew who it would be. The former Ambassador Pope and the Prince of Mennary. It was their suite they stepped out of, stopping in the hall with their heads bowed to one another, the language on their tongue foreign. I wondered if Pope spoke Mennarian for the prince's sake, or if they were intentionally hoping to not be eavesdropped on.

I told myself it was part of my role, my position, to know minute details of what went on with Princess Bryony. I was the head of her royal guard here in the north. I had been appointed to protect her while she stayed here. Still, it may have been wishful thinking on my part to believe that it was within my duties to know that these two particular Chosen were...

Not quite what their title implied.

I wondered why the princess made no use of them. Was it that they were lovers themselves, and their relationship didn't appeal to her? Did she keep the prince on for the sake of diplomacy?

"We'd better just go in before they get started again," Wendell Pope hissed as the men passed me and headed for the princess's suite. "We won't make any progress if we never see her."

I narrowed my eyes on their backs until the prince—Thao—

glanced over his shoulder at me, eyes glaring back. My gaze dropped and I swallowed hard.

Progress in what? In making their way into her bed, or was it something else?

You're bored and jealous and paranoid, I thought, my jaw grinding. *But it* is *my responsibility to protect her, and if their motivations are political, or if they—*

Boots stomped up the hall and I shook myself, straightening in front of the princess's door as the new shift guard came to relieve me in the hall. I would remain near, ready to follow and guard Bryony if she moved from her rooms, but it was Yorley's responsibility next to guard the door.

"Did the new steward finally arrive?" Yorley grunted. "Seems like the repairs are happening quickly."

"There've been no repairs," I answered.

Yorley scoffed and stared at me, his face its usual shade of red beneath his helmet, eyes bloodshot. In time since our appointments started, I realized that I didn't like my fellow guard. In fact, I didn't like *most* of the men assigned to me. Not one of us had been a royal guard before, there hadn't been need of one in the north for decades if not longer. I'd assumed that meant we might work well together, adapt to the new situation and build rapport. Now it appeared as though I'd been given a group of men who were no longer of any use to the army, and asked to prop them up against walls and make a show of it.

"There's new tiles on the floors, the chandelier's been replaced, cracks have been mended, and you want to tell me that there's been no repairs?" Yorley asked.

I straightened even further, moving away from the wall and glaring as I watched him take my place with a slouch. "You want to tell me that you think there are tradesmen at the palace that you just haven't *seen*? Unless you've been working with your eyes shut and your ears plugged, Yorley, I don't think you could've missed them."

I would not have put it past Yorley to work with his eyes shut and his ears plugged, actually, but I knew he'd never admit to it if he did.

"S'pose our little hands on princess must be enjoying the work herself," Yorley said, yawning and filling the air between us with the stench of stale ale. "Speaking of, you managed to convince her to put her hands on you, yet? Was thinking of taking a crack at it myself today, just slip in during a pause and fill her up."

He reached down, cupping himself through his uniform, just in time for the door to open from the princess's suite. I moved in front of him, more for the sake of whomever stepped through than Yorley's dignity. With a little afterthought, I would've let Bryony catch him in the gesture, just for the joy of watching her toss him out like she had Sir Hubert.

It was Wendell Pope in the lead, a slight furrow in his brow as he stared over my shoulder at Yorley before his eyes flicked to mine. "Sorry, do you know where the breakfast is laid out?"

"In the greenhouse, I believe," I said. I didn't believe. I knew because that was where I'd told the maid to have it ready as I tried and failed not to listen to the sweet sounds slipping through the now missing cracks in the walls. Princess Bryony liked her meals in the greenhouse, so it had seemed like a safe guess. "Should I call for the maid to come and help dress her?" I asked, all too aware of Yorley listening behind me.

"No, I think it's being managed," Wendell said, lips twitching as he glanced over his shoulder before looking back to me. "Thank you, that will be all."

Dismissed. Like a *servant*. When *was* the new steward coming? Everything was topsy turvy in the palace in the meantime.

I left the hall, moving toward the stair as Wendell shut the door. I would be waiting there, listening for their footsteps before I moved again, making my way ahead of them to the greenhouse. The newly and inexplicably *repaired* greenhouse.

❧

*...*THE PRINCESS'S *head was tossed back, throat stretched and chest heaving in her dress as she pinned me to the floor.*

"Either they want her to disappear up here, or she'll leave soon..."

I bit off my groan as I woke in the middle of the night to the sound of the guard's dormitory door slamming shut.

"Shhh, he's in his bunk room."

I stiffened in my bed and then released a slow and audible breath. My back was to the open doorway that led to the general dorm. I had my own space as the head of the guard, but it was a flimsy door that offered little privacy, and more often than not I elected to leave it open in case I was needed.

"He's sleeping, it's fine."

My cock was still stiff from my dream, and if it weren't for their words and the strange echo of the conversation that had bled its way into my fantasy, I might've stood and shut my door just to relieve myself of the pressure begging to be touched. Instead, I suffered on my side, waiting to see if they'd continue.

"Why send a perfectly good member of the queen's line up to this shithole province? Something's wrong with her, I'm telling you."

I knew the voice, but couldn't place it amongst the men. They were still all new to me.

"Council says she's missing the Hunger."

"She looked plenty hungry for it in the library the other day. Anyway, the Hunger's just royal bullshit. An excuse for queens to spend their lives with their legs spread."

My fist clenched in my sheets, arousal dying off the longer I listened.

"Think it's more likely that they want her away from the capital and the crown. A princess who cancels taxes? Doesn't suit the council, does it?"

"Saved my uncle from having to sell his apothecary though," the second man said, a little sullenly.

"For *now*. But what do you think will happen in a few months? Taxes will start up again twice as bad, and the council will claim there's no money to put to the roads to bring in doctors. They'll just hit us hardest in the worst months."

"There never was money put to roads. No, you're right. I know. It's probably just a device to win temporary favor before they do something worse."

"Exactly."

The voices hushed as I huffed and tossed over onto my other side, my eyes shut, my mouth hanging open in feigned sleep. I heard the quiet clunk of armor being removed, uniforms unbuttoned, and tried to remember who was coming off guard duty at this time of night. Slowly, *slowly*, I opened my eyes just the slightest bit, only enough to get a rough impression of who was in the dormitory.

One figure was medium to short height, stocky but not round. That would be Brummer, and he would've been the voice who had an uncle who was saved by Bryony's halt on taxes. I waited, and waited more, but whoever the man was urging the conversation against Bryony, he never stepped in front of my door. Brummer slunk away into his bunk, and I lay awake in my bed, running the conversation through my head.

Did they think Bryony was conspiring with the council, or was the council conspiring *against* the princess? I couldn't make heads or tails of it.

Either they want her to disappear up here, or she'll leave soon. The words from my dream—overheard and bleeding through fantasy—echoed again.

I wasn't even sure I'd really heard the words, or if the dream had impossibly manufactured the thought. With the first raucous snores from the guard's sleep, I sat up and moved to dress. The sky was still black with the middle of the night and my shift wouldn't start for hours. I was familiar with the slight purpling shift of color that meant dawn was approaching and it was still a long way off, but I was too uneasy to go back to sleep. I dressed in my uniform and my belt and sword sheath but left my armor behind. I moved better without it, and it was more for show than function.

I stopped in the doorway of the dormitory, waiting to see if Brummer or his conversational companion woke. There were others sleeping in the room. Yorley was missing, likely down in Rumsbrooke drinking at a tavern. I studied the men in their beds, running through a checklist of who I could *not* have heard, and who it might've been, landing finally on Nicholas Walsh. Nicholas Walsh was older, but good looking, and had been a well-respected captain in the army until he aged out without promotion. He never looked me in the eye when he spoke to me, and I wasn't sure if it was because I was darker than him and he didn't like it, or because he thought he should have my position instead. I'd be watching him now.

I moved softly through the dorm and up to the palace, checking every guard in their station on my way, ignoring their glares. I was their nanny, checking needlessly on her charges. Except I wasn't so sure it was needless. My instincts as a man told me most of these guards didn't see any nobility in their position. My instincts as an animal told me there was a threat, vague and distant, and that it was time to keep an eye on what was important.

"What are you doing up?" Stanley Piper whispered as I joined him in the princess's hall.

"Not sleeping. You can stay or you can take a free night off," I answered, keeping my voice low.

Stanley's brows bounced at the offer. I didn't dislike Stanley, he was young and quiet and had a slight limp that was always worse after a night standing on duty.

"Fine," he said with a shrug and a nod.

I took his place in front of the doors as I waited in the dim candlelight for him to leave. The hall was silent and still shining like new. I stepped forward, just slightly peering through the crack in the door to the suite. It was dark, quiet. My hand turned the knob slowly, waiting for a rustle of activity. Nothing.

The moon was bright enough in the sky, light falling in through the windows of the sitting room to reveal that it was empty, that the bedchamber doors were shut and a little warm light slipped across the floor from inside. It wasn't *outside* my duty to take a position in the sitting room, even if I'd never instructed anyone to do it before. Princess Bryony had made it clear she preferred a level of privacy and I was willing to give it to her, or at least grant her a good illusion of it.

Right now, I needed to know she was safe.

I stood in the heart of the room, my ear turned to her door, my eyes on the hall, my hand on my sword, and waited for dawn.

21.
WENDELL

Thao blinked smugly at me as Bryony dug her fingers into his thick fur, scratching behind his massive ear as she lounged against his ribs. Golden eyes met mine, and breath puffed through his giant nose, whiskers twitching and tail thumping against the grass.

I was jealous...*again*. And this time, the reason was a little less clear. I was jealous of the way Bryony was cuddled up against Thao, irritated that she seemed so comfortable doing so while he was a tiger when she never had been in his human form. I was even more jealous not to be in *my* tiger form with Bryony curled up against me. I had softer fur than Thao. Fluffier too. She'd bury her fingers in it, and I would purr for her.

"Oh, should I—" Bryony sat up, and Thao made an irritated but quiet growl at her movement as she looked between us. "I hadn't even thought."

I laughed and shook my head, digging my hand through my hair and tugging on the strands as I realized Bryony had caught some sourness in my expression. "Not at all. He likes having you there. I was only thinking how nice it would be to be in his place."

Bryony blushed, and I stared avidly at her soft smile as she sank slowly back into Thao's side, watching me all the while. Thao blinked at me, eyes slitting drowsily as Bryony went back to petting him. He understood, I knew he did. It was up to me when I wanted to reveal to Bryony that I was also a shifter. I would, someday soon. When I knew our place with her was secure.

We were picnicking by the lake, Cosmo with a sketchpad on his lap, drawing Bryony and Thao in their langor, Owen asleep across the blanket, a plate of half-eaten cakes on his chest and some hideous straw hat over his eyes. Who knew where he'd found it. I planned on throwing it to the lake for the geese—who wouldn't come anywhere near us with Thao in his tiger form.

"I had a dog when I was a girl. Or there *was* a dog when I was a girl, at least. He used to sleep in my bed with me, and I'd fall asleep while running my fingers through his fur," Bryony murmured, resting her cheek on the back of Thao's enormous head.

"I'm sure Thao would be happy to lie next to you at night," I said, grinning as Thao rumbled and Bryony laughed.

She was growing used to our flirting, accepting even. It was slow progress, slower than Cosmo and Owen's certainly, and it made my craving for the young woman that much more keen.

"The bed is plenty big enough," Cosmo said under his breath, eyes sliding to mine with a soft tip of his head.

Was *I* being flirted with too now? I glanced at Thao, who turned over his paw and flexed his claws out, licking them and staring meaningfully at Cosmo. I just wasn't sure if the meaning was threat or invitation.

I didn't know our *place* with this group. Cosmo, Bryony, and Owen had become a threesome, and I wasn't sure what kind of boundary there was between them and Thao and I. For myself, I would've gladly broken all the walls down. Thao wanted Bryony, I knew that. But his form of flirtation usually involved sparking up her frustration with him like some schoolyard boy, and I hadn't been brave enough to correct him again.

"Perhaps in winter you would come in handy during the cold nights," Bryony said, patting Thao's massive paw.

My cock twitched, and I raised my knee to hide any arousal that might pop up as I tried to battle down the thoughts of the four of us warming Bryony at night. Thao's tail swung wildly through the air before thumping down hard over Bryony's lap, an almost possessive drape, twitching and flicking at her skirts provocatively. Cosmo grinned down at his notepad.

❦

"I'm just saying, you've already taken on a great deal of the organization in the palace," Thao said, tying his hair back and wiping the sweat from his brow after his sparring match with Bryony.

She'd escaped the room as quickly as I'd arrived, eyes bright and cheeks flushed, no doubt running off to Cosmo or Owen to satisfy a craving I was beginning to wonder if Thao had been the one to create.

"I don't see how being her steward gets me any closer to being her lover," I muttered, frowning at myself. It was up to Bryony entirely whom she took to bed, and if it weren't for the hints of interest I caught from her, I would've dropped the matter. Anyway, I didn't *want* to be a steward. I had been an ambassador for six years. I understood the diplomacy Bryony was striving to navigate now, and where she was willing, I was happy to shepherd her through. Planning where a meal would be taken was less exciting to me.

"It secures your place in the court at least," Thao answered, equally snappish and quiet.

I crossed my arms over my chest, leaning in the doorway and watching him strip out of the tight fencing jacket. "What secures your place?"

I bit my tongue after the words came out, watching the clouds darken Thao's expression as he looked back at me. Sunlight was streaming through the open windows, the air crisp today—fall threatening the end of summer.

"You," Thao said softly. He sighed and rolled his shoulders, head falling back. "Hopefully. I'm sorry. I know we're not...she's not..."

"She's not tossing us out," I finished for him, raising an eyebrow.

He nodded, eyes shut, skin golden under the sun. "You're of more use to her than I am at the moment."

His jacket was hanging open, sweat darkening the thin shirt beneath, and I groaned at the perfect picture of him. Thao was always temptation personified. He had been my weakness since the moment I stepped into the Mennary court and he watched my every step from his high seat with the rest of the royal family.

I pushed off the door jamb and moved to his side, helping pull him free of the jacket.

"This is her court, not the one in Mennary. I don't think Bryony sees people as tools to be used. Besides, she has plans for you in winter," I said, grinning.

Thao huffed and gazed at me out of the corner of his eye. "Don't remind me. How will we wait that long?"

We. I loved him, and he loved me, and it was always *we*.

"Have I grown so boring in bed?" I teased, raising an eyebrow.

Thao growled, a familiar and favorite low sound at the back of his throat, and I stiffened for a moment—like the prey waiting for the predator. He lunged forward, hot hands holding my face as he stole the kiss from me, a deep and rough claiming of his mouth over mine. I pressed into him, laughing a little at the feel of the protective cup he wore while fencing, grinding into my leg.

"Never, you know that. It's just the anticipation. Let's go jump in the lake," he breathed, eyes bright on mine. His brow bounced. "Naked. If we're loud, she might see us out the window."

I laughed and Thao nipped at my jaw, cupping and squeezing me through my pants. "I want to tell her the truth soon," I moaned, bucking into his hand. "I hate not being able to shift with you. I miss my tiger."

Thao nodded and shrugged. "It's your decision. I trust her too."

I slid my arm over his shoulder as we left the room, my hand digging into his hair and making him groan as he palmed my ass. We were running for one of the southern exits toward the lake when I saw movement from the corner of my eye, a guard rushing forward to us, Cresswell Stark. My steps stalled, Thao glancing at me in confusion.

"Is the Princess in the training room?" Stark asked.

I shook my head. "She left a few minutes ago. Probably to her rooms or..." Or wherever her other Chosen were.

"There's a council carriage arriving." He looked so...*dire*, as if this were unexpected or terrible news.

I glanced at Thao, who was glaring back at the guard. "The council may wait on the princess," he said. "She doesn't answer to *them*."

I sighed and straightened. So much for our swim in the lake. "If there's more than three of them, we should see them in the grand hall, otherwise I think an informal visit in the greenhouse is more than suitable. Your Hi—" I paused, blinking at Thao, who only raised an eyebrow. "Would-would you go and see if you can find her, just to let her know there are guests?"

Thao grinned at me, and I resisted the urge to roll my eyes. I was playing steward again.

"Of course," he said, heading for one of the side halls that would take him past Cosmo's studio.

"We'll await their arrival at the door," I said to Stark, who nodded as I moved to follow him. I was dressed carelessly, and the visit had obviously been intended to catch us off our guard with no warning of their arrival. "Who would've been following the princess?" I asked Stark as I fell into step with him.

"Guard Yorley. I'll track him down when this is done."

"Thao may run into him on his search," I said, and watched as Stark's hackles lowered and he nodded. He was *genuinely* protective of Bryony. That was good. If I had the opportunity, I would share that with her. She deserved to have devoted guards. "It's better that she's not at the door to receive them. A woman of the queen's line is expected to be...occupied."

Stark relaxed again, shoulders lowering, and he nodded once more. He was extremely handsome, with beautifully full lips and green eyes that were especially striking against his brown skin. *Cosmo should sculpt him*, I thought, my own lips twitching with my smile.

"I should be in armor," he said, more to himself.

I'd noticed him wearing less of it as the days went by with our stay in the castle, usually when he wasn't on duty directly in front of us. "You should behave as if you are performing exactly as Her Royal Highness has ordered you to," I offered. "Princesses are expected to be eccentric, and Bryony will never know to correct any false impression you give."

His head turned to me, and his eyes flicked over me head to toe before he looked stiffly ahead again.

"Perhaps you wear less armor because her Hunger demands a better view of you," I said, mostly to watch his reaction.

His steps stumbled and his cheeks darkened, a scowl taking over his features as he straightened again. "I think her ambivalence proves otherwise," he muttered.

I hummed in sympathy, and we reached the front entrance at the same time that a sharp black carriage pulled up to the front steps. I glanced down at the marble and blinked. The steps were whole again. Not just whole, but shining white and laced with shimmering gold veins. An oddly amused jealousy struck me as I realized *how* and when those steps might've been mended. I wanted to make magic with Bryony *too*, damnit, although I didn't really care what the repairs were.

"Who is that?" Cresswell asked with a huff of irritation.

I dragged my eyes up from the steps and found the subject of his question, two women arriving on horseback behind the carriage. "Rebecca Sanders and—oh!—Lady Prudence Whitehall."

Lady Prudence was the only daughter and last in line of a once prominent and now obsolete noble family. Her grandfather had lost most of the family money in overseas investments, and then her father the remainder during card games with other nobility. Lady Prudence had some connections, mostly childhood friends like my mother who offered up their homes for her to visit at length, but I hadn't heard any news of her in years.

She was thinner than I remembered, but still a dignified presence even in humble clothing. Her hair was fully gray now, and she had a wince in her expression that I suspected had more to do with the horseback riding than her mood—she'd always been warm but firm with me as a child.

I turned to the guard stationed at the door. "Go to the kitchens and have them prepare some good, strong tea and scones. A tray of meat and olives if there are some to spare."

The guard, an older man with a gray-speckled brown beard, only blinked back at me. "I'm not a servant."

"Go, Walsh," Stark ordered for me. "Tell them to deliver it to the grand hall."

I caught the flash of anger and the clench of the guard's jaw, and then he turned on the heel of his boot and stomped away.

"The palace is understaffed," I murmured, and Cresswell grunted in agreement.

"That's hardly her fault," Cresswell whispered back. "Do you know the men?"

I watched the black carriage unload its passengers with a frown as I studied the distant faces. They were generally less familiar to me than Lady Prudence, but with a glance at their cloaks and the crest on the carriage, I made my guesses.

"The oldest is Lord Roderick, Earl of Swansbury, head of the Northern Council. The man helping him up the stairs is his son Jonathon, also a council member. The one with the black hat is Sir Speares, and the young one..." The young, handsome, ridiculously broad shouldered man who followed the others at the back, his eyes drinking in the palace before him.

"Is bait," Cresswell said under his breath.

I hummed with agreement. "He'll be their choice of the new steward," I said.

The council was going to dangle that man in front of Bryony like a treat for a well behaved dog, hoping to install him in her household. Bryony was smart enough to see the ruse for what it was and entirely the wrong princess to be set up for temptation. With a quick glance at Rebecca Sanders and Lady Prudence sliding down from their saddles, I suspected the council was going to leave disappointed.

"Get the door," Cresswell said to the second guard stationed.

"You greet them outside, I'll wait in here. Please include Rebecca Sanders and Lady Prudence," I said, and Cresswell granted me the faintest smile of appreciation with his nod before stepping out into the sunlight.

I moved back, under the transformed chandelier that fluttered and chimed with the breeze from the open door, over to the staircase to wait. Jonathon and Lord Roderick moved through the door first, their eyes widening as they took in the entrance of the palace. I didn't blame them, Bryony's magic had wrought enormous changes. The room wasn't just brighter and less in disrepair, there were new strange and whimsical touches too. The bannister of the staircase was carved with vines and blossoms, the crown molding now contained cherubic faces peering down from the corners, gazes gilded and glittering. The space was almost eerie in its beauty. This was no longer a man-made palace. Magic had changed the walls and the energy of the place; it was all now brimming with life.

"Lord Roderick, Lord Jonathon," I greeted with a slight bow. I was Chosen, so a bow was more of a courtesy than a demand of society now. Chosen had no clear political power, but they had the nobility of their mistress. I watched with a surprising satisfaction as the men returned the gesture, a little deeper.

I stepped forward to meet them halfway and shake their hands, placing us over the tiled mosaic of a suggestive wreath of flowers. "Sir Speares," I added with a faint dip of my head.

"I'd heard you were Chosen, Pope," Jonathon greeted, his eyes tracking me. Jonathon was married and ineligible for the choosing, but I was sure plenty of his peers had attended. "Gents say it was a strange kind of ceremony."

"Not at all, my mistress simply knows her own mind," I said. It was true, although maybe not of Bryony's mood during the choosing ceremony.

"She certainly must," Sir Speares muttered with a glance at Lord Roderick before returning to gaze around the room, his eyes cataloging every change.

"Pope, let me introduce Daniel Farraque," Lord Roderick said, stepping aside to reveal the fourth man.

Ah, so that was who he was. I'd heard of Daniel, the bastard and only son of Duke Farraque. He would likely receive his father's title, but there would always be a disparity in dignity for the family line now. A royal steward would be a good position for him. A member of Bryony's Chosen would be *ideal*. Being Chosen erased every inequity of rank one might be born with.

Daniel was as tall as I was, with a stronger jaw and brown hair. He had sharp blue eyes that ignored me in favor of studying the palace, and a mouth that belonged on a woman, swollen and bow shaped, made for kissing. He was handsome—not more so than Owen or I—but he had an animal quality about him that invited sexual thoughts. I didn't like him, but I wasn't sure if his company was to blame, or the fact that I knew he was meant to ensnare Bryony.

"She's made improvements," Lord Roderick said, as Daniel and I dismissed each other.

"I take it you were aware of the state of the palace then," I answered, watching Roderick's ice blue gaze strike me.

"Not recently," he said, extending the words carefully. And vaguely. He wouldn't admit to being fully aware of Sir Hubert's neglect. "Daniel has been the steward of his own father's estate for the past five years. He'll have the experience to see to any needs that arise for the princess."

"Perhaps," I said, waiting to see any kind of life in Daniel's gaze, any reaction to the way we were speaking of him. But there was nothing. Maybe he was used to being spoken of as if he weren't present. "I believe Princess Bryony may have already made her own inquiries for the position."

Roderick's mouth parted, pale brow furrowing, and I moved around him as Cresswell returned, Lady Prudence's hand around his arm and amused glitter in her gaze.

"Lady Prudence," I said, offering her a full bow.

"Ahh, Wendell. I'm not surprised to see you here, now that I think of it. Your mother must be pleased to have you back in Kimmery," Prudence greeted, pulling me in by the shoulders to kiss my cheeks as I rose.

"I've written, but not seen her yet," I admitted. Thao and I had only just managed to arrive in time for the choosing ceremony.

"Of course," Prudence said. Her warm gaze sharpened as it trailed over my shoulder. "I am glad to see you again, especially now that I'm wondering if Rebecca and I wasted the trip."

Rebecca Sanders watched the men behind me with a wary stare, and I leaned forward to whisper in Prudence's ear. "Can't tell yet, but I doubt it was a waste." I spun on my heel to face the room. "I think we might all adjourn to the great hall to await Her Royal Highness."

"This is...council business, of course. Perhaps the ladies

wouldn't mind waiting in a garden somewhere," Sir Speares offered.

Prudence scoffed and rolled her eyes at my side, and I did my best not to look delighted. "In fact, Magistrate Sanders and Lady Prudence are here at the *request* of Princess Bryony," I said, adding privately, *Instead of showing up without any warning.*

"Magistrate...Sanders?" Roderick asked, a white brow arching. "Your late husband, I believe, Mistress Sanders."

"My late husband," Rebecca agreed with a dip of her head. "And recently myself as appointed by—"

"As appointed by me."

My breath caught in my throat as I stared up at the vision on the stairs. Bryony was there, flanked by Owen, Thao, and Cosmo, with two guards at their back. She wore a gown in a tender and gleaming shade of pink that complemented the color in her cheeks and the plush and bitten quality of her lips. Her hair was down—not mussed, but in glossy waves that held the softest halo and slightest suggestion of being bed rumpled. She didn't look debauched, but perfectly sensual. But her Chosen...

My lips twitched as Thao smiled at me. He was still in the thin undershirt he'd been wearing, but he'd managed to change his pants to a looser and informal pair. Cosmo's shirt was half undone, revealing kissed bruises on his throat and chest, and Owen...Owen had very obviously been recently fucked stupid— there was no disguising the dizzy smile on his face or the fresh sweat on his brow.

I forgot to bow, but no one noticed except maybe Prudence. The men in the room were too busy trying to stare up at Bryony while also bending themselves nearly prostrate to the floor. She looked exactly as she ought to, regal and sexual all at once, the ideal woman of the queen's line.

"Councilmen, I'm glad to see you. You've saved me a missive," Bryony said, her eyes smiling even as her lips did not.

Roderick straightened first, and even though the man was a human ice cube, it was obvious that the sight of Bryony in all her sweet glory had caught him off guard.

"Our arrival was overdue, Your Highness," he said, a soft rasp in his voice.

Bryony's head dipped in a nod. "I'll be frank with you Lord Roderick—" I glanced to Cosmo, who nodded once at me. Good, someone had briefed her. "I'm not overly impressed with the council's work here in the north."

The spell of beauty cracked, and the men all straightened, Daniel slower than the others. His attention had been on the palace up until now, but it was wholly Bryony's now, and that made my fists clench at my side for some inexplicable reason.

"Sir Hubert—"

"Sir Hubert is an example, but not the entirety," Bryony said. Her voice echoed around us from her position on the stairs, or perhaps it was her power at work.

"Naturally, we'll be glad to discuss any number of matters with Your Highness. For today, we've come with a new steward for the palace," Lord Roderick said, his next bow stiffer and briefer. "Daniel Farraque would make you an admirable and trustworthy steward. The council has voted and—"

"Her Royal Highness has, I believe, already sought candidates for the position of steward," Cresswell Stark announced, gathering startled stares from around the room, his own face flushing in answer.

"You don't speak for Her Highness," Thao announced in a sharp and quick tone. "Not only has Princess Bryony managed the restoration of the palace without a formal steward, she has those already in her court who are in a better position to see to her needs. Wendell Pope makes an admirable steward already."

My throat squeezed shut, a ringing in my ear sounding over the silence that fell over us all. Bryony's head turned to stare at Thao, who was too suited to haughtiness and dignity to seem remotely embarrassed by the response to his outburst. And Bryony...

It never failed to amaze me all the facets that she possessed. The sweetness, the concern for others, the tender shyness—I understood that woman. The cold and demanding princess who made firm and absolute orders? I knew her too. But the fact they both existed in the same person was incredible.

Bryony was almost unreadable, at least until her hand slid out from the crook of Thao's elbow. She stepped down and I spared Thao the briefest glance, just enough to watch him pale faintly.

"My Chosen is correct. No one speaks for me," Bryony said, the words flat and firm. She gazed over the group of us on the main floor. "It appears I have three candidates for the position of steward. I should like to interview each of them."

"Your Highness, with all due respect," Lord Roderick started, but his voice stuttered as Bryony's eyes widened.

"All due respect? Lord Roderick, I understand it is the council's role to offer advisement to the queen's line to better allow them to tend to the Hunger."

"Yes, Your Highness."

"And you advise me to take on Daniel Farraque as steward?"

"We do, Your Highness."

"I acknowledge this and will now make up my own mind," Bryony said, staring down the head of the council until his head dipped, looking as though it physically cost him to do so.

Oddly, and for no clear reason, I suddenly found myself wishing Aric Martin was here too. He would've at least enjoyed the show while I was busy perishing of mortification.

"Let us move to the great hall, where you might each make your case privately," Bryony said, taking not one outstretched hand to help herself down the stairs and out of the hall.

⚜

"I'm sorry," Thao whispered.

I didn't answer, scratching my index finger over an aching hangnail on my thumb. Cosmo and Owen had escorted the council out through the gardens after Bryony's interview, and Rebecca and Prudence were alone in the room with the princess and Guard Stark now. There was the occasional soft laugh from inside that set me at ease. Bryony would choose Prudence, and the lady would make Bryony a perfect steward, if not an unconventional one.

"Wen," Thao murmured.

"You're lucky she's so—"

"I know."

I huffed, annoyed at the interruption, although I wasn't sure there was really just one word for what Bryony was. The door to the great hall opened, and I straightened, stepping forward as Lady Prudence appeared grinning.

"Oh, Wendell. I like her so much, don't you?" Prudence asked, eyes bright.

"Very much," I said, feeling myself soften at the thought.

Prudence hummed, and Rebecca Sanders followed her out the door, glancing at both Thao and I. "She's asked to see you both."

I stepped in without him, heading directly for the throne, prepared to bend down to one knee and apologize for the awkward position she'd been left in. But I wasn't quick enough. Bryony stood from the throne and skipped down the steps, meeting me in the center of the room. Her hand found mine, her face smooth, and she squeezed my fingers. Somehow, that only made me feel worse, my tongue tied in knots as Thao approached us with slow steps that echoed on the marble.

"Forgive me for my outburst, Your Highness," Thao said softly, bowing.

"Don't demure to me like that," Bryony snapped, and Thao straightened, red flooding his cheeks. "We are friends, and when we argue I don't want to have you suddenly treating me as a royal. That said, I am angry."

"I should have spoken to you privately on the subject," Thao said, a little less demurely.

"It should not be a subject at all," Bryony answered, and his eyes widened. She squeezed my hand again and looked up at me. "Do you *want* to be my steward?"

My mouth fell open and nothing came out for a moment, both their eyes on me. I swallowed hard and shook my head. "No." I swallowed off her title, not wanting to be chastised.

"I didn't think so," Bryony said, more gently and with a smile. It was gone by the time she looked at Thao again. "I understand that things have changed and that the role of a Chosen that I offered you may appear different now. But I consider you all equal, regardless of what shape our relationship takes privately. Thao, you will always be a prince, but in *my* court you are Chosen. Wendell is Chosen. *Owen* is Chosen. There is no other rank between you."

Thao was at my side, and his tension was like a vibration of energy against me as he listened to Bryony. I wanted to soothe him, but I didn't want to interfere with the weight of Bryony's words.

"The two of you have already proven your worth in helping me navigate this journey, but if you cannot accept your role and that *I* am your superior, then you won't be satisfied here. I am the princess. You are Chosen."

My heart broke in that moment. Partly for Thao. He was the youngest male heir in his family, but he was raised prepared to lead a kingdom if the day ever came. To be Bryony's Chosen had seemed a blessing, but perhaps she was right. Maybe Thao would be better suited in a royal alliance, king by marriage in some smaller kingdom. It broke for myself too. If Thao left, I would follow, but how much further could we really travel together?

"I understand," Thao said, with a stiff bow.

Bryony sighed, her expression falling as he turned on his heel and headed for the door. I made to follow him out, and she stopped me with a touch on my chest, waiting for the door to shut behind him. Should I have pushed past her?

"I'm sorry for the position that put you in," she said, sucking on her bottom lip.

I shook my head. "I'm sorry for the added complication regarding the steward. You're choosing Lady Prudence?"

Bryony's nose wrinkled, and she reached her hand up and rubbed at the spot. "I'm taking them both. I know, I know. Farraque is obviously meant to report on me to the council."

"And to find a place in your Chosen," I added, and she shrugged. "You want to keep him close and hope it persuades them to stay out of your affairs?"

"That, and that my grandmother will hear of me possessing the Hunger."

"You aren't afraid they'll be successful and the Hunger will claim him?" I asked. I was afraid of that, or at least, I was if Daniel wasn't sincere as the rest of us had become.

Bryony laughed. "Wendell, if my Hunger was persuaded by

charm or seduction or good looks, it would've claimed you from the very beginning." I swallowed, ignoring the flush of my cheeks as our eyes met, and her smile faltered. "I hope I haven't fractured anything between the two of you."

I sighed and tried to roll the tension out of my shoulders. "I think you only pointed out the fractures. Thao and I will be all right. We are used to trials and skilled at overcoming them."

Her shoulders eased, and I gave myself a moment before the inevitable confrontation with Thao to drink her in. Some of her glow had worn away since she gazed down at us from the stairs, but she was no less beautiful for looking a little wearied. There was nothing specific, nothing concrete between Bryony and I, but the thought of leaving her troubled me.

"Thao and I have belonged to one another almost since the beginning," I said, and Bryony nodded with a faint smile, a slight wince in her gaze. "But we *are* your Chosen, and there is..." I studied her eyes, wondering if continuing might interrupt whatever there was between us. "There is room in our hearts made for you."

My hand reached out of its own accord, fingertips settling against Bryony's jaw, tilting her face up. I was bowing before I knew my own plan, Bryony's eyes widening but her own chin lifting just enough for our mouths to graze together. She tasted sweet and smelled like a meadow, and she leaned into the kiss, our eyes falling shut in the same moment. My heart was hammering in my chest, but the rest of me was steady. If Thao was genuinely insulted by Bryony's speech, I might've lied to her, and perhaps this was a goodbye instead of an invitation.

I stood up straight again and wondered if I imagined the understanding in her gaze.

"I should speak to him," I said.

She nodded, hands shaking slightly as she twisted her hair off her shoulders, smoothing it around her fist. "And I have to go and finish with the council for the moment. They're going to give me more trouble, aren't they?"

"This is only the beginning," I agreed.

Bryony's shoulders squared, and the soft girl from a moment ago became a regal woman again.

"Good luck," I offered.

She arched an eyebrow at me and I grinned. Yes, I needed luck too, probably. We turned in opposite directions and I headed for the door, wondering how far Thao had gotten already.

Not far at all, as it turned out.

He was waiting outside the door, propped up against the wall with a storm on his expression and a loose strand of black hair kissing his cheek. His head lifted as I stepped out, glower digging into his brow, and I resisted the urge to flinch.

"I understand that you're angry," I started.

"Of course I'm angry," Thao snapped, and my shoulders sagged. His jaw ground and we stared at one another, weight sinking from my chest down to my stomach as I waited. Thao frowned, and then his eyes fell shut with a long groan, hands lifting to cover his face. "I'm angry with *myself*, Wen."

"Oh." Relief rushed through me.

"Am I so bad, really? You seem surprised by this."

I winced and stepped forward to him, still cautious. "It's only that I...I've never seen anyone speak to you that way and..."

Thao's hands lowered, and his eyes were wide and worried. "I..." He cursed and shook his head. "I am not always the prince, Wen. I don't mean to be with you. And I will learn not to be with Bryony as well. I embarrassed her, I embarrassed *you*, and in so doing, myself."

Well, this was...a minor revelation. I'd always believed that Thao and I had an understanding of sorts. He didn't flaunt his authority in our personal relationship, but I also didn't break the rules of our positions.

"I know that I have too much pride," Thao said softly, lowering his hands.

"You were raised to be a king," I said, with a shrug.

Thao scoffed. "No, I was raised to *act* like one. An unfortunate distinction that's causing me grief recently. I was never going to really rule, not in Mennary nor in any marriage for politics."

I hummed, and my arms opened automatically as Thao leaned forward to fill the space. They wrapped around him, and I took a deep breath of his warm, spicy scent. "But...can you stand to be equal to Cosmo and Owen...to me?"

Thao stiffened for a moment before leaning back in our embrace, frowning up at me. "Wen, I am more than aware of the ways in which you are superior to me. It's been a long time that I've considered you my equal, and I'll do better to demonstrate it."

I stared at him, my smile growing and twitching with a restrained laugh as Thao rolled his eyes and sighed.

"Yes, the others too. I will do better. And I give you full permission to remind me of my place," he said, grinning.

I dipped my head to hover over his, seeing the love and desire in his gaze. "Your place is with me," I said, kissing him at last, licking at his lips and sucking on the bottom one gently. "And now, with her."

"Yes," Thao said, rising to his toes for another, deeper kiss.

22.
BRYONY

Hunger stirred in my veins, little glowing remnants from Wendell's gentle kiss. I wasn't sure his words would remain true after speaking to Thao, but I didn't regret what I'd said. Thao's slights seemed to roll comfortably off Owen and Cosmo's shoulders, but that didn't mean they ought to bear them. And I refused to tolerate someone speaking over my own opinion when I didn't ask for the help.

I pushed my hands into the pockets of my gown to resist the urge to fidget as I stepped out of the palace, spotting Owen and Cosmo with our guests by the water.

"Your Highness."

I startled and looked over my shoulder. Of course! The guard, Cresswell Stark, was at my back. I hadn't *forgotten* about him exactly, I just wasn't really used to noticing palace staff around me.

"Guard Stark—"

"I apologize for my outburst earlier."

"Oh...yes. It's... You're forgiven," I said, watching him frown in response.

"Prince Thao had every right to correct me," he said.

"You were both out of turn. I manage my own opinions very well," I said, turning away again and feeling him at my back this time as I walked. "You were at least right about them, where Thao was pressing his own. I'd rather forget it and address the situation in front of us."

"The council only has their own interests at heart," Cresswell said, but it was low, as if he wasn't quite sure whether he was being inappropriate in speaking.

If I was going to insist my own opinions being heard in

public, I ought to at least grant others the same courtesy in private. "I suspect the same, yes," I offered, glancing over my shoulder to see Cresswell nod.

"I'll keep my eye on him," Cresswell growled, glaring past me to where Daniel Farraque watched my approach, his hands on the back of an empty chair.

I ignored the implication of the empty seat as I arrived, passing by the outstretched hands and moving toward Owen. He was standing at his own seat—an overturned log by the shore of the lake he was sharing with a few of his usual guests, birds and critters—and he grinned at me as I reached him, immediately settling and drawing me onto his lap. My own mother and Camellia were rarely out of reach of one of their Chosen, and I was more than happy to use their example in this case.

"Sit, gentlemen, please." I watched them with Owen's arms banded loosely around my waist, Cosmo joining us at my side.

Daniel Farraque remained standing, moving away from the chair for Lady Prudence to seat herself, and his eyes were fastened to me in a cold examination. Perhaps the council had not briefed him in charm. That suited me fine.

"I take it you've had adequate time to make your decision, Your Highness," Lord Roderick said, with a cursory nod of his head.

I sucked my teeth, debating on if it might be more enjoyable to say I hadn't, and then decided it would be better to have the council out of my hair sooner rather than later.

"Lady Prudence has the position of my steward; she is exactly what I was looking for," I said, turning and nodding to Rebecca. "Thank you Magistrate Sanders for the introduction."

Rebecca dipped her head in answer but she was stiff, her eyes trailing to the councilmen, awaiting retribution no doubt.

"She is..." Roderick's son sputtered and gestured to the older woman, who smiled beatifically back at him. "She is elderly, and a *woman*."

"I am, indeed. Well spotted, Jonathon," Lady Prudence cooed as the men of the council stirred irritably in their seats.

"She is therefore perfectly suited to anticipating my needs," I said. "However, she is not well equipped to maintain all areas of the grounds and estate. We both understand that," I said with a nod and a smile at Lady Prudence. "So I should like it if Daniel Farraque were to remain in position as a second steward."

"He should be head," Sir Speares cried.

"I don't see why either need be in charge of the other if their domains are clearly divided," I said with a shrug. "However, if you object, Mr. Farraque, I'm sure we can find someone else to assist Lady Prudence."

"He does not—"

"I don't object, Your Highness." Daniel bowed with the words, cutting off Lord Roderick and speaking at last. He had a rasp in his voice, an almost gentle whistle in the low notes. It was a pleasant sound with a bland delivery, and I wondered who the man in front of me really *was*.

"Is there...is there something we might do about the *barn* animal?" Lord Roderick scoffed.

I frowned and then looked on Owen's other side to discover a raccoon had joined us, sitting on its hind legs and shaking its hands at Owen.

"Sorry," Owen murmured to me. "Shoo. No, not now."

I pinched my lips between my teeth but it was no use, a giggle rising. The raccoon was urgent, although respectfully silent as it glanced over at the rest of us. I twisted on Owen's lap and reached into his pocket, pulling out the handful of seeds and nuts he always seemed to carry.

"They come because they know you have food," I murmured.

"I have food because they always come," Owen corrected, but the raccoon was appeased as I spread the treats out on the log, gifting me with a chitter of thanks.

I looked up again and found a mix of amusement and horror on the faces watching us. "We are in his domain, really," I said shrugging.

Lord Roderick scoffed and released a beleaguered sigh. "Your Highness, I appreciate your energy and tenacity, it speaks well of your ability to rule. However, we in the council have the highest duty of making your work *easier* with our counseling."

"I don't see how it should be easier for me to make a decision than for you to finally accept it, Lord Roderick. I'm not in the habit of finding independent thought taxing," I said.

Cosmo choked on a laugh and Lady Prudence snorted, making Rebecca Sanders's smile appear at last. And *still* Daniel was impassive, only studying, and not in the pleasant way Cosmo always managed. He left me feeling like a bug under a magnifying glass, and I wondered if he planned on angling the lens to burn me.

"Of course, Your Highness," Lord Roderick said. "Naturally, you are in charge of your own household."

"Lord Roderick, I am the princess inherit," I said softly, watching the older man stiffen in his seat. "My influence extends beyond this palace. I am not here to holiday in the north, I am here to see to my people's needs now that I find them neglected."

Owen's hands were tight around my waist, the raccoon taking off toward the lake behind us with a nervous flurry of chatter, and Cosmo was tense at our side. I kept my eyes on Roderick's as they bored coldly against me.

"Yes, Your Highness," he said, every syllable as sharp as if it were cutting his tongue and leaving his mouth bloody. "I assume you mean your reprieve of the taxes. They *will* have to resume, you understand."

"I do. After the harvest. And while I remain here I will oversee where the money goes."

Lord Roderick's smile was poisonous. "If you insist and the crown permits."

Ah. Yes, that little snag.

"Naturally," I said instead, stroking gently over the back of Owen's hand until he eased.

⁂

"But will the queen support you?" Wendell asked, leaning forward to keep his voice low as my Chosen and I dined alone in my suite.

The council had, thankfully, left not long after the tense discussion by the water, leaving Daniel Farraque in our company.

Wendell, Owen, and Cosmo took it upon themselves to run Daniel through the palace and grounds to introduce him to his duties, while Thao and I accompanied Lady Prudence in finding a room. I had full confidence in the older woman, who seemed thrilled to manage the young maid and eager to meet the cook. Prudence was friendly and agreeable, but also obviously happy to exert control where it was needed, and I gave Rebecca Sanders the most sincere thanks before sending her back to Rumsbrooke in a spare carriage.

"My mother probably *would* support me, if she's the one who hears of this, but she leaves most of the ruling to my grandmother and..." I paused, drawing up a bite of pheasant doused in a herbal sauce to my lips. "I'm afraid my grandmother will take this as a sign that I still don't possess the Hunger and instead am only meddling in politics."

"Is that so bad?" Cosmo asked, wearing a half smile.

"It's not what I was raised to do," I said with a heavy sigh. "I should've seemed more interested in Farraque so the council felt more secure. How annoying to finally have the Hunger and still not appear so."

"You looked the part, trust me. No man could take their eyes off you as you stood at the top of the stairs," Wendell said, and I blushed under his stare, glancing warily at Thao.

Thao only grinned at us both. He seemed...comparatively docile now. I'd watched him leave the great hall with his spine iron straight and eyes blazing, but by the time he and Wendell returned to the rest of us before the council left, all the fire had burned out of him. If he'd been angry with me or with Wendell, it was gone now, and he was...

"The hair was my touch," Thao said proudly. "She looks just a little debauched with it down, doesn't she?"

"She looked a little debauched because she had been," Owen said, his ankle nudging against mine.

Thao only laughed and shook his head. "Yes, I heard you. I was waiting to come in."

I puffed a breath and choked on my bite, heat flooding my cheeks. I wasn't *surprised* exactly. Thao and Wendell often appeared in the morning shortly after I'd just finished sating the

Hunger with my Chosen. It was just a little galling to have it mentioned plainly.

"What are you going to do with the spy now that you've let him in?" Cosmo asked.

"Farraque's a spy?" Owen murmured to me, brow furrowing with concern.

"The council would be mad not to try and place one in Bryony's court," Thao said, shrugging. "She's making changes, and ones that will seriously affect or nullify their power in the kingdom."

Owen hummed and nodded, and I found Wendell's eyes in time to exchange a small smile. Thao was being polite to Owen, and patient. There was a kind of peace amongst us now, and it left me warm and buzzing in spite of the day.

"He has duties to attend to now. I'm sure the council wants my Hunger to make me useless against him but..." I shrugged and grinned. "They'll be disappointed."

"Especially if Farraque's going to continue to be such a wooden board of a human being," Cosmo said.

"Don't underestimate what he might see, what he can learn from others," Wendell said, watching me. "You may need to..."

"Dangle fruit out of his reach," Thao finished for him with a nod. "Not let him in, but not shut him out entirely either. Your Hunger is real, but it's also—"

"It behaves differently," I agreed with a nod. I focused on my plate for a moment, thinking, my eyes sliding to Owen on my left and to Cosmo on my right. "I'm more modest than my family, but it might help to be..."

"Demonstrative," Wendell offered.

Cosmo leaned toward me, his hand resting on my thigh. "If you're comfortable, it's easily managed."

"I won't make my pleasure a performance for the sake of the council, but I suppose we can stop trying to be quite so sneaky," I said, leaving Thao and Wendell scoffing to themselves.

"It won't take a great effort," Thao muttered but he flashed me a warm smile when he looked up from his plate.

"I've made another decision," I said, trying to change the subject but only finding myself blushing under the general attention. "I want to restore the harvest festival. It's short notice, I know. And usually managed by the people, but they have so little and they receive so little from the harvests—oh! I should've spoken to Lord Roderick about that horrible law."

"I think if you'd pressed another issue to Lord Roderick, he would've had a heart attack or started a rebellion," Wendell said. "A harvest festival is an innocent but symbolic gesture. The crown princess organizing it will imply your best wishes to your people."

"Exactly, and to be honest, I think I could probably... I think the magic of the Hunger could ensure a better harvest," I said, blushing and tilting my chin up.

Cosmo coughed, a wine glass raised to his lips, his eyes wide.

"You want to..." Owen's eyebrows waggled, and his lips curled up.

I nodded and resisted the impulse to giggle."I want a private tent at the festival. It should be out in the fields, or near them. I don't think anyone needs to *know*, well, aside from us, but since we don't really know the range of the Hunger's power, it might be better to be close when we..."

When we have sex. For magic. To ensure good crops.

It sounded like a ridiculous plan when I spelled it out in my head, but if it didn't work, it wouldn't do any real harm. It probably wouldn't do any real harm. I didn't really know for certain, but it hadn't done any yet.

"A trial might be in order in the meadow," Cosmo said, wiping his smiling mouth. I reached out and pinched his ribs, and his laugh broke free. "What? We should just be sure that you don't create giant ears of corn or wheat strong enough to break the scythes."

"A royal harvest festival it is then," Wendell said. "That should keep Farraque busy at least."

23.
DANIEL

"A festival?"

"A harvest festival," Owen echoed. He was big and handsome, and he reminded me of a stud in a horse stable. It was obvious by a glance at his trousers why the princess favored him. It was the same reason the council hoped she might favor me.

"There should be performers. Dancers and fire eaters and jugglers," Prince Thao mused, craning his neck to look around Wendell Pope to his lady, who beamed at him.

The princess and her Chosen had called on me from the greenhouse the next morning, interrupting my breakfast in my rooms. I was used to interruptions, to summons and dismissals. Lady Prudence was there already when I arrived, seated at the table with the princess as if she were royal or Chosen herself. There was a chair open for me too, although I had yet to take it.

"There is a budget, Thao," Wendell murmured.

I pulled the chair back from the table and lowered myself slowly, half expecting someone to correct my impudence. No one said a word.

"I know a few performers from Rumsbrooke. Let them hold their hat out for tips, and they'll attend for the joy of it. It's been a long time since the north has seen any celebration," Cosmo said.

Cosmo Pianetta was an artist of some kind from what I'd learned. He and Owen sat on either side of the princess, free with their touches, occasionally feeding her bites from their own plates. They were the favorites, and I needed to find my place amongst them. Two commoner favorites did the council no good in the princess's ear.

"The same might be done with food vendors. If the festival is free to the people and their coin purses are heavier without any recent taxes, there's bound to be cooks and craftsman who would be glad to put up a stall for the event," Lady Prudence said. She had a bound notebook in her lap and scribbled there with a fountain pen.

I stared at the princess, waiting for her to speak the mind she'd so readily laid out the day before. Instead, she looked happy to let the others lead the conversation. She appeared to be the same woman, still petite and pretty, still flushed with pleasure, but all the iron had melted away overnight.

"I can get the word out in Rumsbrooke," I offered, catching the princess's eye.

"Musicians too," Wendell said, perking up.

That was it, just the briefest glance. Looking at the princess's small collection of Chosen, I wondered if I needed to shave my beard to catch her eye, or if Lord Roderick needed to find another candidate. Women usually noticed me, and Roderick had perhaps mistakenly assumed that the princess's Hunger would manage the work of setting the bait to have me in her ear.

"Daniel and I will speak to the farmers and choose a date for the festival once the fields are cleared," Lady Prudence said.

"Before the harvest!" Princess Bryony sat up abruptly in her seat, blushing a little and pressing her lips together before continuing. "I think...I think it might be nice if it were before. Like a good luck charm."

"Before then," Lady Prudence said with an indulgent smile, turning to me. "We'll work quickly."

"At Your Highness's pleasure," I said, bending in my seat and then preparing to stand.

"Stay, we've interrupted your breakfast. You deserve a share of ours," the princess said.

It was sweetly spoken, although delivered in equal share to Lady Prudence, and I wasn't sure if I should take her in earnest or not. *You should charm her*, Lord Roderick's voice hissed. But with a quick survey around the table, seeing the suspicion on the Chosen's face, and Lady Prudence helping herself to a cup of tea that had clearly been set out for her long before my arrival, I shook my head.

"I'll ride out and look for a suitable location," I said. "The start of the harvest season isn't far from now. Better to begin now. Your Highness." I bowed as I stood and heard the soft hum of acknowledgement.

There would be time to try and seduce her soon. She'd made it clear that she didn't trust the council, and the best remedy might be to go about the actual work of being a steward.

Besides, it was the only part of this arrangement with the council I actually liked.

THREE DAYS BACK AND FORTH, up and down the mountain, and the festival was set for two weeks away. It would still feel like summer in the fields, but Princess Bryony would fall out of her small favor if she asked the farmers to *delay* the harvests.

I saw her in brief moments, and usually in the company of Lady Prudence: with the announcement that I'd found a village commons that was central and could host the festivities, to tell her that a local leader had been more than happy to take up the organization of vendors who were piling up quickly now that the word was out, to inform her that her particularly requested private tents would be prepared.

Every visit involved waiting outside a door under the glowering stare of the Head of the Royal Guard, before being admitted in to find a rumpled princess and a disheveled man. But it was only ever Owen or Cosmo, which would be an interesting fact to share with Jonathon later.

I marched now toward the training room, smirking slightly at the guard's dark stare at my approach. He and I should've been friends, I thought. He looked like someone's bastard too, although probably not one who would get to inherit his father's estate. Not that mine had been worth anything but a title no one felt the need to grant me.

I heard the grunts from within the room first, not unfamiliar, but then an unexpected crash of metal on metal. My steps nearly stumbled as the guard opened the door to me rather than making me wait, and my eyes widened as I took in the scene inside.

Not love-making but sword-fighting. I stared, paused in the doorway, as I watched Princess Bryony snarl and swing a sword in Prince Thao's direction, his own quick to block her blade. The weapons were unfamiliar, longer and broader than a Kimmerian fencing sword, and their fighting was more fluid in movement.

Well, Thao was fluid. Bryony stumbled back at the force of contact, a gasp on the air, before quickly going into an attack again. The difference was clear between them, Bryony was fast and aggressive, but her face was red with exertion and she was sweating and slowing, while Thao moved only when he needed to, efficient and graceful. With her next strike, Thao caught the crook of her arm with his, swinging her around until her back hit his chest with an audible *oof* and the flat side of his blade rested against her throat.

"You're moving too much, wasting energy," Thao said.

"If I don't move, and you don't move, are we really sparring?" Bryony asked tartly, breaths gasping.

I fought myself, but Thao only laughed. They were close, and they seemed comfortable with one another's bodies, but also uncertain of each other. Thao lowered his own sword slowly, and Bryony's head turned in his direction.

She saw me first, and stepped away.

"Mr. Farraque," she said, and I fought the urge to glare. It was what she always called me, her and everyone else.

"Daniel, please, Your Highness," I said, bowing for her.

Thao whispered something, too quiet for me to hear, but I understood the meaning as Bryony shook her head.

"No, go on. I'm fine."

Thao nodded and sheathed his sword, swinging the harness over his shoulder and heading for the exit with a cursory glare in my direction.

"What did you need?" she asked, rolling her shoulders.

She was wearing fencing pants and what must've been a shirt from one of her Chosen, and it was a curiously tempting sight. I knew two kinds of women mainly. The gentlemen's daughters who wanted me whispering filth in their ear but never their beds, and the whores my father had introduced me to to slake my appetites. This princess was an entirely foreign creature from what I'd seen so far.

"I need nothing but to serve you, Your Highness," I offered, painting on a smile as I approached her. "I only came to say that the word is out in the villages and the festival is already considered to be a success."

Her brows raised. "A success? It's still weeks away."

"Your people have faith in you," I said, finally earning a smile.

"I'm happy if they are," she said, and my steps paused.

She's being sincere, isn't she? I glanced over my shoulder and realized we were still alone. Thao had left, and the guard remained outside in the hall. *Here is your opportunity.*

"I didn't recognize the fighting style," I asked, moving closer to the wall, finding the fencing swords resting in their places and picking one up that looked weighted for me. I loved fencing. It was one of the rare avenues in schooling where I could excel against the wealthy—and legitimate—peers, without anyone trying to stomp me back down into the dirt.

"Thao is training me in inukat." She'd been wiping her palms on her pants, rocking her head on her long throat to work the tension out, and she paused, watching me with the sabre. "You fence?"

"Mm, in school."

"And you prefer sabre," she said, eyeing it with an almost predatory interest.

A real smile spread over my lips. "Have you been missing a proper match?"

She glanced to the door, but only for a second before hurrying to the wall, grabbing up a whip of blade and setting the broader sword aside. "Maybe a little. One touch winner?"

My eyes widened, and I glanced down at myself. I was fresh off my horse, and she was only half dressed for a match.

"I won't scratch you, just a little poke," Bryony said grinning, bouncing on the balls of her feet.

I laughed and rolled my shoulders. If I put so much as a scratch on the princess, I'd probably guarantee my head on a platter. But she wasn't really so delicate, was she? I could act defensively and let her win, see if it gained favor. Or...

I stepped back, sinking into position, knees bent and blade extended, body balanced. Bryony flashed me a feral little smile that sent heat running through me, and then moved into position.

"At the ready," I said, watching the slow release of her breath, the subtle shift in her shoulders. "Begin."

She was lightning quick, it was her obvious advantage against me, but I met her at center, blades clashing and tangling. Any consideration I'd had to let her win went out the window in the sudden spark of the match, and I took an opening against her left rib without thinking.

She gasped, and we jumped back from one another. I thought at first I'd used too much force, but there was barely a snag in her loose shirt.

"Point," I said, shrugging at her eyes.

"Out of three," she said immediately, gaze narrowing.

Well, this was a different kind of seduction than I might've expected, but I liked it better, my blood hammering through my veins as we moved back into position.

Her brow was furrowed in concentration, lips pursed in a pout of frustration that I was sure she would've pressed to a flat line if she'd realized it was there.

"Begin."

She learned quickly, charging and lacking any hesitation, taking an opening on my right shoulder that most of my schoolmates had never bothered learning. The tip of her blade bit into the skin of my arm, but it just raised my excitement, the little pinprick she'd promised to deliver.

"Point," she said, arching an eyebrow.

She blinked at my answering smile and backed away, our steps a reflection of one another. "At the ready," she murmured, sinking into her knees.

Now was the moment, fuck the third point. I'd have a victory either way.

"Begin," I said, and we both made quick steps to center.

I held my blade wide, dodging out of regulation as she aimed for me. I appeared in front of her before she knew I was coming. Her breath caught as I wrapped an arm around her back and hauled her roughly against my chest, her head rearing back to look up at me.

"I wonder why your Chosen didn't stay. If sword-fighting doesn't satisfy you, I can promise a better way to make your heart race..." I trailed off as I watched her, felt her stiffen in my arms, watched her eyes widen, pupils contracting as she tried to lean away.

Fear. Just for a moment.

Perhaps I knew three kinds of women because this was a familiar sight too. My mother had startled and cowered this way when she found herself abandoned in our cottage, alone with a man and only me as a little boy to bear witness. I was ready to pull away, but Bryony was quicker, and I stilled as a long blade slid neatly up through the space between us, the sharp tip kissing the underside of my throat.

"Apolo—"

"Are you my Chosen, Daniel Farraque?" Princess Bryony asked, eyes narrowing to slits.

"No, Your Highness," I said, quick to drop my hands to my side, all the purr I'd tried to gather in my voice fading away to flat.

Bryony took a small fraction of the offered space, the sabre tip digging just enough for me to feel the heat of pain. "Have I requested your attention in some way?"

"No, Your Highness."

"If you touch me again without my express demand, I will cut your hands off and courier them myself to Lord Roderick, do you understand?"

I understood, but my cock didn't because it jumped with a horribly timed interest and nudged against the princess's waist.

"Yes, Your Highness."

"Leave the room," Bryony said, almost a growl, as she stepped back from me.

I made my exit quickly, and with a strange thrill coursing through my veins that had nothing to do with my hands still being attached to my arms.

The door was cracked open when I reached it, and the guard outside was smirking.

⚜

I'D BEEN to Rumsbrooke often enough, although it wasn't a place one generally looked forward to visiting. The people were unfriendly and guarded, the streets were filthy, the buildings were decrepit, and I always left feeling as though I was covered in a thin but invisible layer of grime.

It'd been months since my last visit, and I took a deep breath of the moderately fresh air before approaching the gate. Except the city inside wasn't quite what I expected. It was still dirty, still close, still crowded, but the people seemed busy now and...

"Oh, excuse me, sir," one young girl cried before dashing through the street, grinning and giggling as she reached her friends on the other side. And no one cursed after her.

Not everyone was in high spirits, but tempers seemed a little brighter than usual, and there wasn't half the trash and refuse lying about that there usually seemed to be. I nudged my horse forward, waiting for the city I remembered and not *quite* finding it. I glanced up at the sky and decided to blame the sun being out, which it almost never seemed to be in Rumsbrooke. Maybe I had only ever been here during bad weather.

I reached the Yawning Pig and guided my horse to a stand, finding a small boy sitting under an awning nearby.

"Coin to watch the horse," I called, rousing him from his nap and pulling a coin from my pocket. "I'm a friend of Emory, and there'll be more coin if you don't swindle me."

"You're the new palace steward," the boy said, eyes widening.

Hmm, I hadn't expected that particular news to spread so easily or swiftly. "I am."

"What's she like? My friend Asher says he'd seen her, but I don't believe him. Is she really so pretty?"

Bryony, eyes dark and teeth gritted with her sword to my throat flashed in my mind. "Can barely look at her and remember to speak," I said. "The guards say she can make flowers bloom just by walking by, but I haven't seen it yet."

The boy mouthed amazement and pocketed my coin as I left him by my horse and headed for the entrance.

The Yawning Pig really only came to life at night, lit up by candles and lanterns, full of whores and men who could barely pay for a kiss on the cheek, let alone the full service. By daylight, it was an odd kind of space, with an empty stage that looked like the yawning maw of an enormous pig, and a bar that I could usually help myself to without anyone being the wiser.

Today there were two men seated, drinking from foggy glasses.

Jonathon Roderick and Emory...who the hell knew the man's last name, if he even had one.

"You've started without me," I said, moving to join them and shaking my head at the offered bottle. I didn't like alcohol, for myself or for most men. The indulgence only seemed to bring out ugliness, even in smaller doses, and larger ones made it a poisonous habit.

"How go your efforts with Her Highness?" Jonathon asked as I helped myself to a barstool.

"Your father didn't give me an easy start of it. It's obvious there's hard feelings for the council." *And apparently, sword fighting isn't a way into the woman's bed.*

"Of course there are, that's why we've put you in the position," Jonathon scoffed.

"I always said it should've been me," Emory said with a grin and shrug.

Emory might've had better luck if the princess were tempted by elegant looks. Women had never made their interest in me secret, but even I knew that Emory was as beautiful *and* handsome, with vivid auburn hair and eyes to match a sky in a prettier place of the world.

"Not if Martin really is one of her Chosen, although we think that might've been a bluff," Jonathon muttered.

"Aric Martin?" I asked, eyes flashing between the two men.

"King of Thieves, proprietor of the Wing and Rook," Jonathon said with a nod and a roll of his eyes.

I'd heard of him but never bothered venturing that far into the heart of Rumsbrooke, especially not after meeting Emory, who more than satisfied my limited interest in thieves and barkeeps.

"King of dusty old pick-pockets," Emory scoffed, combing fingers through his fiery strands. "As if he could get it up and keep it hard long enough to satisfy the Hunger."

"I haven't seen him at the palace," I offered. I debated saying more, that while I'd seen evidence of Princess Bryony's passions, I hadn't seen real proof of the Hunger itself. For all I knew, she was only bedding two of her Chosen, which seemed contradictory to what I knew of the queen's line, but I hesitated and let the others fill the silence.

"Her festival seems to be a hit," Jonathon said.

"For now," Emory added.

"I take it you have a plan," I said, glancing between them.

"Nothing I intend to know anything of," Jonathon said, grinning and raising his hands in unconvincing innocence.

"My court will attend, of course, most of Rumsbrooke will," Emory said, leaning back against the bar. "We'll be...working."

Stealing. They'd be stealing from people attending the festivities.

"Am I...meant to be doing something about the guards?" I asked, frowning.

Emory scoffed, tossing his red hair to the side. "We can manage the guards. You don't need to have a hand in it. However, if you happened to *see* something, undoubtedly it was from one of Aric Martin's men. Not mine. And you can tell Her Highness as much."

"Speaking of the imperious little bitch," Jonathon said, clearing his throat.

"It's in progress," I said, keeping my face impassive. It was an expression I'd learned to wear at a young age when a scowl could earn me a belt and laughter was too spirited and tears were weak. Better to remain blank. "I see enough from the outside. She's only claimed two of her Chosen."

"The others are lovers," Jonathon said, waving a hand through the air. "We knew as much already. What? You think you're our only man in the palace? You're not there to see, Dan, you're there to fuck the princess until she's too busy wetting your cock to think about taxes and festivals and Kimmery. If you can't do the job—"

"It will happen soon," I said, holding Jonathon's gaze, pretending I didn't feel the cold kiss of sharp steel against my throat.

"Good," Jonathon said, eyes narrowing. "You're replaceable."

"He knows," Emory said, his grin stretching wide.

As a younger man, I would've clenched my fists, ground my jaw, and fought the urge to punch them both. That fire had more or less burned out of me by now. Emory was right. My father could pass his name and estate to a different bastard or some eager cousin. Jonathon and Lord Roderick could find another cock to ensnare the princess.

I was going to end up losing my hands at this rate.

24.
BRYONY

"**C**lose," I whimpered, digging my fingers into Owen's curls as his hands pressed my knees out like wings, his hips rocking into mine, cock gliding wetly inside of me.

"Fuck, the feel of you," Owen rasped, his mouth sucking my collarbone, teeth and tongue scratching and laving every inch of me.

I didn't know where the magic began and ended, or where I was really putting it at this point. It was meant to be outside of us—into the ground beneath us or up into the sky overhead, but there was a heavy charge everywhere our skin touched, flames of power licking between us.

"Owen," I gasped, tugging on his strands, drawing his face up to hover over mine as my body rolled to meet his.

Owen's eyes were glassy and unfocused, his brow furrowed and pupils full and black. "I'm here," he said, but it was a gasp. How long had we been out here in the sun like this? How many times had I come and taken Owen down with me, only for us to start all over again?

His mouth landed against mine, the kiss clumsy as we both groaned, bodies growing frenzied. I wanted to clutch Owen to me, to tie my legs and arms around him and cling to him as we both fell over the edge, but my skin felt heavy with magic and Owen was already soaking so much of it up—*had* already. I sobbed as the gentle tremble began to start in my muscles, and threw my hands back, digging my fingers into the grass and pressing my heels down on the blanket we lay on. Owen bucked, rising up on the palms of his hands and his knees, watching the quick slap of our flesh where we were joined, before his eyes slammed shut and his head was thrown back, the both of us crying out.

I kept my eyes open, watched the soft flash of color ripple out of us, the ground trembling and then suddenly bursting with a flash of red poppies rising up in the tall grass.

Owen's arms shook and he fell forward, collapsing heavily on my chest and knocking the breath from me. He groaned, tongue lapping at my breast as he started to continue to fuck me, hips stuttering and a low moan in the back of his throat.

"Owen, wait. Wait, love," I panted, wiggling beneath him, dirty fingertips pulling up from the earth to press to his shoulders.

He took the nudge as an invitation, rolling onto his back and pulling me with him, hissing as I sank a little further onto his cock.

"Owen, stop," I said, gently, reaching up to his brow to push his hair back and find his eyes.

He blinked at me, gaze foggy, and then again, a little clearer, eyes wincing.

"Ah, ow!" His hand left my hip to reach under himself, touching the back of his shoulder, his eyes widening. "I'm...oh. How long have we been..."

It probably wasn't funny, but a giggle slipped free at his startled expression. "I have no idea," I said, rising up off his lap, gasping at the hollow feeling as Owen whimpered.

"Oh, fuck," he breathed, grimacing.

"Are you all right?" I asked, moving quickly down to his side, my thighs squeezed together to try and ignore the soft throb of craving.

"I'm..." He laughed, and his head dropped to the ground, tilting to face me. "I don't think I realized what you were so worried about before. Don't worry," he added, leaning in and kissing between my eyebrows. "I'm all right. Definitely sunburnt and a little...over sensitive. I remember everything, I just remember not being able to stop."

"I tried not to—"

"Shh, Bryony, it's fine. I didn't *want* to stop. That *was* me.

But perhaps there are reasons why cocks should go soft," he said, still smiling. He started to shift on the blanket and then immediately stilled, eyes narrowing. His closer hand lifted and brushed against my cheeks, revealing a soft stinging sensation. "I know a cure for our sunburns too we can use later. For now, come here."

I scooted closer, pressing against Owen's bare side and resting my cheek against his shoulder.

"It's late in the year for poppies," Owen said, and I could feel his chuckle against me.

"I worry about the magic sometimes—"

"Sometimes?" he asked, teasing.

I pinched his chest and Owen laughed. "We don't know what it will mean for the poppies next spring. Have I forced them to grow too soon and now they won't come back?"

"These poppies will leave seeds for the spring, too. I don't think you're taking life from the earth, I think you're just giving it a boost. The birds don't seem to mind," he added, passing a hand through the air above us.

The birds *were* especially noisy, but it was just a kind of music, and a few came down to the blanket and grass to root around in Owen's pockets. "Perhaps they're offended by our performance," I said.

Owen made a sweet *pft* of dismissal. "This? This is applause. They would've flown away if they disapproved."

I laughed and rolled to lean over Owen for a kiss when I discovered that the birds weren't our only audience. On the balcony overlooking the meadow behind the palace, stood Daniel Farraque. He was sitting on the ledge, leaning against the wall, one leg hanging down and the other bent and perched, his eyes turned to Owen and I.

"We're being watched. Not by birds," I said, fairly certain that Farraque and I had locked gazes, although it was hard to tell from this distance.

"Are you sure it wouldn't be better to get rid of him? Send him back to the council?" Owen asked, craning his neck to see.

Owen was the only one I'd told about what had happened in the training room between me and Farraque. Owen had caught me in my bluster directly afterward, before I'd decided that it would be a secret. What would Daniel Farraque do next under such a direct rebuffing? Apparently...nothing but observe.

"They'll just send someone else," I said to Owen.

"Do you want your dress?" he asked.

I shook my head. "Not until we get ready to go back in. I don't want him thinking he affects me."

"Does he?"

I hummed at Owen's question. "Not in the way the council was hoping. I do find him curious though. He's a bit like one of Cosmo's statues. Beautiful, intriguing clues, but ultimately unknowable."

"No one is unknowable," Owen said, toying with a strand of my hair that had fallen loose.

"Perhaps not. But it was a strange attempt at seduction, and yet somehow, the most personality I've seen out of him yet. I suppose if I were Camellia, it might've worked. Not that she would've bothered with the fencing in the first place."

"Mmm, but you are *my* princess. My Mistress," Owen purred, arching up to kiss my chin.

I gave up my staring contest with Farraque and let him watch as I bent to kiss Owen, gently and slowly to make up for the slight frenzy we'd just woken from.

"My Chosen," I murmured, pecking and sipping at Owen's kisses. "My pure-hearted man. My..." I blinked and pulled away briefly, staring down at Owen, resting a finger against the dimple on his chin to hold him still.

I sat up slowly on my knees so I could take him in, the defined planes of muscle, the taper of his hips, the long nose. Owen was some odd and perfect creation, aristocratically beautiful and undeniably rustic. He was steady as a rock and as open with his heart and mind as anyone I'd ever met.

"My love," I said, a bright smile blooming.

Owen's eyes brightened and he sat up, arms looping around my waist and pulling me into his chest. I was on my knees, cupping his cheeks as I pulled long kisses from him, Owen humming happily with every press.

"Never been in love before, but I think this must be it,"

Owen murmured, his grin making our kiss more of a bump and nudge of our noses. "Bring the Hunger back so I can make love to you properly."

I laughed and shook my head. "No! No magic now, I just want this with you." I kissed his cheeks and forehead and chin and back to his mouth.

We stayed like that for a long time, smiling at one another, kissing when we could, careful not to irritate Owen's burned back or to stir up my Hunger again. It was there, of course, but it let me have the moment as I needed it, purely ourselves.

When I looked up at last, ready to dress and move inside, Daniel Farraque was nowhere in sight.

❧

"Even if you dismantle the land law now, there's no reason why the merchants should sell it back to the farmers, or means for the farmers to purchase it back," Wendell said.

"Can't we make them *give* it back?" I asked, but I raised my hand and shook my head before anyone could answer me. "No, I know. That isn't fair either."

My Chosen and I were tucked away in my suite, our new ritual of the evening. I spent my days with Cosmo or Owen, enjoying the pleasures of the Hunger and making a minor spectacle of myself. And then my nights now went like this, working over matters of legislation and politics in secret and away from the watchful eyes of Daniel Farraque.

Wendell and Thao shared a bench, Wendell's lap full of texts on the laws of Kimmery as Thao studied our maps.

"Some of the land lies fallow," Cosmo said. "Merchants don't make good farmers, but they dictate the crops that are planted. The ones that don't listen to the men who work the fields lose ground by not rotating their crops. If you dismantled the law and the crown was willing to buy the land, I bet the merchants would sell it cheap."

"And then it could be returned to the farmers, but fallow?" I asked, frowning.

"It can be made rich again," Owen said with a shrug.

I blushed. "Are we back to the method where I go about the country using the Hunger to make the crops grow?"

Owen laughed and I enjoyed the sight of him, propped up against my pillows, snacking on candied nuts with his thighs spread—almost in invitation. "No, although I'm sure they wouldn't mind the help. The right rotation of crops will help restore nutrients. It would take time and a great deal of work, but if the land was their own again, the farmers would probably be glad for it."

"You could import olive trees," Thao said, drawing the room's attention and smiling. He shined under our focus, and I was discovering a new itch of interest. Thao had always been beautiful, it was undeniable, but ever since I'd lost my patience with him, he'd been changing. He was elegant, princely, confident, but the burn of pride had softened in him.

"Olive trees?"

"They grow on the mountains in Mennary," Wendell said, nodding. "There's land on the mountains here in the North that could be allocated, and an olive...*orchard* might remain private."

"Mother would send us trees," Thao said, sitting up as if he were ready to write the letter now.

"Won't it be too cold this far north?" I asked.

"Ah," Wendell said, face falling.

Thao frowned and glanced between us. "Are the winters very harsh?"

Cosmo laughed softly at my back. "You'll find out soon enough. But the idea is right. What about apples, or pears? Those grow here in the mountains."

Wendell brightened again. "That's true! They're not fashionable, but Kimmery imports so much of its fruit. Apples and pears could be made more popular, and an orchard is not farmland so..."

"So it falls outside of the realm of the law!" I cried, brightening. "I should think a crown princess could make an apple more popular, but even if I can't—"

"Your people won't complain of good fresh food to eat," Owen finished for me, and I grinned at him.

"There is an old orchard on the palace grounds," Cosmo said, scooting forward to press against my back, resting his chin on my shoulder.

I didn't know why it should feel like such a temptation—shivers running through me and goosebumps appearing on my skin—just to have his breath on my neck, but I blushed at his closeness with Wendell and Thao staring at the pair of us.

"It's overgrown, and I don't know what the trees are producing now but..."

"But you think I should see if I can bring it to life again?" I asked, my breath catching.

"Is that—" Wendell paused, surprise painting over his face as if he hadn't meant to speak. He cleared his throat and started again. "Is that all it takes? Just...just thinking of it?"

Thinking of what? Sex?

"The magic takes effect with her release," Cosmo explained, his arm sliding around my waist, my body automatically leaning back into his.

I swallowed hard and found myself shy under the heavy stares of Wendell and Thao. Since when had I balked so much at discussing my sex life with them? *Since you began to consider including them in it*, a little voice whispered. Thao leaned forward, his elbows on his knees, the loose collar of his shirt falling open to reveal tan planes of smooth chest.

"If you came right now, you could make the orchard grow?" Thao asked, eyelids growing heavy over his gaze.

"I...we don't know. We haven't really tested distances like that," I said, wiggling back against Cosmo, only to find him half hard against my back, his legs stretched out to frame me.

You could prop your legs over his and invite Thao to help you test the theory, I thought, and it was the most I'd ever felt like the rest of the women in my family.

"You healed the front steps to the palace," Thao said, brow arching.

"Only from the entryway," I said.

"Let it be a challenge for another day then," Wendell said gently, although he looked no less interested than his lover.

Thao glanced back at him, smile wry, and sighed. "Very well, but you know how impatient I am."

Wendell hummed and watched me fidget, and I wondered if we were still talking about the apple orchard or not.

⁂

"I CERTAINLY UNDERSTAND YOUR CAUTION, but I've put a great deal of...well maybe not labor—" I stumbled and looked back over my shoulder for support from the others.

"Planning," Wendell said, nodding to me.

"And hopes," Cosmo said.

I swung back to face Cresswell, my argument renewed. "Yes! I don't want to take credit for the festival, but I think I deserve to *enjoy* the evening."

Cresswell's brow furrowed, and I was sure that he *wanted* to relent, that he would finally allow me freedom at the festival. "I'm sure you'll find the festivities very pleasant from within the tent where you can be safely guarded," he said at last.

Cosmo released an exasperated puff of breath, and my Chosen shifted behind me. Lady Prudence made the next effort, stepping forward from the back. As I glanced at her, I saw Daniel out of the corner of my eye, back against the wall of the warm study room where we were gathered. He was watching us all, his usual hobby when not assigned with a task, and as usual, I had no way of reading his mood or what he thought of the conversation.

"Guard Stark, it's absolutely to your credit that you take our princess's safety so seriously. But surely it will do her and her people good to mingle, just a little. You will be on hand, and there will be dancing—"

"And drinking, and rowdy men, or disgruntled citizens," Cresswell said, rushing to add, "Unjustly so, of course, Your Highness."

"My people have plenty of cause to be disgruntled, Cresswell," I said, shoulders sagging and resisting a childish urge to stomp my heel and demand he obey me. I *could* order him, but it was the man's duty to protect me.

"He has a point, Your Highness," Daniel said, his low voice still able to cut through our conversation, quiet as he was. "There's going to be alcohol, people will be in high spirits. Merriment can swiftly transform to temper in that situation."

"I didn't know he had opinions," Thao murmured, and the others coughed in quiet laughter.

Daniel's color changed, but only slightly, as if he had mastery over his blushes *and* his expressions, and he looked down to the ground.

I looked around at everyone gathered in the room and then up at Cresswell. "Could I have a word alone with Guard Stark, please?"

The room hushed, and Cresswell's eyes widened. Daniel might've been able to control his blush, but Cresswell couldn't, and for the first time since we'd begun the discussion of my going to the festival tomorrow, he looked uneasy and anxious as one by one the rest of the room moved to the door.

"Good luck," Cosmo said, kissing the corner of my jaw.

"But maybe listen to his advice," Owen added in a whisper, his hand cupping my waist briefly before he too left.

"Your Highness," Cresswell started.

"Please sit with me," I said, stepping to the side and gesturing to the two armchairs that faced one another by the window.

He hesitated, but gave in as I helped myself to a seat. He was in uniform and out of his armor, and while I seemed to grow smaller in the large chair, Cresswell Stark filled it up, his long legs trying to shrink in the space between our seats to avoid bumping his knees against mine. Instead, I leaned forward, settling my palms against his knees and watching him freeze in place.

"I do understand your concerns, and I'm not blind to how little favor I might hold with my people in spite of the changes I'm endeavoring to make. I'm sure the safest thing would be for me to not attend at all, it's only that I've never been to a festival. Not even the ones held in the capital. I want to dance, and drink stale beer, and eat the questionable meat on a stick that Owen keeps talking about. I'm not asking to pretend that I am not a princess and that I don't need to be cautious. But *please*, Cress-well. If there is any way for me to do just a little bit of those things tomorrow night, I promise to be very cooperative to your rules."

Cresswell cleared his throat, cheeks rosy and eyes trying and failing not to flick down to the collar of my dress or where my hands rested on his knees. He cleared his throat again. And then once more.

"Only a *little* dancing."

"Just one or two dances!" I said. I beamed, and Cresswell growled in a pleasant way, sagging back into the chair, a hand raising to cover his eyes.

"You'll have a food tester," he added. "You should keep either Owen or preferably Thao at your side, they're the strongest and the prince should have his weapon on him. I and another guard will be close at *all* times. If it's too crowded and unsafe and I change my mind about *any* of this—"

"Yes! Yes, I promise," I rushed, laughing and trying to stop myself as he glared at me through his fingers. "Thank you, Cresswell."

His sigh was almost comically heavy, fingers sliding down from his full mouth to land near my own hands. "Of course, Your Highness. But listen," he said, catching my hand before it could draw away. His hands were warm, fingers calloused against my wrist and palm, eyes pale and crystal green as he leaned forward. "Don't be careless, princess. If you are the only person with the power, position, and desire to help those people, you must be here to see it through."

Cresswell's gaze was earnest and almost frightened, enough to dampen the high of my victory. I swallowed hard and nodded.

"I will arm myself too. You know I can fight," I said, prepared for him to dismiss the idea.

He nodded solemnly. "I do, and it would bring me a great deal of comfort to know you had a weapon on hand. I don't want you to expect the worst, but only be prepared for it."

"I will. I promise, Guard Stark."

I don't know if I meant to cut the intimacy of the moment by using his title, but it did the trick, Cresswell stiffening and leaning back before standing and slipping out between the chairs with a quick bow.

"Excuse me. I'll go and find a tester for tomorrow night, Your Highness," he said, voice rough.

I managed a brief sound of assent before he was out the door, with me left blinking as it swung shut after him.

25.
ARIC

I passed Douglas the small vial of sea water from the south, charged and buzzing in my palm with enough magic to leave me weary at the loss.

"Keep it safe and close to her until you can have a charm fashioned," I said, my eyes over his shoulder on his middle daughter Hannah. Her hand rested over her chest, eyes wide as she tested her breathing. I'd done what I could for her immediately. Having the charmed vial would do her more good.

"Thank you, Your Majesty," Douglas murmured. "I'll be back out there soon."

I shrugged and shook Douglas's offered hand. "Just take care of your family now, and the court will do everything it can."

I tried to make the words plain. The last thing the man needed—with a recently deceased wife and a daughter on the brink—was more pity. His jaw worked, eyes blinking quickly before his head jerked with an uneven nod.

"You do us right, no matter what anyone say," he said gruffly, stepping back.

I wanted to ask *who* was saying *what* exactly, but I let it be, turning away from the door. Scrapper was meant to be waiting for me back at the Wing and Rook, and with any luck, he'd have the answer to that question.

I pulled my hood up, on the off chance there were any city guards about, or just folk who wanted my time, and headed for the nearest shortcut back to my bar.

"Martin?"

My pace didn't falter at the question, but I heard footsteps slapping on the brick to catch up with me.

"Aric, I've been looking for you."

I slowed as I dipped into the narrow walkway between two massive patched together buildings. Rumsbrooke used to have breathing room between the houses, I remembered it as a child, but as more families lost their land outside of town, Rumsbrooke had begun to swell, threatening to split at its seams.

"Your mistress needs a favor," the man following me said, and finally my steps faltered, my eyes growing wide.

I glanced over my shoulder and squinted at the man. Tall, with golden brown skin hinting at some mixed heritage, and a pale gaze that seemed to cut into me. Familiar but...

"The princess needs protection," he said, stepping closer into eerie shadows made by the candlelight from a low window.

"Head of the Royal Guard," I said, eyeing him up and down as I recognized him at last. "What are you doing out of uniform?"

"I assumed you wouldn't want to be seen with me in it," he said, shrugging.

I grunted and looked back ahead of me to the end of the alley. That much was true, but it would take more than a change of clothes to fool most of the eyes in Rumsbrooke, and especially those in my court.

"What danger is she in?" I asked, thinking over the letter still in my possession. The alley was as good a place as any to talk, although I continued farther down, away from the windows.

"The most immediate I can tell is her own insistence on attending the harvest festival," he said in a low grumble.

My lips twitched as I scanned around us. Bryony was giving her head guard trouble then, stubborn little creature.

"She has me, her Chosen, and she's not incapable of defending herself," he rattled off, stuttering as I spun to face him.

"What's your name?"

"Cresswell Stark," he said, standing straight and proud.

"You said she has you, what about the rest of her guard?"

"I don't trust them."

"But you trust me?"

"*She* trusts you," he said.

I frowned down at my boots at the swelling sensation in my chest, waiting for it to settle or pass, but it lingered in the quiet.

"The festival is tomorrow, and I'm fresh out of trinkets from the south to use for any magic so—" I was about to offer myself in the crowd when Stark pulled something from his pocket.

It glowed in the dark alley, and my palms itched at the sight of it, a pretty little stiletto dagger just thrumming with power.

"It's hers," Cresswell said.

I frowned and reached out, expecting to find some trace of a charm, perhaps some palace magician's signature spark. Instead I just found...*magic*. No form, no function, just power clinging to the blade as if it were a sponge left to soak.

If I'd known Bryony had something like this, I'd have...

Steal it, I thought. *It's a fortune of magic, if not outright gold too.*

I sighed and released the impulse, glancing up into Stark's rare gaze. "Come with me. I can fashion something for that and...we can speak more on your concerns with the guards."

"It's not just the guards—" Cresswell started.

"Just save it," I said, holding a hand up. "And put that away for now."

He tucked it back into his jacket, and I was relieved to see the magic seemed willing to hide. Magic was fussy, like a living creature almost able to make its own decisions. The blade could've been a beacon with that kind of magic, at least here in the north where power came in thin scraps. Hopefully, whatever I fashioned out of it would be equally content to go unnoticed.

We reached the Wing and Rook in silence, and Cresswell had the sense to keep his head down and look the other way as we entered the bar. Unusual looks weren't rare in my court, thieves and outcasts often finding common and comfortable ground together here, and Cresswell managed an unassuming slouch to his posture that invited being overlooked as we moved to meet Otto behind the bar.

"He's in there waiting for you," Otto said, good eye tracking Cresswell.

"You know better than to leave Scrapper unattended. What's he giving you? A cut of what he steals?" I asked, but I grinned with Otto.

Scrapper probably would help himself a bit while alone in my office, but he was always careful never to take more than I could spare or anything I might actually notice was gone.

Otto cranked the keg closed behind as we entered the tunnel, and I heard the scuff and scramble of Scrapper giving up whatever he was investigating. By the time we stepped into my office, he was lounging in a chair in front of my desk, one foot propped up. I gave him a good once over, looking for any new scratches or scrapes. Scrapper was generally the master of his own body, but sometimes it gave him troubles, usually with balance, or joint pain. I squinted at the foot on my desk and decided not to comment, it was gingerly placed and probably had more to do with a twisted ankle than Scrapper being a presumptuous little shit.

"What's he doing here?" Scrapper asked, sitting up, but confirming my suspicions by not moving his foot down.

"You have a mutual friend," I said, gesturing to the free chair before moving around to sit behind my desk. "Her Loveliness," I added, more to see the look on Stark's face when he realized I meant Bryony and that Scrapper beamed at her mention.

"Ah, well," Scrapper said with a sigh and a sidelong glance at Stark, who perched stiffly in a chair. "Yes, word is he goes mooning about after her around the palace."

Cresswell flushed and glared at Scrapper, mouth working, but he didn't deny the taunt.

"But as far as I can tell, he's more interested in doing his duty of service than *serving* the princess," Scrapper said.

"Where are you getting this information from?" Stark barked, and Scrapper sneered back at him.

"Tell him, Scrap. We're here to exchange, not flaunt," I said.

Scrapper huffed and rolled his eyes, shifting in his seat before meeting Stark's eyes again. "Your man Yorley talks too much in the bars here in Rumsbrooke. Whores about a fair bit too. He's reporting to the crown, as well as one named Piper—"

"*Stanley* Piper?" Cresswell growled, pushing back in his chair and grinding his jaw as he looked absently around the room.

"Mm, but Piper's not a fan of Yorley and he likes the position," Scrapper said.

Cresswell blew out a long breath and slanted his gaze back at my spy. "And who's there for the council?"

Scrapper pursed his lips and shrugged, but I cleared my throat and nodded at him.

"Nicholas Walsh," both men said at once.

"And that new steward," Scrapper added, miffed at not having the news exclusively.

"Everyone knows about Farraque already," Cresswell answered with a wave.

"And Camphrey, Blunt, Sapian," Scrapper rushed out.

"*Shit*!"

Scrapper leaned back, smug once again as Cresswell covered his mouth with his hand.

"She's practically surrounded," I murmured, frowning.

"All the Chosen are clear," Scrapper said with a shrug, and Cresswell and I exchanged a wide eyed glance. It was hard to imagine Pope or Owen working for the council, but it was even more concerning that we hadn't even *considered* the possibility.

"If you...if you hear anymore," Cresswell murmured.

"We'll inform you," I said with a glance at Scrapper, who nodded. "And I'll...keep an eye out at the festival tomorrow."

I hadn't planned on attending, more interested in having a bit of peace in the city, and maybe a bit of spying of my own on Hubert's house. But if Bryony couldn't trust most of her guards...

"Hand me the blade," I said.

Cresswell sat up and pulled it out of his jacket, and I tsk'ed at Scrapper and his greedy gaze, reaching across my desk for the blade, my eyes growing hooded at the just the pulse of power it left against my palm. I had a few ideas of what kind of protections to give it, glamours to help keep it secret, maybe even a warning charm.

It should be pretty too, decorative and charming...like her.

I closed my eyes and focused on my work instead of the woman in my thoughts.

26.
BRYONY

osmo leaned into my side, kissing the curve of my neck
to my shoulder. "Breathe, Bryony."

I huffed and caught my breath, sharing a smile with him. The carriage bumped along the road the next day, myself and my Chosen squeezed in together for the ride to the festival.

"We're still too far from Indiva for you to hold your breath that way," Owen agreed, kissing the crown of my head.

This carriage ride was significantly more comfortable than our last one as a group. I was perched on Owen's lap, my legs hooked over Cosmo's, while Thao and Wendell were cuddled together on the opposite bench. Our knees all bumped together in the center, but no one seemed to mind. Privately, I was finding the closeness a little *too* comfortable, especially with the rhythm of the carriage. My mind and body couldn't quite make the decision on whether or not it would be all right to fool around on the ride with Thao and Wendell watching, or if I wanted them *involved*, or if I was still shy of them in that regard. I only knew that there was a simmer of interest that started the moment the carriage door shut with us all inside, and it only grew warmer by the minute.

Cosmo lifted my arm from my own lap, running his fingers up and down the inside of my arm, lips curling as he watched me.

"I'm excited," I said, a little breathlessly.

"I know," Cosmo said, arching an eyebrow.

Oh, he thinks he's very clever, I thought, knowing my observant Chosen was as aware of my growing feelings for Thao and Wendell as I was.

"We're nearly there now," Owen offered. "I used to make trips to Indiva in the summers with my father for extra work."

Owen's arm was banded warmly around my waist, and I settled my hand over his there, feeling the smooth check marks of old scars on his hands. "Did you like farming?" I asked.

"Mm. No," Owen said, laughing a little. "I liked being around the animals, but the days were hot and long, and it always took my hands forever to get my callouses back for the tools."

I turned his hand over and looked down, rubbing my thumb over the raised callouses, rough and stiff even after Owen's time with me.

"Used to have blisters that would bleed after a few days. Mom would wrap me up with rags like I was wearing mittens, but I'd always take them off again by the end of the day after dropping something or getting too hot."

"You went with your father because..."

"We'd get two portions of pay and a midday meal. Mom had four more at home to feed. I was the oldest, I had to help."

"Where is your family now?" I asked, already wondering what I could do for them.

"Three of the older girls are married, and two of my brothers are in the army. Dad died not long after I went into the army, so Mom and the littler ones now are split between my sisters to help bear the load. We might see some today, I bet," Owen said, voice cheerful.

I looked up from his hands, and my eyes met Thao's first, his expression subdued. Wendell was watching me too, and even without words passing between us, I think he understood where my thoughts went. I'd find a way of helping Owen's family. It wasn't really enough, not when there were other families like his, but I didn't care if it was partiality or favoritism. Owen deserved to know that his mother and siblings were as comfortable and safe as he was, and he'd never ask me for it himself.

"I'd like to meet them," I said, simply.

Owen nuzzled against my hair, probably mussing all the effort the maid had gone to. "Mom's not as strong as you, but she's sweet and patient. I think you'd like each other."

I would absolutely give Mistress Dunne very good reason to like me. I already appreciated her immensely.

In my quiet musing over Owen and his family, I caught the

first notes of the festival from outside the carriage, down in the valley.

"Oh!" I leaned forward, Owen's arm keeping me from falling right off his lap as I pulled the window of the carriage down to look out. There wasn't much at first, just a few wisps of smoke, but then the breeze turned in our direction and brought with it the soft murmur of voices with a few high notes of music and the smell of meat cooking.

Cresswell Stark rode forward until he was level with the window. "Nearly there," he said, his usually stern expression softening at the sight of my smile.

"Does it sound like people are enjoying themselves?"

Wendell leaned forward, his shoulder brushing against mine as he cocked his head to listen. "Sounds like a successful festival to me. What kind of fanfare would you like as you arrive?"

"Oh, none!"

"There should be some announcement," Thao insisted.

I drew back into the carriage shaking my head. "I think it's going to be a little too obvious as it is."

"We're driving the carriage up to the princess's private tent where there is a platform she can greet the people from," Cresswell said. "When the excitement dies down, we'll see about taking her down for the dancing and food."

Suddenly, I found myself wanting a bit of fanfare. If only so I could walk through the market stalls and mingling people right away. Cosmo laughed at my face and leaned forward, distracting me with a gentle press of his mouth to mine.

"A little distance might suit the people fine to start with," Cosmo said quietly. "They won't know how to relax with you amongst them."

I sighed and nodded, falling back into Owen's arms as Cresswell fell back from the window, and I watched the slow roll of the countryside as we traveled closer. We were in the foothills of the mountains now, the view rolling around us slowly, vast potato and corn fields divided with thin tree lines. We passed a few houses, small and humble handmade buildings, but there was no one to watch us as we passed this time, everyone down in the valley for the festival.

"There's been one harvest crop so far this year," Owen said, pointing out the opposite window to a low cropped golden field. "Wheat is always first. My dad said when he was a boy, they still had the occasional Lammas festival to celebrate the first loaves made with the wheat harvests."

"That's what that sweet smell on the air is," Wendell said, blue eyes widening. "Honey and wheat. Our cook used to make fresh loaves for the staff, and she would always give me the first slice with the best portion of crust, all slathered with honey and fresh butter."

"You're making my mouth water for something I've never tasted," Thao groaned, his brow furrowing.

"You can see it now," Cosmo added.

I turned, swatting Owen in the face with a whip of my hair as I craned my neck to look down in the valley. "Oh! They've made it look so sweet!"

The large, low meadow designated for the night's merriment had been given a boundary made of tall wooden posts, twined with flower and wheat stuffed vines, crowned with wreaths. Strung between the posts were hanging ribbons of softly dyed fabric. But the boundary couldn't really hold the full mass of people on the ground, so many my eyes widened and I was suddenly glad to know that I wouldn't have to walk through the crowds. I'd never seen so many people in one place. There was a large raised stage in the center, a cluster of musicians standing—and sitting with their legs dangling over their edge—with their instruments, the music loud and playful. They were just tall enough to see over the crowd, and I watched as sunlight caught on a glittering flying coin that landed at the feet of one of the fiddlers who bowed and played even faster in thanks.

"I've never seen anything like it," Cosmo murmured.

"We have a great many festivals in Mennary," Thao began before stuttering and shifting directions, "And this one is just as impressive."

I snorted and granted him a brief teasing glance. I very much doubted the view below us was half as beautiful as one in Mennary, but that didn't stop my heart from racing as I turned back to the window.

"I see many smiles, Bryony," Wendell said, his hand finding mine briefly for a soft squeeze of my fingers.

I did see smiles, and laughter, and shouting, and snarling expressions that quickly melted back into a grin. And slowly, I saw faces raising at the sight of our procession, eyes narrowing in curiosity, peering through the glass as avidly as I was gazing back at them.

"I think I'm nervous," I whispered. I was absolutely nervous.

"One minute at a time, Mistress," Owen whispered back in my ear, and I softened in his hold, nodding.

We circled almost the entire festival on the curving road that led down into the meadow. I saw the backs of the vendors' stalls, the slow turning roasts of meat on low fires of the food stalls, and eventually, the small cluster of tents at the far end of the meadow. There was the shaded platform where I would appear, guards stationed around it in their shining armor. My eyes widened as I realized that people were already there, crowded even tighter against the gate, waiting for my arrival.

My heart was in my throat, clogging my breath. I must've made some soft squeak of distress because a moment later Owen was pulling me back from the window, turning me on his lap to face the others.

"Am I just supposed to stand there and be stared at?" I asked, eyes growing wide.

"If you are, we'll do it with you," Owen said, which was sweet but not quite soothing.

"Bryony," Cosmo purred, cupping my face in his hands. "You don't need to worry. This is a festival; they're only waiting to see their princess. Most of these people have never seen a royal in their entire lives unless they made it to a choosing ceremony."

"If it was Camellia's, then they've seen a great deal of a royal," I blurted out, and Wendell snorted.

"Let them stare a little, speak if you feel you have something you'd like to say to them, but they'll get hungry soon and move along for more ale or food," Cosmo said, flashing me a grin.

"Your presence is a great honor," Thao added, but he said it in a gentle way.

"I'm only me," I said, shaking my head.

"Well..." Wendell raised an eyebrow at me.

"Princess, future queen, wielder of the magic of the Hunger," Owen counted off, one finger at a time.

"Oh, all right then," I snapped, softening my tone by turning and pressing a kiss to his rough jaw. "I'll figure out what to do when the moment comes, as usual."

"Seeing as how the carriage has stopped, I think that moment may be now," Wendell said, his brows bouncing, a grin growing. And then he pushed open the door.

The crowd was loud, but it wasn't shouting or laughter, just the volume of many people packed together in one space. We were stopped behind the tent, a small collection of guards surrounding the carriage, some watching us while others checked the empty room of the field behind us. Wendell stepped out first, followed by Thao, and together they reached up to take my hands and guide me down. Cresswell was quick to join us, holding out a decorative, woven belt with a sheath about as long as my forearm, bearing a golden blade. My promised weapon.

"Where did you get this?" I asked, eyes widening as I fingered gently down the ornate sheath covered in gilded enameled white flowers. Bryony flowers, just like my name. The blade was my own stiletto dagger but the sheath was new.

"I had it made," Cresswell said, voice sharp.

"By *whom*?" I pressed, gazing up at him. I'd only offered to be armed yesterday, how could he or a craftsman have had time to make—

"Your Chosen," he said, and when I glanced over my shoulder he added, "Aric Martin. I went to see him yesterday evening. It's made of magic, but he says it will hold for you. He says it's charmed to warn for a few dangers, so if it grows hot—"

"*Aric* made me this?" I asked, nearly squawking.

"I thought if he was really your Chosen, he might have an opinion on your safety," Cresswell answered, cocking an eyebrow in challenge.

I swallowed the rest of my questions. Had Aric made this for me so he could keep the convenient protection of being my Chosen? Or had he made it for me, charmed it to help protect me, because he had similar concerns to Cresswell? Concerns for *me?*

"I thought his magic was a secret," I said instead.

Cresswell scoffed lightly. "Only enough of one to keep him off the registry. And now he doesn't even have to worry about that as Chosen."

"Thank you," I said, taking the pretty belt and wrapping it around my waist, watching the way the dagger seemed to nestle into my skirts. It would be difficult to see if you didn't know to look, and even the curling hilt looked more like a decorative element to the belt than part of a dagger.

"Just use it if you have to," Cresswell said, voice lowered.

"She will."

I looked up from my skirts at the sound of Daniel's voice. He and Lady Pru stood at the parted opening of the bright canvas tent, Daniel's arm offered for Lady Pru to lean against, his lips curled just the faintest amount as I met his eyes. I'd held a blade to Daniel's throat and he was right, I could protect myself if I had to. It might be different, I'd known I wasn't in serious danger from Daniel and that he wasn't in real danger from me, but I wouldn't be too shy to draw my weapon.

"Your people await you," Daniel said.

"Are you ready, dear?" Lady Pru asked, smiling warmly at me.

I wasn't. Not mentally, at least. Wendell moved away from my side and Owen took his place, giving me his steady arm to lean briefly against.

"Ready," I said with a nod.

Cresswell was first, along with another guard, ducking into the tent, with Lady Pru and Daniel at his back. I followed, my arm linked with Thao's, Owen's palm warm on my back, Wendell and Cosmo close behind us. The tent was dim, especially after standing in the afternoon sun, and for a moment, I moved blindly through. Then someone flicked the flap by the platform open and I could see the space, full of comfortable furniture, including a small curtain on the far right that would lead to a private room where I could be alone with my Chosen. There was a table dressed with food and bottles of wine, but I didn't see anything that looked like a fresh rustic loaf or a stick of meat, so I planned on still exploring the food vendors.

"Just smile and wave and nod to start with, like you would to your people outside the southern palace. They'll be too loud to hear you," Thao said in my ear, and I nodded. "Remember what you've already done, what you plan to do, and show in your smile your love for them."

We were nearly to the steps leading up to the platform, and my fingers were digging into Thao's arm, he and Owen all but carrying me forward. I turned and looked at Thao, his chin lifted high and face relaxed. Today was not only a familiar process for him, but also possibly less pressure since these weren't his citizens. His confidence and calm radiated, and I did my best to take a deep breath and share it with him.

"Thank you," I whispered.

And then we stepped into the light, ascending the stairs. The sunlight was bright again, the quick transition from in and out again confusing my eyes, but I saw the dark blur before me and knew it was the audience.

"Her Royal Highness, Princess Bryony of Kimmery," some booming voice announced as I stepped onto the stage.

I couldn't feel my feet beneath me, but Thao and Owen were careful in their guiding, taking me down the steepled platform to the bottom level.

The crowd was silent, or not quite, but they weren't cheering, just staring up at me, muttering to one another, and it took me a moment to remember to smile, the expression fragile and shaky.

It was as if we were trapped on two sides of glass, as if I were an object displayed for their curiosity. I couldn't greet them from here, not in any real way that mattered, and they couldn't know me from where I stood on the stage. Sudden humiliation rushed through me. I wished there had been some way I could've mingled with them, unknown as Bryony.

My knees wobbled and an unconscious impulse struck quick. I pulled my arm free of Thao's and stepped forward, looking out over the vast crowd, the musicians who'd turned on their stage to watch, the vendors and cooks who watched from their stalls.

I fell into a deep curtsy, my head bowing low, my hand over my heart, and listened to the soft rush of collected breath.

A roaring cry of cheers followed, thunderous and shocked, lewd and happy words thrown in my direction that made me rise with a laugh and giant smile to match the faces that stared back at me.

"Make merry with your princess, people of Kimmery," the crier yelled, but it was lost in the din.

27.
BRYONY

"It's the best cut, I kept it fresh just in case you might stop by, Your Prince—princess, highness— Your—"

"Thank you," I pressed, smiling at the short, heavyset man who stumbled over my title. I bounced on my toes as I waited for the quiet taster Cresswell had found for me to take his bites, before finally passing me the skewered, still steaming meat.

Fat and salt struck my tongue first, making my eyes widen with the first bite. The meat was crispy around its edges and perfectly tender inside, hot and seasoned with a hint of unusual spice. I hummed my pleasure, eyes falling shut, and the cook in front of me chuckled from the other side of his stall.

"I can pass the recipe along to your cook, Your Highness," the cook offered.

"Oh, no, you should come to the palace and make it yourself and sit with us for dinner," I said, waving a hand and smiling as the man's eyes widened and he spluttered through his thanks.

Thao was at my side. I didn't know if Cresswell had mentioned to him that he should stay close to me, or if Thao wanted to be there anyway, but he was taking the task seriously, his hip pressed to mine and his arm around my shoulder. I turned the skewer in his direction, raising an eyebrow in invitation as I licked my lips. Thao ducked, helping himself to the bite I'd offered, sharing my groan of appreciation. I watched as he licked the char and fat and salt from his own bottom lip, staring avidly at the flick of his tongue and not looking away as he found me watching, his grin growing.

"Another?" the cook asked.

"Please," I said, even though this was the last stall we were visiting and I was far too full of good food already.

It took an hour or more before the crowd at the platform grew bored of my waves and nods and the little words I was able to exchange with them. Once, and only once, someone threw a tomato toward the stage, but they missed me by quite a bit and it was Owen who caught it in his palm, giving thanks and then eating it like an apple. Our audience cheered for him, and a small fight broke out near where the tomato was thrown from.

When the sun began to set and the music grew loud and wild again, the crowd thinned and Cresswell relented and let me wander the festival grounds, surrounded by a ring of my Chosen and a second of guards.

Once I'd started visiting the stalls, I couldn't stop. I purchased woven baskets, corn husk dolls, hand knitted sweaters, wooden bowls, miniature paintings, and a beautiful glass figurine of a horse from one of Cosmo's artist friends. I'd eaten tarts and honey wheat buns and shucked corn dressed with butter and cheese curds and ground spices.

"I love festivals," I said, sinking into Thao's side with a sigh.

Oh, and I'd drank a fair amount of mead.

Owen laughed and took the mug from my other hand, finishing the contents and grabbing my attention as a little dribble ran down his cheek. He gasped and waggled his eyebrows at me as he finished.

"You'd better get your dancing in before you have any more of that," Owen said.

"Your Highness should return to the tent, surely you could dance there," Cresswell argued.

"Nooo! Cress, you promised, you *did*. Just one or two dances," I said, slipping free from Thao and squeezing past a cuddly Cosmo to face my head guard. "Please," I said with wide eyes.

One of the other guards muttered something under his breath, scoffing lightly, and I watched as Cresswell turned a genuine growl in his direction, before clearing his throat and settling to face me again. "The crowd is still heavy and you are..."

I was drunk. A *bit* drunk. Pretty drunk.

"I'm fiiiine!" I cried, my arms swinging wide, the skewer still in my hand prodding the guard who'd scoffed at me.

"Ow!"

"I wouldn't trust you with that blade right now," Cresswell said firmly.

"Can I be of some help?"

Just the soft, velvety rasp of his voice, and suddenly the Hunger was there, as if she'd been lying in wait the whole time.

"Aric!" I spun, and there he was, standing outside the ring of my guards, the firelight from the torches around the festival catching in his gaze as he smirked at me.

"Princess," he said, nodding.

"Bryony," I corrected. "Come here."

He raised an eyebrow, but the guards stepped back and Aric joined us in our little nest of company inside their bronze ring of armor.

"Where have you been?" I asked.

"Working," he answered, brow furrowing with confused amusement. "And you?"

"Working," I mimicked, crossing my arms over my chest.

"Would you like a little sobriety? Just enough to dance," he asked.

He was beautiful, wasn't he? Strangely so. Grandmother was right, he was too old for me, too rude, too completely uninterested. No, not completely.

"Thank you for my sheath. It's beautiful," I said, reaching down and finding it right at my hip, the gold still warm to the touch.

"You're welcome," Aric said, with the slightest dip of his waist. Not a bow, but a polite answer, and there was a kind of friendliness in his eyes that he didn't show elsewhere. Or at least, that was what I wanted to see. "You didn't answer my question."

"Will you be my dance partner?" I asked.

For a moment, that warmth in Aric's stare shuttered, and I cursed my too loose tongue for even thinking of asking him to dance with me, but then he bowed softly again.

"For one dance," he said, lips twitching as I vibrated with my restrained shout of victory.

I stilled as his hand lifted to my face, fingertips brushing loose strands of hair back before sparking gently against my skin. The familiar tight feeling passed over me, as well as a cool rinse of clarity that made the lines of the world sharper again when I hadn't even realized they'd begun to blur. I looked down and found my dress simplified, and my dagger hidden.

"You've made me plain again?" I asked, grinning.

"Never plain, but safe," Aric said quietly, and the Hunger in me prowled impatiently. He looked up over my shoulder to Cresswell. "Stay close, but not so much so it will make it obvious who she is. I'll return her to you shortly."

I glanced back over my shoulder to find Cosmo wearing his usual knowing smile and only Thao looking irritated by the interruption. Aric's hand found mine and I followed his tug, a sudden sense of freedom hitting me as we left the circle of guards.

"I thought you'd say no."

"Did you want me to?" Aric asked, pulling me closer to his side as we wove through the mingling crowd.

"No, I got what I wanted," I said. *Mostly*, I added to myself.

I wanted *Aric*, which was terrible because he'd made it clear he found that impossible. Maybe it was worse to get to see him, to call him my Chosen and have him make me beautiful magical charms and give me glamours so I could experience small frag-ments of a life that didn't really belong to me. Moments with a man I couldn't really possess.

"You deserve to dance," Aric said as we neared the surging mass of dancers, the ground stamped down to mud from the day. "You've given the north its best day in a long time, princess."

The music and the shouts of dancers were growing too loud, making it harder to hear Aric and his scratching soft tone.

"You don't know how to dance like that, do you?" he asked, leaning to my ear.

I watched the men and women leaping together, practically running past one another, women hooked to their dance part-ner's chests with strong arms around their waists, heads thrown back with laughter. It wasn't how people in court danced, and even that I'd done very little of aside from some instruction. I looked to Aric and shook my head, and he grinned, his arms squeezing tighter around my waist, his free hand scooping mine up.

"I'll lead," he said, and then we were galloping into the mass of the crowd.

I screeched, my arm wrapping around Aric's shoulder, clutching to the dense leather of his vest as he drove us straight towards a dozen other couples. I was sure that at any moment we'd crash into them, but Aric just spun us into the movements, my feet racing to follow his, my eyes as wide as they could go as I laughed in my joy and panic. There was no logic to it that I could find, not while I was trying to keep up, it was only wild movement, but it was as if every person who followed the pounding rhythm of the musicians was in some kind of connected understanding with one another, moving like air currents or rushing water, constantly spinning around like mad planets in orbit.

Many partners changed hands, tossing women into new arms, but Aric kept a tight clutch on my waist, turning us away before we could be interrupted. I thought I could feel his heart pounding against my chest for how tightly we were pressed together, the buttons of his clothing catching on the embroidery of my dress. He was laughing with me, his breath against my ear and throat, my toes barely touching the earth before he would swing me around again, my skirt pooling out behind me like a lady's fan.

There was no room to speak, even if I *was* able to catch my breath; we were going too fast, the music was too loud. The longer we moved, the more relaxed I grew, the easier I was able to dance and move for myself. I quit watching over Aric's shoulder for the moment we crashed into someone and decided instead to trust him to lead. It gave my eyes room to turn to his face, see the wide grin he wore and the way he was watching me too. His cheeks were brighter from the activity, his chest brushing against mine as we fought for breath, hair bouncing and flying, and those gray eyes falling to my lips, my throat, back up to lock with my eyes.

It hurt. It hurt to want him *so* much. It made my eyes burn and my throat tight and my heart beat too hard and my cunt ache. It turned my hands into claws as I tried to hold onto him. It drew up ugly thoughts of *demanding* he serve me, submit to me, accept his role as my Chosen. It wasn't a convenient lie for Aric's sake only, that was what he was to me. I had Chosen him first, and now my Hunger did as well. The music was slowing, and I was taking grateful gasps of air as Aric slowed our spinning, his face now frowning. Maybe he read the desire in mine and it irritated him, or maybe he was angry with himself for the way his eyes kept dropping down to my lips or my breasts.

"Bryony." I read my name on his lips, his voice too low, and we both stilled as his hand came to cup my hips.

The sheath was hot, warmth bleeding through my skirt and warning me against my thigh. Aric's eyes were over my shoulders now, spinning us slowly as he studied the crowd.

"Here comes Thao," Aric said, head bending to my ear. "Keep dancing until Guard Stark interrupts. I'm going to search the crowd."

I nodded but my fingers wouldn't release Aric's shoulders, and his smile was tense as he pulled my hands free, raising one to his mouth and leaving a scant kiss against the heel of my palm. "Be careful, princess," he whispered as he passed.

Too late, I thought, but I lowered my hand to the hilt of my dagger, and in the next moment the music was starting again, a more mellow and playful tune to allow dancers to catch their breath. A warm arm looped around my waist, and Thao caught my free hand in his.

"There was a masked man moving toward you in the crowd," Thao said gently. "We're going to dance in the direction of the tent."

I nodded, my head still too full of Aric to really wonder about the threat at my back. I was safe with Thao and...

And Aric was hunting with my guards for whoever the man had been.

"You don't need to worry," Thao said, slipping between two close couples.

"I'm not. I'm just..."

Thao wore a slow, wry smile. "Ah. I admit I don't understand his appeal, but I am more impressed with him than I initially expected."

"He doesn't want me." It didn't feel vulnerable to speak it out loud with Thao. The prince would understand what I wouldn't want to admit to anyone else. There was something deeply *irksome* about not being able to simply take what I wanted from Aric. That my position as princess was a hindrance and not a help in making him mine.

"He may choose not to accept you, but believe me when I say that it's clear that man *wants* you, Bryony," Thao said, frowning over my shoulder.

"I don't know if that makes me feel better or worse," I said.

"I'm jealous of him. That's uncomfortable to admit," Thao said.

We weren't really dancing now, just turning slowly away from the crowd and the music, closer to my tents. My dress was growing heavier, Aric's charm lessening, and the sheath was cool again. At the corners of my vision, firelight glinted off the armor of the hovering guards who followed our slow progression.

"Why would you be jealous?" I asked.

Thao paused us in place, pulling our joined hands up to rest against his chest. He didn't have me pinned against him the way Aric had, but we were close enough to share breath, for me to feel the press of his hips against my stomach.

"Could any of your desire ever be for me?" Thao asked, voice small, frown fragile, eyes tracking my expression.

I stilled and stared up at him. It'd been weeks since Thao had been *cocky,* but I'd never really seen him insecure in this way. Not since the night I'd chosen him as he sat anxiously at the banquet table with the others. He'd always been beautiful, but beauty didn't really make my pulse pound.

Thao did though, lately when we were sparring, dancing, arguing. I enjoyed arguing with him as much as I did with Aric, their opinions opposite but equally willing to clash with mine. I was grateful for his confidence when mine faltered. I craved the depth of connection he shared with Wendell.

"Forget that I—"

I cut him off, rising to my toes and pulling him down to meet me for a rough and sudden kiss. There was none of Wendell's tentative gentleness. As soon as Thao met me in the kiss, he was greedy for more, clutching me close and sweeping his tongue in to taste me with my gasp. My Hunger was equally eager, and I groaned as Thao's hips pressed into mine, wanting to rub myself against him in full view of everyone around us.

Speaking of, the crowd was laughing and cheering.

"That's our princess! It's about time the north was blessed with the queen's Hunger!" someone shouted.

Thao was only encouraged, tongue thrusting against mine, his hand untangling from my fingers to hold the back of my head for his kiss. The magic of the Hunger purred at his insistence, and Thao's own rumble shook and teased against my chest. I was clinging to him, barely restraining myself, when he finally pulled away, scooping me up from the ground with a giant roar of approval from the crowd.

I laughed and pressed my face to his throat, nipping at his pulse.

"There is something you need to see first, Bryony," Thao whispered. "And then Wendell and I will take our place in your Chosen at last."

"I chose you from the start," I said, lifting my face to catch his eye briefly as he strode quickly through the parting crowd. "I'm just slower when it comes to the claiming. You both want—?"

"Yes. *Yes*," he rasped, eyes growing dark. "We *want* you."

Two guards were loitering in the tent near the neglected table of food, and they scurried quickly out the back, their cheeks puffed with pilfered food as we appeared. Thao put me on my feet, his hands around my waist, but he stepped back as I moved to steal another kiss, his face smooth and serious.

"There's something we've been keeping from you. We felt it was important at first, and then when we realized it wasn't, the moment never appeared and—"

The front of the tent opened again and the rest of my Chosen—minus Aric, *always* minus him—entered.

"About time the three of you sorted this—" Cosmo started, smiling.

"Wen," Thao said, catching his lover's eye and making Wendell's smile melt away. "It's time, I think. I'm sorry, you should've been the one to say."

"No. You're right," Wendell said softly, nodding.

We were standing in the open doorway. Cresswell and Daniel were both missing, and Lady Prudence was napping on one of the low couches at the other end of the room, a pair of guards watching over us from the field entrance. In spite of Thao's reassurance and Wendell's calm, they were both obviously tense and nervous, and I didn't think the audience helped.

"Let's go speak in...in relative private," I offered, tugging gently on Thao's arm toward the conjoined tent meant to act as a bedroom.

"We'll be out here," Cosmo said, kissing my cheek as I passed and nodded at him and Owen.

Wendell moved ahead of us, his head hanging low and his shoulders hunched as he moved for the hanging curtains.

Lady Pru had been in charge of organizing the room for me, and she'd made it a warm and romantic space for myself and my Chosen, fresh flowers arranged in every corner and a large mattress nestled on the carpeted floor, a canopy of gauze hanging from the peak of the tent. Heavy curtains separated the two spaces, enough to mute sound but not to block it out entirely.

"Whatever it is, you needn't worry," I said as the barrier swung shut behind us.

Thao and Wendell exchanged a loaded look between them, worry and hope mixing together as well as that beautiful support they seemed to share between them with just a glance.

"It's overdue is all," Wendell said. "I hope you'll forgive me for not trusting you with this sooner."

I tried to keep my expression calm for his sake, but I itched with curiosity. Luckily, I didn't have long to wait, Thao pulled me back toward an open spot of the carpet, making room between us and Wendell. The tall blond rolled his shoulders and took a deep breath, releasing it slowly and seeming to melt as tension bled out of him, a small relieved smile spreading over his lips.

And then magic buzzed in the air around him, giving it a

shimmery blue glow that was difficult to stare at, as if everything in focus around him was moving at a sudden and rapid rate. I'd seen magic like that before, and my lips parted as the glow spread out and then down, replacing Wendell with a massive and beautiful white tiger.

The festival carried on, bodies churning in the field, barely noticing as their princess was bundled away, spinning through the grass. I watched Bryony go with Thao toward the tent, before turning and tracking the stranger she'd been dancing with. He was headed in the opposite direction, toward Cresswell, and I pushed off the stall I'd been leaning against, moving to join them.

I didn't recognize the man who'd been running for Bryony, but I had a sneaking suspicion this was related to what Emory and Jonathon had hinted. At the very least, it was something I might blame on Aric Martin as I was asked to do.

I was at the edge of the festival, searching through the dark, when I heard a hiss of whispers beneath the raised voices of the revelers. I moved behind a closed stall and found the three men.

"Was jus' lookin' to dance with a pretty girl, lads," the man groaned as the tall stranger pressed him to the wall of the stall, rifling through pockets and loose clothing.

I'd seen this new man approach Bryony and her Chosen earlier, and the way the princess seemed to bloom under his stare, batting her lashes in a way I'd never really seen from her before. She was certainly a far cry from the ferocious creature who'd held a sword to my throat, all girlish and sweet, giggling as the man had escorted her to the dancing.

He was older, tall, and dressed like a rogue but with an air of authority. I wondered if he was some secret kind of security, perhaps someone from the south meant to protect Bryony in the shadows.

"What are you doing here, Farraque?" Cresswell snapped at me.

The older man gave me a cursory glance before going back to digging in his captive's clothes.

"I came to see what the commotion was about. Could he be telling the truth?" I asked, eyeing the raggedy man they held.

I didn't recognize him either, but Emory had plenty of wastrels hanging about he might call on.

"The charm warned danger," the stranger growled, and then he stiffened, eyes widening. He twisted the wastrel's arm back and up, making the man yowl in complaint, before plucking a long pin pierced through the fabric of the sleeve.

"Doesn't look harmless," Cresswell said, eyeing the sharp tip dubiously. "But..."

But it didn't really look deadly either.

"Maybe he stole it," I said, thinking of my conversation with Emory and Jonathon.

"It's not *jewelry* though is it?" the stranger muttered, lifting the pin to his nose and frowning. "Smell that."

Cresswell took it from the man's fingers, barely bringing it closer before coughing and shaking his head, making the stranger's eyebrows tick up briefly. "Is it..."

"Lady's Slip."

I stiffened, staring at the pin, moonlight glinting off the edge where I could see an oily coating. "You think he was trying to *poison* her?"

"One good stab and she'd be close to death if not meeting him directly," the stranger said, ignoring me and staring at Cresswell, who growled but looked unsurprised.

The man they held captive abandoned his jovial persona upon realizing how thoroughly caught out he was, snarling and struggling in the other man's grip.

Poison. Poison is not *petty thieving*, I thought. This was an entirely different matter than what Em and Jonathon had suggested, but I knew my line.

"He looks familiar," I said, eyeing the scowling man pinned to the wall. "I think I've seen him around the Wing and Rook. Perhaps he is...one of Aric Martin's men?"

Cresswell and the stranger both leveled sudden and attentive stares in my direction.

"Oh, you think so?" the stranger asked in a smooth and dark tone. "Spend much time at the Wing and Rook?"

"I... No. I've only passed by and—"

Cresswell arched an eyebrow at me before looking to the stranger. "Well, Aric? Is he one of yours?"

Fuck. *Fuck Emory, specifically.* My guts turned to lead as the stranger, Aric fucking Martin, smirked at me.

"He's made no vows to me, I swear it," Aric breathed, eyeing me up and down. "Can't vouch for whether or not he's ever been in the bar though. Let me take him back there now, question him properly where we're less likely to be...interrupted."

I ignored the sensation of ice scratching through my veins under Aric's stare and looked to Cresswell, whose narrowed eyes were focused on me.

"Fine, but I'll need to speak to him as well. Go now, before the festival starts dispersing."

Aric nodded and ropes appeared, binding up the slight and ragged man in their custody. "Tell the princess she ought to rethink her choice of steward," he said to Cresswell, glaring at me, before dragging the other man away.

I gaped at Cresswell, hands open at my sides, my head shaking. "How was I to know?"

"How were you to know whose thieves are who in the first place, Farraque?" Cresswell hissed. "Just get back to the tent. I'm rounding up the guards."

I turned gratefully, hurrying away from the scene, my hands clenching to fists. Fucking poison, meant for the princess. No wonder Emory and Jonathon wanted fingers pointed at Aric Martin, but it would've been helpful if they'd warned me he was *aligned* with Bryony.

I stormed through the crowds, face hot and heart thumping wildly in my chest. Had I just shown my cards so obviously? Fucking *Emory*. I was nearly back to the stage where Bryony had charmed her people with her humble bow when a hand snagged at my sleeve.

My fist swung, muscles coiled so tight with tension, I was ready to spring at the slightest provocation.

"Ho! Careful now." My fist slammed against a ready palm

with a bright slapping sound, and the man I'd been cursing in my head stumbled back from the impact, grinning at me. "Slow down, Danny boy."

I growled, looking around, searching for any sign of guards watching us, before grabbing Emory by his loose collar and dragging him into the shadows.

"Tell me I didn't just witness a failed attempt to *poison* the girl, Em," I hissed, throwing him aside as we slipped away from the crowds between two stalls.

"Ahh, was that what that was all about?" Emory asked, eyes wide with feigned innocence. "She got lucky then."

"What she got was *protection* from Aric fucking Martin," I whispered.

Emory's gaze flinched and he stared out into the hills for a moment, hands resting on his hips. I followed his stare as his lips twitched with a smile and realized there was a couple fucking in the grass. *Be quiet, be calm*, I chanted in my mind.

"You told me theft," I breathed, keeping my eye on the festival, on the open air around us, waiting for someone to come.

"No, I didn't. Never said what would happen. And there *was* some theft," Emory said with a shrug. His head tilted as he watched me turning, waiting to be caught, waiting to be dragged off by guards or Martin, or Bryony's fucking tiger Chosen. "You never really ask questions, do you, Dan? That's why Roderick likes you so well, right where you are."

I stiffened, chest heaving, trying to get control of my breath. Emory was right. I knew as much myself. I'd been raised, shaped, to do as I was told. Accusing Martin of mishaps at the festival seemed easy enough. Taking the role of steward at the Winter Palace was promising. Finding my way into a princess's bed wasn't unappealing.

And now look at what it's all adding up to, a voice in my head whispered.

"You fuck her yet?" Emory asked. "You know, I thought your delay might've been that she was ugly, but she's a delectable little thing, isn't she? Still, maybe you won't have to in the end."

Just get back to the tent before Cresswell finds you.

I stumbled away, ignoring Emory's taunts at my back.

An assassination plot. Is this what my father's estate is worth?

"We'll speak soon, Dan," Emory said behind me as I rushed back into the melee of the festival.

The tent was quiet inside, Owen and Cosmo talking and lounging together, Lady Prudence snoozing. The quiet left too much room in my head, and I searched the room three times for Bryony before I realized she was in her private area with others, their voices soft.

"Hey. Hey, Farraque, wait!" Cosmo jumped up, hurrying over and catching me by the arm as I marched for the curtains.

"I need to speak with Her Highness," I said, not entirely sure what would come out of my mouth if I did.

"Not a good time, I'm afraid," Cosmo said, exchanging a grin with Owen. He looked back to me and frowned, shaking his head and pulling me back a step. "Seriously. She's busy speaking with her Chosen. Leave them to it."

She was alone with Thao and Wendell? Could they be trusted? *Can I?*

"Leave them, Daniel," Cosmo said, words growing hard.

Outside the tent, the sound of armor approaching echoed in my head. I eased back, glancing one last time at the curtain as a soft, feminine gasp sounded. I rolled my shoulders, pulling free of Cosmo's grip, and headed for a seat to wait the night out. Rushing in and spilling my guts to the princess was probably the surest way to have my guts spilled for real. I just needed time to think through all the pieces and sort out where I fit in the mix.

29.
BRYONY

"**O**h!"

The tiger blinked a set of pale eyes, silver with blue near the pupil, and his head hung shamefully low. He was as big as Thao, perhaps a little more, or maybe it was only that his fur seemed fuller, wider around his face and a little shaggier on his sides. I reached out in an automatic impulse to touch, so fond of doing so with Thao, and then paused and clenched my fingers back into fists.

"We didn't want him to register when we came back." Thao spoke slowly, stepping forward and kneeling down so that Wendell could butt his massive pale head against his shoulder. "And in Mennary, this was a secret. Only my family and royals by marriage are given the bite of our bloodline so they might take their second nature. But Wendell and I are...we are—"

"More than lovers," I said, resting my hand against Thao's shoulder. Wendell released a low, pleased rumble and nuzzled a warm nose against the back of my hand, his massive jaw and brutal teeth brushing against me.

"It was his right to share this gift with me," Thao said, nodding. "He is first in my heart."

I smiled at that and the way Wendell was leaning his weight into us both. "You missed this, didn't you? All these weeks without getting to be this other part of yourself? Wendell, you were never at any risk with me."

Wendell continued to purr as I sank to my knees, although it was closer to a roar than the sweet rumble the castle cats made when they sat next to my chair at dinner and begged with wide eyes.

"I think you both know you are welcome to express your love

for one another however you choose in my court, and that includes your second natures," I said, digging my fingers through Wendell's fur, feeling the rough vibration of his purr thrumming in my fingers. "I am sorry we didn't find time to say as much earlier."

The sensation of their magic against my hands was like the needle pricks of blood rushing back into a limb, and I held my breath as Wendell's handsome face and full smile appeared before me.

"I'm the only one who owes you an apology," he started, the blue in his eyes a perfect match for the tiger's.

"You don't!" I rushed ahead of him. "You are *all* my Chosen as much as you wish to be. I don't want to hold dominion over you, you owe me no explanations."

Wendell's eyes slid to Thao briefly and then back to me. "That goes both ways, Bryony. Thao and I are yours as much as you desire us to be."

My breath slid into my chest, and it was full of them both, just a hint of the animal still left on the air, as well as Thao's spice and Wendell's clean aroma.

Thao scooted closer on his knees, an arm moving around my hips. "It's not our title as Chosen that gives you power over us, Bryony. You gained that yourself with your kindness, your beauty."

"Your care and open heart," Wendell added gently.

"Your ability to tell me when I'm being a terrible lover and friend," Thao added, cutting through the tightness in my chest to make me laugh.

My head fell back with the giddy sound, and then it strangled in my throat as Thao leaned in, his mouth pressing to my shoulder and neck, wet open kisses pressed over my skin. Wendell rose up on his knees, his hands framing my ribs and pulling me into his chest.

"It's said that the Hunger's magic has a harder time affecting shifters and sorcerers," Wendell said as Thao continued to dress my neck and shoulders in kisses, shifting slowly to press against my back, pinning me between them.

"I didn't—" I gasped as Wendell's thumbs swiped over the

underside of my breasts through my dress. "I didn't want to come between you."

"Hmm...maybe not *between* the first time," Thao murmured, and I laughed and turned my head to bump it against his, craning my neck for another kiss.

His kisses were deep, starving things, and I was already being devoured when it occurred to me to feel shy for doing so in front of Wendell, but that passed quickly. Wendell gasped as I moaned, his hips pressing hard into me, letting me feel the growing ridge of his excitement through my skirts.

I found it easier to forget about the Hunger from one moment to the next lately. The more I grew used to my magic, the easier it was to ignore the way it seemed to lurk at the edges, just waiting for the opportunity to be fed. I wasn't sure if what Wendell said was true, if he and Thao would be less affected by the Hunger's demands, but I was too busy being consumed between them to try and control my power.

With Thao taking control of my lips, pulling me along to his demanding rhythm, Wendell was free to taste the kisses Thao had left behind on my neck. Wendell licked softly at my skin, breathing over the marks and drawing out goosebumps as cooler air breezed over. His hands stroked my sides in soft passes up and down. I'd given up wearing corsets because it was too wonderful to feel a hand against my side rather than the bite of boning, and I swooned into his skimming touches as they teased around my breasts.

With some unspoken command, the men lifted me from the carpet, my shoulders braced against Thao, as Wendell pulled me up to straddle his lap, squeezing roughly at my ass and making me cry out into Thao's mouth. Suddenly, the grazing gentleman was gone, Wendell rocking up between my hips, his palms gripping on their way up to clasp my breasts and massage them roughly.

"Yes!" I gasped, pulling away from the kiss, wrapping my arm around Thao's shoulders as I met Wendell's churning hips with my own, the friction muffled by too much fabric and leaving me whimpering and squirming.

I'd lost track of Thao's hands, until I felt his knuckle graze against my spine and I realized he was undressing me. Wendell's head lifted from my shoulder, and I pressed forward, arching for his kiss. He was perfect in contrasts, his hands firm and claiming, even as his kiss was gentle and explorative, a steady groan of pleasure echoing against my begging lips.

Thao wrestled down the bodice of my dress, and they both pulled away for a moment, Wendell leaning back and staring down at my breasts with a glazed and happy expression that made me laugh.

Thao's hands passed up and down my back, warming my skin in slow passes. "What do you want, Bryony? Tell us how to please you."

"You do please me," I said, simply enjoying the trance of Wendell's stare for the moment. I wasn't especially plentiful when it came to my breasts, but he was watching me catch my breath with absolute interest, his tongue flicking out over his bottom lip.

"He's very good with his mouth," Thao whispered in my ear, reaching around to pluck my nipples to points. "And he would look so pretty with his ass in the air and his face between your thighs."

"Oh! Yes," I said, nodding loosely. "Yes, that's what I want. I want him to make me wet for your cock."

I was already wet, but my suggestion made both men groan, Thao leaning away to part the gauze surrounding the pillowed mattress. "Get her onto the bed."

Wendell's arms went around my hips, his movements clumsy as he wobbled us over the few feet to the bed, my hair and skirts tangling with the thin netting around the bed. I laughed as I fell onto the dense mattress with an *oof* of breath, Wendell rising up briefly to stare down at me, his hair rumpled. Then he dove down again, lips latching onto a bare breast with a moan. I arched and joined him in the sound, my eyes falling shut, and then giggled as Thao fumbled with the latch of one of my shoes and the lace of a stocking at the same time.

"Tastes like spun sugar," Wendell gasped, pulling away.

"I do not," I laughed, wiggling backwards as Wendell held my skirt, helping me worm my way out of it.

"The belt," he said, as I grew stuck.

It was a jumble as I undid the belt Aric and Cresswell had gifted me, while Wendell continued to pull the dress out from under it as if he might leave me with my dagger on just to get to me faster.

"You undress too," Thao ordered, only a little more collected than Wendell and I. He'd managed to get both shoes off, but only one stocking, before he was untying the laces of his own vest.

When I was stripped of all but a stocking, and Thao and I had wrestled Wendell out of his own clothing, Wendell tackled me back to the mattress with quick and messy kisses, his bare body grinding over mine. He was a great deal taller than me, and I had to crane and twist in odd directions to kiss him and rub myself against his stiff cock at the same time, but I liked the weight and length of him on top of me, the same way I liked when Owen would pin me to the bed with his whole body and fuck me so slowly it made me want to cry with frustration.

"Don't fuck her yet," Thao said, sliding down to lie at our sides, his hand moving between us to cup at my sex, like he was trying to prevent Wendell from finding his way inside me.

"He can if he wants to," I whined, sagging against the bed and stroking at Wendell's chest as he stiffened and held himself up over me.

Wendell's cock was as long as Owen's, although not quite as thick, and I spread my legs a little wider, ready for the stroke of him inside me.

"No," Wendell sighed, shaking his head. "No, he's right. I know what I want to do."

I whined, but only for the moment it took Wendell to move back towards the edge of the bed on his knees, bowing down so his face hovered over my sex. He grinned up at me, his face poised between my thighs, framed there like a perfectly erotic picture.

"Bite the pillow if you don't want the others to hear you," he said, and then he opened his lips wide and wrapped them around the sensitive folds of my pussy, his tongue lapping and thrusting into me.

I shouted at the first warm rush of pleasure of his mouth, trying to squirm away until Wendell hooked his arms around my legs to hold me against him, one palm pressed to my stomach.

"Ass up," Thao ordered, kneeling at Wendell's side, and Wendell laughed as mine tried to bounce up in response.

I bit my lip, forcing my eyes to stay open in spite of Wendell's teasing, swirling tongue, as he hummed against me and raised his hips, giving me a beautiful view of the corded muscles of his back shifting, leading to the two rounded, dimpled globes of his ass. Thao's hands passed over the dense muscle, a dark shroud of hair falling across his cheek as he bent his head and kissed down Wendell's spine.

For all that Cosmo and Owen shared me between them and were comfortable with one another, they never gave me a view like this, touching and caressing one another. My fingers slid into Wendell's hair, my eyelids heavy at the drowsy, liquid heat he stirred with every teasing flick of his tongue against my clit, the press of his lips there in a tender kiss.

"Who are you teasing? Me or her?" Thao growled, scratching down Wendell's back and making him moan, which in turn made me moan and squirm.

My breaths panted and I tugged on Wendell's strands, trying to pull him into me, trying to force the friction he was only giving in tiny doses.

Thao leaned back, pulling his own shirt off over his head, shimmying out of his pants, a shorter, thick cock bouncing against his stomach.

"Come here," I pleaded, wanting someone to kiss, to touch me everywhere Wendell couldn't.

"Ah ah," Thao said, shaking his head, returning to his spot at Wendell's side. "I want him to hurry, and to do that..." He trailed off, his hand sneaking underneath Wendell.

Wendell's face lifted, chin and lips glossy, as he shouted, hips bucking, and I tried to twist to watch Thao touch him. "Fuck! Does it have to be all at once, Thao?" Wendell laughed, cheeks going bright red and brow furrowing as if he were trying to fight the pleasure.

"If it were all at once I would do this too," Thao said, his other hand vanishing behind Wendell's ass.

Wendell groaned and tensed, and then dove back down between my legs. I shrieked and shivered as he sucked and licked and fucked me with his tongue, more determined than before, growling from the manipulation of Thao's touches.

"I want inside her," Thao said, voice low. "I want you inside me. You know how impatient I am."

Wendell didn't bother answering and if he'd tried, I might've screamed and pulled him back to me. I was impatient too. I wanted to come, my bones ached with the Hunger's ravenous appetite for pleasure. Wendell's grip on my hips was too firm to let me ride his mouth the way I wanted, but Thao was right, he knew exactly what to do, driving me high and then holding me there as I panted and whined.

"Always teasing," Thao murmured. "Let her come. I want to feel her magic on our skin."

Wendell hummed agreeably, and his lips latched onto my clit, sucking and not letting up until I had a pillow over my face as I screamed and trembled in his arms. The force of my release was as strong as the shudder of magic bursting out of me. I didn't know where it went or if the ground trembling was just my orgasm, and I didn't care.

Wendell's arms loosened around me as I gasped into the velvet pillow.

"Let me feel her just a little?"

"Get that soaked and then fuck me with it."

Their words were filthy but the tone was tender and affectionate, almost whispers. I pushed the pillow aside just in time to watch Wendell on his knees, pulling my hips up and drawing me onto his swollen cock, rocking softly into me, a dizzy smile on his lips that parted on a moan.

"Silk?" Thao asked.

Wendell laughed. "Silk wishes. Bryony, you are decadent." I squeezed on his length with his third stroke, grinning as he choked and pulled out. "Fuck. She nearly made me come. You worked me up too much."

"Oh, well I feel terrible," Thao said, rolling his eyes and

pushing at Wendell's shoulder. Wendell fell back and Thao's hands wrapped around my ankles, yanking me towards him.

"I'm confused. Who is fucking who exactly?" I said, laughing and rising up to my elbows.

"Are you?" Thao asked, an eyebrow lifting as he settled over me. "Here, let me show you."

I could not have been more ready for him, but it was still a surprise as he thrust in with one quick and rough motion. My arms clutched around him as I shouted. Owen and Cosmo were always slow and patient at the start of our lovemaking, and the suddenness of Thao's possession was shocking and delicious. My body trembled with the force but adjusted quickly, and before I'd gotten over my surprise, I found myself digging my fingers into his shoulders and starting to ride him from below.

"Listen to your little whimpers," Thao purred. "Desperate little thing aren't you? Sweet little cunt sucking on my cock. Go on, take what you like."

My eyes were wide, staring between us at where Thao's girth stretched the lips of my sex. His words were rude and I loved them, wanted more.

"Please," I whined, looking up and finding Thao's dark gaze watching me.

"Wendell is right, you are decadent, slippery and slick and begging. So impatient, can't even wait for me to fuck you. Is that the Hunger, Princess Bryony? Or are you just wanton?"

I gasped and bucked faster, suddenly too embarrassed by my own pleasure to look him in the eye. But Thao wouldn't have it. One of his hands clutched at my chin, turning my face back to his.

"I think you would let me tie you up and blindfold your eyes if I promised you would come," Thao said, grinning wickedly, and I moaned at the thought until he added, "But I think you would like it even better if we were tied up and you could ride us to your greedy little cunt's content."

"You are the most depraved," Wendell said fondly. He appeared briefly at my side, bending and kissing my forehead. "Don't worry, I'll make him shut up in a moment."

"I-I like it," I whispered, craning my neck to kiss Wendell and then Thao's chin.

"Of course you do," Thao said lightly, finally starting to sound a little winded as he watched me bucking up onto his cock, taking exactly what he'd described— what I wanted.

"I would ride you now, if you let me," I gasped.

Thao grinned and groaned. "Soon, another time. Now though —" His words faltered as Wendell reappeared behind him, a crack of flesh to flesh sounding on the air. Thao's hips stuttered into mine, slapping wetly, and he groaned and laughed. "Now you learn who is fucking who," he groaned out.

"With the way you're carrying on, it's just you getting fucked," Wendell said. "Treat our princess as she deserves. Show her how good you can make her feel."

I felt divine and I would've said so, but then Thao's mouth was on mine, claiming me again. His hips rolled like waves into mine, occasionally faltering but always returning to a rhythm that left me breathless and clinging to him, sucking on his tongue the way I did his cock.

"Ready?" Wendell asked.

"Yes, yes, I've been—" Thao's answer ended with a groan, his body growing heavy on top of me, his hands grabbing my wrists and raising them above my head and into the pillows.

"Oh!" I said, watching Wendell's face over Thao's shoulder as it twisted with pleasure, Thao's hips grinding into mine. "Ohhh, yes."

Thao whimpered, and his head fell to my shoulder as a new and slow rhythm took over, Wendell's movement in and out of Thao sinking Thao in and out of me. Now all of Thao's filthy poetry failed, his voice weak and senseless. I caught his mouth with mine, kissing him through his groans, spreading my legs and trying to remember to breathe as his body rubbed perfectly against my clit, the pressure explosive.

I forgot about the Hunger, the festival, the people outside of our little nest who must've heard the explicit cries and groans of our union. I probably forgot my own name until Thao whispered it and Wendell's together, his fingers tight around my wrists. My legs wrapped around them both, heels in Wendell's ass making him buck and groan. As fire seemed to race through me in a syrupy slow rush, I came with a long cry of praising and pleads.

It was a chain reaction, Thao stiffening and then bucking suddenly between us, making Wendell's steady and slow strokes fail. For a moment, I was buried beneath them, unable to catch my breath, and I didn't even care. Then Wendell slowly fell to one side, Thao to the other, their lips eagerly catching against my shoulders and then meeting in the middle. Wendell's hand made gentle passes from my breasts to my hips before finally finding its way to covering my sex, fingers dipping inside of me and drawing out a flutter of aftershocks.

"Mm, you could have more, couldn't you? We should've paced ourselves better, Thao," Wendell mumbled.

Thao scoffed, resting heavily on my side, his arm draped over my stomach and his breath puffing against my jaw.

"I am satisfied," I said and then laughed as Wendell's smile took on a humorous version of a frown. "I mean, I don't need more. That was *wonderful*."

"Of course you need more," Thao mumbled agreeably. "That's what the others are for."

"She's been managing with two quite nicely," Cosmo announced, ducking carefully into the bedroom, Owen following closely at his back before making sure to pull the curtain fully shut again.

"Lady Pru slept through that, but I think Cresswell might've died twice and Daniel certainly seems to be suffering," Owen whispered, helping himself under the gauze of the canopy to reach my feet on the mattress. "Oh. Can we come in?"

Thao sighed and rolled onto his back, arm over his eyes. "By all means."

I glanced at Wendell, but he was smiling widely and he leaned in to whisper in my ear. "Ignore him. He loves to watch. So do I for that matter."

Well in *that* case. I pushed up to sitting, watching through the canopy as Cosmo began to undo the buttons of his shirt, his eyes drinking in all of us on the bed with eager anticipation.

"Did anyone find out what happened with the man in the dancers?" I asked, rising up to my knees, leaning in to let Owen kiss the corner of my mouth, smiling as Thao's hand rose to cup my ass. I glanced over my shoulder at him and found him peeking from beneath his arm, but his eyes were watching Cosmo. I checked on Wendell and when I realized his were too, I let it be. As long as everyone was comfortable with the directions of interest, I was happy.

Owen tiptoed his fingers down from my chest to my pussy. "I think Aric dragged him off. Are you ready for me too?"

I grunted, eyes falling shut as Owen pressed two fingers into me bluntly and started to pump. I *was* wanton, wasn't I? "Aric?" I gasped out, trying to focus instead of just crawling closer to Owen so he could fuck me properly.

"He and Cress had him as we made it back to the tent," Cosmo said. "We'll learn more in the morning. For now..."

My eyes opened and I watched Cosmo duck under the canopy, naked and grinning, watching Owen's fingers work me over.

"I think you should take her first," Owen said to him before blinking and grinning sheepishly at me. "That is, if you want, Mistress."

I let out a guttural groan as Owen curled his fingers inside of me. "Yes, yes, someone touch me, *please*."

"I'd be offended if I hadn't heard the two of you trying to keep up with her in the past few weeks," Thao said, sitting up and scooting closer.

"I'm about to be offended with the way you talk around me," I said, arching a brow at him.

Thao blushed and smiled, dropping a soft kiss on my shoulder and then leaning in for another, uncharacteristically delicate one on my lips. "Sorry," he whispered.

"Forgiven," I answered softly. "Especially if you promise to speak like you did earlier."

His eyebrows rose high. "You really liked that?"

"You couldn't tell?" I asked, glancing down at his cock, which was still a little glossy with my release.

"Mmm, dirty girl," he hissed in my ear.

I shuddered and then gasped as Owen stroked inside of me, drawing out a shallow but sweet orgasm that left me melting into the cluster of arms surrounding me. Cosmo pressed in closest, and I found his face with my hands, turning into him for the deep, drinking kisses he always gave me.

"Did you enjoy today?" Cosmo asked, nuzzling my cheek.

"I'll enjoy it more when you're inside me." He laughed, and I blinked, blushing under his studying gaze. "Yes. This was... I think this has been my favorite day yet."

Cosmo hummed, and then his smile stretched wider as he leaned in and pecked a kiss at the end of my nose. "Mine too. Or..." He waggled his eyebrows. "It's about to be."

I hadn't noticed the blurred line of where the Hunger had abated for the moment, but Cosmo must have, and he'd drawn it out again with his sweetness and his humor. I took his face again in my hands, kissed him until my lungs burned for breath, and then let him turn me around to face Wendell and Thao, his cock hovering at my ready entrance.

"Let's make the harvest rich this year," he whispered in my ear, and then he began to thrust.

Wendell and Thao pressed in close so that I was folded between the three of them, dizzy between their hands and mouths, clinging to whoever was close at hand as Cosmo turned his hips to find the perfect angle inside me. Every gentle buck of his hips made me cry out, made my hands flutter, made the magic of the Hunger buzz in my blood. I wanted to fall forward on my hands and rock back into his thrusts, but Wendell and Thao were there, sucking on my breasts, my collarbone, Thao pouring wicked words in my ear.

"You like that splash of cum on your thighs don't you?" Thao whispered in my ear before glancing down. "I bet you'd like it even more if Wendell cleaned you up."

Cosmo and I both groaned as Wendell laughed and moved down to lie on his stomach.

Cosmo shouted then too, growing rougher behind me, pushing my thighs apart so Wendell could lick at us both. I forced myself to open my eyes, to watch the explicit act of Wendell sucking on me, and then Cosmo's sac. And with my eyes open, I caught the moment that Thao released my throat and moved to kiss Cosmo, their mouths meeting with a shocking force and twin groans.

I looked over my other shoulder, and Owen was there, having undressed while we were busy, stroking on his thick cock and watching me, his eyes meeting mine again with his perfect fondness.

"Love you," he mouthed.

I came before I could answer, Wendell sneaking a finger up inside of me alongside Cosmo's cock, making us both collapse with sudden cries, magic rushing out of me and into the air, bleeding through the gauze of the canopy. I hoped it did the earth good, and the people at the festival, and all of Kimmery. I wasn't surprised when Thao moved to steal Cosmo away from me, but I demanded licking kisses from them both, Wendell rising and claiming one for himself, gentle and flavored with my own taste.

Owen moved to my side, surrounded me up in his strength and heat, drawing me into his chest and away from the others, peppering kisses over my face, my neck, my shoulders.

"And how shall I serve my mistress?" he whispered.

I lifted his face with my shaking hands, sucking softly on his full lips. "I want to feel every inch of you and beg for more," I answered.

Owen growled and then pushed me down to my hands and knees. "And do you want them to hear?" he asked.

I might've claimed I didn't know who he meant—the others in the bed with us, the crowd outside of our tent, it might've been anyone—but that would've been a lie. Or maybe I only thought of them first—the men just beyond the heavy curtain, Cresswell and Daniel listening to us.

Aric, if he were here.

"Yes," I hissed, and then I shouted as Owen lined himself up and drove into me.

I was noisy, obscene, vivid in my begging for more as my Chosen touched me everywhere they could. Owen kissed and licked down my spine as he fucked me down to my elbows and then to the mattress, covering and weighing me in place, pushing me through one orgasm and then the next, until the air was thick with magic and the earth groaned with the weight of the promise.

"More," I whined as Owen sucked on my throat and trembled and gushed inside of me.

This was the Hunger. This was what it was to be one of the queen's line.

EPILOGUE

The hills rolled by the carriage windows the next morning, the colors rich and vivid, the ground bursting with renewed life. There'd been a great thunderstorm during the night, after my Chosen and I had finally started to settle and the music and crowds had grown quiet. The fresh rain had made the entire north greener it seemed, although with a coy glance at Wendell, I wondered if we could take a little credit.

"How are you?" Wendell murmured in my ear. I was perched on Owen's lap, but this time it was Wendell sharing the bench with us closely, as Thao and Cosmo cuddled together on the opposite side.

"Perfect," I said, a shy smile growing.

Owen was sleeping behind me, it was only Wendell and I awake, and even that was by a thin margin. I was looking forward to getting back to the castle and dragging them all into bed with me for more rest on a better mattress.

"You are, aren't you?" Wendell said, kissing the corner of my jaw. "Have I mentioned yet how happy I am you let Thao and I into your bedroom the night of your ceremony? Where would we be now if you'd refused?"

"Where would I? It was the two of you who gave me the idea of taking you all to the north. I might've been shuffled into a corner somewhere in the castle as an embarrassment without you."

"Mm, I doubt it. Sooner or later, someone would've managed the work of making you fall in love with them," Wendell mused, turning back to gazing out the window.

But who? One of Camellia's Chosen? There were almost no other men allowed access to us in the castle, aside from during choosing ceremonies. No, I'd been blessed with a rare kind of luck during my choosing ceremony.

"Not the right ones," I said, and watched Wendell's face grow bright with his smile.

We were almost back to the palace, and I lowered the windows to listen to the sound of the woods. I'd grown up with the smell of roses and sea air, but I already preferred the heavy and deep damp of the mountain forests, the sound of song birds in the trees, mingling with the cries from the forest floor.

I don't want to go back to the capital, I realized. *I love it here. I am falling in love with these men, with the north, with my people.*

And rather than worry, comfort followed. We had time here. I shifted a little so I could fit more neatly between Wendell and Owen, Wen dropping an automatic kiss to the top of my head.

"Nearly home," he murmured, and I ignored the flare of Hunger at the affection our shared thoughts drew out.

A horse hurried past the carriage window, Cresswell Stark sitting stiff as a board, eyes directly ahead as he passed us.

"I'm afraid I embarrassed him," I whispered.

"He's not embarrassed, maybe jealous. Or mourning what he can't have," Wendell said, shrugging a little.

The gate to the Winter Palace groaned gently as it parted for us, more of the sound of a lover than the warning cry we'd heard the first night.

"We have so much work to do still," I said, my eyelids already growing heavy at the proximity to my bed.

"And we will, but not today I think."

I hummed in agreement and dozed on the way to the front steps, happy to accept the permission for a short break. There were orchards to plan, laws to rewrite, councils to wrangle. But surely it could begin tomorrow? Or at least after a little nap?

"Your Highness."

I startled in my seat and found Daniel Farraque at the window. His brow was furrowed, eyes slightly wide with surprise.

"The Winter Palace has guests," he said softly.

The others stirred as Daniel opened the door to the carriage. I gave myself the briefest time to fuss over my appearance, rumpled as it was after yesterday and the carriage ride, and then

I took Daniel's hand, squinting under the bright glare of the sun as I emerged in front of the steps.

"Bryony."

My blood froze at the bite of my name from her voice, my eyes growing wide as I stared up at the figure of my grandmother at the top of the stairs. And there, impossibly, at her side was Camellia.

"What on earth have you been doing all this time?" Grandmother snapped.

"Oh fuck," I breathed, as Daniel Farraque covered his shocked laugh with a cough.

To Be Continued...

The Kingdom's Crown

Sweet Pea Mysteries
The Baker's Guide To Risky Rituals

The Rooksgrave Manor Series
Esther: A New Beginning - Book 1

ACKNOWLEDGMENTS

When your whimsical little standalone idea grows into a behemoth...well, here we are.

This is absolutely thanks to my family, my friends, my Moongazers. Most especially my parents whose belief in me fuels so much of my progress and is the backbone of any success I find.

Thank you to the readers who let me run around in genre playgrounds, rearranging all the pieces into something completely different, and are still happy to come and play with me after I've made a strange and interesting mess of things. My books will never be for everyone, but if *this* book was for *you*, then I'm so happy!

Now specifically onto the people who keep me on track and in the best possible shape-

Gorgeous cover compliments to Covers by Combs for the exquisite work on the cover!

Proof-reading amazingness thanks to Bookish Dreams Editing!

My alphas - wink wink - Chloe, Lana, and Desiree, who chased me down for more!

My beta babes who absolutely devoured and protected this story; Jami, Ash, Kathryn, Helen, Enid, and Elle - thank you so much for all of your input and for helping to shape my stories!

And thank you, lovely reader, for taking this journey with me, Bryony, and her Chosen. Buckle in, it's about to get bumpy...

ABOUT THE AUTHOR

Kathryn Moon is a country mouse who started dictating stories to her mother at an early age. The fascination with building new worlds and discovering the lives of the characters who grew in her head never faltered, and she graduated college with a fiction writing degree. She loves writing women were are strong in their vulnerability, romances that are as affectionate as they are challenging, and worlds that a reader sinks into and never wants to leave. When her hands aren't busy typing they're probably knitting sweaters or crimping pie crust in Ohio. She definitely believes in magic.

You can reach her on Facebook and at ohkathrynmoon@gmail.com or you can sign up for her newsletter!